STRANGERS ON A PATH

By

Susanna Cooke

Copyright © Susanna Cooke 2023
This book is sold subject to the condition that it shall not, by way of trade or otherwise, be lent, resold, hired out, or otherwise circulated without the publisher's prior consent in any form of binding or cover other than that in which it is published and without a similar condition including this condition being imposed on the subsequent publisher.
The moral right of Susanna Cooke has been asserted.
ISBN-13: 9798376512524

This novel is entirely a work of fiction although some of the historical details and characters are factual. Persons named within the script are fictional and are the product of the author's imagination. Apart from those in the public domain, any similarity to persons past or living is coincidental.

To Michael.

CONTENTS

1. AMY 1
2. AMY 9
3. LYNN 20
4. LYNN 30
5. AMY 38
6. TOM 43
7. AMY 51
8. TOM 61
9. AMY 67
10. LYNN 79
11. AMY 89
12. LYNN 102
13. LYNN 110
14. AMY 114
15. AMY 124
16. AMY 130
17. TOM 138
18. LYNN 144
19. AMY 157
20. TOM 165
21. AMY 170
22. LYNN 181
23. LYNN 194
24. AMY 202
25. LYNN 215
26. LYNN 221
27. AMY 230
28. TOM 237
29. AMY 245
30. TOM 260
31. LYNN 264
32. AMY 275
33. LYNN 281
34. AMY 285
35. LYNN 292

36. TOM 298
37. AMY 301
EPILOGUE 311
ABOUT THE AUTHOR 314

ACKNOWLEDGEMENTS

Many thanks to Vicki, Chris, Magda, Keith and Frances.

1. AMY

'Can I help you, madam?' There was a hint of a question in the receptionist's voice: *What is someone like you in a jacket like that doing in a hotel like this?*

I leaned against the black marble reception desk and lifted one throbbing foot off the floor. 'Mr and Mrs Santini are expecting me.'

In my bag was the invitation Beth had sent, a pale blue card with the words '*Amy and Richard, please come to my first birthday party*' written in her neat cursive script. Either that or she and Paolo had a child prodigy on their hands.

'It's just me,' I added. *Just,* as if I wasn't enough. I would have kicked myself if my feet weren't hurting so badly.

She looked down at her watch. 'You're a little bit late. Most of the other guests have arrived.'

'Yes, I realise that, but you try walking from Bond Street Tube in these shoes. Next time my heart is broken, I'll stay well away from the shopping channel.'

No, I didn't say that. You don't admit failure to someone who looks so efficient. What I actually said was, 'I've not been here before. How do I find the manager's flat?'

She gave me the kind of smile you give someone you feel intensely sorry for and pointed over to the lift. 'Top floor. The manager's flat is to the right as you come out, madam.'

Madam thanked her and managed to hobble over to the lift without crying out. Once the doors slid closed, I slipped off the crippling heels, collapsed back against the wall and breathed out a long sigh. 'Shhhhhhhit!' That's when I noticed the security camera in the ceiling.

It was eerily silent as the lift swept upwards, giving me time to study my blurred reflection in its stainless-steel wall. Too much lipstick – a bit over the top for a child's birthday party and besides, there was no need to put on a brave face when these were my closest friends. Well, Beth was, and had been for years. Paolo had earned the title simply because he and Beth came as a unit these days, a kind of buy-one-get-one free arrangement.

There was just time to wipe my mouth with a tissue before the lift gently stopped and opened to reveal a carpeted corridor. The muffled sound of voices punctuated by little ripples of laughter floated towards me from a door halfway along – a disconcerting sign that the people who'd arrived on time were obviously settled in and at ease with one another. Oh great.

Moments later, the door was opened by six foot two of Irish affability in the shape of Joe Walsh, Beth's father.

'Well, Amy Lewis! Is it yourself? You're looking grand!'

He wrapped his arms round me in a massive hug then stepped back to let me into the hallway. I was twelve years old again, back in Bruford on Sea having my tea at Beth's and wishing that Joe was my dad and that when I got home, my own wouldn't find fault with almost everything I did.

'They're all in the kitchen, love,' Joe was saying. 'Let me take your lovely jacket then go through. Herself will be delighted to see you.' He smoothed the velvet where it had creased before hanging it on a hook. 'That's a lively sort of pink alright. Just your colour, I'd say.'

'So, how are you, Joe?' I asked. 'I hear you've adopted Florence.'

Beth had messaged a few months ago to say that her beloved tabby cat had gone to live with her dad.

'She's good company,' Joe said. 'The house doesn't seem so empty now there's another living thing in it.'

'I suppose it's for the best. Cats aren't always that good with babies.'

He smiled. 'Yes, but they're very good with pensioners.'

Hobbling into that room full of people engrossed in conversation, I put on my 'Hello, what fun!' face before realising that none of our old friends were there. Normally, such a situation wouldn't throw me but I had a strong sense that my usual cheerful efforts to mingle wouldn't work here. They all seemed to fit snugly together leaving no room for a stranger.

Noticing me, Beth rushed over and we hugged and moaned about how long it had been and how time flew by so quickly until her attention was commandeered by a couple who arrived even later than me. 'Catch up with you in a minute, Amy,' she said, moving away to welcome them before I had a chance to tell her about Richard.

The kitchen was huge so I took the glass of wine that Joe offered me and hovered by the wall, surreptitiously easing my shoes off and standing in my stocking feet while pretending that it was perfectly enjoyable to watch other people deep in conversation.

A few minutes later, amid waves of shushing and clapping, Beth carried a large Thomas the Tank Engine birthday cake to the table. Little Luca watched with periwinkle blue eyes from his highchair, kicking his plump legs in excitement as his mother lit the candle in the middle of Thomas's boiler. That was our cue to gather round the kitchen table like the shepherds in Bethlehem to admire the birthday boy as Joe led the singing of 'Happy Birthday' in a rich Irish tenor. When Beth removed the cake to slice it, a frighteningly elegant young woman standing beside me turned and gave me a smile that didn't reach her beautiful eyes.

'Are you a friend of the Santinis? I'm Sarah from the babies and toddlers group – that's how Beth and I met. She's become such a good friend; I absolutely adore her.' Her voice was high and sharp.

I introduced myself and was about to explain that I'd known Beth since primary school when Sarah continued as if she'd merely paused for breath.

'I bought Luca that outfit he's wearing. They have such adorable baby clothes in Harrods, don't you think?'

'Oh yes, I suppose so.' Did they? No idea.

The gift bag I'd passed to Beth contained some hand-knitted mittens and a romper suit that I'd bought from a woman who ran a clothing stall in the market at Kingston. With winter only two months away, I'd thought she'd be glad of them but now I wasn't so sure. Luca's blue and white sailor suit certainly looked expensive but I couldn't help wondering how long it would stay that pristine on a one-year-old child.

Sarah lowered her voice conspiratorially. 'Beth was thrilled. Between you and me, I don't think it's something she would have bought him herself.'

My hackles rose. 'She's very practical, actually. Beth is always careful with her choices.'

'So where do you live, Amy?' she asked, imperiously.

'Kingston upon Thames,' I said.

'Oh. Where's that?'

Was she serious? Surely her London geography didn't just cover the Ultra-Low Emission Zone? Swallowing my astonishment, I explained that if you followed the Thames for long enough, you'd eventually find Kingston, a deceptively ancient town sitting behind some modern concrete buildings and a beautiful stone bridge.

Sarah's eyes glazed over. 'So how old are yours?' she asked.

'My what?'

'Your kids.' The look on her face suggested a hint of impatience.

The question momentarily stunned me. 'I don't have any, Sarah.'

She cocked her head to one side like a dog who doesn't quite understand what its human is saying. 'Do you and your hubby want them, though?'

I forced myself to smile in spite of being shocked by the intrusive nature of the question. 'No husband either.'

A look of pure sympathy crossed her face for the fraction of a second it took her to think of a suitable reply. 'Lucky you, being free and easy.'

'Don't you think that in this century we should have moved on from obsessing about the marital status of women? And is our value measured solely in our ability to reproduce? I hope you don't mind me saying this, Sarah, but it's not a question you would have asked me if I were a man.'

I wish I'd said that but it only occurred to me much later on the tube home. No, I just mumbled something about women having so many more options these days.

Sarah looked flustered and apologised, the kind of apology that inferred that I was being oversensitive. It was a relief when she excused herself and went to join the group by the sink, leaving me discarded. I looked around for someone else to talk to but Joe had sat himself down at the table with a can of Guinness and was engrossed in a football conversation with Paolo while Beth was surrounded by women who were watching with rapt attention as she plated up the birthday cake slices. What was that all about?

Eventually, one of them emerged from the group with two plates of cake covered with blue icing which she placed on the table a little too close to the delighted Luca. Too late – he reached out, dug his plump little hand into the soft sponge and opened his mouth wide like a chick in a nest. Fortunately, most of the cake missed its target and ended up in a colourful smear on his chin and cheeks. Paolo immediately got up from the table, hoisted the baby out of his chair, grabbed a tea towel, turned and noticed me for the first time.

'Amy, come, sit,' he called, pulling back his chair for me at the table. It was typically thoughtful but I felt a twinge of embarrassment that he'd seen me standing by myself. 'Come,' he said again, pulling out a stool from under the worktop for himself.

He still looked handsome, like one of those beautiful Roman gods carved in stone with their sculptured lips and strong arched noses. His eyes were a rich dark brown and his voice warm and expressive with an accent that gave it a musical lilt. My heart beat a little faster as he beckoned me over.

Beth, meanwhile, was still swamped by the attention of some of her new friends. Their excited chatter filled the kitchen, bubbling with the sheer joy of owning babies and all the paraphernalia that came with them. Snippets of infant information flew into the air. What the hell was baby yoga all about? Was it even safe? How does an infant do the downward dog, for heaven's sake? And the baby masseur was obviously making a packet out of these women. I longed to drag Beth away from all this cloying nonsense, back to her real self.

'How are you, darling?' Paolo asked when I'd sat down beside him.

'Fine thanks, Paolo,' I lied. There was a raw patch of hurt inside me that his kindness was in danger of exposing.

'And how is your new flatmate getting on?' he asked.

I swallowed back the threatening tears. 'Richard couldn't make it.'

He smiled. 'Oh, but actually I was thinking of the one with four legs.'

Relief flooded through me. 'Max? Yes, he's fine. He's a bit wild sometimes but I'm working on it. He hasn't learned all the house rules yet.'

'You must bring him here one day,' said Paolo. 'We'd like to meet him.' He looked up at the gaggle of women by the sink then back at me. 'She misses you.'

'Does she?' Was he just being kind? Beth hadn't looked once in my direction since her initial greeting.

'I miss her too. And you, Paolo? How's it going here?'

He had taken over the running of this hotel and it took up a lot of his time. The bonus was that the job came with this spacious flat with its elegant Edwardian features.

He shrugged. 'Mamma mia, it's a challenge! Maybe I will be a very old man before business improves.'

I laughed at the dramatic face he made.

'And your love life?' he asked, gently. 'How is Richard? He couldn't make it today?'

'We've split up. Last weekend, actually.' The scene was still playing and replaying in my mind with the volume turned right up.

'I'm sorry, darling,' Paolo said. 'Come to dinner one evening. I will get Beth to ring you.' He patted my hand and for a moment, I allowed myself to imagine what it must be like to live with such a loving, compassionate man. Some people have all the luck.

While we'd been talking, Luca had been busy transferring some of the cake from his face to his hair. Ignoring the squeals of protest, his father used the tea towel to firmly wipe the mess off the child's face, hands and sticky spikes of dark hair. Luca scowled at me as if being cleaned up was all my fault until his father kissed the angry little face.

Joe grinned at me from across the table. 'Are you getting some tips on babies, love?'

'No, Joe,' I said. 'It would be like giving crochet lessons to a crocodile.'

He laughed but I could tell he'd taken my flippant comment at face value. Joe was old school when it came to marriage and family. 'And how are your parents?' he asked.

I explained that they'd had a late midlife crisis and had sold up the house in Bruford on Sea in order to buy a ramshackle cottage in Devon with two acres of paddocks where they could 'reconnect with nature' as they put it. Thanks to their undying devotion to David Attenborough, my mother was becoming an expert on goats while my father had morphed into a competitive vegetable grower who knew all there was to know about compost.

I didn't mention the fact that I was keeping a massive secret from them, a secret that would only confirm my father's poor opinion of me.

Paolo glanced up as Beth set some plates of cake on the table and the two of them exchanged smiles that sent a secret message only they understood. 'Join us, Bethy,' he said. 'Come, sit down for a moment. You've done enough work.'

Beth passed us each a fork. 'I will but Sarah and Paul have got to go in a minute. Their babysitter couldn't stay the whole afternoon.'

As if on cue, the couple appeared behind her. Sarah flashed me a fraction of a smile like the flicker of a light bulb about to blow and, seeing Paolo, pursed her perfect lips into a pout of a kiss. A spark of annoyance lit his eyes.

But then something wonderful happened which lifted my spirits no end. With excellent timing, a stream of creamy sick erupted from Luca's mouth, flowed down his chin and onto the snow-white collar of his sailor suit, staining it pale yellow.

'Oh dear,' I said. 'Is it washable?'

'Dry clean only,' Sarah snapped before turning on her heel and dragging her husband away. Beth picked up the baby. 'Back in a minute. I'm going to change him.'

'I'm sorry, Amy,' Paolo said, 'but when you come to dinner, you two can have a good talk.'

A good talk was what I missed now Beth was living up in town instead of fifteen minutes away on the other side of Kingston Bridge and along the riverside; that accessibility of having a friend you're completely at ease with and can easily reach. I was glad she and Paolo were so happy but their marriage had left a huge, empty space in my life.

It was still on my mind later when I emerged from the Royal Mayfair Hotel into the cool of early evening to struggle back up Bond Street to the tube. Those bloody shoes; bloody Richard.

And I hadn't had a chance to tell Beth what had happened. She was the only person who could put me back together again.

2. AMY

Nearly home, I stopped to give my crushed toes a break and leaned on the cold stone wall of Kingston bridge. I thought about hurling the crippling shoes over the parapet and into the water until the guilt at polluting the river with non-biodegradable footwear made me think again.

It was a relief to get home to my rented flat on the ground floor of a Victorian house a stiletto's throw from the river. The first thing I'd done after moving in was to cover the insipidly pale walls in colour: a soft lilac in the sitting room and hall, English rose in the bedroom, mint green in the bathroom and sunshine yellow in the kitchen because it faced north and needed warming up. Ok, it was a bit overwhelming in such a small room but I thought my landlord's comment that it looked like an explosion in a custard factory was so rude. He'd arranged to come round to have a look at my washing machine which had developed an entrancing new habit of flooding the floor but had spent most of the time insisting that I restore the flat to its 'original tasteful colour' by Christmas. Two large tins of magnolia emulsion were parked on my hall floor gathering a thin layer of dust – well, it was still early September so I wasn't in any hurry.

Hearing me come in, Max careered along the hallway, yelping with high-pitched excitement and skidding on the wooden floor, knocking my discarded shoes flying. Through the open door of the sitting room, I could see that he'd rampaged among the turquoise and purple cushions on the sofa, tossing them all over the carpet before turning his bored attention to the magazines on the coffee table.

Shreds of paper were scattered around the room like giant confetti.

'Shit, Max!' I exploded, but it was hard to be cross with him for long. Max might be a vandal but at least he was faithful, affectionate and had the decency to look embarrassed when he'd done something wrong unlike some men I know and one in particular.

While I was still tidying the mess, my mobile rang. 'Hi Mum,' I said, pushing the dog off the sofa for the fifth time.

My mother's voice, sharp as a glass shard, cut into my ear.

'Darling, I just had to phone you with the news.' She sounded breathless with excitement. 'Daddy won first prize at the produce show with his marrow. He's over the moon. Alas, the onions didn't come anywhere but the runner beans got a second so not all bad. Better luck next time, eh?'

'Congratulations. And second is good.' I tried to sound interested but really, my parents' intellectual capacity seemed to be withering now they were spending so much time with vegetables.

'Oh and Merlin's had a bit of a tummy bug but then he will eat rubbish.'

'Merlin?'

'Our new billy goat. Keep up, darling. You're ok I hope?'

'Yes but Max has wrecked the place while I've been out at Beth's.'

'Dogs are like children. Even a small one like Max needs attention. You can't just go off flibbertigibbeting, dear.'

It was tempting to remind her whose dog it was. So I did.

'Well, if Marcus hadn't flibbertigibbited off to Australia, I wouldn't have been lumbered with his bloody dog.'

I looked down at Max and mouthed the word 'sorry' at his mournful face.

Max was a mistake on two counts: firstly, his Pomeranian mother was accidentally impregnated by the neighbour's poodle and secondly, he was an unwanted, surprise present from Marcus to his then girlfriend. The same day, Marcus had FaceTimed me in a panic.

'What am I going to do, Sis? She hates this thing. Turns out she's allergic to fur so when I took it round to her place, she came out in this itchy rash. Now she hates me too.'

He had held up a small scrap of squirming white fur and made it wave hello with one paw like a scruffy glove puppet.

'He needs a haircut, poor little thing,' I said. The puppy was looking straight at me with round black eyes just visible beneath spiky strands of fur. 'Help me!' those appealing eyes seemed to say.

'Well, it'll get one in Battersea Dogs Home,' Marcus said. 'I'm taking it over there tomorrow.'

'No, Marcus, you can't!'

'Come on, I can't keep it. I'm off to Australia in a couple of weeks and anyway, they'll probably re-home it with any luck.'

'Yes but what happens if they can't?'

He'd made a slicing motion with his hand across his neck and grimaced.

'I'll take him.'

Who said that? Apparently, it was me.

'I thought your lease stipulated no animals?' Marcus asked.

'No, it's ok. My landlord will never know if I'm careful.'

Easy to say but much harder in reality. Fortunately, the landlord was legally obliged to give me notice if he was calling round and on the one occasion he'd surprised me, Max had been at the vets having a wound stitched up after an altercation with a bad-tempered dachshund.

'No, I'm sure it will be ok, Marcus. You can't just dump him.'

'Great. I'll bring it over to your place tomorrow. Thanks, Sis.'

The screen had gone blank. He'd done it again. He always got what he wanted.

His preferential treatment was written in the annals of our family history. When Marcus reached eighteen, he was given driving lessons and a decent second-hand car while I was queuing at bus stops and saving as much as I could from my college holiday jobs to pay for a yellow shopper bike in the Argos catalogue. My brother rewarded our parents' funding of his education and transport by accepting a banking job in Australia which came as a complete shock to all of us.

I'd expected them to be devastated so wasn't surprised when my mother complained about what she called 'the slavery of parenthood' and 'the hurtful ingratitude of one's offspring'. There were no statues to commemorate her sacrifice but she did her best to keep it alive with the tools of the martyr: sighs, raised eyes and hurt silences.

Her voice cut across my thoughts. I'd almost forgotten she was on the other end of the phone.

'So,' she continued, 'how is Richard?' The question I'd been dreading.

I told her that we had agreed to go our separate ways which made us sound like reasonable, mature adults when the truth was much uglier. But I wasn't ready to share the awfulness of the break-up with my mother or with anyone except Beth who would have totally understood.

'Oh,' she said. 'So now that Richard has left you, any new boyfriends on the horizon dear?'

Her lack of sympathy stung. Not only that, but the disappointment at not yet being a grandmother hung in the air, unvoiced yet heavily present. I thought about telling her that it was me who threw Richard out but it wasn't worth the effort.

'Not yet,' I replied, 'but the big department store in town is having a sale of men next week. I might trot up there and see what's on offer.' Spurred on by sheer devilment, I added, 'Or I might decide to have a change. These days, relationships have so much more... variety. Why stick with the conventional?'

No, that was cruel. She would fret about that. My mother took everything literally.

There was a distinct intake of breath on the other end of the line.

'All I'm saying, dear, is that your biological clock is ticking. Don't leave motherhood too late or you'll regret it.'

'Look, Mum,' I protested, 'I haven't got time to use my ovaries at the moment. I'm too busy using my brains.'

There was a horrible silence. Then a sigh, deep and wounded.

Why couldn't I tell her how awful the break-up had been? How it had left me feeling so wounded that I couldn't face any more relationships? The fact is, she would have blamed me, asked me what I'd done to upset Richard. To my mother, men were like gods, infallible. She should have been born a hundred years earlier.

'So,' she continued. 'Is everything all right at school? No Ofsted inspections coming up or anything?'

'No, no inspections.' *Please don't ask me anything else about school.*

'And are you going to go for the deputy headship? Remember you mentioned there'd be a vacancy at the end of the year and you might apply?'

'That was a while ago. I... changed my mind.'

'But why, Amy?'

'Listen, I have to go, Mum. Someone's at the door but I'll call you next weekend.'

'All right. Daddy wanted me to tell you about the marrow, that's all. Take care, darling. Ciao.' She hung up.

I looked down at Max, the patient receiver of my moans and musings.

'Max, I'm thirty-one years old, fairly intelligent – if you ignore that lapse into insanity with the bargain shoes – so why is it that every time I talk to my parents, I feel...'

What exactly? It was hard to put it in words, especially to a dog. 'On edge' captured it pretty well. After all, every conversation was a minefield when at any minute I might let slip my guilty secret.

A year ago, on my way home from work, I'd stopped to peer into the dusty window of an empty drapery store on the south side of the market square in Kingston. The 'For Sale' sign had been up for ages but nobody seemed interested in buying it. That's when it happened: my 'St Paul falling off his horse' moment. Suddenly, I had a vision of what the old shop could be. All it needed was someone to rescue it, someone perhaps a bit insane. Not only that but I knew I had the funds to buy it and set it up as my dream business thanks to my grandmother. In her will, Granny Lewis had left all her money to me, much to my parents' disgust and the appalled disbelief of Marcus, who was only left £1,000. In his eyes, this was an unforgiveable insult.

Granny had owned a string of department stores on the south coast which earned her a fortune so you could say that retail was in my blood. It wasn't until that evening as I stood outside 'Hooper's Fine Drapery and Linens' with its dusty brown window shelf scattered with wasp and fly corpses that it struck me how much I needed a new challenge.

It was a huge risk. I would be leaving a well-paid, pensionable job in teaching to take an enormous leap in the dark. All I could do was pray that my father never found out what I'd done with his mother's money.

But… 'Rescue me,' the shop whispered. So I did.

For months afterwards, I'd wake up in a panic, asking, 'What have I done?' Too late. My resignation for the end of the summer term was in, the shopfitters were at work and gradually, the old place was being transformed. Glass shelves were fitted into the huge window, the existing floor to ceiling shelving was painted forest green and two large matching display units were positioned in the centre of the shop floor. The original oak counter lived on, polished with beeswax to a soft honey glow. I decided to keep the old shop bell on the back of the door because it was a bit of history as well as a means to alert us to incoming customers – hopefully.

Then began the exhausting work of finding stock, weeks and weeks of researching suppliers and negotiating deals while at the same time, updating my class records and marking tests.

I renamed the shop 'Earth Song', a name Richard scoffed at as being too precious.

'It's topical,' I told him. 'Greta Thunberg would love it.'

'Exactly,' he'd scoffed in those rich overblown tones of his. 'It's a teenage girl's fantasy.' He should know. It turned out he was one himself.

My beautiful phoenix of a shop would offer gifts which were natural, eco-friendly and ethically produced by talented local craftspeople – everything from jewellery to herbal skin creams, soaps, potpourri, cosmetics and even beautiful silk cushions in luminescent colours sewn from sari material by a women's cooperative in Southall.

My customers would take their purchases home in strong paper carrier bags since plastic had become an anathema. As a reminder of its crimes, my friend Roz, who was going to help me run the shop, stuck a large poster on the wall behind the cash desk showing a sad-eyed seal swooping torpedo-like between bloated plastic bags dangling on the tide like jellyfish.

Yes, Greta would have been pleased; it might even have put a rare smile on her face.

So here we were in the middle of September, up and running at last. Every morning when I unlocked the shop door, I took a deep breath, inhaled the smells of lavender, bergamot and geranium and felt a rush of happiness. It was my achievement, my beautiful creation.

But keeping it a secret was weighing me down. Pretty soon it would get too heavy.

I grabbed my trainers. Max needed to get out on his favourite walk along the river, off the lead to enjoy a bit of freedom, and I needed to clear my head of negative thoughts now my toes had stopped stinging.

As usual, a collection of houseboats were hugging the bank close to the bridge. The one at the end, *Serenity*, was a converted Dutch barge painted pale yellow with black stripes like a floating wasp. Three months ago, I'd been wandering past when I came across the couple who were living on it for the summer. He had set up an easel on the grass near the water's edge and was busy sketching out shapes on a large canvas while she was engrossed in drawing the swans that had clustered near the bank hoping for food.

Being nosy, I stopped to ask the man what he was working on. Stupid question. Even with the rough markings you could see the outline of the bridge and the far riverside and the beginnings of the broad sky. It would be an oil painting of the river at sunset, he told me. Hopefully, someone would want to buy it.

Casual conversation had eventually led to friendship and one Saturday, Jan and Kyle had invited me aboard *Serenity* to see their work and join them in a fish and chip supper. Both had retired and were enjoying this break down south away from their home in Durham to indulge in their love of nature and art and would I like drawing lessons?

That's how I swapped hot yoga (too much like hard work and far too sweaty) for a nice sit down in a cosy cabin on a Wednesday evening.

I was touched when Jan presented me with a small portrait of Max painted in acrylics that perfectly captured his indignant expression, lopsided ears and soft fur the colour of Cornish ice cream. But then that's what artists are good at, I suppose. They have an eye for detail.

I was about to tap on their window just to say hello when a large white cabin cruiser with darkened windows glided to a stop further along the bank and a boy of about fourteen jumped down from the rear deck to secure the mooring rope. Max immediately rushed towards him, ignoring my command to heel (what a waste of money those training sessions were), and began jumping up at his target's legs until he knelt down and ruffled his ears.

'He's cute. What is he?' he asked, looking up at me.

'He's a Pomeranian mixed with poodle.'

'Never heard of one of those.' His reward for all the fussing was ecstatic licking until Max turned his attention to the canvas bag slung from the lad's shoulder.

'Sorry,' I said. 'He has no manners.'

He grinned up at me. 'Nah, he's all right, aren't you, fella?'

I was looking into a pale face with freckled skin stretched over sharply defined cheek bones and eyes that looked as though they were meant to be blue but had had some of the colour washed from them. His sandy coloured hair was cropped close to his head which could have given him a hard look but for the easy smile at the dog's antics. To be honest, seeing him on the street, you might think he was a bit of a teenage thug, especially with that hoodie.

'Did you choose him because he's blonde like you?' he asked. He seemed disarmingly frank and innocent in a way that made it impossible to take offence at this remark but I still needed to put him right.

'He's not a fashion accessory if that's what you think.'

'No, I didn't mean... oh man, I only meant...'

'It's ok,' I said. 'I was given him by my brother who was going to Australia and couldn't keep him and I didn't have the heart to dump him on Battersea Dogs Home.'

'Sick. So what's his name?'

I told him. 'Good,' he said. 'I hate some of the stupid names people call their dogs but Max is ok.'

I smiled. 'Mine's Amy. Pleased to meet a fellow dog lover.'

'Mine's...' He paused as if struggling to remember his own name then, with a glance up at the cockpit of the cabin cruiser, he lowered his voice. 'Ben. It's Ben.'

'Nice to meet you, Ben.'

There was something moving in the way boy and dog were so delighted with each other. It made me wonder if he had one of his own at home and I was about to ask when he fingered the red collar around Max's neck and said, 'This is a good colour, my favourite, actually.'

'It's made of recycled leather,' I told him. 'We sell them in my shop, Earth Song. It's in the marketplace.'

'Oh yeah, I know it, that weird place.'

I was about to protest when there was a muffled cough from somewhere inside the boat. The boy stood up, checked his watch, straightened his rumpled grey top then brushed the legs of his jeans.

'I'm sorry about the hairs,' I said. 'I keep meaning to get him clipped.'

'No problem. It's fine. Better get going.'

He adjusted the strap of the canvas bag so it hung across his body, pulled the grey hood of the sweatshirt over his head and set off along the path towards the bridge without speaking again or looking back. I watched him go, feeling strangely disappointed that our conversation had been cut short. Don't get me wrong – I'm not in the habit of speaking to strange teenage boys but he seemed so easy to talk to, so unlike the monosyllabic offspring of some of my friends, kids who could barely grunt you a greeting and then only on the insistence of their parents. Take my friend Jenny whose son had just reached fourteen.

'Say hello to Amy, Matthew.'

'Uuuum.'

'Yes, nice to see you too, Matt. Looking forward to a proper conversation in about six years' time.'

Ben's accent sounded northern so I presumed that made him more communicative and outgoing. Most of the northerners I knew seemed perfectly at ease with strangers.

By now it was getting dark. The sun was a mere glimmer, sinking low behind the distant buildings; the red-and-gold-streaked sky had dulled to a dark grey chilling the air. I walked on for several yards but as it grew colder, I called Max and turned to go back because at this time of year, evening could plunge into night without much warning.

Along the road on the other side of the river, the streetlamps flickered to life one by one, forming a chain of yellow dots all the way along to the corner of Beth's old road. Nostalgia for the old days flooded over me with memories of giggly evenings in Beth's flat and of driving home past those lights lining the riverside like a string of bright pearls.

Quickly, I looked away and focused instead on the path running along the riverbank to the slope that led up to the road. The white cabin cruiser was still at its mooring. Close up, it was stunningly beautiful, sleek and streamlined with a long, pointed prow, gleaming paintwork and a broad sweep of black along its side giving it a racy appearance. Definitely a rich man's toy. On the stern was a name written in an elegant, navy blue cursive script: *Sea Swift*. Such a pity that it found itself on the brown, plodding waters of the Thames when on the sea it could have opened its throttle and swooped and flown across the waves.

I stopped to get a closer look and to fantasise about what the interior might be like. Pretty plush, I guessed, picturing red leather sofas, glowing walnut fittings and glasses of chilled champagne perched on gleaming side tables.

Then, as if a breeze had suddenly blown up from the river, I felt a cold sensation in my spine. Someone was watching me from behind the darkened windows of the cabin. Even though I couldn't see them I could sense their presence, feel the intensity of a stare focused solely on me.

Embarrassed to be caught snooping, I clipped on Max's lead and hurried away without looking back, forcing the dog to trot along beside me until we reached the end of the path and the welcome bustle of the main road. When I turned to look back, there were lights glowing in the windows of each houseboat along the row. The exception was the beautiful cabin cruiser which skulked in darkness beyond them.

I didn't know it then but that meeting with Ben was to change my life.

3. LYNN

I marched straight through reception and down the long, straight corridor without looking left or right or glancing up at the overhead signs. No need. I'd been here a few times in my professional capacity you might say. If I'd been brought here with my eyes closed, not only could I feel my way to the casualty department, I'd also know it from the clinical smell that clings to your nostrils.

A nurse stepped out of the lift.

'Detective Inspector Morris! Not another stabbing?'

I raised my eyebrows to show my exasperation. 'No, this time it's my son. He's had an accident at school.'

No time to elaborate. Being dragged out of the office in the middle of a crucial investigation and then having to spend a fraught half an hour trying to find a space in the hospital car park had exhausted my patience. And the menopause wasn't helping either, unless they'd ramped the heating up to maximum in this place.

Halfway down the corridor, a sharp left turn took me through a pair of swing doors into A&E and a noisy, bustling area lined with curtained bays. 'Jack Morris?' I asked as a weary looking nurse approached, swerved on her heel and led me to a cubicle further down the row.

Jack was sitting on the edge of the bed with a blood-stained bandage wrapped round his head. His face was the colour of the sheet he was sitting on. 'Hello, love,' I said, trying to sound calm but shaken by the sight of so much crimson seeping through the white gauze. I've seen many a blood-soaked victim in my time with the Met but there's something shocking about seeing your own flesh and blood in that state.

Behind me, the nurse tutted. 'Looks like we'll need to dress that wound again, Jack. I'll come back in a minute and do it.' She smiled at me. 'Won't be long.'

When the school secretary rang my mobile to say that Jack had viciously attacked another boy during the art lesson, what could I say except yes, it was totally unacceptable behaviour and I'd have a word with him? It was only when I was driving to the hospital that I realised this was totally out of character. He might be morose, moody and uncooperative but never violent. Besides, he got hurt too. How did that happen?

I sat down on the bed beside him, gently put my fingers under his chin and turned his face to inspect the damage, forcing him to look into my eyes.

'So tell me about it,' I said.

'Good to see you too, Mum.' It was the most he'd said in a while and almost a complete sentence.

I reached up and smoothed down the spiky strands of blood-encrusted hair protruding above the bandage.

'Come on, love. I'm in the middle of a crucial case so I'd appreciate an answer.'

Immediately, his grey blue eyes narrowed and I cursed myself.

'Besides, I was worried sick about you,' I added, all too aware that it sounded like an afterthought.

The surly look on my son's face darkened. 'Don't pretend you care,' he muttered.

I felt as if he was moving further and further away from me like a piece of flotsam floating away from the shore and out towards the open sea. Soon he'd be so far away I wouldn't be able to reach him.

His father was no help. Graham was always full of creative excuses for not having Jack to stay. Mostly he blamed constant deadlines or urgent meetings with his publisher. I blamed the woman he was living with. She seemed to be allergic to children in the same way that some people can't be anywhere near cats.

'Jack, the school told me you attacked James Gresham with a piece of wood during the art class.' I was uncomfortably aware that I sounded as though I was interviewing a suspect so I tried to soften my tone. 'Is it true?'

'Yeah, I did.'

'Why?'

'Dunno.'

I took a breath. *Keep calm.* Getting angry would only send him back into his shell where he'd seal himself in for days, sometimes weeks.

'So if you attacked him, why is it you sitting in A&E with a gash on your head?' Surreptitiously, I glanced at my watch. *Would there be time to get home, settle him and get back to the incident room for a couple of hours?*

'Hit me back, didn't he?' Jack said, looking down at the floor.

'But what on earth was it all about?'

Jack kept his life at school secret. If he was having problems then he'd hidden it well.

'Nothing. Can we go now?'

'You don't attack someone over nothing. You need to tell me why.'

'You're not in your fucking police station now – leave me alone, Mum!'

The nurse, returning at that moment with a fresh dressing, raised her eyebrows; to my amazement, Jack actually looked shamefaced and mumbled an apology. I stood up to make room as the young woman slowly unwound the bandage and removed the scarlet, sodden wadding revealing a stitched wound surrounded by dark blue and purple bruising.

I flinched. James should answer for this. The following morning, I'd get on to the school and put in a complaint because this amounted to GBH. James might be the son of a wealthy local businessman but there was no way he was getting away with it. Then a troubling thought crossed my mind.

The nurse, meanwhile, had cleaned the wound, checked the stitches and wound a new bandage round Jack's head. 'There,' she said, pinning the ends, 'all ready to go home now.' She spoke gently as if he was about six years old and the expression on his face softened in a way that pulled at my heart. He used to look at me that way – when I wasn't public enemy number one.

His response was polite, almost meek. 'Thanks,' he said, looking up at her with doe eyes. 'Thanks for, you know, looking after me.'

She gave him a bright smile. 'You're welcome, sweetheart. Take care, now.'

Jack's eyes followed her as she went through the plastic curtain and out of his life.

'Come on then, let's go,' I said, with a brightness I didn't feel. 'Are you ok to walk?'

I held out my hand ready to support him but he brushed it off and hauled himself up, wincing. That's when I noticed the bruising on both his legs, a reminder that James's returning blow had knocked him to the floor.

When we finally reached the car, I asked the question that had been bugging me.

'So you admit that you attacked James first?'

'Yeah. So?'

'Did you hurt him?'

He said nothing for a moment and I could tell he was debating with himself whether to supply the details. Finally, he looked me in the eye with his chin raised in defiance.

'Yeah, I did.' He sounded almost proud.

'And? What's the damage?' *As if I haven't enough to deal with.*

'He's been in A&E too. I think I broke his nose.'

We got into the car without a word. It was only while I was waiting for the exit barrier to lift that the impact of Jack's statement hit me. Finally, I exploded. 'Oh bloody hell, Jack!'

As soon as we got home, I rang my ex-husband. Time he remembered that sharing his sodding genes with a child came with some responsibility.

*

'Graham, I'm not asking you to be father of the year. All I need is for you to have Jack tomorrow. He's not well enough to go into school and I can't get time off because we're in the middle of an important case.'

I shifted my mobile into my left hand, inserted a ready meal into the microwave oven with my right and braced myself for the usual excuses. Sure enough, Graham would have loved to have Jack ordinarily but he was at a crucial stage in writing his latest novel, his agent's deadline was looming and having a kid around would have ruined his concentration. *A kid?*

'He's not some kid – he's your bloody child!'

Too late. Jack had come into the kitchen from the sitting room where he'd been slumped on the sofa. I turned to apologise but the boy was fiddling with his phone, probably relaying his adventures and making himself out to be an injured hero. He reached up into the cupboard, extracted a chocolate digestive then paused by the door to take a selfie, pointing to the blood-spotted bandage and fixing a pained expression on his face, obviously unaware that the heroic effect was completely ruined by the biscuit sticking out of his mouth. I was about to caution him against public boasting considering the circumstances but before I could say anything, he'd gone back into the sitting room and I was left to deal with Graham and his frantic, important life.

'Please, Graham, just this once.' Begging was beneath me but needs must. 'Clare's gone back to uni and there's no one else to ask.'

Our daughter was twenty. Even if she'd been available, the idea of hanging out with her fifteen-year-old brother would not have gone down well.

In the background at Graham's end of the line, I could hear

Monique, his literary agent and lover, chipping in with her comments, urging him to stand firm. Mademoiselle sodding perfect, she of the bee-stung lips and high cheek bones, stole my husband from right under my nose before abducting him to her expensive five-bed detached in Surbiton. It was at one of those tedious book launch parties that I always felt duty bound to attend in wifely support that I realised what was going on. As usual, I'd been glancing at my watch to see when I could realistically leave when Monique had appeared at Graham's side and guided him away, leaving me marooned in a large room full of strangers caught up in their own cleverness. When I looked across, Monique was standing close to Graham, so close that their bodies were touching. Then Graham put his hand on her back and slowly slid it down until it was resting on the curve of her backside.

So that's how he swapped me for a woman who was ten years younger with smooth skin, a single-digit dress size and no stretch marks. Oh, and a sodding jacuzzi in the basement.

'I don't know,' Graham was saying. 'Won't the boy be alright at home on his own? He's fifteen for God's sake.' He sounded impatient, as if time was literally running through his fingers.

'Look, Graham,' I said, between my teeth. 'I may be your ex-wife but no way is Jack your ex-son.'

I checked my watch – one hour twenty minutes and we'd either have to let the suspect go or apply for an extra twelve hours custody.

In the end, the best Graham could offer was a promise to pop in for half an hour the following day. A feeling of intense weariness overcame me as I peeled the boiling hot cellophane from the top of the bubbling ready meal with the finger and thumb of one hand.

About two minutes later, my mobile rang. It was the headteacher at Jack's school, Martin McDonald. Could I make a meeting with James's parents, himself and two of the senior management team the following day at eleven o'clock? A thought flashed across my mind: *Does he think I'm home all day in a flowery apron dusting the sodding ornaments?*

Drawing myself up to my full five foot seven inches, I put on my formal voice, the one I use for the public. 'I'm afraid not, Mr McDonald. I'm working. As you may be aware, I'm a DI with the local police force and we're working on an important case at the moment.' *Stuff that in your pipe.*

'I see.' He sounded unimpressed.

I tried an even lower and more serious tone. 'However, I would like to come and discuss what's happened. Can we arrange a convenient time?' There was a pause on the other end.

'Do you understand the seriousness of this incident, Mrs Morris?'

Stupid question. I spend my days dealing with the darkness of adult criminality. Did he really think I couldn't recognise bad behaviour in a fifteen-year-old? But I bit my tongue, took a deep breath and eventually we managed to arrange an appointment for five o'clock the following Thursday.

The cause of all this trouble, meanwhile, was back on the sofa and busy tapping away on Instagram. I stood in the doorway and then, apparently invisible, moved until I was in his eye line.

'I've left you a TV dinner, Jack. Just let it cool for a minute then turn it out onto a plate, ok?'

Cooking him something from scratch would have made me feel like a proper mother but time was running out. Fifty minutes left to get back to the incident room and check progress.

Jack's eyes were glued to his screen. 'Mmmm,' he murmured.

'I'll be back as soon as I can – probably in a couple of hours.'

'Mmmm.'

'It's your favourite – spaghetti Bolognese.'

'Ok. Don't fuss, man.'

My tether, already stretched, began to fray dangerously. 'Number one: I am not a man, thank God. Number two: don't ever call me that again if you want to live to see sixteen. Ok?'

Just lately, whenever he'd been talking to his friends, Jack had started to call them things like 'bruv' or 'blood' just like a gang leader we'd arrested who was now residing at Her Majesty's pleasure. He'd sent his minions out peddling hooky drugs that left a trail of poisoned, maimed victims who'd smoked, injected or inhaled the toxic rubbish he'd produced.

But drug dealing operations are like worms – you cut them in half and the pieces wriggle away. There's always someone ready to take over. What I didn't need was a son who reminded me of the problem that was haunting practically every police station in the country.

Forty-eight minutes to go.

I picked up my bag and paused to look at Jack from the doorway. 'See you later then. You'll be ok, love?'

He grunted something unintelligible that got lost as I shouldered my guilt and walked out of the front door.

*

The smell was the first thing that hit me when I walked into the office. Two of the DCs, Kai Chauhan and Sam Clinton, were tucking into take-away meals at their desks. Sam was picking at an enormous portion of cod and chips in white, grease-stained paper, inadvertently filling the room with the seaside smell of hot fat. I wrinkled up my nose and opened the nearest window, ignoring the look that passed between the two men. They're all right though. I may give them stick every now and then but I'd trust them with my life, Sam especially. His grandparents came over on the Windrush and worked their socks off to bring their children up to believe in God, Work and Truth in that order. In spite of his laid-back appearance, those beliefs were inherited by Sam, running through his core like words through a stick of rock.

Kai was a different kettle of fish. He was his mother's brown-eyed boy – intelligent, wiry, slim, always wore a suit, kept his nails immaculately trimmed and checked his hair every time he passed a reflective surface. But the lad had eyes like a hawk and a police officer's instinct for trouble.

At her desk at the other end of the room, DS Stephanie Davies was beavering away on her computer but looked up and smiled as I entered.

The minute hand on the clock above the office doorway clicked onto the six to show five thirty. Fifteen minutes left.

'Good to see you two aren't neglecting your stomachs,' I said, sitting at my desk. My own appetite had vanished.

Sam broke off a crisply battered chunk of cod. 'How's your son?'

I told him, withholding the fact that Jack was the aggressor.

'Kids, eh?' said Kai. Finishing his burger, he wiped his mouth with a tissue, crunched it into a ball and threw it into the exact middle of the waste bin.

'So, did you have any joy with our friend Swinford in the interview room?' I asked.

Sam swallowed his fish and looked serious.

'We're going to have to let him go. We've got nothing on him apart from the fact that he obviously doesn't want to compromise himself. We've both tried our best to get him to talk.'

'The bastard is guilty as hell; I can feel it in my water,' said Kai. 'Guy Swinford is a pro at acting innocent.'

Sam vehemently stabbed a small wooden fork into a chip. 'I don't know – he's acting the big man but you can tell that underneath the bluff he's shit scared of someone. I've got a feeling this guy is just a small fish in a big pond.'

I sighed. 'Ok, we can't keep him any longer, anyhow. He's been here for twelve hours and I don't think it's worth asking for another twelve when we're shooting in the dark.'

Kai was now cleaning his hands with a wet wipe but looked across at me. 'This guy knows it. They know the rules better than we do.'

I had to agree. I don't get to see the smug look on suspects' faces when we're forced to let them go but Des, the custody sergeant, describes it pretty well: 'Like a pig who's fallen into a pile of shit, Ma'am.'

'Somewhere out there is a shark running the whole operation,' I said. 'We need to find him.'

'Or her,' said Stephanie who is all for equality in the workplace.

'Whoever. Sooner or later, he or she will trip up.'

The man in custody was a small-time drug dealer and number one suspect in the murder of a rival who had strayed onto his patch. Hours of scouring CCTV footage and following up dud leads had only led us to a dead end. After the day I'd just had, the last thing I could face was the look on DCI Cavendish's face when I told him we'd run into a cul-de-sac with this investigation.

'Kai, you better get down there and tell Des to let the suspect out now you've finished stuffing your face,' I said. 'Time's up.'

The smell of hot fat and fish was still lingering in the air.

'And is there any chance that someday soon, one or both of you will be civilised enough to use the canteen?'

'Only when they start serving edible food, Ma'am,' Kai replied, receiving a nod of agreement from Sam.

'Point taken. Ok, I better go and see the DCI and hand in my resignation.'

I looked at the startled faces in front of me and grinned. 'As if.'

It was only half a joke.

4. LYNN

When Graham rang, I knew it was something serious since it's usually me who calls him. The only time he's ever bothered to ring me since our divorce was when he asked me to return the rest of his CD collection. I didn't tell him it was languishing in a box in the garage waiting to be taken to the local charity shop in the hope that somewhere in Kingston there was at least one fan of acid jazz.

Graham was using his concerned father voice, the general subtext of his conversation being my inability to cope with an adolescent boy. Apparently, the fact that he had popped in for an hour to check that Jack was ok awarded him several brownie points in the paternity stakes.

'I thought you might be interested in what our lad had to say about that incident at school,' he began. 'He told me why he'd lashed out at that other kid.'

Instantly, I experienced a hot flush of irritation. So far, I hadn't been able to get any explanation out of Jack so that came as a blow.

'Ok, so what story did he give *you*?' I asked, in an attempt to put Graham in his place.

'That James has been teasing him about you being a copper,' he said, almost accusingly.

'Excuse me? This isn't one of your pathetically inaccurate crime novels,' I retorted. 'I don't work my guts out just to be called a copper. Anyway, why should that bother James Gresham?'

'I don't know but he needles him every day about it, whatever opportunity he gets. Not only that, but he knows that we're divorced and teases him about that too. So, in the end, Jack couldn't take it anymore. Can't say I blame him for hitting out – that's the way to treat a bully, if you ask me.'

'Oh yes, Graham, nice parenting. I presume you'll be the one to pay for his bail when he's arrested for GBH one day.'

He gave a deep sigh. 'I thought you ought to know, Lynn, seeing as you've got the meeting at the school. Forewarned is forearmed.'

'Yes. Well, thanks. You're not free to come along, I suppose?' *Ha. Who am I kidding?*

'Me? No, sorry, my agent is tightening the thumb screws.'

'Thought so.' I snapped my phone shut.

'Who was that?' asked Jack, trooping into the sitting room in his pyjamas. He slumped down on the sofa with his iPad and a cup of coffee.

'Your dad. Are you thinking of getting dressed before lunch?'

'What did he want?'

I risked sitting down beside him and ignored his tutting. 'Is everything alright at school?'

'Whaddyamean?'

'Look, I've got this meeting on Thursday with Mr McDonald and I need to know why you lashed out at James.'

'What's Dad been saying?'

I told him. 'Do you hate me being in the police, Jack?'

He shrugged. 'Dunno really.' *'No comment' in other words.*

'It's my job that keeps this roof over our heads,' I said, firmly.

He moaned. 'Ok, ok, m—.' Seeing the look on my face, he stopped himself from saying the forbidden word just in time.

'And I know it was hard for you, but your dad and I were having problems, Jack. If we'd stayed together, we'd have made you and Clare as miserable as we were. The thing is, if you're having problems with James because of all that, then you need to tell me so I can fight your corner.'

Jack was silent for a minute so I waited, wondering what was going on in my son's mind and wishing I could turn the clock back to a time when there were no secrets between us. In primary school, he'd been a different child: funny, ebullient and enthusiastic. When he transferred to St Saviour's High School, it was as if someone had doused his optimistic spirit in ice cold water.

'Are you being bullied?' I persisted. 'Jack, you have to tell me.'

He stood up, picked up his coffee, tucked the iPad under his arm and left the room.

***

At the head of the table, Mr McDonald leaned forward and joined his broad hands as if in prayer. On the office wall behind him was a large shield with the school's mission statement written in bold italic script: *'St Saviour's: a place where every student can aim for the stars.'*

Mission statements are my pet hate. In my opinion, they're completely meaningless, a sop to convey unrealistic positivity. If we had one at the station, it would be something along the lines of *'Three out of ten convictions isn't great but we live in hope.'*

My gaze lowered back to the headteacher.

'First of all,' he began, 'I want to thank James's parents and Jack's mother for attending this important meeting. I truly believe that by honest communication we can move forward with this situation but I can't emphasise enough that this was a serious assault on a fellow pupil and it cannot be tolerated.' He spoke with slow emphasis as if we would find it hard to comprehend otherwise.

Although irritated by his insistence on stating the bloody obvious, I managed to reign myself in while surreptitiously looking around to gauge the reactions of the other people present. James's parents, Mr and Mrs Gresham, were sitting opposite me, moulded together in parental unity, and at the other end of the table, Sharon Bailey, Jack's form tutor, a petite blonde, gave me a weak smile of support. The smile was totally unnecessary. I'm in my element in confrontational situations.

Mr McDonald turned towards me. 'I'd like to give each of the parties a chance to express their views. Perhaps you'd like to start

Mrs Morris?'

Clearing my throat I began, focusing on the two people opposite.

'I've spoken to Jack and he knows that what he did was an...'

Just in time, I stopped myself from calling it an offence.

'He knows it was wrong but I believe there was provocation. James was goading him about my being in the police force as well as the fact that Jack's father and I are divorced, and although I'm not justifying my son's actions – far from it – he's always been close to his dad so the split has been traumatic for him.'

The Greshams were sitting in bolt upright indignation. I know it's wicked but Mr Gresham reminded me of a large white slug. The sickly effect wasn't helped by the sharp contrast of his coal-black hair which, suspiciously for a man in his fifties, lacked a single flick of grey. The eyes fixing mine in an unblinking, challenging gaze were a clear bright blue, like sapphires in the snowy setting of his face.

According to Jack, they lived in a large, detached house in a gated estate near the river and, judging from the rings on Mrs Gresham's fingers and the gold Rolex on her husband's wrist, they weren't short of a bob or two, as my dad used to say.

Mrs Gresham, immaculately made up and resembling a middle-aged Russian doll with pursed scarlet lips and fake eyelashes, narrowed her glittering eyes at me.

'We've brought James up to hold Christian values. He's a gentle boy; he would never say anything unkind or aggressive.'

'He hit my son,' I said, firmly.

'*Back*,' she snapped. 'He hit him back. Your son struck first.'

The slug-like man beside her stirred to life.

'Jack is out of control, that's the trouble. It's not your fault, Mrs Morris, but a teenage boy needs a male role model. Nowadays, they're exposed to all sorts of evil influences, let's face it. Half these kids going round knifing each other belong to single mothers. We understand how difficult it must be for you to manage Jack by yourself.'

His cut-glass accent and attempt to patronise hit a nerve, jangled further by his outrageous generalisation.

'Excuse me? You know nothing about our situation or how I'm bringing up my son.'

At the other end of the table, Miss Bailey gave me another of those placating smiles. 'I don't think Mr Gresham meant it that way, Mrs Morris.'

'In my job,' I persisted, 'we deal with evidence. Conjecture is not enough without solid evidence to back it up.'

Mr Gresham's thick black eyebrows twitched and his wife raised her spidery-lashed eyes and looked away. If James was as smug as his parents, I would have happily handed Jack that piece of wood. *Stop it,* I scolded myself. *Stop being a prize bitch. Their son was injured.*

At the end of the table, Mr McDonald cleared his throat to command our attention. 'May I remind everyone that we're here to resolve the situation in a civilised way with the best result for both boys?'

He reminded me of a judge I used to see in court, a man who was so reasonable that the defendant more often than not got away lightly in spite of the prosecution's evidence.

'Our James's nose will never be straight again,' said Mrs Gresham, reaching for a tissue from what looked like a designer handbag.

'So it *was* broken?' I asked.

She sniffed. 'No, but it won't ever be straight.'

'And Jack will have a scar on his forehead for the rest of his life.'

Miss Bailey shifted in her seat. 'How awful.'

'I think we could go round the houses with this one,' said Mr McDonald. I'd noticed him surreptitiously glancing at his watch a few times since the meeting began.

'Never mind the houses, what punishment is our son's assailant going to have?' Mrs Gresham asked, receiving a nod of agreement from her husband.

The head turned to me. 'I'm sorry, Mrs Morris but I intend to suspend Jack for two weeks starting from tomorrow. He will have some work to complete. You'll see to that, won't you, Miss Bailey?'

She nodded. 'Of course. And I think it might be a good idea when he returns to put him in a different set for art.'

She shot me a sympathetic glance and, begrudgingly, I agreed, swallowing the temptation to suggest that ideally, the two boys should be in separate buildings. As if.

A hint of a flush tinged Greg Gresham's white cheeks. 'Two weeks? Is that all? Two weeks' suspension for nearly maiming our son?'

'It's disgraceful,' his wife agreed. 'No wonder the country's going to the dogs if hooligans are getting off scot free!'

'My son is *not* a hooligan,' I said between gritted teeth.

The head held up a hand. 'Nobody is suggesting that but I think we're all agreed that teenage boys sometimes find it hard to manage their feelings. Part of growing up is learning how to choose and control your emotional response. We call it emotional intelligence.'

More of the sodding obvious. I glanced at the Greshams.

'I'd like to talk to James. I'd like to hear his side of the story.'

'What? No way!' A bead of sweat dripped down from the black thatch of Mr Gresham's hairline.

Mr McDonald looked alarmed. 'Not a good idea. Leave this to us, Mrs Morris. This isn't one of your criminal investigations, after all.'

He grinned at the others around the table but the smile melted away when his eyes rested on me.

I held his gaze firmly. 'You do have a bullying policy at this school, I presume?'

'Are you calling my son a bully?' Mr Gresham leaned forward and a whiff of expensive aftershave crossed the table and headed up my nose.

I returned his glare without flinching. 'What would you call it when a child torments another child?'

'This is ridiculous. Our son gets injured and you're excusing his attacker. No wonder Jack doesn't know right from wrong.'

I was about to reply when Mr McDonald jumped in quickly.

'Mrs Morris does have a point. Now I'll tell you what I intend to do. When Jack returns to school I will speak to the boys and try to get to the bottom of what happened in the hope that they can put this behind them and move on. If there are issues of bullying, then we will of course deal with that in accordance with our zero-tolerance policy and give them both the support they need.'

It was stalemate. After an awkward pause, I reluctantly thanked him, ignoring the glares from the opposite side of the table.

'And as their form tutor, I will also work with both students,' added Miss Bailey with a glance at either side of the table.

'That's settled then. We have an agreed plan of action so thank you all for your cooperation.' Mr McDonald failed to prevent an expression of intense relief from covering his face.

A question crossed my mind. 'What did the teacher in charge of the class have to say about the incident?'

I noticed a look flash between the head and Miss Bailey at the other end.

'Mr Brennan, our art teacher, is extremely competent. What happened could have occurred in any of my teachers' lessons.'

'I just think it would have been helpful to have had him here.'

To my surprise, there were nods of agreement from across the table.

'Mr Brennan is not in today, I'm afraid. He works three days a week,' said Mr McDonald. 'Though point taken, Mrs Morris. I can assure you that I've questioned him about the incident and am satisfied there was nothing he could have done to prevent it.'

He stood up and held out his hand to the Greshams who begrudgingly shook it in turn. He ignored their sceptical expressions.

'I think you'll find that after a couple of weeks, young Jack will come back ready to apologise and make amends and, hopefully, Mrs Morris will find a way to help him manage his anger.'

My spirits plunged.

Sharon Bailey accompanied me down the corridor towards reception. 'I'm sure it was a one-off. Jack is normally a well-behaved boy, very amenable.'

I stopped dead in my tracks. 'Amenable – Jack?'

The young teacher was looking at me as if I was mad. 'But of course, Mrs Morris. I wish they were all like Jack.'

Maybe she'd like to adopt him since it's only me he hates, I thought.

'Well, thanks for that, Miss Bailey. You'll sort out some work for him? I don't want him to fall behind.'

'Sure. I'll liaise with his subject tutors. He's a bright boy, Mrs Morris. I'm predicting straight As in his GCSEs so we'll keep him at it.'

She smiled then walked away, leaving me to my thoughts. Jack could get straight As? How did I not know that?

Leaving the building, I headed towards my dark green Toyota parked along the road as the Greshams swept out of the school gates in a sleek black Mercedes, nearly clipping the 'Staff Parking Only' sign attached to the wall. As they drove past, studiously ignoring me, I was forced to suppress a childish impulse to hold up two fingers.

5. AMY

So far, we were just keeping our heads above water in the shop but then we'd only been open for a few weeks. Roz and I were busy developing a website to broaden our customer base but even so, we were all too aware that the business had an unpredictable future.

Tuesday had been an unusually profitable day thanks to Max. Since the doggy day care woman had flu, I'd been forced to bring him to work and, unexpectedly, the sight of a small, cute dog asleep in Earth Song's sun-warmed window had drawn in several people who might otherwise have walked past.

'We should put Max on the pay roll,' Roz remarked at the end of the day. 'Sales are well up for a Tuesday.'

'Trouble is, he's not always this well behaved,' I said. 'By the way, did I tell you I went to that exhibition at the art gallery in Thames Street?'

Roz looked up from tidying the shelves. 'Oh yes, any good?'

I told her about the amazing ceramics I'd seen, the work of a local craftsman who specialised in making bowls with unusual shapes and dazzling colours.

'I was wondering whether he'd consider selling some here. Maybe we could come to some arrangement.'

Roz was about to reply when Max suddenly jumped down from the window, yapping frantically, and began scrabbling at the glass in the shop door. I went over and was about to drag him away when I realised what had caught his attention.

On the other side of the square was Ben, the boy I'd met on the riverbank on Saturday evening. He was leaning against the wall at the entrance to a passageway that led to the river. I watched as he took out a mobile from the bag slung across his thin body. He was studying it with total absorption, seemingly unaware of anyone or anything until he glanced up and immediately jammed the phone into the pocket of his jeans. Someone was obviously standing beside him but I couldn't see who it was since the person was mostly in shadow and half hidden from my view by a market stall. Whoever it was seemed to be doing all the talking because nodding and shrugging were all Ben seemed able to do.

Roz had put her coat on and came up behind me, disturbing my thoughts.

'I'm off home if you don't mind. It's open evening at Nathan's school.'

'Oh yes, you go.' I stepped aside to let her through the door, keeping a firm grip on the dog's collar.

'What's up with him?' Roz asked, as Max continued to whimper.

'He's seen someone he recognises,' I explained. 'Someone he's taken to I think. Good luck with Nathan's teacher.'

'Thanks. The teacher's lovely but sitting on those small chairs cripples me.'

When she'd gone, I looked back across the square and was surprised to see Ben ambling across it towards the shop. He stopped and peered in at the window so I opened the door.

'Hi again,' I said, holding tight to the struggling dog. 'Ben, isn't it?'

He seemed pleased to see me. 'Hiya, Amy, hiya, Max.'

'Were you looking for something to buy?' I asked. 'I'm about to close up but you're welcome to come in and have a browse.'

He shrugged. 'Nah, just looking, just curious like.' He turned away as if to leave then seemed to change his mind. 'Ok, maybe I will. Thanks.'

I stood aside to let him in, restraining the ecstatic Max who was obviously overjoyed at seeing his young friend again. The feeling seemed to be mutual. Ben's pale, pinched face broke into a broad grin seeing the dog's backside careering from side to side as his joyful stub of a tail lashed against the bottom of the display units.

'What a nutter! You'll hurt yourself, boy.'

I waited while he walked slowly around the shop eventually coming to a stop by the shelf of cashmere scarves and reaching out to stroke a red one on the top of the pile.

'These are sick,' he murmured.

'Yes, they're very soft and I think you said red was your favourite colour.' I dragged the dog into the back room. When I turned around, Ben was standing by the door.

'Thanks for, like, letting me look around,' he said.

'You're welcome to stay a bit longer if you want. Have a good look round.'

'Nah, you're ok. Thanks but I better get going.' He turned and went out then walked off towards the High Street.

I watched him for a moment, wondering what he'd made of the place, then went into the small back kitchen to wash up the tea mugs. I was drying them when I heard someone cough in the shop. Annoyingly, I'd forgotten to turn the closed sign on the door. I shut Max in the kitchen then went to investigate.

A tall, stocky man in a black leather jacket was whistling softly to himself as he moved about among the displays, picking things up and checking labels. Judging from the breadth of his shoulders and the width of his upper arms straining against the sleeves of his jacket, this guy worked out with weights. He had thinning brown hair cropped tight to his scalp and a face that would have been handsome but for the eyes which were small, dark and too close together. An overpowering smell of aftershave was clashing with the scent of lavender and bergamot soap and really getting up my nose in more ways than one.

'Can I help you?' I asked. 'I'm closing in a minute but if you need more time to browse, we open at nine in the morning.'

'Thanks darling.' He gave me a twitch of a smile and looked me up and down unashamedly. 'Thing is, sweet cheeks, I need a present for the wife. These are unusual.'

He stopped by the stack of neatly folded cashmere scarves and began to thumb through them, picking out a green one from the bottom before changing his mind and holding up the one remaining red scarf from the top, leaving the rest in an untidy heap.

'Unusual colour – like a corn poppy,' he said, holding it up to the light then dropping it carelessly onto the pile. I watched nervously as he moved onto the display table and picked out a long necklace made of hand-carved wooden beads with a matching set of earrings.

'Ok, this'll do. The old girl likes jewellery. How much love?'

He took a thick wallet out of his pocket and handed over a wad of notes, obviously wanting me to sort out what I needed and give him back the rest. Either he was showing off or he just couldn't be bothered to use his card or find the right money. Whichever it was, I felt insulted. His arrogance had both annoyed and flustered me and I couldn't wait to get rid of him. Retreating behind the counter, I quickly wrapped the jewellery in tissue paper, put it in one of our gift bags, gave him his change and watched him walk towards the door, feeling distinctly sorry for the 'old girl'.

Meanwhile, in the kitchen, the dog was yapping in high-pitched protest. The man paused by the door. 'Maybe you should let Max out before he bursts a blood vessel.'

He turned and left, strolling across the marketplace as if he owned it, hands in the pockets of his jeans, elbows stuck out at right angles.

'You arrogant –' I stopped abruptly. How the hell did this complete stranger know my dog's name?

Later that evening, still uneasy, I decided to tell someone what had happened.

Beth's mobile was answered after only three rings but not by Beth.

'Hiya, this is Sarah. Beth's busy right now. Can I take a message for you?' She said it with a slide of the voice upwards that set my teeth on edge.

'No thanks, I'll call her back.' What was she doing answering someone else's mobile?

'Who shall I say called? I can take a message because, as it happens, Beth is my absolute bestie.'

'It's Amy, her friend Amy.' I stressed the word 'friend' but stopped myself from adding 'her absolute oldie'. Beth and I had known each other since childhood.

'Oh yes, I remember you. I'll tell her you called, Amy.' There was a muffled sound; she had obviously covered the phone with her hand for a moment.

Beth cut in. 'Hi Ames, sorry about that but Luca just won't go down tonight. He's being a right little grizzler. Paolo's great at settling him but he's working late.'

I could hear the front door of their flat closing in the background. Stupid, I know, but I consciously relaxed.

'Why did Sarah answer your phone?' I asked, trying not to sound petulant.

'Yes, that was a bit cheeky,' she agreed. 'She was here hoping to catch Paolo.'

Yes, I bet she was.

'She's learning Italian at an evening class and struggling with the homework.'

'Really?' I said, dryly. Surely Beth could see through that? The trouble was she expected other people to be as honest as she was.

'I was just wondering when we could get together for a catch up, just us. It's been ages,' I continued. 'And there's something I wanted to get your opinion about.'

I heard her sigh. 'I'll call you back, Ames. It's a bit tricky now – Luca just won't settle.' She sounded frazzled and unlike her usual placid self so, reluctantly, I let her go.

I hadn't even had a chance to tell her what had happened in the shop.

6. TOM

My mother rang me just as I was washing the clay off my hands and getting ready to go and pick up my daughter from school. So the last thing I needed was the parental panic streaming down the phone line from County Sligo. She's the kindest, most loving woman in the world but her timing is terrible.

'I've been thinking a lot lately, Tom, and you know, creativity doesn't pay the bills. If it did, your father and I would be millionaires.'

That was her opening gambit. Instantly I was reminded of something my ceramics tutor at art school was always warning us about: 'When Mr or Mrs Average go shopping for art, they're looking for pictures not pots.'

Actually, as we students quickly found out, Mr and Mrs Average hardly went shopping for art at all, unless it was a mass-produced bargain on Amazon.

'We're doing all right,' I said, deliberately keeping my voice level to give the impression of calm and order on this side of the Irish Sea. I knew how she'd sit and fret that her son and only grandchild were starving to death in the wicked wastes west of London. You see, I was a late, much-wanted child, a miracle according to my mother, who, in her words, had been 'minutes away from the menopause'.

Trying to sound upbeat, I explained that I was exhibiting in a local gallery now as well as online. 'People seem to love my work, Mam.'

The gallery was about the size of a fish and chip shop and was tucked away in a back street in Kingston upon Thames but it was a start.

'That's good but if it's not enough, maybe you should go back to teaching full time,' she said.

The same thought had occurred to me but I'd pushed it to the back of my mind. Three days a week at the local high school was enough, especially after what had happened in one of my lessons the previous week though I'd avoided mentioning that little incident to my mother or she would have had a meltdown.

'Don't worry, Mam, we'll be fine,' I reassured her.

God, I'm a good actor if I do say so myself.

'Sure, isn't it a mother's job to be worried about her son?' she insisted. 'I'll get a mass said, love.' Her answer to everything. 'Your father can go down to the church and arrange it. It'll do him good to get out for a bit. He's under my feet all day.'

I pictured my father in the old armchair by the range in the kitchen, still bewildered by retirement and wondering where the years of productivity had gone. He was a man who needed to be useful. Take that away from him and there wasn't much left.

If I could get the money together, I'd take Orla to Ireland in the summer holidays. It would lift my parents' spirits and give her a bit of spoiling from her granny and grandad. Besides, I was yearning for a bit of home-baked soda bread fresh out of the oven and dripping with soft butter.

'Tom? Are you alright, love?' I suppose my silence worried her.

I came to my senses. 'Yes. Listen, I have to go now, Mam. Orla… you know…'

'Of course. Trust me to call you at the wrong time. Off you go then, Tom.'

She was packing me off to school again, watching me go down the path and all the way up to the bus stop as if I might disappear if she went inside and closed the door. I could feel the fragile thread of her concern as she said goodbye and hung up.

Twenty minutes later, I was taking up my usual position by the edge of the kerb at a safe distance from what I call 'The Power

Mothers', the major players in school gate politics. Today, I could hear murmurings about the headteacher's decision to ban crisps and chocolate bars from lunch boxes – the poor woman was in for it as soon as that gate opened. As if that little group of women with their designer jeans and cut-glass accents would ever let E numbers or an overload of sugars and fats pass their precious children's lips. I suspected it was more to do with their right to choose. If she'd banned celery sticks and hummus, they'd still be furious.

'You must be Orla's dad,' someone said.

When I'd recovered from the shock of being spoken to, I turned to find a small, plump woman peering up at me, one hand shielding her eyes from the sun. She looked older, probably one of the grannies, and she had a kind face, lived-in – a face that strangers want to speak to, even the lone male among this pack of lionesses.

'Yes, Orla's mine all right. How did you know?' I asked.

'Well, there aren't any other dads here today and besides, you have Orla's lovely thick, dark hair.'

'No, actually, she has mine,' I smiled.

Oh lord, she was embarrassing me. But then I did a better job of embarrassing myself when I said, 'You wouldn't say that if you had to plait it every morning. Sure, it has a mind of its own.'

A puzzled look crossed her face until I hurriedly explained that I meant Orla's hair not mine.

'She's in the same class as my grandson,' she said. 'Benjie and Orla sit next to each other and apparently Orla's given him the impression you're some kind of superhero.'

I couldn't help chuckling at that – which was great because I could feel my shoulders drop slightly, easing the ache at the back of my neck.

'Then I better make the most of it while she's young enough to be deluded,' I replied. 'Shame children have to grow up and discover all your faults.'

The woman raised her eyes. 'And constantly remind you of them.'

Until recently, my daughter had harboured an ambition to be either a princess or a mermaid but since reading a book about the moon landing, her ambition was now focused on becoming an astronaut which meant that I had to paint over the fairy-tale castles on her bedroom wall and create a dramatic diorama of planets, moons and stars on the ceiling. Ok it wasn't exactly the Sistine Chapel and I'm no Michelangelo but it was worth the effort just to see Orla's face when it was finished. Sometimes, when I sneaked in to check she was asleep, she was just lying there staring up into space and I wondered what or who she was thinking about – although I think I know the answer to that one. Compared to her mother, I would always be second best, muddling along like an amateur pretending to know what he was doing. The thought stabbed at my heart.

'They're going to get married you know,' Benjie's granny announced.

'Who?' I asked, wondering if she'd done that thing that older ladies sometimes do, that flitting from topic to topic like absent-minded butterflies.

'Apparently, Benjie proposed to Orla during the outing to Bird World in the spring.'

'Really?' My laughter attracted darts of curiosity from the direction of the school gate. 'Then if we're going to be in-laws, I'd better introduce myself: Tom Brennan, father of the bride.'

'Babs, granny of the groom.' She shook my hand and we laughed at our silliness.

Meanwhile, the caretaker had unlocked the gate and a flood of children was erupting onto the pavement. Babs turned to look up at me.

'Do you mind if I say that I think you're marvellous, you know, in the circumstances? It must have been so hard for you when…'

I could see the struggle written on her face but she persisted, unfortunately.

'Someone here told me what happened and I'm so, so sorry Tom.

Not that it helps but –'

I had to force myself to smile. 'Thanks, Babs, you're very kind.' *Please God she'll let it go at that.*

Luckily, at that moment, she spotted her grandson in the crowd and moved away to meet him, leaving me ripped open with her sympathy and needing a moment to recover. When I turned back, Orla was charging at me, waving a piece of paper.

'Daddy, look – it's called "Starry Night".'

I took the painting from her and studied the yellow and white whorls of colour dabbed thickly onto a midnight blue background.

'Let's see. Who did this? Was it Van Gogh, by any chance?'

Orla's nut-brown eyes widened. 'No, it was me!'

I gave her my best look of astonishment. 'No! So it wasn't Van Gogh?'

She hopped from one foot to the other in her excitement. 'We've been trying to paint like him. He's a famous artist, you know. He chopped off his ear.'

'Not all of it, Orla, just a bit.' My personal bugbear is the teaching of gruesome details to engage children's interest in historical figures.

Orla looked downcast for a moment then said, triumphantly, 'And he shot himself.' She handed me her red book bag and took back the painting.

I sucked in a deep breath through my teeth then forced a smile. 'Well, that picture deserves a smart frame. I'll make you one, if you like.'

A woman with a mobile phone clamped to her ear barged past us, ignoring her child who was frantically trying to get her to look at his painting. Without even looking down at him, she grabbed the paper and crumpled it in her fist.

'Shut up, Daniel, can't you see I'm talking?'

'*Can't you see you're an arsehole?*' I said under my breath, taking my daughter's hand and drawing her away from the throng and along the road towards the park. She skipped along beside me, waving her picture like a flag and singing, her voice high and clear in the September afternoon. It was both painful and a wonder at the same time. Such bubbling happiness, as though nothing terrible had happened in our lives, as though brush-loads of thick blue, white and yellow paint could obliterate the memory of the worst day of our lives. How I envied her.

'I think that kind of quality artwork deserves half an hour on the swings,' I said solemnly, leading her through the iron gates and towards the children's playground. Immediately, Orla slipped away from me and ran towards the slide where a plump toddler was screaming his way down to the mat at the bottom. I watched with pride as she patiently waited for the little boy to climb the ladder and slide down again before taking her turn. Anna had taught her well.

There was a battered bench at the edge of the playground so I sat down and waited. When Orla switched her attention to the swings, it would be my job to push her hard and high so she could imagine herself soaring towards the moon. The ritual was for me to shout, *'One small step for Orla Brennan, one giant leap for mankind'* in my best American accent as she raised her slim brown legs and pointed her toes to the sky, leaning backwards until almost horizontal, her thick chestnut plaits flying out behind her.

A teenager, his face shaded by a grey hoodie, looked across from the path and quickly looked away again as I caught his eye. The park was a notorious place for shifty types to hang about thanks to the council cuts that had left local amenities sorely underfunded. There was an air of sad decay about it now. The grass was blotched with bare patches, flowerbeds were brown with the crisp corpses of last year's hydrangeas and the once vibrant café was just a graffiti-covered shell whose windows had been gleefully smashed in. When you walked past it, the smell of pigeon droppings and ancient fat encrusted on kitchen tiles was enough to force you off the path and onto the parched, scrubby expanse of green that had once held tennis courts.

I watched the boy amble up the path and towards the building before disappearing round the back. Obviously up to no good. Why else would anyone tolerate that smell?

'Daddy,' shrieked Orla. 'Push me!' While I'd been distracted, she'd run across to the swings and was ready for the next excitement.

'Coming,' I called, hauling myself up. 'You start the countdown and I'll be there for lift off.'

She'd just reached two when my mobile rang.

'Sorry, need to get this,' I said. 'Abort lift off while I see who it is.' I ignored her moans – there was no way I could afford to ignore possible business opportunities.

Mr McDonald didn't wait for me to say hello. The man had a way of charging straight into a conversation as if he had no time to spare, as if a stopwatch on his imposing desk was ticking away the seconds. He was just updating me on the two boys who'd had the fight in my art lesson. It wasn't my fault, he tried to reassure me, but the inference in his tone of voice was that this was not expected to happen in a school like his. Great, just call me teacher of the year.

Apparently, he'd excluded the quiet one, Jack, for a couple of weeks, having discovered there was a bullying issue that had tipped him over the edge. It made a lot of sense – I'd noticed that the Gresham kid was fond of throwing his weight around, even trying it with me until I threatened him with detention. Spending an hour or two sweeping up the art room after school didn't seem to appeal and when he realised that getting his father onto me had no effect either, that put the fox among the chickens, to quote my dad.

I thanked the head for ringing and was relieved when he added that the two kids would be put in separate groups. Once was enough. It's not good for a teacher to take sides but I knew who I was going to look out for from now on.

'Who was that?' asked Orla when I pocketed my phone. She was impatiently digging her heels into the dry, impacted earth at her feet.

'Mission Control,' I said. 'Wanting to know what the hold-up was.'

'Did you tell them it wasn't my fault?' She laid a freshly picked bunch of dandelions down on the bench. 'I'm going to paint these later.'

'Come on,' I said briskly, 'before someone else takes your place in the command module.' I took her hand as a teenager in the navy and grey uniform of St Saviour's sped past on a bike and headed up towards the deserted café. Thank God he didn't look over at us because I recognised him instantly. He still had the plaster over his nose.

About ten minutes later, as Orla was getting off the swing, he cycled back down the path at such a speed that he narrowly missed colliding with the mother and her toddler as they left the playground.

I heard Orla tutting to herself and turned to see her scowling. 'That boy doesn't deserve a bike.'

7. AMY

Roz was busy arranging a new display of vegan cosmetics when I arrived at the shop the next morning and apologised for being late.

'No Max today?' she asked.

'No, his carer's better, thank goodness.'

'You look like you could do with a strong coffee. Did you sleep last night? There are dark circles under your eyes, sweetheart.'

'No, it wasn't a good night.' I went to put the kettle on in the tiny staff kitchen.

'I'll have a coffee too, please,' Roz called. 'I had to tidy up this morning. Some of the stock was in a bit of a mess. Did you have some kids in here last night?'

'No,' I called, feeling guilty because I'd been too tired to refold the scarves. 'But this flashy guy came in late and was rummaging around for a present. He paid in cash. I was expecting to take his credit card but he just fished a load of notes out of his wallet.'

'We could do with more customers like that,' Roz said. 'But it would help if they were tidy as well as wealthy.'

'It was weird because he called Max by his name,' I told her.

'Oh? Is he someone you know?'

'No, I've never seen him before yesterday evening.'

The kettle clicked off. 'Corn poppy red,' I said, spooning the coffee into two mugs. 'That's how he described the colour of the red scarf. To me, it's more like tomato.'

'Talking of which,' Roz said, 'it's your turn to go to the bakers for the sandwiches today and mine's a mozzarella and tomato on sourdough.'

Around twelve, I left the shop and strolled round the corner onto the broad pedestrianised High Street, a place of buzzing friendliness thanks to the buskers playing amplified music in the centre of the precinct.

It's strange how outdoor music softens the world. For a few precious moments, all my worries about Earth Song's survival seemed to melt away in the melodies that floated into the air around us all. The mournful treble of South American pan pipes gradually merged into the singing of a young man sitting against the wall of a large sports shop. I stopped to listen, allowing myself to be momentarily lost in his hauntingly sad love song. On the way back, if he was still there, I would drop a couple of pound coins into the open guitar case to thank him for making me feel so deliciously sad.

When I emerged from the bakers, the whole marketplace was bustling with lunchtime shoppers filling the pavement in criss-crossing drifts. I threw the coins into the young man's guitar case, listened to his rendition of 'Perfect Day' for a few minutes then hurried on, remembering that Roz would be coping with the rush on her own.

But then an unexpected sight made me stop so suddenly that a woman following behind walked straight into me, apologising profusely as only the English can do when something's not their fault.

A familiar figure, dressed in a black leather jacket, dark blue, baggy denims and what looked like brand-new, glowingly white trainers, was approaching from the opposite direction, strolling among the crowds with what was almost a swagger. Coiled around his neck and tucked into the top of his jacket was a red cashmere scarf, the colour of a corn poppy.

Ben had spotted me. I expected a smile of recognition and certainly not the look of panic that came over his face. In seconds he had dodged sideways into a narrow alleyway running down between the shops; by the time I drew level with it, there was no sign of him.

To cover the length of the alley and disappear so quickly, he must have sprinted like a gazelle.

The scarf worried me. The colour was so distinctive – that orange-red was peculiar to the dyes used by our supplier in Southall and nothing like it was on sale anywhere else in the town. Had Ben been into the shop and helped himself to it while Roz was busy? It would certainly explain the guilty look on his face and the need to escape. No, I didn't want to think that of him. He just didn't seem the sort to go shoplifting.

'You've been ages – what kept you?' Roz asked when I got back. 'I've been rushed off my feet.'

Immediately, I went to check the pile of scarves on the shelf, half afraid of what I might find. 'Only the green scarves are left. Did anyone buy the last red one?' I asked.

'No,' Roz said. 'It was there this morning when I tidied the shelves but after you left, it got really busy. I had a crowd in the shop but nobody bought a scarf.'

'Did you notice anyone hanging about?'

'Listen, you know what it's like; I haven't got eyes in the back of my head,' Roz snapped. 'That's why we need CCTV in here, Amy. And another assistant, come to think of it.'

I said nothing, just stroked the soft green cashmere, wondering how I could have misread Ben so badly. The cocky teenager in the precinct seemed a mile away from the frail, waif-like boy on the riverbank, and besides that, it hurt to think that after letting him in to browse the evening before, he'd come back the following day to steal something. Where had the new jeans, jacket and expensive trainers come from? Had he taken them from one of the other shops?

That evening, my mind was still mulling over what had happened as I tapped at *Serenity*'s window and waited for Jan to let me in for my drawing lesson. Further along the riverbank, the cabin cruiser loomed ghostly white over its neighbours. A sudden movement there caught my attention. A man climbed down onto the bank and began to walk along the path towards me. Even in the darkness I recognised the swagger, as if he alone owned the space. As he came closer, my heart began to thump against my ribs. I turned away, not wanting him to recognise me. But I recognised *him* alright. He was wearing the same leather jacket with the collar pulled up over his ears. As he passed behind me, leaving a pungent smell of aftershave hanging in the air, he gave a low whistle which I was obviously supposed to be flattered by but which just annoyed me intensely.

It was a relief when the houseboat door opened and Jan appeared.

'Come in,' she said. 'Kyle's been putting the finishing touches to his painting so the place is a bit of a mess, I'm afraid. Up you come, trouble.' She hauled Max aboard then held out a hand to help me on. 'Kyle's hoping to find a buyer in one of those riverside places over there.' She pointed to a row of small restaurants on the other side of the Thames.

The fumes of wood smoke and oil paint caught in my throat as we entered the living area of the boat. Jan put the kettle on while I settled myself on the bench near the wood-burning stove, opening my sketch pad at a page of hastily drawn bottles.

At the other end of the room, Kyle wiped his brush on an old towel and glanced over. 'Is that your homework?'

I already knew what to expect, having completed the drawing at ten thirty the previous night.

Jan grimaced. 'Did you look carefully? You need to spend more time just looking, Amy. Art is about what you see as much as what you draw.'

'I was in a bit of a rush to tell you the truth. I'll do better next time.'

I accepted a mug of tea while Max curled up at my feet. The warmth of the cabin and the company of friends was easing the tension I'd been feeling since discovering that Ben was a shoplifter but it still hurt that I'd been so easily duped.

Propped up on a shelf was one of Jan's charcoal portraits of an old man who lived on a dilapidated, home-made houseboat further upriver. She had obviously studied him carefully judging from the photographic quality of the portrait which had captured his wizened, sunburned skin, toothless grin and black eyes glittering like two chips of jet.

Seeing my interest, Jan said, 'When you've mastered ellipses, you can have a go at drawing people.'

'Talking of boat people,' I said, 'do you know who owns *Sea Swift*, that fancy cabin cruiser further along the bank?'

Kyle shrugged. 'No, never seen him. He keeps himself to himself behind those tinted windows. Why do you ask?'

'I just wondered who could afford something like that.'

'It's a flashy boat for this part of the river,' Jan agreed. 'A few times now we've seen a young lad get off. Must be the son of whoever owns it but he looks as if he could do with a good meal. He's so pale, isn't he Kyle? His face is deathly white.'

'Yeah, titanium white. He has a luminous skin like someone who avoids the sun… or a ghost.'

'He haunts the riverbank,' Jan said, opening a packet of custard creams and slipping some onto a plate.

Kyle lifted his painting off the table where it had been resting and studied it, deep in thought for a moment, before holding it up for me to see.

'What do you think?' he asked.

'Wow! That's come on since you did the sketch!'

'This old river of yours is kind of moody. Sometimes it's calm and placid, flowing along gently, then other times, fast and aggressive, rushing along as if it can't wait to reach the sea. You paint it one way then the next day it's different.'

'Not the ideal sitter at all,' Jan smiled. 'Terrible at keeping still.'

It never ceased to amaze me how a talented artist could capture a scene so vividly. He had perfectly depicted the texture of the arching stone bridge, the movement of the water and the way it ruffled up around a flotilla of swans sailing in a line towards the bank among ripples splashed with red, gold and white by a fiery sunset. In the foreground was a surprise: he had painted the cabin cruiser *Sea Swift*, heading towards the bridge, causing the wake that the birds were riding.

But there was a sad atmosphere to the scene too, the feeling of a day drawing to a close, of light soon to be drowned by darkness.

'Do you mind if I take a photo?' I asked. It was cheeky of me but it would be a reminder of this talented couple. They both posed beside the canvas while I took the picture with my mobile phone.

'Actually, I have to be honest,' Kyle said, laying the painting back down on the table. 'I got Jan to paint *Sea Swift* because I'm not much good at boats.'

'It's fabulous,' Jan sighed. 'And probably a lot more comfortable than this old tub. Still, we'll be off home soon.'

By now, I was drowsily relaxed by the warmth of the wood-burner and the soft glow of the lamps. The subject of how long Jan and Kyle would be staying had never arisen and I'd lived in hope that the 'adventure' would last as long as they could manage it so the news was a blow.

'I thought you were… I mean, I just assumed you were staying around here for a while.'

'It's been great,' said Jan, 'but we miss home.'

'So when are you going?'

'Probably the end of November. We'll keep in touch, though. Maybe you'll come up and see us, Amy.'

'Maybe.' The word felt ephemeral, like a ghost of a word with barely a meaning.

Later, walking home, I waited at the end of the river path while Max relieved himself against a lamp post and turned to look back at the glimmer of light behind *Serenity*'s windows wondering how I could have forgotten that it would never be a permanent feature of the riverside. A nagging feeling that all the colours were gradually being washed out of my life was making me feel bleached and abandoned.

Max began to tug at the lead, straining to reach someone who was coming up behind us. I looked round in time to see Ben ruffling the dog's ears. 'Hiya, Max boy,' he said, gently.

'How are you?' I asked, coolly.

He was back in his usual clothes, the crumpled grey jacket, jeans and black trainers. Gone was the swaggering adolescent and no sign of the red scarf either. I wondered where he'd hidden it.

I was about to say, 'You've got a bloody cheek, you little rat,' when something made me stop. Under the cool light of the lamp post, I could see an angry purple bruise spreading under his right eye, like a dark stain on the pallid skin. The top lid was swollen, almost black.

'I'm ok, thanks,' he said, avoiding my gaze.

'How did you get that bruise?' I asked, trying not to sound like a teacher on playground duty and totally forgetting that I was talking to the boy who'd stolen from my shop. Had he been in a fight? If so, why? He just didn't seem the aggressive type.

All was not well with this kid, I realised. We'd been trained to spot the signs of abuse when I was teaching, the little things like changes in behaviour or the physical signs like under-nourishment, dirty clothing... or bruises.

Ben stuck his hands in his pockets, the look on his face telling me that I'd overstepped the mark. He'd pulled down a shutter between us.

'Gotta go now, sorry.' He started to walk away.

I called after him. 'Ben, if you need help, you can have my mobile number if you like.'

Was I stepping over an invisible line? After all, I wasn't the boy's mother. Who was though? More to the point, did she know that her son was out on the riverbank at this time of night?

Ben had stopped on the path and was looking back at me. 'Thanks, Amy,' he said, so quietly that I barely caught the words.

'For what?' I asked, surprised.

'For, like, worrying about me.'

He kicked a stone at his feet then turned and strode off towards the white cabin cruiser. Before I could think of a suitable reply, he had climbed aboard and disappeared down into the cabin. Immediately, the engine roared into life and *Sea Swift* growled away from the bank, did a broad U-turn in the middle of the river and glided away, leaving behind a white trail of rippling foam on the ink-black water.

I was still thinking about Ben when I got home that night until my mobile rang and my mother's number appeared on the screen. I thought about ignoring it until guilt got the better of me.

'Hi, Mum. Is Merlin ok?' Pretending an interest in the welfare of an overindulged goat took more acting ability than Richard had ever been capable of.

'Oh yes, completely fit now and showing a lot of interest in our nanny.'

'Oh, that must be embarrassing.'

'Poppy the lady goat, you silly goose.' My mother sighed as if in pain.

'And how are you and Dad?' I tried to inject a note of interest into my voice.

'That's why I'm ringing,' Mum said, breathlessly. 'It's very exciting but we've been invited to a do at the Albert Hall on the first of November. One of Daddy's old piano pupils is performing in his first solo concert so we were wondering…'

An uncomfortable sensation of being drenched in ice-cold water soaked into my body. I waited, holding my breath.

'Would it be possible to stay with you for a couple of days?' she continued. 'No need to go to any trouble; we'll bring sleeping bags and camp out in your box room, darling.'

'I don't have a box room; this is just a small flat, remember? Maybe you'd be better off booking into a hotel. I could ask Beth to book you a room in the Royal Kensington where she works. It's handy for the Albert Hall.'

'Oh no, no, no dear! We won't be any trouble. Daddy and I will be just as comfortable in your sitting room.'

I struggled to control the tremor in my voice. 'So what day are you coming?'

'The concert is on Saturday so we'll come on Friday 31st and go back on Sunday 2nd if that's all right.'

'So you're coming on Halloween?'

She laughed. 'That's right but we won't be in fancy dress.'

The image of the pair of them appearing at my door in fright masks and witch hats flashed into my mind.

'You'll be home on Saturday, of course, so perhaps we can go somewhere nice for lunch,' Mum added.

Saturday, the busiest day of the week at the shop. I had to think quickly.

'Um, the thing is, Mum –'

'Now, before you start panicking,' she broke in, 'we won't interrupt your schoolwork if you have any to do at the weekend. We'll be quiet as mice while you get on with it.'

'It's not that exactly, but –'

'And we'll be out of your hair by teatime Sunday. So that's settled then. Thank you, Amy. Your father will be thrilled – you know how much he hates hotels.'

'Paying for them, yes,' I muttered under my breath.

For a second, I considered telling the truth about giving up my school job for the shop. I even opened my mouth to confess before remembering in the nick of time that confession would mean admitting what had happened to the several hundred thousand pounds of my grandmother's inheritance. The fallout would be enormous simply because Dad had pleaded with his mother to leave the bulk of it to Marcus. So they'd be apoplectic, seeing it as a complete waste of money when Marcus would have put it to much better use. Love truly is blind sometimes.

From his perch on the arm of the sofa, Max released his grip on a cushion and cocked his head quizzically as if to say, 'Are you mad?' I swallowed the confession and let out the breath I'd been holding. The time was not yet right.

'Um, I'm afraid I have to be out all day that Saturday but maybe we could go out to dinner on Friday evening.'

'Oh? Is it something you can cancel? After all, we don't see that much of you, darling.'

'Sorry, it's been arranged for ages.' It wasn't exactly a lie.

By the time the call ended, I was even more exhausted. Max had gone back to chewing the cushion which, much to his satisfaction, had resulted in tiny puffs of stuffing emerging from a hole in the corner. I went out into the kitchen to get a chilled glass of white wine, pausing for a moment to stare at a photo on the fridge door of Beth and me at a party a few years ago. We had our arms around each other and were making hideous faces, spurred on by an invisible presence behind the camera. I leaned against the fridge and closed my eyes, listening to its purring in the silence of the room for a few moments before yanking open the door to extract a new bottle of Sauvignon blanc.

8. TOM

As we walked home on Friday afternoon, Orla stamped through the crisp leaves piled up beneath the plane trees, covering her white socks and black school shoes with a mess of brown and orange crumbs. I pretended to be cross and tutted at her, 'You're the one who'll be cleaning those shoes, young lady,' but secretly, it lifted my spirits to see her get as much pleasure from leaf crunching as I did at her age, smashing through the golden piles and watching them fly up like sparks of gold. It was those little moments of light and joy that kept me going.

Just in time, I managed to drag her away and across the road before we reached the large bike shop on the corner. Thankfully, she seemed to have forgiven me for not buying her the pink bike with the multi-coloured streamers on the handlebars but it was still in the window so I wasn't risking it. Anna had bought her blue Raleigh there, a second-hand, reconditioned road bike that she used for the journey to her office in Richmond. It was always a relief to turn our backs on Edward and Sons Bike Emporium.

'Dad...'

Oh no, I recognised that whiny tone, the one that Orla always used when she wanted to get round me.

'Yes, sweetheart?' I asked, wondering what was coming considering that she practically had a master's degree in adult manipulation, male adults in particular.

She slipped her small hand in mine. Little girls know all the tricks.

'Can we have fish fingers for tea?'

Foolishly, I relaxed. 'Of course but I don't know any fish that have fingers. Do you?'

She giggled. 'You're silly. And...'

'What? Do you want some chips as well?'

'Can I have a bike for my birthday in February? When I'm seven I'll be able to ride it properly.'

My stomach lurched. 'We'll see, Orla.'

'What does that mean? Does it mean yes?'

'It means I'll think about it. Bikes cost a lot of money, sweetheart.'

So she hadn't let go of the bike dream after all and, having resurrected it, she would nag and worry away, hoping I'd weaken. But no, I wouldn't – not on this.

'So what reading book have you got for tonight?' I asked, determined to divert her. I held up the red book bag. 'What's in here? *War and Peace* or something longer perhaps?'

'*Kipper's New Bike*,' said Orla, sulkily. 'I read four pages to Miss Thomas this morning.'

Shit. Why the hell couldn't she have chosen a different title?

'And what did she say about your reading?'

The question was weighted. Miss Thomas had informed me at the last parents' meeting that Orla had fallen behind because she wasn't practising enough at home. *Mea culpa, mea culpa, mea maxima culpa.* It was no good admitting that my wife was the one who had always heard her read. Such a lame excuse would never wash with a woman like Miss Thomas who looked as if castration would be the least I could expect for such a crime.

So I'd left the school that evening weighed down with guilt but determined to put in the work, reading Orla bedtime stories every night, listening to her stumbling attempts with her schoolbook, holding my tongue when she got stuck on the simplest of words even though I felt like yelling, 'That word is *was* for crying out loud! How can you not know that?'

But lately, she'd been speeding up a little, sounding less robotic and recognising a lot more words on sight so there was both hope and dread in my heart as I waited for the answer to my question.

Orla looked up at me, solemnly. 'She said I can go on to green level next week.'

'Fantastic! That's my girl!'

A heavy weight had been taken off my shoulders. 'Astronauts have got to be able to read, sweetheart,' I said. 'See, if you can't read the instructions, you might overshoot the moon and end up lost in space. So, green level, eh?'

I had no idea where green level was in relation to the standards expected for her age but thank God she was getting off brown at last because I was so thoroughly sick of the repetitive, simple language and the way nothing exciting ever happened. *Please God,* I thought, *on green level, Kipper will perhaps have an affair or get arrested for shoplifting or, best of all, get kidnapped by Somalian pirates.*

'That's good news to tell Granny Maureen when we ring her,' I said, patting her head. 'Now, what about fish and chips from Mr Patel's chippy? His fish don't have fingers but we need to celebrate the artistic and literary genius of Orla Brennan.'

Later, while she was getting ready for bed, I went into the sitting room to shift the newly ironed and folded clothes off the sofa, adding several pairs of small white socks which I'd draped over the radiator to dry. I was too tired to put it all away properly so I just dumped the whole pile onto the kitchen table.

Anna hated mess. Exhausted or not, she would have taken the laundry upstairs and refolded everything neatly and put it away in the relevant drawers or wardrobes. Everything had its place; everything was clean, tidy and ordered. I often wonder now how she did all that and why I just assumed she would and whether I ever thanked her. Did I help or just sit around while she did every fucking thing?

When Orla was finally asleep, I went down to the workshop. The kiln was packed with bowls waiting to be unloaded but tonight my focus was on the small rocking horse standing on the woodwork bench. My friend Kenneth hired a stall every year at the Christmas market on the South Bank selling wooden toys, and in a typically generous gesture had invited me to sell something of my own. The horse was glowing honey yellow beneath the lights, waiting to have its saddle finished and fixed to its curving back.

There's such pleasure to be had in shaping wood. I watched the shavings curl up from beneath the plane, running my hand along the smooth, warm curve of the saddle every now and then. For a while, I could forget that Orla would be up at seven demanding cocoa pops and complaining that the way I plait her hair was never as good as 'when mummy did it'.

My grandfather's carpentry tools, worn and familiar under my hand, felt like old friends who knew exactly what I wanted them to do. Time melted away as I became lost in the work. Somewhere outside in the darkness, a vixen screamed. Curls of wood were piling up on the floor at my feet and a smell filled the air like that of an ancient beech forest on the slopes of the Chilterns, a rich, musty smell of damp earth and rotting leaves that took me back to my childhood playing among the trees behind our house.

The next morning, both Orla and I overslept and when I finally woke it was to the sound of a heated exchange on the *Today* programme between Nick Robinson and the Home Secretary. The clock radio was tuned to Radio 4 because I needed to hear voices; somehow, they made the bedroom seem less cold and quiet. I missed my wife's warm body stirring beside me, her sleepy mumbling as she rolled over into my side and slipped her arm over my chest. I missed holding her and feeling her heart beating against mine. I missed... I missed... her.

I lay for a while listening to the verbal tennis as politician and presenter rallied in bad-tempered, interruptive conversation until the crisp tones of Mishal Husain announced that it was 8.15 which shocked me to my senses. Although it wasn't a school day for me, there was only half an hour to get Orla up, washed, dressed, fed and delivered to the school gate in time for the bell.

Predictably, she was grumpy at being woken so suddenly. Already stretched thin by exhaustion after a late night in the workshop, I struggled to keep my temper as she whined her displeasure.

'Today is going to be like the Olympics,' I said, forcing myself to be patient. 'Imagine that you're a star athlete and everything you do has to be at top speed so you can beat everyone else in your class.'

'Like sports day?' she asked, sleepily.

'Sort of, yes. This is the "be out of the door by eight thirty-five championships" and you're going for gold, Miss Brennan.'

It was wearying to be so positive and upbeat when actually, I was panicking at the thought of having Orla's name entered in the dreaded Late Book which was what happened if you got there after the gate had closed. Another red mark from Mrs Thornton in the office would set in concrete her conviction of my failings as a parent.

I'd hoped for an enthusiastic response to my Olympic fantasy but Orla was in a stubborn mood necessitating a firmer tone.

'Ok, I'm going to go downstairs and start the stopwatch on my phone. Your cereal will be on the table in exactly ten minutes.'

'But you have to do my plaits,' she wailed.

'Just for today, you can leave your hair loose.'

I braced myself for protest, knowing that Orla's hair would bother her all day, rebelling against all efforts to flatten it.

'We just don't have time, sweetheart, and it's all my fault I know. I'll make it up to you tomorrow.'

Her bottom lip projected in disgust. 'Mummy always did them even when I was late.'

'Yes, but Mummy's not bloody well here, is she?'

I left her then, slapping the bedroom door closed more in anger at myself than her.

When the child appeared in the kitchen ten minutes later, she sat down and began to eat her cereal in silence, studiously avoiding my eyes by staring down into her bowl. I could see the glistening of tears on the curl of her dark eyelashes and felt a rush of shame. None of this was Orla's fault. Come to think of it, it wasn't mine either.

'I'm sorry, sweetheart,' I said, feeling like a right bastard.

'That's ok,' she said in a small voice as if she'd shrunk. 'You swored.'

'Yes, Dad got out of bed the wrong side this morning.'

'What's the right side then?' she asked, looking up at me with wide, wet eyes.

I sat opposite her and buttered my toast. 'You did well to get down here in that time.'

Orla gave me a sad smile. 'You don't like it when I talk about Mummy.'

'No, it's not that, Orla, it's just…' Words failed me. It was too early for psychoanalysis with a six-year-old.

'Why did she leave us?'

The question came out of the blue. I thought she'd understood but here she was bringing it up again when in five minutes we needed to leave the house. Why, after all this time, had she chosen this moment? I checked my watch, not because I wanted to know the exact time but to gain some thinking space.

'We should go.'

'Ok,' she said, her voice still small. 'Was it my fault?'

Now it was me that was struggling. I wanted to scoop her up into my arms and tell her that sometimes life is an absolute bastard and there's nothing anyone can do about it, least of all me.

'Orla, what happened to Mummy is nothing to do with anything you or I did,' I said at last. 'It was a bad man driving too fast who took her away.'

The spoon clattered into the bottom of her bowl. 'I hate him,' she said.

'He probably hates himself, love.'

Oh yes. He hated himself enough to drive away and leave her. Nobody could hate him as much I did.

Orla nodded solemnly and went out into the hall to fetch her coat, leaving me to pull myself together.

9. AMY

Halloween crept up and jumped out at me far too soon.

'We've been round that bloody one-way system three times thanks to that bloody useless satnav,' Dad growled as I opened the front door on Friday evening.

'Nice to see you too, Dad.'

'And we got that satnav from a very reputable store,' Mum added. 'They're usually so reliable. Hello dear, we had trouble parking at first because there are a lot of children milling about your street dressed as wizards and witches.'

'Running all over the place like maniacs,' Dad said, still frowning.

'Oh, they're the neighbours' children. They always go out trick or treating on Halloween so they're probably full of sugar and high as kites,' I explained, stepping back to let them in.

They came into the hallway bringing with them a smell of cold, fresh air. Max, shut in the kitchen, became hysterical.

'Oh, I'd forgotten about *him*,' Mum said. 'We've become a bit allergic to fur since we moved. Sometimes we come out in these rashes, don't we, Ian?' She gave me a brief chilly kiss on the cheek.

Dad grunted, manoeuvred his bag into the sitting room and began shifting the cushions to one end of the sofa to make room for himself. He'd put on weight, probably due to the cream teas they treated themselves to on Saturdays.

'Maybe you should do an allergy test,' I suggested. 'Could it be the goats causing you problems?'

A look flashed between my parents, an exasperated expression that hinted at incomprehension at my stupidity.

'Hardly,' Dad sniffed. 'Our goats are hypoallergenic; they're a special breed with short hair that doesn't moult.'

'So, who's looking after the animals this weekend?'

My mother explained that the transgender farmer up the road was sending his teenage son down to feed the animals and keep an eye on the place.

'He's very reliable that Sandy and he's had a lot to cope with, poor lad, what with his mother becoming another dad. A cup of tea would be nice, dear.'

'I've made you a nice beef stew,' I said. 'I thought you'd be hungry.'

Dad punched a turquoise sari cushion into submission and settled back on the pink velvet sofa looking incongruous and uncomfortable.

'We stopped at one of those dreadful motorway places and had something unrecognisable with chips,' he grunted.

'Very filling, though,' said my mother.

Already, the flat seemed over-full and not mine anymore. Beth's husband, Paolo, once said that when you're with your parents you feel like a child again. He was right. On the rare occasions we were together, I seemed forced to walk a tightrope of unspoken recriminations that sent me straight back to childhood. It felt as if at any minute, I might be sent to bed without any supper for having a string of unreliable boyfriends, for being unmarried and childless and for having a job that was nowhere near as important as my brother's, money earned being apparently the only marker of success, beating the education of children by a mile. Oh lord, how would shop-keeping rate in their opinions?

This time, I'd promised myself that things would be different. Time for reconciliation. Over this weekend, I would make them see that I was a competent, autonomous adult. Pity about the stew, though. I'd spent ages shopping for quality ingredients and simmered it slowly in a pint of Guinness. It smelled delicious.

So far, they hadn't mentioned the colour of the walls which was a blessing. I took a tray of tea and biscuits into the sitting room and put on a bright smile, like an actress emerging from the wings to greet her audience.

'I've put Max in the garden for a while so you can relax. You must be exhausted after that journey.'

Seeing my parents slumped together on the sofa, the grooves and shadows of fatigue drawn on their faces, I felt a sudden rush of love that made me determined to take care of them no matter what they threw at me.

'Thank you for putting the dog out,' said my mother. 'I was beginning to feel a bit itchy.' She took the mug of tea. 'No cups, dear?'

'What's going on with this colour?' Dad asked, looking around at the lilac walls. Above his head was a large ceiling rose which I'd painted a vibrant pink, picking out the plaster leaves in a soft moss green. I explained about the landlord's instruction to repaint the whole flat magnolia but omitted to mention his threat of eviction if it wasn't done by Christmas.

'Ever the non-conformist, our Amy,' said Mum. 'So unlike Marcus. By the way, he Zoomed us last week to say he's had a pay rise, quite a substantial one actually.'

I forced myself to look pleased. 'Good for him.'

No doubt there was a self-satisfied look on my brother's face as he made his announcement and waited for their excited coos of approval. Personally, I felt it was unbecoming for a grown man of twenty-eight to constantly elicit his parents' admiration.

'You two are *so* different,' my mother continued. 'Marcus has always been so grounded and focused on his goals whereas you seem to flit about with your head in the clouds.'

She said it kindly but it hurt. Their opinion of me was so fixed that it made me feel like a specimen butterfly pinned down in the glass cabinet of their minds, forever a cabbage white to Marcus's red admiral.

'How's school, dear?' The question I'd been dreading came out of the blue.

'Still fine, thanks. More tea?' I hoped they couldn't hear the catch in my voice.

It was a burden this inability to be honest with them. People changed jobs all the time without feeling terrible guilt as if they'd let down generations of their family. Although they probably hadn't gambled their beloved grandmother's hard-earned money in the process.

The previous evening, I'd thoroughly cleaned the flat and stored anything incriminating in a box in the boot of the car, including the pile of 'Good Luck' and 'Sorry You're Leaving' cards from every class in the school with their hilarious and occasionally touching messages. Most precious among them was the giant card the nursery children had made, covered with small handprints in primary colours and names scrawled in wobbly capital letters, some of them almost recognisable.

Other things had been stuffed in the boot too. My parents had come up for the day a couple of years ago to visit me in my old flat and Dad had opened one of the kitchen drawers. Unfortunately, it was the messy drawer, the one crammed with the paper detritus of everyday life, stuffed to jamming point with old bills, supermarket vouchers, cab company cards and local take-away menus. Even worse, he'd spotted a final reminder for the electricity bill and had delivered a ten-minute lecture on the perils of being cut off from sources of power, completely ignoring my protestation that if I wanted to live in the cold and dark like a Victorian pauper in an attic then it was my choice and yes, I do realise what a feeble argument that was.

Anyway, this time, I was ready for him. There was nothing in the drawer except a small pile of paper napkins and a set of posh cake knives, an unused gift waiting for a cake that came up to their standards. I had also scrupulously tidied my bedroom because it was far easier to let my parents sleep in there while I slept on the sofa.

Shortly after drinking their tea, Mum and Dad both expressed a need for an early night after the long journey. They weren't getting any younger, I realised, and one day they wouldn't be there at all which set me off wondering what that would feel like, whether I'd spend the rest of my life regretting that we were never close enough or wondering what I could have done to be a better daughter.

When I showed them into the bedroom, Dad's eyebrows twitched at the sight of the strawberry pink quilt and matching pillows (bought brand new from the market the day before and, to be honest, dirt cheap) while my mother just exclaimed, 'Oh… bright!' In my attempt to be hostess of the year, there were new white towels on the bed and a small vase of scarlet artificial poppies on the bedside table beside a pot of rose-scented hand cream from Earth Song. A spritz of lavender 'Serene Sleep' bedroom mist (sprayed just before their arrival) still hung in the air, adding to the general effect of a comfortable, welcoming oasis of calm.

'This is lovely, dear,' said my mother. 'You've made it so nice for us.'

I glowed secretly until my father asked, 'Does the window open in here? There's a funny smell.'

I left them to their bedtime routines and retreated to gather up the tea things from the sitting room. One evening down, one to go. While I was doing the washing up, Dad padded into the kitchen in his slippers and dressing gown.

'You know, Amy,' he began, 'you can't be a skittery little thing forever. Sometime, you're going to have to grow up.'

I turned to face him. 'What are you talking about, Dad?'

'This bloody stupid rubbish,' he said, holding up the one object I'd forgotten to hide – a book I'd left in the bedside cupboard. 'Who the hell is Rollo Moonshine when he's at home? Some hippy, pseudo-scientific charlatan making pots of money from gullible airheads, no doubt.'

Not far from my flat was a musty old second-hand bookshops

smelling of damp and mouldy paper owned by an ancient man in brown wrinkled corduroy trousers who specialised in the odd and the occult. I'd spotted this battered copy of *Protecting your Aura* by Rollo Moonshine and bought it as a joke to give Beth when she was pregnant with Luca but got so engrossed in its ridiculous hokum (you always have to read a gift book first just in case) that she never received it. Probably just as well because Beth is a sensible down-to-earth type firmly rooted in reality.

I wanted to explain all this calmly but being called an airhead as well as a 'skittery little thing' caught me off guard.

I lowered my voice to sound more authoritative. 'Dad, I'm thirty-one years old and what I choose to read is my business. Do you think I'd criticise *your t*aste in literature?'

His taste tended towards expensive volumes with handsome spines that looked good on a shelf of mainly unread books arranged to impress. 'Look at this beauty,' he'd say, delicately running his fingers over the faux leather cover of his newest acquisition.

'What's it about then, Ian?' someone once dared to ask.

'Not sure yet but I'll get round to reading it some day when I've finished the others in my pile,' he'd said, replacing the book on the shelf with its virgin comrades.

He was looking at me sadly, as if deeply grieved by my very existence. 'Sometimes, I worry about you, Amy,' he said, quietly.

'There's no need, Dad. I'm perfectly fine.'

Breathe in to the count of five, breathe out to the count of ten. Be calm and at peace. (Rollo Moonshine in Chapter three: 'Connecting to the Universe'.)

'Are you?' Dad moved closer. 'Marcus, well, he can take care of himself and, let's face it, he'll always look out for number one. But you're made of softer stuff, Amy. You're more gullible.'

Where the hell did he get that idea? For a minute I just stared at him, wondering how we could have become such strangers; how had this fantasy daughter of his filled his mind and replaced the real one?

I held my hand out for the book. 'I'm stronger than you think. There's no need to worry about me.'

'We brought you up to be a good Anglican,' he said. 'What do you think you're doing with this alternative stuff? You know, I worry that you could end up in some awful cult having your mind destroyed by a weirdo like this.' He jabbed a finger into the photo of the dreadlocked Rollo on the front cover.

'Then you really don't know me very well, Dad,' I said, still holding out my hand.

He hesitated before passing it to me. 'Bin it,' he ordered. 'That new age nonsense will do you no good.'

I threw the book onto the kitchen worktop. He was still standing there with that worried look on his face and I so wanted him to give me a hug and say that he was proud of me.

'It was a joke,' I said, quietly. 'I know it's nonsense but I wanted to make Beth laugh.'

'Ah, Beth,' he said, half smiling at last. 'Now there's a lass with her head screwed on.'

I nodded. 'That's why she's my closest friend. Good night, Dad. I hope you sleep well.'

'Why do you have to be so stubborn?' he sighed. 'I don't know what we're going to do with you, Amy Lewis.'

The insult stung. 'You don't have to do anything and someday, I'll prove it.'

I turned away and, hearing him scuffle off back to bed, opened the kitchen door and went out into the garden. It was bitterly cold under a clear black sky pitted with faint stars – not a night to be outdoors but the sharp, fresh air was what I needed just then.

Max was shivering and whining pathetically at my feet so I picked him up and held him close, tolerating his enthusiastic face licking as tears ran down my cheeks and into the thick ruff of fur around his neck. He was used to it. The night Richard left, Max ended up soaked to the skin.

When I went into the kitchen at seven the following morning, I could tell immediately that my parents had been discussing me because Mum glanced sideways at Dad, flashing a sharp look of warning that blocked whatever he was about to say.

'Morning,' I said, more brightly than I actually felt but still determined to keep the atmosphere positive. 'You're up very early – did you sleep ok?'

It was a relief to hear my father say that he had quickly 'dropped off' as he put it in spite of the ultra-feminine, pink bed linen. In fact, they both looked fresh and rested after a long night's sleep in the king-size, memory foam bed bought with another chunk of Grandma Lewis's money. Although, had they known about that, they wouldn't have slept a wink. I, on the other hand, was feeling exhausted after a cramped, restless night on the sofa with Max curled up in the crook of my knees so I wasn't in the mood for any more scathing comments from my father. Just in case, I'd hidden Rollo Moonshine's book under the sofa, pushing it way back where Max wouldn't be able to drag it from its hiding place.

I left them sitting knee to knee at my small breakfast bar tucking into boiled eggs and wholemeal toast and set off for work taking Max with me, thankful that they seemed to have swallowed my explanation for being absent all day.

'I hope your friend's all right after her operation,' my mother had said. 'It's so good of you to pick her up from the hospital and stay with her for a while.'

Dad, on the other hand, had looked decidedly suspicious. 'Wasn't there anyone else who could do it?'

'No, I'm the only one she trusts,' I said, firmly. A cloak of guilt fell onto my shoulders but I shrugged it off. Needs must as Granny Lewis used to say.

At eight o'clock on a Saturday morning, the town centre had a calm stillness about it; the air was cool and fresh as if it had been washed clean over-night. This was my favourite time to walk through

Kingston while the streets were spacious and quiet and even the brown river seemed rested and unruffled. The day was full of possibility because it had only just started, like an empty page newly turned, not yet creased or marked. Gradually, the pain of my father's remarks the night before was easing away and a new optimism was replacing it. Today would be different.

As I crossed the pedestrian precinct to enter the marketplace, the sight of a large yellow police sign brought me to a halt. The words 'Fatal Incident' were picked out in white letters followed by the date and time: 2.00 a.m. Friday October 31st and a contact number. Halloween night in any town can be lively at closing time when warm, drunken people erupt into fresh, cold air. I speak from personal experience.

In the shop, Roz had no clear idea what had happened apart from rumours flying around the square.

'The manager of the coffee shop thinks someone may have drowned when they accidentally stumbled into the river, probably while they were drunk. It's happened before.'

I vaguely remembered seeing grainy CCTV pictures on the news a few years ago showing a young man stumbling out of a nightclub and down a dark street towards the river.

'Do they know who the dead person was?' I asked.

'A young boy, I think,' said Roz. 'Some guy in the marketplace told me there was a teenager involved. He thought it might have been another stabbing.'

'A teenager?' Immediately, Ben came into my mind.

'Honestly, these young kids seem to want to wipe each other out,' Roz said. 'I don't understand it. Thank God my Nathan isn't that age yet.'

'Did he say what the teenager looked like?'

'No, nobody knows the facts yet. You know what it's like when these things happen – everyone has their own ideas.'

Once we were open there wasn't time to think about the incident but during the lunchtime lull, as Max was worrying to go out, I clipped on his lead and headed off across the marketplace and along one of the side streets that led to the riverside. Halfway along on the left-hand side was my favourite charity shop which was about to be the recipient of my brand-new, hardly worn sky-blue stilettos. Hopefully, someone else would be able to wear them without the crippling pain they'd inflicted on me.

The shop had once been a butchers and still had, beneath its large front window, a decorative tiled panel depicting a sturdy bull surrounded by rolling green fields. Unusually for a Saturday, it was closed with all the lights off. I stopped to look through the window and was just about to turn away when I noticed a large bouquet of white chrysanthemums propped up by the door beside a candle flickering in a red glass. A small white card was tucked between the creamy heads of the flowers and as I bent down to get a closer look at the writing, the words 'Rest in peace' came into focus.

'Sad, isn't it?' said an elderly man behind me. He dropped a large black sack down beside several others that had been left by the tiled bull and straightened up. 'Some kid, some teenager, I believe. They're all on drugs, of course. In my day, you thought yourself lucky if you got your hands on a bottle of cider. Now look at them.' He shrugged and shuffled away, hands in pockets.

I was about to leave when something caught my eye. Half hidden by the bouquet was a red scarf, coiled up on the scuffed black and white floor tiles. I bent down and lifted the end of it, finding the familiar cream-coloured label with the word Earth Song picked out in green cursive script.

'Ben!' The word just erupted out of my mouth.

I saw him in my mind's eye strolling through the lunchtime crowds dressed in what looked like brand-new clothes with the poppy-red scarf tucked jauntily into the neck of his jacket. Then, under the pale light of the lamp, looking gaunt and battered. Surely he couldn't be dead?

'Did you know this lad?' a voice behind me asked.

A middle-aged woman in a navy-blue coat was fending off Max's enthusiastic attention so I straightened up and pulled him sharply back, apologising. The woman reached into her bag and held up an ID card.

'Detective Inspector Lynn Morris, Kingston CID. If there's any information you have about this incident, we'd be very grateful for your help.'

'I recognise that scarf,' I said. 'I know a boy who has a scarf like that. We sell them in my shop but he…'

The detective was studying me keenly with cool, grey eyes. She reminded me of my old headmistress – the same severe bob-cut dark hair and penetrating stare that had reduced many a child to a quivering, confessing wreck.

'He took a liking to the colour. It was his favourite,' I finished lamely. I wasn't about to accuse him of shoplifting in front of this woman.

'Tell me about this Ben.'

'He's about thirteen or fourteen I'd say but he could just be small for his age.'

Lynn Morris narrowed her eyes. 'So is there any reason why this particular boy might end up dead in this doorway?'

The blunt question took me by surprise.

'Do you know who it was?' I asked, anxious to know for sure. The police had a habit of skirting round, trying to find out what you knew before telling you the facts of a situation. When my car was stolen and ended up being used in a raid on a jewellery shop in Richmond it had taken fifteen minutes of questioning before they admitted they'd found it and apprehended the thieves just as they were loading it with bags of jewellery. I wasn't in the mood for that sort of technique now. I needed to know whether Ben was alive or dead.

'I'm sorry but I don't know the facts yet,' she said. 'I'm on my way to start my shift at the station but is there anything I should know about this boy you mentioned?'

I hesitated for a moment then decided to tell her what I'd noticed about Ben's general appearance and demeanour, his link to the cabin cruiser and my hunch that he wasn't attending school. She thanked me and jotted something down in a notebook produced from her shoulder bag.

'We're up to our eyes in cases but I'll get one of my team to talk to you about this boy. In the meantime, it would be useful if you could write down all the times and places you've seen him and any details you remember about this boat.'

'The boat's called *Sea Swift*.'

'Nice name. Just jot your name and number down for me and I'll get one of my team to call you.'

When she'd gone, I stood looking down at the white flowers and wondering if I'd done the right thing because, after all, Ben was none of my business. Partly, it was a relief to share my concerns but I couldn't help feeling guilty at involving the police and possibly getting him into trouble. If he was still alive, that is.

'Shit, have I done the right thing?' I said, looking down at Max. He looked back at me then suddenly cocked his leg up against the tiled wall. A thin yellow stream slowly flowed across the black and white tiles towards the crisp cellophane of the bouquet.

Later that afternoon, I left Max with Roz and made my way back, intending to leave the bag of shoes at the front of the charity shop. But as I reached the top of the narrow street, I saw something that made me pull up sharply.

Ben was standing by the shop doorway, looking down at the white flowers. He was motionless until, as if emerging from a trance, he suddenly bent down, pulled out the red scarf, rolled it up into a ball and stuffed it into his jacket pocket. I was about to call his name when he turned away and ran off down the street and round the corner, leaving me wondering what on earth was going on with him.

10. LYNN

As soon I got to the incident room that morning, I asked who the dead boy was.

Sam Clinton looked up from his computer. 'Are you ready for this, Ma'am?'

'As ready as anyone can be when it comes to the death of a teenager. Who was it then?'

'It's James Gresham, the son of Greg Gresham who owns that fancy car dealership on the main road, the one that sells motors most of us can only dream about. The dad has made a positive identification, poor sod, but at the moment, only the family know. It's not public knowledge and we're respecting their privacy.'

'Until the press get hold of it,' added Kai. 'They're like bloody ferrets.'

'It'll be all over social media as well,' Sam said.

'James Gresham? Are you sure?' I sat down at my desk, feeling weak.

Sam frowned. 'You ok, Lynn?'

'My son knows him. They are... were... at the same school. Do we know what happened?'

He checked his notes. 'Apparently, his parents rang the station around three a.m. when their son hadn't arrived home from a Halloween party. You can imagine their reaction. We've sent someone over there to act as family liaison.'

I could feel the blood draining away from my face.

'Are you sure you're ok?' Kai asked. 'You've gone very pale.'

'Is there anything on the town centre CCTV?' Chances were that

James had shown up and, hopefully, anyone who was with him.

'Sure. Take a look.' Sam plugged a memory stick into his computer. 'I went over to the control room and downloaded it this morning. The operator on duty last night called the emergency services. It'll be clear when you see it.'

On the screen, strings of small ghosts and witches were scampering about the marketplace on their giggly quest for tricks or treats.

'Sorry,' said Sam. 'I need to fast forward a few hours.'

As the nightclubs and pubs of the town began to close, spilling their customers out onto the streets, the atmosphere changed and became more edgy. Then, at around two o'clock in the morning, a lone figure appeared in the deserted square, looking at first glance like just another drunken lad lurching his way home through the dark streets until Sam zoomed in to get a closer look and we could see it was James. A scarf was hanging loosely round his neck and over the front of his padded jacket. Although, in the grainy greys and blacks of the picture, it was impossible to discern the colour, I knew it was red.

'So that's James Gresham,' I said under my breath.

Sam zoomed further in to get a good look at the boy's face.

'It's shocking to see how young this lad is. Look at his eyes; they're staring wildly as if he can't focus properly. Now, he disappears then turns up again on another camera at the corner of this side street. You can see he's slowing down.'

I leaned forward to get a better look. James was struggling to stay upright. Every now and then, he bent double as if trying to catch his breath before suddenly collapsing sideways into the doorway of the charity shop where he lay still in a slumped heap beside the black sacks piled up along the front of the shop.

Within minutes, the screen was lit up by the glare of flashing lights, and a couple of paramedics ran over and knelt in the shop doorway. I watched, mesmerised, as they worked frantically to resuscitate the boy.

'Apparently, they worked on him for about twenty minutes,' Sam said.

On the screen, one of the paramedics sank back onto his heels and shook his head at his colleague.

Suddenly, I felt sick. 'What the hell were the Greshams doing letting a fifteen-year-old boy stay out till that time of night?'

I'd imposed a strict curfew on Jack. If he wasn't home by eleven, he was in deep trouble. My friend Jane often accused me of being old-fashioned and far too strict. 'These kids are street wise, Lynn,' she was fond of saying. 'It's not like when *we* were fifteen. We were more like children at their age whereas, these days they know it all.'

'They *think* they do,' I always insisted. 'And that's the trouble.'

'When my kids are that age, I'll be checking up on them,' Sam was glancing at the small photo on his desk. His wife and two kids smiled back at him.

'I'm twenty-nine and my mum still rings to check I got home alright,' said Kai.

Sam shot him a look of disbelief. 'More fool you for telling her about your social life.'

'So do we know what the cause of death was?' I asked, still trembling.

Kai checked his notes. 'Possible drug overdose but we're waiting for the results of the toxicology test.'

'Drugs then?'

I remembered Greg Gresham and his wife sitting opposite me at the head's meeting with that superior expression on their faces, with that unspoken inference that I was a failing single parent. It was outrageous but no one sodding well deserved this.

'Maybe the kid had taken something that was contaminated,' Sam suggested. He had studied drug-related offences, driven by a personal hatred of dealers after losing his nephew to a cocaine overdose. I respected his opinion.

'Do we have any evidence for that?' I asked.

'The paramedics said his lips were blue and that's one of the signs that a drug has been cut with a dangerous chemical. Or it could have been something that caused a heart attack, of course. Whatever it was, someone out there is dealing death.'

'How the hell did James get hold of it?'

I'd repeatedly drummed into Jack the dangers of alcohol and drug abuse, not sparing him the details of what we'd seen: the wrecked lives and zombie-like states of the unfortunates trapped in a vicious circle of addiction. How could the Greshams have missed the signs that James was using?

My thoughts were interrupted by DC Chauhan.

'These bastards are probably dealing in front of our very noses outside local schools. Is it worth checking their CCTV and talking to staff to see if they've noticed anyone hanging around?'

'Good idea.' I got up and headed for the coffee machine, a leaving present from a colleague who'd recently retired. Hopefully, the next person to leave (me?) would treat us to a new set of mugs. I picked the one with the least brown stains and no chip in the rim and waited for the machine to work its magic.

'Should we bother with the faith schools?' asked Sam. 'I mean, the girls at the convent are hardly likely to be indulging, are they?'

'Check them all and don't take anything for granted. Start with St Saviour's, James Gresham's school.'

And Jack's. Something he'd said had been bothering me ever since the incident with James the previous week. Sod it, I thought. By the time I got home, he would probably have heard the news on social media.

The coffee was predictably disgusting but it did the trick. My brain shifted up a gear.

'Sam, there's something else I need you to do.'

I told him about meeting a young woman called Amy Lewis outside the charity shop and about her concerns for a boy she'd seen a few times on the riverbank. I scribbled down Amy's phone number and passed it to him.

'It could be something or nothing but have a chat with her anyway.'

At lunchtime, I reached for my coat, told my colleagues I would be out for a couple of hours and headed home, texting Jack that I was coming and to stay where he was.

He was waiting for me when I got home and had even made some doorstop sandwiches with wedges of thick cheese shoved between roughly cut slabs of bread. He was just arranging these on plates when I walked into the kitchen.

'What?' he asked, seeing my look of surprise.

'Thanks, Jack, much appreciated.'

I decided not to ask if he'd washed his hands. Talking to my son often felt like treading a narrow path through a minefield in which one false move or careless word could release an explosion of rage. So this welcome felt like a truce. Better not to spoil it for the sake of hygiene.

'S'all right.' He picked up the plates and led the way into the sitting room.

I eyed the thick crusts warily. Just lately, I'd been suffering from toothache and often woke up with my jaw tightly clenched. My dentist was always warning about the terrible effects of teeth grinding. Well, he should sodding well try doing my job and see if he could avoid gritting those perfect white teeth of his.

We settled ourselves side by side on the sofa in what seemed an unusually peaceful atmosphere. I told myself to be careful, take it slowly and definitely avoid sounding as if I was interviewing a suspect. So, to begin with, I broke the news about James as calmly as I could.

Jack looked me in the eye for the first time in ages. 'He's dead?'

'Yes, love.'

'How? I mean, why? I mean, how could that happen?'

'At the moment, we don't know exactly why he died but there'll be an autopsy.'

The colour drained from his face.

'Even though you two didn't get on, it's still horrendous,' I persisted, reaching for his hand. It was cold so I rubbed it gently.

'He was a druggie,' Jack said.

'What?'

'I've seen him buying cannabis off this kid in the park and about two weeks ago, when I was hanging about in the old café, I heard them talking outside. He asked the kid to bring him some ecstasy tablets.'

'Ecstasy? Are you sure?'

'The kid said he was only supposed to sell it to adults but James beat him up and took his scarf off him so he gave in.'

'So you're telling me that James Gresham was taking drugs regularly?'

'Yeah. And he told this kid that he wanted the ecstasy for this Halloween party he was going to.'

'How old was this other lad?'

'Thirteen, fourteen maybe. He's small and skinny like he doesn't eat properly or something. I wanted to help, Mum. I wanted to go outside and stop James hitting him but I just couldn't. I was scared he'd beat me up too.'

How is it possible to feel glad that your child wasn't beaten up when another child was? It's a strange morality. Graham would probably have told him off for not pitching in and standing up against a bully. I, on the other hand, knew that he would have come off worse. Jack was not a fighter.

'Does this younger kid go to Saint Saviour's?' I asked.

'No, I don't think he goes anywhere. He's never in school uniform.'

'Would you recognise him again?'

'Yeah, I think so. He has a northern accent too.'

'That's useful information, Jack.'

'So James really is dead?' He sounded as if he hadn't believed it first time round.

'Yes, I'm afraid so.'

I was surprised to see tears welling up in the corner of his eyes. Could it be the two boys hadn't been such enemies after all?

'It's over.' He said it quietly as if I wasn't there sitting beside him.

I pushed the fringe out of his eyes, surprised when he didn't protest. The scar on his forehead was fading but there would always be a line of paler skin to remind us of James Gresham.

'What's over, Jack?' I asked, praying that the shutters wouldn't come down.

'I can't tell you, Mum.'

He turned his head away, breaking the fragile connection between us. I was in danger of losing him again.

'What can be so bad that you can't talk about it? You said he was bullying you. Is that it?'

'Yeah, but that's not all and I can't tell you. I can never tell you, Mum.'

'Listen, I've heard it all in my time with the police force. You can't shock me, I promise.'

'You'll hate me,' he said, still avoiding my eyes. 'You'll hate me even more than you hate Dad.' He shifted further along the sofa.

That stung. 'Listen, I don't hate your dad, ok?' A lie but needs must. 'And I could certainly never hate you. Is it about the drugs?'

Please God, he wasn't smoking cannabis. So many kids were these days but surely I'd know. My friend Linda had recently found some wraps hidden in the bottom of her son's sock drawer so I'd done a search of Jack's room while he was at football practice. I'd found nothing, but the relief was tainted by guilt at mistrusting him.

In the silence that followed, we waited. Years of experience in interview rooms had taught me patience. Very few people had the nerve to sit out a prolonged silence, not even a teenager with the capacity to stay sulkily mute for hours. Finally, when I couldn't stand it any longer, I said, quietly, 'Keeping it to yourself is going to eat you up.'

He sighed. 'Ok, but you won't like it.'

'Try me.'

I sat back, desperately trying to look more relaxed than I felt. When he finally began to talk, the words poured out of him in a rush so that all I could do was listen without interrupting until he finished. As Jack's story unfolded, I couldn't help wondering how one boy could torment so many other children without being detected by the school staff. Apparently, James Gresham had been demanding money from several of the kids in exchange for not being beaten up after school by his little gang of cronies.

'How long has this been going on?' I asked, determined to keep my tone neutral. Inside though, I was shaking with anger.

'Since we started at St Saviour's – in Year 7,' Jack said. 'But it seems longer, like forever.'

'What? And nobody ever reported it?'

'You don't understand, Mum. We were all too scared and then he started on the nerdy guys in my year group.'

'So, did *you* pay up?' *Great. You just lumped him in with the nerds.*

Thanks to his dad's complete refusal to contribute, how on earth would Jack have ever been able to pay off James with such a small amount of pocket money?

'No, I never gave him anything. I told him it was blackmail and he was a criminal.'

'Good for you.'

It was the first time that my son had shown any sign of being a chip off my block and a courageous one at that. DI Jack Morris – it had a ring to it.

'I'm proud of you for standing up to him,' I said.

He shrugged. 'Oh yeah, what a hero. He found other ways of making my life hell, didn't he? I didn't get beaten up but he'd pick on me every day doing dumb things like throwing my books down the toilet or spitting in my lunch. Then when you and Dad split up, it got worse.'

'But how did he know about me and your dad?'

'Dunno.' He shrugged again, harder this time.

'Oh no, you didn't tell everyone on Facebook did you?'

To say that I was suspicious of all things social media would be an understatement. The trouble is, I'd seen the harm it could do to fragile young people. A few months before, a young girl had committed suicide after being persistently bullied online about her appearance. On the news, they showed a selfie she'd taken. Her pretty, shiny-eyed face with its wide, lip-glossed smile was doing a good job of hiding the hidden pain.

'Jack, is that what you did?'

He looked away. 'Might have. Not Facebook, though, but I wanted to tell my friends. I needed to tell someone.'

More guilt. Of course he did. 'Go on.'

'Anyway, I'd had enough. Then, when I overheard James buying cannabis from this kid in the park, I stopped him in the corridor the next day and told him I knew he was on drugs and if he didn't lay off me and the other kids, I'd tell Mr McDonald everything. It felt so good, Mum, like for once *I* had power over him. Anyway, it was great for a while cos James avoided me and I thought that was it, no more hassle.'

'But I'm guessing it wasn't the end?'

'No, he was just working out how to really screw me.'

'Screw you? How?'

He put his head in his hands and groaned. 'I can't tell you what he did,' he mumbled through his fingers.

Searching my mind for all the possibilities, I was only too aware that if I mishandled this, Jack would slope off to his bedroom and that would be that. So we both sat quietly, me stroking his back while he struggled with his emotions. After a few minutes, I said, more calmly than I felt, 'Remember, whatever it is, I'll always love you, Jack; I'll always be proud of you.'

Jack sat up straight again. 'I'm too embarrassed,' he said, looking away.

'Listen, let's both agree not to be embarrassed. Let's be totally pragmatic because that's the only way you can move on unless you want this incident to haunt you for the rest of your life.'

He shook his head.

'Ok, then tell me the cold, hard facts. I'm guessing James Gresham's bullying just transitioned into something far nastier. Am I right?'

By now, he was a ball of tension, the struggle written on his face manifested in his fidgeting fingers and restless right leg.

'It's ok,' I said, quietly. 'Take your time.'

I heard him give a deep sigh. 'No, I can't.'

For several, silent minutes, we sat close together with me holding tightly onto Jack's hand and him leaning against me until he suddenly pulled away as if embarrassed by our proximity.

'Can we have our sandwiches now?' he asked.

I watched as he tucked into his food voraciously then I got up, picked up the sandwiches I could no longer eat and went out into the kitchen to make a coffee, leaning against the worktop as the kettle boiled. How did James keep his drug habit a secret from parents who insisted he was a paragon of virtue? And perhaps the most pressing question of all: what makes a boy who seemingly has a privileged home life turn into a merciless bully?

More to the point, what had he done to Jack that was so bad he couldn't bring himself to tell me?

11. AMY

There was little time to think about Ben after I got back to the shop because we were faced with the busiest afternoon we'd had for a long while. The doorbell clanged constantly in a way that began to be annoying. Had it not been a chilly day, we'd have left the door propped open, although, as Roz pointed out, the bell was a deterrent to shoplifters since it attracted our attention.

'Didn't stop that red scarf from going missing,' I was about to say before thinking better of it. No way would I blame her when I'd been dilly dallying that lunchtime and wasn't there to help her cope with the unexpected rush.

A young man had just bought a box of fragranced hand creams for his girlfriend and, as he'd asked for gift wrapping, I had to reach down to a long shelf below the counter where we kept layers of coloured tissue paper and boxes of glossy, spiralling ribbons. Yet again the shop bell tinkled. Granny Lewis would have been proud to see that business was flourishing.

When I straightened up again, holding two sheets of purple tissue and a length of yellow ribbon, I got the shock of my life. My parents were standing in the middle of the shop looking the place up and down with bemusement. No chance of ducking down again because the young man was growing impatient, waiting for me to get on with the wrapping.

Too late anyway. Mum and Dad swung round and our eyes met.

As they moved towards the counter, a dry croak of a sound emerged from my mouth.

'Oh, hello.'

'Your friend must have recovered extremely quickly,' said my mother, narrowing her eyes.

Roz shot me a questioning glance.

'These are my parents,' I said, trying desperately to send her a warning with my eyebrows. 'Mum, Dad, this is Roz, my... friend.'

'Pleased to meet you,' Roz said cheerfully. Her grin faded when it was met with blank incomprehension. The young man who'd bought the gift checked his watch.

'Could you hurry up with that, please? Only, I've got to catch a train in a minute.'

Three pairs of eyes bored into me from the other side of the counter, watching as I struggled to tape the ends of the purple tissue and fumbled with the curls of yellow ribbon. The result was way below my usual artistic standard but the young man seemed pleased enough which was a relief.

My father waited until the customer had left the shop.

'So, are you going to explain yourself?'

'The operation was cancelled,' I said, desperately improvising with the uncomfortable knowledge that my astonished business partner was hanging on my every word. 'So, I decided to come and help Roz instead.'

'We came in out of curiosity,' Mum said, looking around. 'We thought we'd have a little wander round the shops because Daddy was thinking of picking up a little present to give his old pupil after the recital tonight.'

I flinched, embarrassed by the fact that even though I was thirty-one years old, Mum still insisted on referring to her own husband as 'Daddy'. *Daddy will be home soon and then you'll be in trouble, young lady.* In front of Roz it was excruciating.

'So we saw this shop and thought it looked rather... unusual,' Mum continued. 'So how about afternoon tea in one of those nice cafes near the river? Our treat to repay you for having us.'

'Um, well...' I was standing in a pit that was getting deeper by the minute, so deep that soon it would be impossible to climb out.

'I hope you don't mind,' said Roz, suddenly, 'but I really could do with your daughter's help for the rest of the day. My usual assistant is off, you see, and we're normally inundated on a Saturday.' She turned and gave me an innocent smile. 'You don't mind, do you, Amy?'

'No, not at all, Roz.' I felt a rush of gratitude that made me want to hug her.

'Shame,' said my father, giving me the same penetrating stare as DI Morris. He would have made a good detective, come to think of it, especially when he added, 'Your friend must be disappointed about the operation. You get yourself all worked up for it and then you have to go through the whole torment again the next time. What did you say she was having done?'

I frantically searched my mind for a medical procedure. 'Oh, a minor operation. You know the kind of thing.'

'No, I don't,' he said, still eyeing me steadily.

'It's a female problem, Dad. She was getting her ovaries looked at.' *Where did that come from?*

'Oh, a laparoscopy,' Roz chipped in.

Barely disguising the relief in my voice, I said, 'Yes! That's it! I couldn't remember the name.'

I was seeing Roz in a new light. This upright, moral, gospel-singing Baptist had turned into a co-conspirator and partner in my deception. What's more, she seemed to be enjoying her supportive role if the expression on her face was anything to go by.

Dad looked from one to the other of us then at my mother. 'I suppose it's just us for afternoon tea then. It's a pity because we needed to talk to you about something but I suppose it will have to wait now until the morning.'

When they'd gone, Roz's bright smile faded.

'Good to know my years with the Surbiton Amateur Dramatic Society haven't been wasted but you've got some explaining to do, Amy Lewis.'

Several minutes later, having revealed my dilemma, I braced myself for the full force of Roz's wide-eyed incredulity.

'Girl, you're thirty-one not thirteen. Your parents can't dictate your life to you anymore. And besides, you've only changed your career not run off to Syria to join an ISIS terror cell.'

Across the shop floor, a browsing customer shot a nervous glance at us both.

'And as for your Gran's money,' Roz added, lowering her voice, 'it's none of their business what you do with it.'

'I know that,' I said between gritted teeth, 'but you don't understand what they're like – they're not like normal parents. If my brother had invested the money in this place, they'd have said he was using his initiative.'

Roz gave me a sad smile. 'So am I hearing you say that sheer stupidity on your part would be sheer genius on his?'

I sighed. 'You've got it exactly.'

***

It was a huge relief to find that by the time I got home after work, my parents had already left for the Albert Hall, leaving a brief note on the kitchen table:

'*Back around 11.30. You've run out of milk.*'

Annoyingly, when I checked the fridge, they were right. Nothing for it but to traipse out again to the local shop. At least it would avoid a catastrophe at breakfast when the lack of morning tea would finally convince them of my total incapacity to cope with life. Never mind, the walk would clear my head and give me time to prepare for the inevitable interrogation over the eggs and bacon next morning.

Max trotted along beside me, delighted to be out again among the street smells with the musty promise of the river in the distance. With the milk bought, I decided to keep going and take him down to the riverbank just as far as the row of houseboats since it was dark. *Serenity* was missing but I knew Jan and Kyle sometimes took it out for a trip along the river although usually they'd be back before dark.

A little way along, the sleek white bow of *Sea Swift* loomed up in the darkness. Max began tugging on his lead, pulling me towards the boat then jumping up, yapping incessantly as we drew level with its curving white side.

Exhausted by the tension of the day, I snapped. 'If you carry on like this, I'm going to bloody well post you to Australia and let bloody Marcus sort you out!'

A woman passing by with a smug-looking Afghan hound gave me a look that should have curdled the milk in my bag.

Eventually, Max allowed himself to be tugged away but every now and then on the walk home, he would stop, look back, then look up at me as if to say, 'It's not me that's being stupid.' Something had definitely upset him.

Around eight o'clock, I left the dog curled up in his basket and went off to meet friends in the pub, the idea being that if I stuck it out until twelve, refused a lift home and walked, with any luck, by the time I got back, my parents would be tucked up in bed thereby postponing awkward conversation until the morning and giving me time to prepare a credible story.

At twelve thirty, I shut the front door quietly, took off my shoes and slunk down the hallway to the kitchen. I don't know why I bothered to be quiet because my father's snoring, punctuated by intermittent grunts and snorts, had forced its way into the hall.

It had been an enjoyable night but I'd lost count of the drinks I'd had and was desperately in need of some painkillers. I still missed the regulating presence of Beth who could always sense when I was about to tip over from being happily light-headed to feeling morosely unwell.

The headache was thumping away at the back of my skull as I slowly opened the kitchen door, trying not to wake Max who would normally be flat out in his basket.

But tonight he wasn't there. Tonight he was stationed at Mum's feet as she sat at the kitchen table in her pale-blue dressing gown and faded pink slippers with a mug of hot milk in front of her.

I found myself under the scrutiny of two sets of eyes: Max with his 'you left me again' mournful expression and my mother's 'what time do you call this?' face, reinforced by the slight lift of the eyebrows. I was fifteen years old again, sneaking in after the agreed curfew and about to be grounded.

'I see you and Max have made friends then,' I said, trying to sound cheerful.

'You're very late,' Mum said.

'I thought you'd be asleep.'

'Sleep? With that noise going on?' she sniffed. 'He's always bad when he's been drinking. I knew I was in for it when he had that double brandy at the bar in the interval. It's like sleeping next to a pneumatic drill.'

I reached into the cupboard for the tablets. 'So how was the concert?'

'Oh, pleasant enough if you like Chopin which I don't really. Your dad's pupil was very good if a little overdramatic. I prefer it when they just put their hands on the keyboard and get on with it without all that flourishing and closed eyes as if they're in terrible pain. Are you not well, dear?'

'A bit of a headache,' I said, filling a glass with water. *Oh to collapse on the sofa and fall into a deep sleep.* 'I'm just a bit tired.'

I was hoping she would take the hint and go off to bed but instead she waited for me to snap two tablets out of the blister pack.

'You didn't fool me you know, Amy.'

'Pardon?'

'Today in that shop, I knew from your face that you were experimenting with the truth.'

'What?' No time to improvise. I took a gulp of water. 'What on earth are you talking about?'

My mother was shifting into second gear. 'I don't know what

you're up to but Daddy and I weren't born yesterday so you might as well come clean.'

Standing there under her piercing gaze I was in danger of morphing into a fractious teenager about to launch a spirited defence. But no. I wasn't having this. I took a breath and prepared to explain myself calmly and with dignity like a thirty-one-year-old.

'That friend of yours wasn't having an operation, was she?' My mother folded her arms and waited patiently during the silence that followed.

I sank down wearily on the other kitchen chair and swallowed the capsules. 'No. I'm sorry.'

In a few months, I'd envisaged having built a fall-out shelter made of Earth Song's fame, success and profit, enough to justify my decision to sacrifice a good career and spend all that inheritance money. But this wasn't the right time. It was early days. Earth Song was built on shifting sand and it could still all go horribly wrong.

My mother gave a long, deep sigh which was echoed by Max as he retreated to his basket and looked up at me with soulful eyes that seemed to say, 'Let's see you get out of this one.'

'Did you think we'd be upset if we knew?'

Uncomfortably aware that the question was about to send me over the top and charging straight into the enemy line of fire, I asked, 'Knew what?'

'About your Saturday job, you silly goose.'

'My... Saturday job?'

'Yes, why on earth do you need it when you have a good salary? We both feel you're overdoing it because being a teacher is stressful enough. You need your weekends off, dear.'

The retreat had sounded, sending me running back to the safety of the trenches so I let out the breath I'd been holding.

'But Roz needs me.' It wasn't exactly a lie.

Mum reached over and grasped my hand. 'You'll make yourself ill, that's what you'll do. Mark my words, burning the candle at both ends is fine when you're very young but for someone your age –'

'Thirty-one isn't exactly ancient,' I protested.

'I know you think Daddy and I are mad old codgers but we're only thinking of your wellbeing.'

I stood up and went to put the glass in the sink. 'Please don't. You stick to worrying about your goats. I'm fine. Now if you don't mind, I need to get some sleep. Goodnight, Mum. Hope you sleep ok.'

'Your dad never stops snoring, you know,' she said. 'Night after night, the same. Sometimes I have to go and sleep in the spare room.'

It was the first time I'd heard her complain about her life with Dad. Sitting there in her dressing gown and flannelette pyjamas in a strange kitchen away from home, exiled from bed and sleep, she seemed so child-like and vulnerable. I had a sudden urge to go over and hug her.

For a moment, I even considered offering her the sofa while I scrunched up in the armchair.

When I sat back down, she reached over and took my hand. 'I don't think you understand how much I worry about you being here alone in the big city.'

'Kingston upon Thames isn't exactly the big city.'

She looked hurt. 'You know, sometimes I feel as if you're a hedgehog, full of prickles, rolling yourself into a defensive ball and rejecting everything I say on principle when all I want is for you to be safe and happy.'

Her words came as a shock. 'I'm sorry you feel that way. I honestly don't mean to be like that.' More guilt.

We were quiet for a moment, listening to the hum of the fridge, the click of the minute hand on my wall clock and the gentle, subdued snoring of Max in his basket. It felt like a truce, as if we were on the brink of understanding each other a little better.

But then the atmosphere changed.

She patted my arm almost dismissively. 'I'll just finish my drink then go back to bed. Off you go.'

I stood up. 'Oh, ok. I'll see you in the morning then.'

'Night, dear. Thanks for getting the milk.'

'That's ok. Night, then.'

She gave me a sad smile. 'We don't see enough of you, Amy.'

'I'll try and get down to Devon some time,' I said. 'It would be nice to meet Merlin.' *What? Now I really had lost it.*

She perked up at that. 'Good, come soon then.'

'I will.' I turned back at the door. 'It's lovely to have you here, Mum.' It surprised me how much I meant it, how much I wished it was just her and me in the flat.

'Thank you, dear,' she said, quietly. Then she looked up at me with glistening eyes. 'Sometimes, I miss Marcus so much it hurts.'

Her words hit me hard in the stomach. 'I know you do but maybe you and Dad should go out there and visit. Australia is a wonderful place.'

'Yes, perhaps we will.'

She got up, put her mug in the sink then stood by the back door, just staring out into the darkness as she spoke.

'You get out of that shop, Amy. You tell that friend of yours that she needs a Saturday girl not a schoolteacher.'

The following morning, they were both up early, too early. Hearing them moving about, I dragged myself off the sofa, pulled on my dressing gown and went out into the hallway, surprised to see their cases standing by the front door of the flat. They were bustling about the kitchen making themselves at home, Dad setting out cereal bowls and packets while Mum tutted over the state of the cupboards as she opened door after door searching for something.

'No teapot,' she remarked, seeing me in the doorway. 'Everyone should have a teapot.'

'I drink coffee mostly. How come you're up so early?' I squeezed past my mother, slotted a pod into the new coffee machine (bought specially for their visit) and waited for the urgently needed shot of caffeine.

Dad had put his reading specs on and was checking the expiry date on a packet of organic muesli.

'Do you realise this is out by three weeks?' he asked, sliding the specs down his nose to peer at me.

Mum snapped the cupboard door shut. 'Never mind, Daddy. I'm sure we won't be poisoned.'

Anyone seeing her the night before would have thought her a very different woman in that sharp morning light.

'So why *are* you up so early?' I repeated, hoping this time for an answer.

'Oh, we had a frantic call from the farmer's son saying that when he went to check up on the goats early this morning, they'd all escaped from the paddock and he has no idea where they've got to,' Mum said.

Dad gingerly poured some cereal into two bowls. 'Could be anywhere. They roam, you know. I've been on at the local handyman to come and mend that fence but he's always got some excuse.'

Mum was holding a teabag between her thumb and forefinger as if it were about to explode. 'I don't suppose you have any loose tea, Amy?'

I shook my head. 'Sorry.' *Who uses loose tea these days? Even coffee comes in bags now.*

Dad settled himself on the stool and poured milk on his out-of-date muesli.

'It's that bloody Merlin; he's the ringleader. Anyway, we've got to get back and recapture the idiots.'

'I was going to cook you bacon and eggs.' It sounded pathetic.

'Sorry, dear, but needs must.'

My mother had a habit of running her fingers through the hair around her forehead when she was stressed. She was doing that now as she waited for the kettle to boil, revealing a startling expanse of grey that had been hiding beneath the sandy gold top layer.

'We'll be off straight after breakfast,' she sighed.

'Out of your way,' said Dad, between mouthfuls of cereal. He looked older this morning. His face had crinkled like thin paper and there were deep bags under his eyes and grooves around his nose and mouth that I'd never noticed before. One day he would be less of a man, his strength dwindling, unable to cope with delinquent goats and a cottage that was too big and too needy, unable even to care for himself or Mum. Then it would be up to me to rescue them both since Marcus would be far away in the sunshine of a Melbourne suburb. Yes, he always won.

'Sometime when you can manage it, we need to have a talk.' The statement came out of the blue as if someone else had spoken for me.

'About what?' asked my mother, as she poured the hot water into two mugs. 'Can't we do it now?'

'No, sorry. I'm not quite ready.'

Max was sitting by the kitchen door begging to be let out into the garden. I unlocked the door and watched him scuttle towards the rectangle of rough grass that the landlord insisted on calling a lawn. It was mottled with yellow patches where the dog had relieved himself – just another job that was to be done along with the painting. There was a packet of grass seed in the hall cupboard waiting patiently for its turn in the sun.

'I knew it, you've got yourself into some kind of trouble. I told you, didn't I, Jean?' Dad pushed his cereal bowl away, clasped his hands and glared up at me. 'What have you done now?'

A look of resignation settled on his face, an expression that disguised his satisfaction at being proved right. I knew it so well.

'Nothing important.' A lie but I needed time. 'I can't talk about it now.'

'Oh, so it's ok for us to drive all the way home with that sentence ringing in our ears, is it?'

I struggled to sound calm and in control. 'Look, there's nothing to worry about. You go home and capture your goats and then when

I'm ready we'll have that chat, ok?'

If Beth had been there, she would have teased me for using what she called 'Amy's teacher voice'. It was, she once told me, the kind of tone a teacher uses when she has deep concerns about a child but doesn't want to unnerve the parents. Spot on in this case.

It was a relief when the coffee machine filled the room with the smell of freshly brewed Americano. Without it, the temperature in the small kitchen would have dropped several degrees while my parents adopted a stiff-lipped silence over their mugs of tea.

Suddenly, Mum looked up. 'You're not...' The question hung in the air unfinished.

'Not what?'

'You're not pregnant or anything?'

'No! Of course not!' I looked from one to the other. 'Is that what you think of me?'

I stirred a small amount of milk into the black, bitter liquid in my mug. Soon they would be gone. *Hang on a little longer.*

'I'm sorry, dear. It's just that we worry about you.' Mum glanced across at Dad.

'Worry about Marcus instead,' I snapped. 'Who knows what he gets up to in Australia?'

'Speaking of Marcus,' my father said, pushing his cereal bowl to one side, 'we need to talk to you about this legacy of yours.'

My heart jumped in my chest. *Please God, no! I'm not ready!*

'He rang us not long ago. When was it, Jean?'

'October the twenty fifth at nine minutes past nine in the evening,' my mother said, staring down into her tea.

There was such precision in her answer that I guessed she'd actually written down the date and time of Marcus's call in her diary.

'Any news? How is he?' I forced myself to ask.

A look passed between them. 'Snowed under at work,' said Dad. 'The thing is, he talked about setting up his own business one day. He's got potential clients so when the time comes all he'll need is the capital to set it up and find the right premises. Which is where you come in.'

My heart was racing uncomfortably by now. 'What's it got to do with me?' I asked. As if I didn't know.

Dad glanced at my silent mother then back at me. 'We've been discussing this and we feel it's only fair that you give your brother at least a half share in the money your gran left you so he can make a success of his new business.'

I opened my mouth then closed it again. Something had happened to my voice.

'He really will need a substantial amount of money,' my mother chipped in. 'Can you think about it, dear?'

'Don't think – *do*!' snapped Dad. 'The boy needs it more than you and if your granny had had any sense, she would have realised that. I hate to say this of my own mother, but she wasn't the best judge of her grandchildren's potential.'

I was stunned at the injustice of his words. My grandmother had always seen the unequal way Marcus and I were treated. She had wanted to redress the balance and I'd always be grateful to her.

'Say something, Amy,' my father barked. 'Don't just stand there like a lemon.'

'I'll think about it,' I managed to say.

'What is there to think about? You need to examine your conscience and help your brother out. It's your duty.' He looked at his watch. 'We should get going before the wretched goats reach the next county.'

Never had I been so grateful to a herd of goats.

And then they were gone and I was standing on the pavement watching as the car receded into the distance, wondering what on earth I was going to do.

12. LYNN

Sam Clinton went to interview Amy Lewis in her flat one evening a few days after Halloween and came into the office the next morning brushing white hairs off the bottom of his coat.

'Any useful information?' I asked. 'Apart from what a sodding nuisance dogs are?'

He took out his mobile and held it out to show us a photo. 'It's a painting of the river done by an artist friend of Miss Lewis. She assured me that it's a pretty good likeness of the boat the lad was on.'

'The lad she met on the riverbank, you mean?'

Sam nodded. 'Ben, yes. Presumably that is his real name and not one he's made up.'

Kai whistled through his teeth. 'That boat must have cost a lifetime's salary.'

'Yesterday morning it turned up again, moving upriver towards Hampton Court, apparently.' Sam took out his notebook. 'She told me it has dark tinted windows. When she first met Ben, she had an overwhelming feeling that someone on board was watching them and listening to their conversation.'

'Her imagination perhaps?' I knew that some people had a tendency to dramatise.

'She strikes me as a sound witness, Ma'am,' said Sam. 'What's more, she says that a man came into the shop the following day who knew her dog's name which could indicate that he was the person listening on the boat. She described him in detail.'

'Sounds strange alright.'

'She asked me whether Ben would be in trouble because of what she'd told me. I wrote down exactly what she said.' He turned the page of his notebook and quoted Amy's words. 'I feel like, a bit like a traitor. I know it's stupid because I don't know anything about this boy but there's something about him. It's just a feeling that he's not happy, not living the way a young teenager should.'

'Good of her,' said Kai. 'She sounds like a decent sort.'

'I'm a dad,' Sam said. 'I certainly wouldn't want my son or daughter hanging around the riverbank at night or bunking off school and if they were I'd be grateful for someone like Amy Lewis reporting it.'

'Worth following up then,' I suggested.

Sam nodded. 'It could be a wild goose chase but I've got this feeling that there's something odd going on. And even if we don't come up with anything, I got the impression that Miss Lewis is worried for the lad's welfare.'

'In the meantime, the toxicology report on James Gresham's death has come through,' I said. 'You were right, Sam. It was MDMA mixed with cocaine.'

'If he'd been drinking at that party, the mixture of ecstasy, cocaine and alcohol would have been lethal.'

The following day, I left the station after the morning briefing and made the twenty-minute drive to meet the Greshams with a heavy feeling of dread weighing down my stomach. How do you tell grieving parents that their son had died unnecessarily, that if he'd stayed home and played computer games on Halloween night, he would still be alive?

Forest Heights was a gated development set between a golf club on one side and a five-star hotel on the other with the river close to its back. As soon as I drove onto the development, the rarefied atmosphere of the place made me edgy. I turned into Woodland Way feeling distinctly unwelcome under the eyes of the security cameras mounted on poles and drove past several grand detached houses pretending to be Victorian with names that recalled the ghost of the woodland sacrificed for their construction: The Elms, The Beeches, The Willows and, finally, The Oaks where the Greshams lived.

I parked my Toyota on the semi-circular gravel drive behind the black Mercedes, got out and approached the imposing front door which was framed by a white stone portico. Standing to attention on each side of the stone steps were two bay trees in tall metal planters, their foliage cut into perfect spheres. I brushed down and smoothed my coat and pressed the doorbell which chimed so loudly and for so long that I wondered if it was ever going to stop. In the top half of the door was a stained-glass panel depicting an oak tree growing on a semi-circle of pale green grass under a royal blue sky and behind this, a blurry shape appeared as someone tried to see who the caller was.

Nora Gresham opened the front door looking ashen. Her face, now devoid of makeup, seemed to be carved into hollows. Without the false eyelashes, her eyes looked dark, small, sunken and red-rimmed. She had obviously been crying.

I apologised for disturbing her and explained the reason for my visit. She moved back and waited for me to enter the wide hallway which was dominated by a central marble staircase elegantly curving up to a broad landing. There were rooms on either side of the hallway. The one on the left appeared to be an office of some kind. The door was open just enough to reveal a large desk beneath the front window, an antique leather armchair on one side of a white marble fireplace and, above this, a large, ornate mirror. A leather golf bag crammed with serious looking clubs was propped up against the wall near the doorway. 'Nob's game,' my dad would have said. He was a darts and football man himself.

'In here,' Nora murmured, leading the way into a sitting room big enough to contain the entire ground floor of my 1960's semi. It was a vast white room, the only furniture being two black leather sofas and a long, smoked-glass coffee table. Three red cushions had been placed vertically at the back of each sofa providing the only touch of colour. On the wall above the longer of the two sofas was a large abstract painting, the kind that has you wondering what the hell it's supposed to be, all sodding lines and scribbles probably costing my year's salary. A TV the size of a small cinema screen filled the wall above a marble fireplace that was the duplicate of the one in the office.

At the other end of the room, an archway led into an enormous kitchen with a glimpse of striped lawn stretching into the distance beyond bi-fold glass doors. The gleaming white worktops were empty except for what looked like a bright red coffee machine, one of those fancy Italian jobs that cost a fortune. The whole effect was stunning and yet there was something so cold and clinical about this house that I couldn't help feeling grateful for the small, untidy warmth of my own.

While Mrs Gresham went to the foot of the stairs to call her husband, I took the opportunity to scan my surroundings. On the mantelpiece, a row of silver football trophies were lined up on either side of a framed photo of a smiling James. A single tealight flickering in a red glass gave the arrangement the aura of a shrine. Glancing quickly towards the door, I went closer to study this frozen moment from James's short life. It must have been taken on holiday since he was wearing a striped tee-shirt and white shorts and was squinting into the sun. But it was the background that was capturing my attention when I heard the rap of Mrs Gresham's shoes against the parquet floor in the hallway. There was just time to go back and sit on the smaller of the two sofas before she came into the room followed by her husband.

Grief had blanched his face as white as the walls beside him. There were dark shadows under his eyes and he obviously hadn't shaved for a while judging by the grey stubble around his mouth. I stood up and waited for them to sit on the larger sofa, noticing how Mrs Gresham moved to the opposite end, leaving a space big enough for two people between her and her husband.

After expressing my sympathies, I cleared my throat as the real purpose of my visit had to be faced.

'I'm so sorry to tell you this but the toxicology report on James indicates there was a high level of ecstasy in his blood.'

Mrs Gresham looked as if she was about to faint. 'No, no… That can't be right.'

Judging from their shocked, outraged faces, neither had any idea that their son had a drug habit. That only made it more difficult when I had to explain that the ecstasy had been cut with a substance that made it twice as dangerous and which was the most likely cause of death since James had also consumed large amounts of alcohol. It was a toxic mixture that caused a heart attack.

His mother began to cry silently, holding a tissue over her nose and mouth. Beside her, Mr Gresham was motionless as if time had stopped for him until, suddenly, he leaned forward and jabbed his finger at me.

'I want to know who did it. I want to know who gave my son that poison. I want to know who murdered him.' He spoke only to me as if the woman beside him no longer existed.

Nora turned to her husband, her eyes streaming with tears.

'Greg, you should never have let him go to that party. I told you he was too young to stay out that late. I told you but you wouldn't listen.'

So she'd been overruled – interesting. What kind of a man ignores his wife and makes completely autonomous decisions about their child? Not even Graham would have been guilty of that.

'Did you know the people holding the Halloween party?' I asked.

'James was a popular kid; he had a lot of friends.' Mr Gresham sounded defensive as if I were blaming him. 'I told him to ring me when he was ready to come home and I'd go and pick him up. I waited up for his call. I waited…' He tailed off.

'Please don't take this the wrong way but did James have any friends that you didn't approve of, someone who might have been at that party and shared drugs with him?'

The answer was a growl. 'Our son did *not* take drugs. If he had them in his blood, someone forced them on him against his will.'

But he did take drugs. Jack had insisted he'd seen him talking to a dealer and I believed him but was this the time to lay more bad news at their door? I opened my notebook.

'If you could give me the name and address of the person who held the party then we'll try and find out if James obtained the drugs while he was in their house.'

Mrs Gresham rose and left the room, returning with a notepad. She tore off a sheet and passed it to me. 'This is their phone number. James left it for us.' She slumped back down on the sofa, turning her back on her husband.

I stood up. 'I know we've had our disagreements but again, please accept my condolences. I'll be in touch to let you know when James's body will be released so you can arrange the funeral.'

It crossed my mind that they had no idea that their son had bullied so many children and had made my child's life a misery every day since they started at St Saviour's. No, they were destroyed enough.

Greg looked up at me. 'Someone killed my son and you better find out who it was.'

'We're working on it, Mr Gresham,' I assured him.

His wife blew her nose, got to her feet and led me to the front door.

'Thank you for telling us what happened.'

'Will you be alright, Mrs Gresham?' I asked. 'Would you like the family liaison officer to make another visit?'

'No, no, thank you.' Nora swung the front door open so rapidly that it was obvious that my time was up.

I drove back to the station with one thought on my mind. How incongruous it seemed that the son of that gleaming, modern house with its clean lines and sharp edges had met a sordid death on the dusty floor of a charity shop doorway. In a home like that, James should have grown up, been successful, earned himself a packet and bought a house just like it.

And yet, he wasn't happy; he couldn't have been. A child who bullies others and takes drugs isn't a happy well-adjusted human being.

DC Chauhan looked up from his lunch as I walked into the office. 'I bet that was tough.' Beside him, DC Clinton had just finished eating a cheeseburger. The air was thick with the aroma of fried meat, synthetic cheese and sour gherkin, made more pungent by the warmth of the room.

'You could say that,' I said. 'Any luck with the CCTV footage? Did anything show up at any of the schools?'

'The convent,' grinned DC Chauhan. 'You can see the nuns taking delivery of a large package of cocaine.' He took a bite of his spicy chicken wing and winked at Sam Clinton.

My nerves were shredded by the morning's visit. 'DC Chauhan, when you've stopped being God's gift to comedy, could you finish that disgusting-looking mixture of fat and salt and give me some useful feedback?'

Seeing Kai's face fall and Sam's look of surprise, I apologised immediately. It wasn't professional to snap at the two colleagues I respected most.

'No, *I'm* sorry, Ma'am,' Kai said, sheepishly. 'It isn't a laughing matter when a kid's dead.'

'You might like to see the St Saviour's CCTV footage for yourself,' Sam said, bringing it up on his screen. 'This was taken by the camera on the front wall of the school. See there, by the railings.' He pointed to a figure in a hoodie just visible on the edge of the picture as the uniformed throng flooded through the school gates.

I realised I was holding my breath as I spotted Jack emerging onto the street closely followed by James. To my relief, Jack looked back over his shoulder then dodged away, losing himself in the crowd.

I leaned forward to get a closer look at the figure in the hoodie. 'It could be someone's brother waiting for them,' I suggested.

'That's what I thought at first, but look.' Sam pointed at James.

I watched as James gestured to the hooded figure who turned and followed him until both were out of shot.

Sam swore under his breath. 'Tragic. I'd be devastated if my kids got involved with drugs when they're that age.'

'You're a good dad, Sam. If I know you, that won't be a problem. Can we rewind and get a close up of that lad?'

I waited while Sam obliged, freezing the first frame. 'Damn – that hoodie really hides his face.'

'That's what they're for,' I said. 'It's the criminal's choice of disguise.' Our job would be a lot easier if they only sold jackets without hoods.

'It's the same story at the other school,' Kai remarked. 'There's a hooded figure that looks like a ghost except that he's in plain sight like those shadowy presences you see in eerie, paranormal YouTube videos.'

'Some of us have better things to do with our time, Kai,' Sam muttered.

'There and yet not there,' I said, half to myself.

'What was the Greshams' place like?' asked Sam.

I gave him a brief but accurate description of the grandeur I'd encountered, adding, 'The photograph on the mantelpiece bothers me for some reason.'

I realised for the first time that what struck me about the photo wasn't the angelic-looking James posing in the sunshine but the significance of what was behind him. Annoyingly, I couldn't put my finger on why exactly it was nagging at me.

13. LYNN

It would be three weeks before I met the Greshams again but in very different circumstances. Their son's body had been released and they'd immediately organised the funeral.

I arrived in time to see the hearse glide to a halt outside the entrance to the crematorium. I wasn't expecting to be shocked at seeing the coffin but maybe it was because of its size – smaller than average, made to fit a teenager. Or maybe it was the large white wreath spelling out the word SON along one side of the hearse with another spelling his name in the blue and white colours of Chelsea football club. James's favourite team, according to Jack.

My son hadn't said much since the day I broke the news of James's death and it took me a while to realise that his obvious relief that his tormentor was gone had been replaced by guilt at feeling so glad. If only I'd married a child psychologist instead of a third-rate crime writer.

I walked slowly over to join the group by the door just as a gleaming black limousine drew up behind the hearse and the Greshams got out, followed by their younger son Paul, a twelve-year-old version of his father in a black overcoat, black leather gloves, dark grey trousers and polished black brogues. An eerie silence fell on all of us until Mrs Gresham moved towards some people at the front of the group. The air was suddenly filled with the sounds of sniffing and muffled sobs.

I followed the procession into the chapel and slipped into a pew at the very back. By now, the coffin was in its place on the curtained bier and one of the undertakers was rearranging the flowers in order to prop up a framed photo of James. It was a blur until I put on my distance glasses and recognised it as the one on the Greshams' mantelpiece. The creaky organ started 'Abide with me' and my neighbour in the pew joined in with a rich baritone, obviously determined to rescue the hymn from the half-hearted efforts around him. I spared the congregation from my singing voice and concentrated instead on what was puzzling me about that photo.

What can I say about the service except that in a strange way it was beautiful? I'm not much of a believer but I could see how the prayers and hymns would comfort someone who was. Funny, I hadn't got the Greshams down as being religious.

Afterwards, we trailed out to a courtyard where all the wreaths had been laid out on the paving around the photo of James. I positioned myself at the back of the group waiting my turn to get a better look at it, aware that the head of St Saviour's was standing close by. Beside the tall figure of Martin McDonald, Miss Bailey, Jack's form teacher, was wiping her eyes with a tissue passed to her by a tall, good-looking man with dark wavy hair and a neat, close-cut beard. Probably her boyfriend. Mr McDonald acknowledged me with a suitably subdued greeting which I returned before nodding at Miss Bailey who tried to speak but couldn't. 'Tragic,' muttered Mr McDonald. 'Should never have happened. I hope when you find the person responsible for giving James that drug you lock them up and throw away the key, Mrs Morris.'

I assured him we were working on it. Gradually, as the people at the front of the queue moved away and dispersed, we shuffled closer until we were looking down at the colourful selection of wreaths. The teachers bent down to study the photograph of James and read some of the memorial cards attached to the flowers while I took out my phone, pretended to check it for messages and surreptitiously took a photo. When I straightened up, I noticed that the tall young man had left the group to go and talk to Paul, who had been standing by himself in the middle of the courtyard looking distinctly alone and awkward. I watched as the teacher shook the boy's hand then patted his arm in a comforting gesture. Whatever he was saying, Paul seemed to be listening intently, nodding and replying, obviously at ease with this man. It struck me how astute he was to notice the isolation of the poor kid.

Several minutes later, I made my way back to the car park and was just unlocking the car door when a tall figure emerged from the side of the crematorium. The young man strode towards an elderly Peugeot hatchback parked at the other end of the row. Obviously teachers weren't getting paid as much as I thought.

On the drive back to the town centre, I couldn't stop thinking about young Paul Gresham who had walked down the aisle alone behind his parents and stood quietly by himself out in the courtyard watching while they received all the sympathy. Did people think that kids weren't capable of grief? Did they really expect the boy to just get on with losing his brother while his parents suffered? Paul's loss should have been recognised. When I shared my observation with Kai and Sam back at the station, both agreed it was odd.

'Poor kid,' Sam said. 'I hope he's going to be ok. Doesn't sound as if he's getting much support.'

'Maybe he'll get it at school. There was a teacher there, a young man who seemed to understand what the lad was going through. I have a feeling he'll watch out for Paul.'

I made myself a much-needed coffee and sat down at my desk. 'Do you know what else I noticed? Gresham tried to put his arm around his wife when they got out of the car but she shrugged it off.' I went on to tell them about the day I visited when Mrs Gresham left a large space between them on the sofa.

'Maybe their marriage is in trouble,' suggested Kai. 'This death might have widened the cracks.'

'You could be right,' I said. 'But it's strange because they were a united front when I had to meet them at the school about something.'

I opened up the photos on my iPhone and found the one I'd just taken at the crematorium. If my suspicion was right, I needed to zoom in closer. It didn't make any sense I told myself, but I needed to know if what I'd seen in the background of James's photo was really what it seemed.

14. AMY

When Beth rang two days later it took me by surprise. I suppose I'd got the impression she was too busy to see me, that our lives had swung off in different directions and I would have to wait patiently for what business-people call 'a window' in her busy schedule. She sounded enthusiastic about meeting up, her idea being that we could both enjoy a morning of retail therapy at the Christmas market along the South Bank, my favourite part of London. I'm a river girl at heart, I suppose.

'They're setting the market up in the second week of November,' Beth said. 'Can you make it? Just you and me and what Paolo calls a "girlie catch up".'

I smiled at that. 'He's getting very English that man of yours. Is he ok babysitting or are you bringing Luca?'

Apparently, Paolo was looking forward to having his son to himself for a while. Beth told me that when she got home, the flat would be strewn with toys and he and the baby would have fallen into an exhausted sleep on the sofa. Uncharitably, it crossed my mind that if Sarah found out he was alone, she might be tempted to call round that morning to catch up on her non-existent Italian but I kept quiet, not wanting to spoil the moment.

Two Sundays later, I was leaning on the railings by the river near the Festival Hall with Max sitting impatiently at my feet when Beth appeared looking stunning, like a model in a long sky-blue coat and black high-heeled boots, her thick chestnut hair swept back in a ponytail and her face lightly made up with just a touch of colour in her cheeks and on her lips. Beside her, I looked like some ragamuffin the proverbial cat had dragged in, having dressed for comfort in blue jeans, a white sloppy joe jumper, black trainers and a pink padded jacket. I'd pulled my hair behind my ears with a couple of hair slides and just dabbed on a bit of mineral face powder because, yes, I'd been in a bit of a hurry.

Within minutes, Beth and I had assumed a familiar ease in each other's company as if nothing had changed in our lives and we'd never been separated. She bent down to stroke Max's head prompting an enthusiastic, over-the-top response that took her by surprise.

'He's the cutest thing on four legs, aren't you boy?'

'I hope you don't mind me bringing him but he's not happy left on his own for too long,' I said. 'Cushion replacement is costing me a fortune; a dog psychologist would cost less.'

'Of course not. So you rescued him?'

'You could say that.' I explained, not sparing my brother's part in Max's story.

Beth raised her eyes. 'Marcus hasn't changed then.'

As we walked along towards the Christmas market, the air became thick with the smell of frying sausages and onions which made breathing in enough to make you hungry. The path was lined on either side by wooden chalets festooned with fairy lights, luring us towards them with their promise of unusual food and gifts and handmade Christmas decorations, a symphony of colours and sparkle. We strolled along clutching beakers of hot mulled wine and talking non-stop as we caught up on what had been happening in our lives while the jangling of a nearby carousel brightened the atmosphere with its schmaltzy Christmas tunes. I was relieved when Beth informed me that a friend had warned her about Sarah and that she was now *persona non grata* in the Santini household.

'I think she's taken the hint. Apparently, she's already wrecked one marriage but she is definitely not going to ruin mine.'

'Quite right,' I said. 'But there's fat chance of that with Paolo. I've never seen a man so besotted with his wife – goodness knows why.'

She gave me a friendly push then linked my arm in hers as we strolled on.

'Listen, Amy,' she said, 'Paolo told me about Richard. I'm so sorry.'

Strange how the mention of his name still stung. 'Yes, more fool me for being taken in.'

'But I thought you two were planning on getting married?'

Up until a few months ago, that had been the plan, I told her. We'd set a date, chosen a venue we could afford for the reception and even made a start on the guest list. But everything fell apart when I went over to North London to see him in a play at the Hampstead Playhouse. It was a two hander with a very young actress I'd never seen before, Julia something.

'There were friends of his in the audience, other actors, and in the interval, I heard one of them say, "So is that who Richard is sleeping with now?" And one of the women said, "We should warn Julia that Richard practically has a Bafta for laying the most leading ladies." They all found that hilarious. "Yeah, leading actor in a horizontal role!" someone else said.'

Beth's eyes widened. 'Oh my god, Ames, you poor thing having to listen to that.'

'Thing is, Beth, doubts had already crept in by then. There were nights he was really late home and I just put it down to the cast going out to dinner or something.'

'What a creep! And here's me thinking he was a solid gold human being.'

'Trouble is, I really did love him. But when he got home that night, I faced him with it, asked him if it was true. Beth, it was like looking at a stranger. He just stood there shouting cruel, nasty, insulting things. I thought he was actually going to hit me at one point.'

The memory had stirred from the deep place I'd hidden it and was about to ruin our special, precious time together. I swallowed and tried to smile.

Beth put her hands on my shoulders and looked me square in the eyes. 'Amy, you are too good for someone like that.'

I nodded. 'From now on, I'm making my own way through life without the help of any man, thank you very much. Unless you get tired of Paolo in which case, send him my way.'

But she was still looking concerned. 'No chance of that. So what did your parents say when you told them you'd broken up?'

'Oh, they were ok. I brushed over it. They don't even know about the shop yet. They think I'm still teaching.'

'What's the worst thing that can happen if you tell them?' she asked.

'Beth, you have no idea. My father already thinks I'm an idiot.'

'Which you are definitely not.'

'I know that but it'll be a case of light the blue touch paper and stand well back, and I just can't face it yet. I'm just a coward I suppose.'

'It's your life, Ames. You have the right to make your own choices and decisions, good or bad. After all, we learn so much from our mistakes.'

I stopped dead on the path. 'Are you saying I've made a mistake buying the shop?'

Beth studied me for a moment, obviously regretting her choice of words. Every decision she made was weighed for pros and cons so she would never dive into the deep end of life without giving it a lot of thought.

'I didn't mean it like that,' she said, obviously choosing her words carefully. 'I wasn't calling it a mistake because, after all, the shop could become a major success. Then you'll have an achievement to be proud of when you present your parents with the truth. She who dares, wins.' She grasped me by the shoulders. 'But are you a man or a mouse, Amy Lewis?'

'Neither, actually,' I smiled.

'Good, then you show them what you're made of and make a

success of this.'

'Aye, aye, sir. I intend to, sir. And, actually, I am, so there!'

Our laughter broke the tension and soon, without realising it, we were deep in conversation again, having walked through nearly half of the Christmas market without glancing at the stalls on either side until a brightly lit chalet with the sign 'Ken's Krafts' over it drew our interest with its fascinating selection of hand-carved wooden toys and terracotta bowls filled with sweets. Beth bought a wooden Noah's ark from the stall holder, a large, bearded man of about fifty who resembled a lumberjack. He seemed only too keen to chat, telling us that his mate was the potter while he only worked in wood. 'Love the stuff. Call it fifty quid for the Noah's ark, darling.'

My eye was caught by a small rocking horse made of honey coloured wood with a red saddle on its back and matching leather reins.

'Nice, eh?' said Ken, noticing my interest. 'Not one of mine, I'm afraid to say. My mate the potter turns his hand to wood carving every now and then. Maybe you've got a little one who'd enjoy riding it, sweetheart?'

I could feel myself blushing. 'Not yet but who knows?'

As we walked away, Beth nudged me.

'I think he fancies you. You could be in there, Ames. Play your cards right and you'll never be short of wood!'

'Very funny. I'll have you know I'm finished with all that. From now on I'm going to live like a contemplative nun.'

The small amount of mulled wine that was left was too cool to be enjoyable, so I guiltily tossed the cup into a nearby bin, glad that Roz wasn't there to witness my shameful contribution to the earth's plastic waste. When I turned back, Beth was smiling.

'What's amusing you, Mrs Santini?'

'You being a contemplative nun. I can't see it.'

'Listen, Beth, you got lucky with Paolo but they're not all like him, believe me.'

'Pity, I can just see you living in a cottage in the middle of a forest while Mr Ken over there chops wood for his next project.'

I gave her a friendly nudge. We had slotted back together again like two pieces of a jigsaw puzzle and it felt comfortable, familiar and joyous. 'Someone will come along one day,' she said, squeezing my arm. 'Someone who truly deserves you, Amy Lewis.'

'Sure,' I said. 'If the reverend mother ever lets me out.'

By midday, the South Bank was becoming crowded, with large huddles of people hovering by the food and drink stalls making it difficult to push through. Progress was made even more difficult by Max pulling back to escape the forest of legs.

'I know a great little Italian restaurant called Rosso's near Waterloo Station if you fancy an early lunch,' Beth suggested. 'It's tucked away in a side street so it doesn't get too full. Paolo and I go there sometimes when we want some quality time together.'

'Sounds good.'

'I can't stay too long, though, because he's got paperwork to do this afternoon.'

I picked up the dog and carried him until there was space to let him walk unhindered. Once free, he shook himself and groaned like an old man. 'Poor Max,' I said. 'He prefers the Kingston riverside and the wide spaces of Bushey Park. He's not really a town dog.'

Beth was looking thoughtful. 'Sometimes I'd give anything to go running again along the riverbank towards Hampton Court. I often feel a bit… cooped up, I suppose. It's one thing working in a busy part of London but another living in it as well.'

I so wanted to say, 'Come back, come and live somewhere we can meet easily, where we can be part of each other's lives again, where the thread of our childhood friendship can be strengthened'. But I didn't, of course. It wouldn't be fair – life is like that, dividing people, sending them in different directions and they can't do anything about it.

Fortunately, Signor Rosso agreed to have the dog in his restaurant as long as we ate outside in the garden where he'd arranged some small booths with outdoor heaters. Before we knew it, two hours had passed, two easy, comfortable hours in which Beth and I slipped back into our shared past as though nothing had changed.

Eventually, she checked her watch. 'I've got to get going. Paolo will be an exhausted wreck! I'm so sorry, Amy. This has been great and we have to meet up again soon.'

We hugged but when she pulled back, she was looking worried. 'Ames, what you said earlier about Richard… well, call me if you want to talk.'

'I will. Thanks for listening, Beth.'

And then, I was waving her up the steps of Waterloo station as she ran to catch the tube. When she'd disappeared inside, I stood for a moment trying to dampen down the hurt and sadness her words had inadvertently resurrected.

A flood of people were spilling down the stone steps from the station almost trampling a couple of homeless men slumped in sleeping bags by the wall. I was about to turn away to give Max the chance to have a walk before we got on the train when something caught my eye.

It took a moment to believe what I was actually seeing. But no, I hadn't imagined it – drifting along among the crowd was a boy dressed in jeans and a rumpled grey hoodie with a flash of poppy-red at its neck. It was Ben.

I stood still and watched as he pulled the hood over his head, rammed his fists into the side pockets of his jacket and hunched his shoulders against the icy wind blowing up from the Thames. Max had noticed him now and was whining and tugging at the lead.

'What is *he* doing up here?' I asked no one in particular as the dog jumped around hysterically at my feet.

By now, Ben had reached the main road and, without waiting for the traffic lights to change, was crossing at a run, dodging the cars and heading towards the long passage that led to the Festival Hall and the riverbank. I picked up the struggling dog and tucked him under my arm before quickly crossing the main road then breaking into an ungainly run, hampered by Max wriggling beneath my right arm and the weight of the full shopping bag over my left shoulder. I ran through the long passageway towards the South Bank, dodging the *Big Issue* seller holding out the magazine with a hopeful expression, a busker playing mournful flamenco music on a battered guitar with a half-empty box of coins at his feet and a group of Japanese tourists taking selfies and finally emerged, breathless, into the bright, sharp light.

Ben had reached the top of the steps beside the Festival Hall. He paused, looked back over his shoulder towards the station then seemed to hesitate about which direction to take before being swallowed by a crowd of people swarming out of the side entrance of the building.

I struggled up the steps fervently wishing I'd picked hobbies that didn't involve so much sitting down and wondering if staying the course with hot yoga might have given me a bit more stamina and flexibility. Ben was young, fit and fast. What hope was there of keeping up with him? This was beginning to feel like a fool's errand especially when, at that moment, a familiar voice in the back of my mind began nagging. As usual it was my father's voice.

What do you think you're doing chasing round after a perfectly innocent boy? Why do you have to make a drama out of everything?

I set Max on the ground and strained to pick out my quarry. To the left of us, a mass of people were surging towards the London Eye while to the right, another crowd were heading towards the Christmas market. Which way did he go? I looked back and forth to both sides and then, as the crowd split for a moment, spotted the grey hoodie as Ben turned to look back from the path leading towards Westminster Bridge. Soon he'd be lost in the thronging streets and then what? My instinct told me the boy was in trouble. Just seeing the shifty way he behaved coming out of that station I could tell that he was running away from something.

There was no time to think logically. I knew what I had to do.

As I followed, keeping Ben in sight, I found DC Clinton's number on my mobile and called him. It was Sunday but if he wasn't at work at least I could leave him a message. But to my surprise he picked up. I apologised for disturbing him and explained what was happening.

'It's the boy from the boat, *Sea Swift*. I just have a feeling he's in trouble.' Oh heck, he'd think I was a lunatic. This kid could just be having a Sunday out.

By now, Ben had reached the enormous wheel of the London Eye and was passing a long queue of people waiting their turn to board. With horror, I realised that standing not far away from the end of the queue, only a few metres away from the boy, was a man in a black leather jacket that I instantly recognised. It was the same man who'd come into the shop to buy the necklace, the same man who I'd seen leaving *Sea Swift* the night of my art lesson. He was standing looking out at the river with his back to the crowd having an animated conversation on his phone.

'What is it?' DC Clinton asked. 'Miss Lewis, are you ok?'

I explained, quickening my pace. I had to get to Ben before that man saw him.

'Miss Lewis,' the detective said, sounding serious, 'you need to leave this to us and get home. You don't know what this man is capable of.'

'But that's exactly it,' I protested. 'If he catches up with Ben, what will he do? I have to help him.'

There was a sharp intake of breath from the detective. A female voice in the background was protesting that his dinner was getting cold, and I could hear children chattering so I apologised for disturbing him and offered to call back later.

'Don't put the phone down,' he ordered. 'You need to listen please. I'll notify the police up there straight away but do not – I repeat – do not try to tackle the situation yourself, Miss Lewis.'

'But this man was on the boat,' I insisted. 'With Ben.'

The pieces were beginning to fit together. I told the detective that I had a feeling that Ben was afraid of this man. I mentioned hearing someone cough and how, after that, the boy had abruptly hurried away.

'I want you to turn around and go back to Waterloo,' the detective said, firmly. 'We've got the description of this guy now so let us handle it. Miss Lewis, are you listening?'

No, I wasn't because at any moment, the man might turn round and then it would be too late to help Ben.

15. AMY

I threaded through the people around me, keeping to the left and ducking to make myself less visible until I was close enough to tap the boy's shoulder. He wheeled round, eyes wide at seeing me but I signalled to him to be quiet and gestured over towards the riverside. A sound like a jet of steam erupted from his lips: 'Oh shhhhit!'

What I did next astonished both of us because before I'd had time to think, I'd reached out and grasped his hand, pulling him with me back towards the Festival Hall while shushing the dog who was beside himself with excitement. We broke into a run, weaving through the pedestrians on the path until, before we knew it, we were in the middle of the Christmas market.

Glancing back and seeing we weren't being followed, we came to a halt by a hot dog stall where, suddenly embarrassed, I let go of Ben's hand.

'Sorry, I didn't think. I just wanted to get you out of there,' I panted between gasps of onion-scented air.

He pulled the neck of his jacket up to his chin in an obvious attempt to hide the red scarf. 'Thanks,' he said, looking everywhere but at me.

'Who is that man?' I asked.

Now the pale eyes were staring right at me with obvious terror. 'He can't find me, Amy. He's going to kill me.'

'Was he on the boat, *Sea Swift*?'

He nodded and looked away.

'Ben, why is he after you?' I persisted.

The voice coming from the phone in my jacket pocket reminded me that DC Clinton was still hanging on, perhaps listening to our conversation. Not wanting to alarm the boy, I ended the call without responding to the detective's urgent demand to know what was happening. No doubt if Ben knew I'd called the police he'd bolt like a startled deer.

When I looked up again, his face was ashen. 'He's coming.'

The sight of the man striding along among the crowds in the distance was enough to freeze us both. If we ran for it, he'd be sure to see us. The only other option was to hide somewhere. Where? Without thinking, I grabbed Ben's hand again and pulled him off the path and down the side of one of the chalets, thinking that if we could only get behind it, he wouldn't see us. That's when I tripped over a pile of boxes that had been stacked along the side, lost my balance and fell sideways through the open door, pulling him with me. The two of us landed in a heap on the floor among rolls of bubble wrap and boxes of tissue. When I looked up, a young man at the counter had swung round and was looking at me with obvious shock.

'What the f—'

Perched on a tall stool beside him was a small girl in a pink parka and purple leggings. She was staring at us with wide, dark eyes, her mouth a round 'o' of astonishment.

The carved wooden toys on the shelves and the counter looked familiar. I suddenly realised that we'd landed in Ken's cabin, although this young man definitely wasn't Ken. He was taller and slimmer with dark, wavy hair that reached to the top of his collar, a close-cut beard and stunning, deep-blue eyes like a summer sky.

I caught my breath. 'I'm so sorry about this but could you please just act as if we're not here?'

For a moment, it looked as if he was going to order us to get out so I quickly added, 'I can explain but there's someone we need to avoid and I'd be so grateful if you'd just let us hide here until he's gone past.'

I described the man we were avoiding without going into detail about why. 'Just trust me, please. He's a nasty piece of work,' I pleaded, looking up at two astonished faces.

This could go either way. The little girl was still staring at us as if we were aliens that had fallen out of the sky.

Ben, meanwhile, had flung himself down in a foetal position with one arm covering his head. Perhaps it was this sight that changed the young man's mind because he turned back to the child beside him.

'Ok, Orla,' he said, calmly. 'You know how sometimes we play secret agents? Well, this lady wants us to play that game now for some reason I can't quite fathom. So, you and I have to pretend that everything is normal and we haven't got two people and a dog lying on the floor of Ken's cabin. Ok?'

'Ok.'

'And this is important: if you spot Ken coming back, you're to report to me immediately. Have you got that?'

'Ok.'

'Good girl. If the astronaut thing doesn't work out, you'll always have MI5 to fall back on.'

Irish, I thought. His voice was warm and pleasantly musical with an accent that made me feel instantly calmer. Perhaps a bit mad if the conversation was anything to go by but who was I to judge?

He laid his hand gently on the child's shoulder so that she calmly swivelled round on her stool and turned her attention to what was out front until Max decided to act like a lunatic by yapping and jumping up at her with a stupid grin on his face. 'Lie down!' I hissed, hooking my fingers through his collar and pinning him to the floor between me and my shopping.

Ben had now pulled the grey hood over his head and was lying so still he reminded me of one of those petrified bodies you see at Pompeii, forever caught in the moment of their death. I crouched as low as I could beside him and closed my eyes, breathing in a spicy smell coming from a box of pinecones under the counter. Since the cabin had been erected over the tarmac path, we were actually lying on the freezing cold ground, feeling the chill gradually sapping the warmth from our bodies. How Ben managed to lie so still I couldn't understand. I was just wondering what on earth was going on with him when I heard the young man speak.

'Can I help you? Were you looking for something in particular or do you need time to browse?'

'I'm not buying, Paddy,' said a voice I recognised, a hard, grating, cockney voice that sent me straight back to that day in the shop. My heart began to thump painfully. I saw Ben flinch and bring his knees up closer to his chest.

'Daddy's name is Tom not Paddy,' said the little girl, scornfully.

I held my breath. The man grunted something I couldn't make out. I looked across at Ben who had now pulled the hood even further over his face as though it would help him disappear into the grey ground beneath him.

'He's gone,' Orla's dad said, turning to look down at us both. 'He's heading off towards Tate Modern. Nice character, very friendly. Still, my girl here put him in his place, didn't you, love?'

Orla nodded solemnly. 'Why did he call you Paddy when it's not your name?'

'Sure, he probably thinks all Irishmen are called Paddy,' her father said, with a wink at me. He held out his hand and helped me to my feet. 'Tom Brennan, nice to meet you… I think.'

'Amy Lewis, and I owe you Tom and you, Orla.'

The child stared at me solemnly. Unlike her father, she had conker-brown eyes and darker skin but they both had the same thick chestnut hair which in Orla's case was held back from her face by a pink hairband.

Ben had got to his feet and was brushing himself down – although it was hardly worth bothering since his clothes were looking distinctly grubby since I'd seen him last. 'Thanks, Amy,' he mumbled.

My phone was ringing now with one long persistent demand for attention and I didn't need to check the caller to know who it was before answering. 'Hello, sorry about that DC Clinton. We had a problem.'

Too late I realised my mistake. Ben was staring at me with a look of sheer panic in his eyes. Before I could stop him, he flung open the door and was gone. I rushed outside to call him back but all I could see was a glimpse of grey as he disappeared through the crowds back towards the Festival Hall and God knows where. There was no way I'd ever be able to catch up. All I could do was swear under my breath at the frustration of losing him through my own stupidity. I said as much to the detective who was still hanging on, waiting to see what was happening. I heard the clatter of plates in the background – he'd obviously made it to the dinner table although he wouldn't let me go until I'd reassured him that I'd ring him back later with a full account of what had happened.

Back at the cabin door, there was nothing left to do now but pop my head round to apologise to Tom Brennan and thank him for going along with my madness.

'Who was that boy?' he asked. 'More to the point, where does Mr Personality come into this? If I never came across his brand of charm again it would be far from disappointing.'

'Ken's coming, Daddy,' Orla called from her perch.

Tom passed me my shopping bag. 'Nice to meet you, Amy Lewis. It was a bit dramatic but you take care now. Will you be all right?' He sounded genuinely concerned and there was warmth in those blue eyes. 'Oh here,' he said, 'take this just in case you're ever in desperate need of a ceramic fruit bowl.'

I looked down at the business card he'd given me. 'Kingston? You're based in Kingston? That's where my shop is.' I produced one of our cards from my bag and handed it to him.

'Small world,' he grinned. 'Maybe we can do some business.'

'Wait, do you have some of your work in an exhibition in Thames Street Gallery?'

He nodded. 'Just a few things, nothing earth-shakingly wonderful.'

I was about to disagree when the bulky figure of Ken appeared clutching a large cardboard box so I made some excuse about Tom being kind enough to let me leave my bag there for a while.

'He's all heart this lad,' Ken grunted.

Tom winked at me then gave me a smile that weakened my knees. 'So maybe I'll see you in Kingston someday, Amy.' He turned back to the counter as more customers demanded his attention. There was nothing left to do but trudge back to the station with a worrying feeling of failure. I'd let Ben down. Now he could be in serious danger.

16. AMY

The guilt had no way faded by the time I got home. Ok, kids do go up to London, and kids do run wild sometimes, but I could still see the terror on that boy's face when he spotted the man from the boat standing so close to us.

And there was that time I had met him after my art class – it seemed odd that a young teenager should be hanging about on the riverbank at night. He didn't look the sort to be making trouble although, of course, there were angel-faced delinquents in every town getting up to no good while their parents either didn't know or didn't care.

Anyway, Detective Clinton had children of his own and seemed a decent man so I had to trust him. Ben's fate was in his hands now.

Max had climbed up onto the sofa and fallen asleep before I had a chance to evict him to his basket but I let him stay there because, after all, he deserved a bit of comfort after what I'd put him through.

I was just contemplating opening a bottle of wine when my iPad signalled an incoming FaceTime call. Wearily, I answered.

'Hi, Marcus. How are you?'

A tanned and rugged version of my brother looked back at me. He'd filled out. *Great, he's taking up even more space now*. I pushed the thought away, ashamed of being so negative about someone I ought to love.

'Nice to see you too, sis,' he said. 'It's been ages.'

A trace of an Australian accent had crept in since the last time we'd spoken. Then he'd been a pasty-faced Englishman, now he looked like someone from the outback advertising his favourite lager.

'To what do I owe this pleasure?' I asked, with a sweetness I didn't feel.

No doubt there was an agenda to this call because Marcus had been so overindulged by my parents that he'd developed an irritating sense of entitlement while regarding both them and me as pushovers, barely worthy of his consideration unless useful.

'Can't I phone my sister just to find out how she is?' he asked. You would almost think he cared.

'I'm fine and so is Max, in case you're interested.'

'Who's Max?'

I turned the iPad so the camera lens was pointing at the snoring dog on the sofa beside me.

'Oh, that thing,' he said.

'Yes, *he* is adorable. I wouldn't be without him now. So how are things there?'

He reached for a cigarette and lit it. 'Fine.'

'Since when did you take up smoking?' Not even Marcus had been allowed to smoke at home. My mother regarded it as a filthy habit more suited to down and outs.

Marcus took a long draw, narrowed his eyes and breathed out a grey, foggy ring.

'Sick, isn't it? A huge swathe of this country is covered in bushfires and here I am, adding to the smoke.'

'That's not funny, Marcus.' It was typical of him to make a joke out of a tragedy.

'Ok sis, I won't beat about the bush – pardon the pun – but I wanted to ask you a favour.'

I slumped back against the cushions. 'I thought as much. What is it?'

He leaned forward and lowered his voice slightly as if afraid of being overheard.

'I need some money.'

'What? But you're earning a packet and Mum and Dad have

retired, remember? They're spending any pension they have on goat feed.'

'Not from them, from you, idiot.'

A panicky feeling rose into my throat. I stared at the screen, wondering what to say, how to escape from the inevitable.

'From me?' Stupid question but it was all I could say.

'Look, everyone's doing it.'

'Doing what?'

He took another draw on his cigarette, pulling the smoke deep into his lungs before speaking. 'Online gambling. I got into a few poker games with people at work. I took a few risks and they didn't pay off. That's all there is to it.'

'Mum and Dad said you needed money to set up your own business.'

He raised his eyes. 'Oh yeah, that's what I told them. Couldn't exactly tell them the truth, could I? Dad thinks bingo is the devil's work so you can imagine his reaction if he knew I was into the heavy stuff. Amy, you have to keep your mouth shut about this, ok?'

'How could you be so stupid? How much do you owe these people?'

He looked up at the ceiling and it struck me how humiliated he was at that moment.

'A lot. I thought I could win it back in other games but I just kept bloody losing more and more and now I'm in trouble.'

'Why didn't you stop before it got too bad?' I asked, frantically wondering how I could extricate myself from the direction this conversation was taking.

He looked at me as if I was insane. 'That's not how it works. You always think the next bet will be the one that makes you rich or at least pays back what you've lost.'

'So you kept on betting and losing?'

'Yep. That's pretty much it. So you've got to help me out.'

My legs seemed to have turned to water. 'How much?'

'A hundred and fifty thou will do it, enough to pay back some loans and get my head above water.'

The room was silent except for Max's gentle snoring. Then I found my voice.

'How could you lose that much?'

Marcus looked furious. 'I just did, ok? Now I need the money a.s.a.p. It's bloody urgent.'

'What makes you think I can afford to send it to you?' Just in time I stopped myself from adding: 'on a shopkeeper's salary.'

'Oh come on! You've got Gran's money tucked away in that savings account doing nothing. It's a mystery to me why she threw it away on the likes of you but she was a mad old bat, probably only half a brain by the time she popped her clogs.'

'Don't talk about her like that!'

Max woke, startled, and sat up as if wondering what he'd done to upset me. I gave him a reassuring stroke. 'It's ok, Max. I wasn't talking to you.'

'Looks as if Gran wasn't the only crazy in this family,' Marcus sneered. 'Maybe it's genetic, sis.'

Now I was furious. It was so typical of him to be insulting and still expect me to do what he wanted without question. Not this time, oh no. So, I took a deep breath and spoke as calmly and firmly as I could manage in the circumstances.

'It's your problem, Marcus. You got yourself into this mess. I'm not bailing you out.' *Please leave it at that.*

He stared at me for a moment than suddenly, shockingly, put his head in his hands. On the screen, all I could see was his fingers running through the hair on top of his head.

'Ok, ok, I know, I know,' he mumbled, all bluster gone.

Good, the lesson had gone home – no more messing about. This time he was on his own. It had been a close shave but I was getting away with it. Now he'd never know that I'd taken an enormous gamble of my own. All I had to do was say goodbye and wish him luck.

Oh, but that would have been too easy.

When he looked up again, there were tears streaming down his reddening face and he was taking shuddering, panicky gasps of air.

'Please, you've got to help me. Please, Amy. I'm... begging you.'

His distaste at using the word was obvious even though his normally powerful voice had become strangulated as if he was choking on his own misery. No, it wasn't misery, it was fear. I could see it in his eyes, the sheer panic, like an animal in a trap. Annoyance turned to shock then pity as I watched him struggle to control himself.

'Marcus, please don't get upset,' I pleaded. 'You'll find a way to put it right. I know you will.'

A thin, transparent stream of jelly was dripping down from his nose, adding to his humiliation. He wiped it away with his sleeve as though he were ten years old again.

'I'm desperate and you're the only person I can turn to,' he whimpered. 'There are people losing patience because I can't pay back the money I owe them and they're not the kind of people you mess about if you want to stay in one piece. Do you understand, Amy?'

When we were children, I had desperately tried to love my brother not only because it was expected of me but because I desperately *wanted* to love and be loved by him. The role of big sister and protector had been firmly laid on my shoulders by my parents and they'd expect it of me now.

The temperature in the room seemed to drop suddenly as if someone had turned off the heating and opened the window to let in the winter. Marcus was staring out of the screen, his eyes wide in desperation.

'Soon as you can, transfer the money into my account,' he pleaded. 'I'll email you my online bank details or better still, I'll give you them now. Have you got a pen and paper handy?'

All I could do was stare back while my mind searched for a solution.

'Amy, get this down now!'

'Wait, I need to think Marcus.'

My business account contained just enough to keep me going until I could weigh up the profits at the end of the month after paying Roz and settling the bills. Things weren't much better with my savings which had shrunk much to the bank's chagrin. On the kitchen worktop was a letter from the financial manager suggesting a switch to a different sort of savings plan with an even more pathetic interest rate. His glee and bonhomie at handling the thousands I'd inherited was a distant memory now that nearly everything had been sunk into Earth Song.

Like brother, like sister. We're both risk takers.

'What's your hurry?' I asked, playing for time. 'You can pay it all back in instalments if you make a plan.'

Marcus thumped the desk in front of him. 'You stupid bitch, don't you get it?'

A low, rumbling growl sounded in Max's throat. 'You're upsetting the dog,' I said, with a coolness I didn't feel.

Marcus scowled. 'For fuck's sake, can't you put that stupid thing in another room?'

'I have to go.'

'No, wait! Look, I'm sorry but I have to make you understand. They're all on my back at the same time, all wanting their money right now or else. Believe me, you don't want to know what they'll do to me if they don't get it.'

Who on earth had he got in with over there? Did Australia have its own version of the mafia? The moment felt surreal, as if we were living in an episode of the Godfather and the mob were about to leave my brother half dead and beaten to a pulp in some alleyway.

I shuddered. 'Who are these people?'

'Look, all you need to know is that you've got to help me, sis. I'll pay you back, honestly. When I can, you'll get every penny.'

I wondered what my parents would make of their blue-eyed boy getting himself into such a predicament. They must never know about this. It would hurt them too much.

'So what happens when you've paid these people? Will you start gambling all over again?'

Marcus was looking desperate. 'No, no, I'll get help. There are places you can go to get...' He hesitated. 'Cured.'

'Good idea. It's as much an addiction as alcohol or drugs, Marcus.'

He nodded. 'I know, sis, and I'm sorry for losing my rag but I can't take much more.' He put his head in his hands again.

Staring numbly at the screen, a memory stirred in my mind. Marcus was four and I was eight and we were playing on the beach at Bruford on Sea while Mum set out a picnic up near the wall of the promenade. We were having a game of football on the flat, firm sand, well away from the tumbling waves, me tapping the ball gently towards him so that he could easily kick it back. It was going well until Marcus was distracted by the barking of a large Alsatian that was tearing round in circles with the wind under its tail. Before I could stop him, he was running off towards the dog, ignoring my yells to come back as I chased after him. Too late. He'd reached the animal and was about to pat it when it bared its teeth and growled menacingly. Marcus froze, one arm held out towards the Alsatian's jaws and his face a mask of surprise as, not stopping to think, I hurtled over and threw myself between him and the snarling animal. In the distance, the owner was racing towards us shouting, 'Tyson! Come!' which had no effect whatsoever. The dog had worked itself up into an angry froth and was totally focused on us and me, in particular. Scooping up my little brother, I staggered away, desperately trying to bear his weight all the way back to the safety of the sea wall. That's when I noticed the slow trickle of blood running down towards my sock, the pain kicked in and I realised I'd been bitten.

Mum was furious. 'What were you thinking of Amy? You never let Marcus near strange dogs again, you hear?'

Yes, I'd always looked out for him, like the time I faced up to the bully who'd beaten him up after football practice for letting a goal through. True, the boy had laughed at the red-faced, angry girl threatening to take his head off if he ever touched her brother again but nevertheless, Marcus had no more trouble after that.

Pity it didn't work the other way round.

'So, these are my account details. Are you ready to write them down?' He had pulled himself together and had adopted a cold, business-like tone.

'What?'

'So you can transfer the money, you silly cow.'

'I can't.' It sounded like someone else's voice.

'What do you mean you can't?' He was angry again.

'I... haven't got it.'

The silence was heavy, filling the room.

'What the fuck are you talking about?' he said at last.

'I can't explain now. I'll call you back.'

I cut him off and threw the iPad onto the end of the sofa.

17. TOM

The annual art exhibition was, in Mr McDonald's words, 'What makes St Saviour's high.' There'd been some surreptitious sniggering at the staff meeting when he said this but I'd managed to keep my face straight since I was seated directly opposite him at the time.

'Yes,' he'd insisted, 'the standard of work we produce puts the "high" in high school.'

This year was no exception. We'd worked hard on setting up the school hall to display the range of techniques used by students across the year groups and the result was an explosion of creativity.

As the babysitter had let me down, I was forced to bring Orla along that evening but sat her down on a chair beside the ceramics table with her reading book and spelling homework; fortunately, she was perfectly happy sitting there watching the art department get ready. Her eyes were large and bright seeing the expanse and range of work on display. Our students had done themselves proud.

'I want to come to this school when I'm older, Dad,' she announced.

It was worrying to think of my girl as a teenager having to cope with the everyday jostling and joshing of secondary school life. And teenage boys, of course. No, I wasn't ready for that. 'That's a long way away yet, Orla,' I said, mainly to reassure myself.

Emily, the head of department, had been bustling round doing a last-minute check before we let the parents in but now she came over and eyed the display of pots and sculptures. If I say so myself, some of them were highly imaginative and skilful for kids who'd not had much experience of handling clay.

She gave me one of her tight smiles. 'It's looking great, Tom.'

Emily was not known for gushing praise so when she did say something positive, you really valued it. 'Would Orla like a little tour, I wonder?' she asked, holding out her hand. Orla meekly took it and went with her, listening intently as Emily explained the ideas behind the art works in words the child would understand. I watched with some pride. Our girl was already displaying artistic talent. Reading might not come easily but splashing colour about with abandon certainly did.

At half six, the doors opened and the first visitors appeared, their faces a picture of amazement as they walked into the transformed main hall. It reminded me of the time I'd gone with Orla's class on an outing to the National Gallery. The tediousness of the coach journey into town was soon forgotten as we walked into the first gallery and a look of sheer wonder came over the children's faces. There it was now as these adults suddenly realised that their children had produced this work and that education wasn't just about achievement in Maths and English.

Around ten, when we were thinking about winding up because everyone had gone, the door opened and a woman came into the hall closely followed by Jack Morris from year 10. I vaguely recognised her but wasn't sure why.

'Sorry,' I heard her say. 'I was held up at work. Am I too late?'

Emily assured her she was welcome but that we would be closing in about fifteen minutes.

'Ok, Jack, where's yours?' the woman asked. She looked frazzled and tired as if the pressures of the day had creased her face. Ah, so this was Mrs Morris. Jack's father had usually turned up for parents' evenings but since their divorce I suppose she'd had to make more of an effort. Mr McDonald had mentioned that she was a detective inspector so maybe it was difficult for her to get the work/life balance right.

Exposed by the emptiness of the room, young Jack desperately looked round for a haven and, seeing me, traipsed over to the ceramics table. Poor kid. I'd been about to tidy up but made an effort to look alert and welcoming as they approached.

'Hi, sir. This is my mum,' he mumbled. 'Mum, this is Mr Brennan.'

'Tom Brennan,' I said, offering my hand. 'Pleased to meet you, Mrs Morris. I'm a part-time member of the art department here specialising in craft and design techniques including sculpture and clay work.' My, didn't I sound grand! My mother would be proud.

She gripped my hand strongly, giving it a firm shake and holding my gaze with her small dark grey eyes while granting me a flicker of a smile. There was a keen intelligence behind those eyes. I could tell she was summing me up in that steady gaze and it didn't feel that comfortable.

'I'm so glad you could make it, Mrs Morris,' I continued. 'Jack here has a lot of talent. I expect him to get a good grade in his GCSE so he should certainly consider including art among his A levels when the time comes.'

'Really?' She seemed surprised.

Jack, meanwhile, had sidled over to the other end of the table where I'd displayed his collection of pottery sunflower bowls on a midnight blue velvet cloth, a deliberately dark contrast with the scorching yellow and orange glazes of the carefully sculpted petals. Earlier, they'd caught Orla's eye and it was all I could do to stop her touching them.

'Did you really make these?' Mrs Morris asked, turning to look at her son.

Jack nodded and I could tell from the glow that came into his cheeks that his mother's reaction had pleased him. Good. About time this kid got some praise.

Orla climbed off her chair and before I could stop her, was tugging at Jack's sleeve.

'Will you teach me how to make sunflower pots, please?'

Jack looked down at her, obviously unsure what to say to this small, determined person who'd glued herself to his side.

'Orla, leave Jack alone. Go and sit down on your chair now, there's a good girl,' I said.

Jack smiled an awkward 'unsure how to handle this' sort of smile then said, 'No sir, she's ok.' He looked down at Orla. 'Umm, you should ask your dad. He showed me what to do.' He ran his fingers through his hair, a nervous habit I'd seen him do before, and I noticed that the scar on his forehead was much paler.

'Do you like Van Gogh, Jack?' Orla asked.

That child was getting so bold. Where the hell did she get it from? I knew the answer, of course. Anna always had that direct way with people; she'd get so impatient with my Irish tendency to go around the houses. 'Out with it!' she'd say. 'Pretend you're English for God's sake!'

Orla slipped her hand into Jack's which, to my surprise, prompted the boy to ask if she wanted to see his painting. She nodded and let him take her over to the other side of the room where a large display board took up most of the wall.

Oh heck, something else to worry about. Would she grow out of this habit of approaching strangers and going off with them? I had visions of some creep asking her to come and see his etchings. *Oh, come on,* I scolded myself, *she's six years old! No point in fretting about what might happen when she's sixteen.*

Mrs Morris watched them for a moment then turned to me.

'Mr Brennan, I'm glad we've got a quiet moment. I want you to know I don't hold you responsible for what happened between Jack and James Gresham in your lesson.'

I stiffened. 'That's just as well, Mrs Morris, because regrettably, these things can happen where teenagers are concerned.'

'But I would like to know how Jack managed to get hold of a piece of wood heavy enough to almost break James's nose and how you didn't notice what was happening until it was too late.'

A shadow had fallen over the buzz and success of the evening. I explained that new clay had to have the air pummelled out of it and we usually put it on a wooden board to avoid having to clean up the work bench. It was one of these boards that Jack had snatched from the pile. Swing it hard enough and it could certainly do damage.

Mrs Morris was studying me intently. It made me wonder what it would be like to be a suspect sitting opposite her in the interview room. Not great, I imagined.

'It all happened so quickly,' I explained, almost wishing I had a lawyer standing beside me. 'I was helping one of the kids whose pot had collapsed and while my back was turned, the situation between the two boys kicked off.'

She nodded, seeming to think this over. 'I'm not a teacher but I can imagine it's hard to manage a class of adolescents.'

'To be honest,' I said, 'teaching a group of teenagers is akin to herding cats.'

'Especially when you have bullies and victims in the same room,' she said, pointedly.

I chose to ignore that remark for the sake of diplomacy but I knew who she was talking about.

Turning to see what her son was doing, she looked back at me. 'Jack told me that he and other kids were being bullied. Or rather, I interrogated him and he confessed.' She gave me that twitch of a smile again which made me wonder if there was a sense of humour beneath that stern exterior. 'Tell me, did you ever meet James Gresham's parents?' she asked.

I told her they'd wanted to sue both me and the school for negligence. It was only when their lawyer informed them that they didn't have a leg to stand on that they backed down.

'They may still try again,' I informed her.

'Maybe not,' she said. 'When I saw the Greshams at Jack's funeral, they looked as if all the fight had gone out of them.'

Now I remembered where I'd seen her. I'm almost sure it was her in the car park afterwards getting into a green Toyota.

'I saw you at the funeral,' she said. 'I presumed you were Miss Bailey's boyfriend.'

I laughed. 'That position has been filled by Will Gordon of the maths department.'

'Well, I'm glad to have met you, Mr Brennan,' she said. 'And thank you for encouraging Jack. If you can keep an eye out for him, I'd be grateful. He misses having his father around and most of the time, I feel like second best.'

Her eyes flickered away for a moment. The admission had obviously cost her a lot but I knew exactly how she felt. Second best was all I'd ever be for Orla too.

'I'm sure you're doing a better job than you think,' I said. 'Your son is a gifted artist, he just needs to have more confidence in himself.'

She gave me that fixed stare that made me wonder what she was thinking. 'Thank you, Mr Brennan. If you can come up with an idea of how I can help him with that, I'd be grateful.'

She turned away and I followed her over to where Jack was solemnly explaining to Orla the technique he'd used to produce his multimedia picture, speaking to the child as if she was on his own level. She was still clutching his hand and hanging on his every word, her eyes darting between his face and the painting.

Mrs Morris turned to me and smiled. 'I think Jack has a new admirer.' Smiling suited her. Her face softened as if someone had airbrushed it.

When they'd gone, Orla solemnly gathered up her books and I helped her on with her coat, tutting about the state of her woollen gloves.

'We're not made of money; I can't keep buying you new ones.'

She held up the damaged gloves and studied for a moment the ragged, soggy holes in the end of the fingers where she'd obviously been sucking and biting at the wool.

'I've spoiled their visual impact,' she said, sadly.

18. LYNN

When Sam told me about the call from Amy Lewis my first thought was that it might simply be a case of a kid on a jaunt up to London, having an adventure, meeting friends then heading back home for his dinner. Then again, the average teenage boy on a day out isn't usually pursued by a man who wants to kill him.

If Ben was truly alone and bent on running with nowhere to go, we both knew that London would swallow him up. After a few weeks, he could end up as just another lump in a sleeping bag, possible prey for drug dealers or sex traffickers. According to Sam, if the guy this boy was avoiding caught up with him, there wouldn't be much chance of tracing him. He'd end up as yet another face on a fading missing person poster.

After talking to Amy Lewis, Sam had immediately contacted the police up in town and phoned her back to let her know what was happening. She'd sounded only mildly relieved and it struck him how extraordinary she was to care so deeply about a young boy she didn't know, let alone put herself at risk to rescue him. 'He got lucky when she crossed his path,' he said.

It just shows how wrong you can be about people. When I came across Amy in that shop doorway, I'm ashamed to say my expectations of her intelligence weren't very high. Not that I have anything against blondes (apart from assuming they're thick) but since my husband decided to have an affair with one, it's made me even more prejudiced. Unfair I know. Still, water under the bridge as they say. I don't care who Graham fancies now and Amy Lewis is a decent young woman. Ok, she might even be intelligent.

A few days later, Sam's mobile rang with news.

'One of the homeless charities reported a young lad sleeping rough in Oxford Street and the local beat officer thinks it might be the boy we're looking for. They're holding him at the station for the time being.'

'You better go up there,' I said. 'Take Donna with you and bring Ben back. We need to ask him a few questions.'

PC Donna Harrington was good with kids, having three lively teenagers of her own at home.

Sam's stomach was rumbling and he wasn't going anywhere without food. 'I'll just grab some lunch before I go.'

'Ok. Oh, Sam…'

'Yes, Ma'am?'

'If you're getting a hamburger, get me one too, will you?'

It was Kai's turn to look at me with his mouth open.

I shrugged. 'Ok, hamburgers are disgusting but they're bloody good when you're stressed.'

*

Around 1 p.m., after we'd sent a photo of the boy in the Oxford Street nick to Amy Lewis and she'd given a positive identification, Sam and DC Harrington went up there to collect him. Sam called me before they left for the return journey.

'This lad took a lot of persuading. He's obviously terrified of someone in this town but I promised we'd keep him safe.'

'Any idea who he's afraid of?'

'He's not saying but maybe we can prise it out of him.'

'Softly, softly,' I warned. 'Take it from me, teenagers clam up tight if they feel threatened.'

Sam chuckled. 'There speaks experience, Ma'am. Anyway, the poor little guy's in a bit of a state. He's been sleeping rough for a few days so right now he's defensive and unwilling to cooperate, but maybe after a hot meal, who knows?'

I was right to trust Sam and Donna. By the time the trio arrived back at the station, Ben had calmed down considerably although he looked ready to fall asleep. Who could blame the poor kid? Some drunken idiots like nothing better than to kick people sleeping in shop doorways or even urinate over them. Most likely, he hadn't slept properly for days. I shuddered to think of a boy close to Jack's age being so vulnerable.

'I bet you'd like a shower and some clean clothes, love,' Donna said, as she led the small, gaunt figure into the office. We'd decided against the interview room and instead found a quiet corner with vaguely comfortable chairs where he wouldn't feel so threatened.

'Are you arresting me?' Ben muttered.

'No, son,' Sam said. 'We've brought you here to have a chat, that's all.'

I introduced myself then gestured to the boy to sit. The grubby grey hoodie was hanging off him and I wondered when he'd last eaten. Donna must have read my mind because she asked him if he'd like some food. When he nodded, she said she'd pop off to the canteen to see what was available.

When she'd gone, I was able to get a good look at this mystery boy of Amy's.

He was small for his age – if he was indeed fourteen as he'd claimed – and being painfully thin gave him a childlike vulnerability. His unusual pastel-blue eyes were large and framed by long, curved lashes; his eyebrows were almost hidden beneath scruffy strands of sandy hair that should have been cut ages ago. The face beneath the fringe was unnaturally pale, almost grey under the eyes. He obviously hadn't been getting much sleep lately, the poor kid. I wanted to wrap him up in a blanket and take him home like the abandoned, muddy puppy Graham and I had once found on the riverbank. But I had a job to do so banished that thought from my mind.

Sam, practical as ever, reached for his mobile.

'We need to contact your parents, Ben. I'm sure you'd like them to be here and they could bring some clean clothes. Give me their number and I'll call them for you.'

'No!' Ben's pale eyes widened. 'Don't. Please.' I noticed his fingernails scratching repeatedly at the knees of his worn jeans.

'You're a minor,' I said, gently. 'You need a parent or guardian here.'

'I thought I wasn't under arrest?'

'You're not but don't you think your mum and dad must be going mad with worry? Don't you want to see them again?'

'My mum's dead.'

Sam and I exchanged glances.

'I'm so sorry to hear that, Ben. When did she die?' I asked.

Ben began to pick at a small hole he'd made in the jeans, white threads beginning to show.

'Last Christmas. She had cancer.'

Sam looked genuinely saddened by this statement. 'That's the pits, son. Very sorry.'

The boy looked up at me. 'I hate Christmas.'

I thought of all the gaudy decorations strung up across the precinct, all the corny piped music and the constant bombardment of TV adverts showing happy families gathered round a table overflowing with Christmas food and how it must all have rubbed salt into this boy's wound.

'What about your dad?' I asked. 'Where can we find him? Does he have a landline or a mobile number?'

'Dunno.'

'Come on, Ben. We have to notify him.'

'He left us a long time ago and I'm not going back to Karl.'

'Who's Karl?'

'My mum's boyfriend. He hates me. That's why I came down here to London.'

'So where are you from?' His accent seemed to pin him down to somewhere up north but I wasn't sure where.

'Fallowfield,' he said. Then, seeing my blank look, he added,

'That's in Manchester.'

Sam raised an eyebrow at me. He knows geography isn't my strong point.

'Ok, but we'll call him later anyway just to let him know you're safe,' I said. 'Anyone else we should notify? Is there anyone in London that you know? Any other relatives, maybe?'

The boy shook his head. His right leg was now moving restlessly as if he had a tremor he couldn't control.

I drew in my breath. 'Ok, for now, I think we better get an appropriate adult to come and support you, Ben. They're volunteers, nothing to do with the law but everything to do with making you feel supported in a police station.'

Sam stood up. 'I'll see who's available, Ma'am.'

When he'd gone, Ben unwrapped a grubby red scarf from his neck, stuffed it into his jacket pocket then folded his arms and looked up at the ceiling. 'Am I here because I killed that boy?'

'What boy?' I asked. *Careful does it.*

'I wasn't supposed to give it to him. I told him but he wouldn't listen.'

At that moment, Donna Harrington returned with a tray. 'I managed to get the lad some fish and chips and some tea from the canteen, Ma'am.'

She set the tray down on Ben's frayed knees, stilling the nervous bouncing, and smiled when he muttered his thanks. 'You're very welcome, sweetheart. Tuck in.'

We waited, unasked questions hanging in the air, while the teenager attacked his meal and the smell of fried food competed for space with the suspect odours coming from his clothes. I was right. Judging by the way he bolted his food, this was his first meal in ages. Eventually, he took a gulp of tea, wiped his mouth with the back of his hand and sat back in his chair. 'Thanks very much,' he said. Whoever his mother was, she'd done a good job on his manners, that's for sure.

Donna took the tray and went off back to the canteen. While I was considering my next move, Sam returned with Moira Fraser, one of our team of appropriate adults and an old hand at supporting teenagers in custody.

'Let's start at the beginning, shall we?' I said, when everyone was settled and Sam had started the tape. 'Please tell me your full name.'

'Ben Webster,' he mumbled, avoiding my eyes.

'So, Ben, what's been happening?'

It's not easy to listen to a story like that from a child Ben's age, to hear him describe in a matter-of-fact way events that just shouldn't happen to anyone let alone a child.

Things went wrong for him after his mother's death when he was left alone in the house with the boyfriend, an abusive and violent individual. One night, Ben ran out of the house, not knowing where he was going but taking enough money to get him a train ticket to London with the vague idea of finding a close friend of his mum's who might help him. Of course, a young lad from Manchester would have no idea about London's sprawling geography. All he had was a scrap of paper with the friend's address somewhere in Finsbury Park along with her phone number, and the confidence of youth that he'd be able to go straight to it.

'London's a big place,' I said, 'as you probably found out.'

The atmosphere in the room had changed. We could see that Ben was kicking himself for telling us that much and had decided to clam up. Our next questions were met with sullen muteness until Sam said, 'I'm guessing that you found yourself in a situation beyond your control. You were alone and lost in a big city, at the mercy of strangers. Am I right?'

The boy looked miserable, avoiding our gaze, like a panic-stricken, trapped animal looking for an escape.

'It's ok, Ben,' I said, gently. 'Whatever happened to you, I'm guessing it wasn't your fault. But if we're to help you, we need to know the facts.'

He looked down at his restless fingers scratching away at the denim fabric. 'You won't send me back?'

When we assured him we wouldn't, the relief seemed to loosen his tongue just a little. With careful, unthreatening questioning we managed to find out that after getting off the train, he wandered around King's Cross with no clue as to how to get to North London and being ignored by any strangers that he asked. After a few nights sleeping in railway and bus stations, he was approached by a friendly stranger who said his name was Dillon, he worked for a homeless charity and was concerned for Ben's safety.

'He said a kid like me could get into trouble. There were evil people around who…'

I almost knew what was coming but sensed the boy's humiliation so kept my voice calm.

'Carry on, Ben. You're doing really well. What else did this Dillon say?'

He looked down again at his restless hands before speaking. 'He was nice to me, acted like he cared. He said there were bad people about who used kids like me for sex but he'd make sure I'd be safe so no need to worry.'

'And you trusted him?'

'Yeah, he seemed ok. He said he lived out west London way and he'd take me home with him and I could stay as long as I liked.'

'Whereabouts in West London?'

He shrugged. 'Dunno. He had this big car, a black Range Rover with leather seats, really cool, and he drove me out to his house. It was ok at first because it was a nice place and I had my own room.'

'What was this house like?' Sam asked.

'Big, like about four floors. You had to go up steps to the front door then there was a big kitchen downstairs where we ate and a sitting room upstairs and then the bedrooms were above that. Then one evening, another man I'd never met brought this Asian boy to the house. He said he'd found him wandering the streets with nowhere to go because he'd run away from home. Chris was just a little kid, twelve years old.'

As Ben unfolded his story, familiar elements crept in. After a couple of weeks, Dillon stepped up the pressure, telling the boys that if they liked living there, they'd have to start earning their keep. If they ran some errands for him, he'd even give them some money.

'What kind of errands?' Sam asked, even though we could both guess what they were.

'Delivering stuff. He gave me a small package and told me to take it to the supermarket car park. A guy would meet me by the recycling bins. So I went and the guy gave me some money in an envelope to give Dillon and then Dillon gave me some notes for doing the job.'

'And did Chris do these errands too?'

He nodded. 'But one day he took a look inside one of the packages and told me it was a plastic bag of white powder and that's when I knew it was drugs. Dillon found out and got so mad I thought he was going to kill us both. He wasn't nice anymore. He'd changed.'

Surprise, surprise. 'What happened next?'

'He drove us to this, like, scrapyard full of junk and there were two big old rusty boxes there and he said we'd end up inside them if we didn't do what he said and then he locked us in this old shed and left us.'

'How big were these boxes, Ben?'

'Like, really big, like what you see on the back of lorries sometimes.'

'How long were you in the shed?'

'A couple of days but then Dillon came back and he'd changed again. He was nice, kind even. He said if we behaved ourselves and carried on delivering for him, we could go and live on his friend's luxury boat on the river. This guy would be our new boss so we had to do whatever he said. Chris started on about wanting to go home so I tried to shut him up because Dillon would get nasty. I knew that now. Then Dillon hit him and told him to shut the fuck up – sorry,

Miss. So I said we'd do whatever he wanted because I needed to get Chris out of trouble. He was just a little kid, missing his mum and dad. I had to take care of him. So Dillon said good, that was the right attitude and the next day he took us out to this really cool boat on the river. So I told Chris we were ok now, we'd landed on our feet. Things would get better.'

Sam looked up from his notebook. 'And did they?'

Ben was now looking even more exhausted, as if the effort of talking about his ordeal was draining him of energy. Like it or not, the kid needed a rest. I stopped the tape and sat back in my chair. 'Let's take a break for a while.'

'No,' he said, looking startled. 'I need to tell you. I need to get it over with before you arrest me.'

I leaned forward. 'Ben, listen, you're not going to be arrested. You're helping us with our enquiries, helping us work out who *does* need arresting. At the moment, from what you've told us, it isn't you.'

The fists on his knees unclenched. 'But if they find me, if they know it was me who told you all these things…'

I did my best to reassure him that we'd keep him safe because he was our most important witness and, after a few minutes, he seemed to gather the energy to continue with his story.

Once on the boat, the two lads were each given a mobile phone by their new boss. They were to answer when it rang and listen carefully so they knew where to go with the package. Ben was given the school run as well. He was ordered to hang about outside a couple of schools to try and get new customers.

I inserted the memory stick into the laptop and turned it so that Ben could see the screen. 'This is the CCTV footage taken from St Saviour's High School. Can you tell us who that is?' I pointed to the hooded figure moving like a shadow between the milling school children.

He glanced up at the appropriate adult beside him. Mrs Fraser had the ability to stay calm no matter what she heard while exuding compassion for the young person she was supporting. A pity she hadn't been around to take this lad under her capable wing. Now she smiled at him reassuringly. 'It's best to tell the detectives the truth.'

He stared at the screen for a while, his fingers resuming their restless picking at the hole in the knee of his jeans. 'It's me,' he said at last.

I froze the video and pointed to the middle of the screen where James Gresham was emerging through the school gate. 'Do you know this lad?'

He leaned forward to get a better look at the screen. 'Yeah. He would follow me to the park and pay me for cannabis wraps.'

'Was it always cannabis?' Sam asked.

The boy shook his head. 'One day, he got nasty and said he wanted some molly for a party he was going to. I told him no, I wasn't allowed to give it to kids his age because it was too dangerous, the boss said. But this kid beat me up so in the end I got it for him. He was bigger and stronger than me – what could I do?'

'Molly? You mean MDMA? Ecstasy?'

He nodded.

'How did you get the drug, Ben?'

'I told the boss it was a special order from one of my regulars and he didn't ask any questions.'

'So what happened when you heard this boy had died?' Sam asked.

'I knew what the boss would do to me if he found out it was me who gave that kid the ecstasy. So the next day when I went out on a delivery I just kept going, slept rough for a bit then got the train into London. I thought if I could get back to Manchester everything would be ok. I could go and see my mate, Anil. Maybe see if his mum and dad could help me.'

He looked away and was quiet for a moment.

'So what happened?'

'That's when Amy found me. I was looking for the right station to get back home.'

I was worried that this was becoming too stressful for him. 'Are you ok, Ben?'

He looked close to tears. 'I left Chris behind. I should have taken him with me. I left a twelve-year-old kid with that fucking bastard.' He looked up at me. 'Sorry, Miss.'

'No need to apologise. I think we all know that's what he is.'

I glanced across at Mrs Fraser who was sitting beside him, noting the slight lifting of the eyebrows and the tightening of the mouth.

'And who was your boss?' I persisted. 'What's his name?'

Ben shrugged. 'We had to call him Boss. I don't know his name. Dillon said as long as we were on that boat, we had to do what the boss said.'

'And the boat's name?' Sam glanced across at me.

'It's called *Sea Swift*. Me and Chris do the river run. I work Kingston and Chris has to do around Hampton and Molesey.'

'Are you serious?' Sam's eyes widened. 'We're talking about respectable, quiet Surrey towns here. Are you messing around with us, lad?'

He and his family lived in a quiet, leafy street in Hampton. The area was a cut above mine, that's for sure, but then I didn't have a wife in advertising.

Ben looked alarmed. 'I'm telling you the truth. The boss takes us up and down the river and drops us off.'

'So does *Sea Swift* belong to your boss?' I asked, with a warning look at Sam.

'Yeah.'

'Can you tell me what he looks like, Ben?'

He thought for a moment then, glancing at Sam, said, 'He's really tall, taller than him even. And he works out with weights so he's got big muscles. He can lift me and Chris at the same time like we're just feathers or something.'

'And his face? How would you describe it?'

'I dunno. He has small eyes and a fattish nose like someone's punched it and he has a tattoo of a knife on his neck. He said he got it because it made him look hard and it does, dead hard.' He looked at Sam again. 'Harder than you, no offence.'

Sam grinned. 'None taken, son.'

I suppressed a smile. 'What about the boss's hair? I presume he has some?'

Ben nodded. 'It's short, really short like Action Man's.' He looked embarrassed. 'I knew a little kid who got one in a jumble sale and the boss looks like that, like a GI or something.'

'Good. You're being very helpful. Anything else you can tell us about this man?'

'Yeah, he's dead mean. One time, he gave me money to buy new clothes, like a really cool leather jacket, a pair of Levi's and some trainers. But when he said I wasn't doing well enough, he took them off me and threw them in the river. Then he hit me round the face and said there was more where that came from if I didn't watch myself.'

I noticed Sam frown but I, on the other hand, was beginning to feel my usual frisson of excitement when we were closing in on what DC Chauhan always called 'the bad chapatti'. It was what kept me in the job. It was why my resignation letter was still in a drawer at home.

'So was it just you and Chris who were working for this guy?'

'No, when me and Chris were taken to the scrapyard, one night, this minibus drove into the yard and these men got out. We saw them through a hole in the door, three of them.'

'What happened to these people?'

'Dunno. One of the guys tried to escape but these other men beat him up and dragged them all away but we couldn't see where they went. Then the yard lights went out and we couldn't see anything at all.'

'Where is this place?' I asked.

He was quiet for a moment. 'I don't know where it is exactly but when we went to live on the boat, sometimes the boss took it up that way to see Dillon and pick up supplies. It took about an hour to get there.'

'Which direction did the boat go in?'

He shrugged. 'Not sure but we went under the bridge first and then we had to go through about two locks further down.'

I turned to Sam. 'Sounds like they went downriver past Teddington and Richmond.'

'Sometimes, we just went under a bridge and didn't use the second lock,' Ben offered.

'Sounds like Richmond lock, all right,' Sam said. 'They raise the sluice gates about two hours either side of high tide and I guess the boat would need to travel on the high tide.'

'The boss was always swearing at other people in the lock, telling them to get off the river and onto the canal where they belonged,' Ben said.

Sam tutted. 'Typical owner of a gin palace who thinks he owns the Thames. So did you ever see Dillon on these trips?'

Ben shook his head. 'We weren't allowed up top when we went there. The boss locked us in the cabin but I could see a bit through the porthole.'

'But would you be able to show us on Google Maps how you went?' Sam persisted.

By now, the boy was obviously exhausted as well as badly needing a shower and a change of clothes but we were so close to getting important information.

I pulled my laptop closer and clicked on the app. 'Just do this one more thing for us and then we'll call it a day, Ben.'

19. AMY

It was just a matter of time. When the phone rang, I was tempted to ignore it. What was the point? Then I realised that it would only delay the inevitable.

'Hi Mum,' I said, brightly, as if this was a routine catch-up call. 'How are you both?' There was the tiniest chance that Marcus hadn't rung them.

'What's this we hear? Marcus says you won't lend him any money.'

'Did he tell you all about it then?' I wondered if he'd actually confessed.

'Of course.'

'So it's a pretty bad situation he's got himself into.'

She seemed remarkably calm considering her son was up to his eyes in debt to a bunch of murderous criminals.

'What on earth do you mean, Amy? All he wants is to get his business going,' my mother said, with a note of exasperation in her voice.

'Oh. That's what he told you?'

'He says you refused point blank. Well, neither of us can believe it of you.' The remark was punctuated with a sniff.

There was a low rumbling in the background as my father added his comments.

'And Daddy is quite frankly very angry that you're not prepared to help out considering you were the one that his mother bestowed her hard-earned money on. Poor Marcus was completely forgotten by his grandmother and now, it seems, by his sister as well.'

I stood up and headed for the kitchen. Only the rich, black liquid from an espresso pod could calm my nerves at this moment. 'You'll end up addicted,' a friend had once remarked and she was right but it was marginally healthier than smoking or taking hard drugs.

Beth's Irish dad, Joe, had a saying that truly fitted my brother: 'He lies like a cheap watch.'

'How do you know Marcus is telling you the truth?' I asked.

'Of course he is! What are you suggesting?'

'It's not what he said when he rang me.'

'Oh? And what did he say?'

It would have been so easy to betray him. Part of me wanted to open their eyes and make them understand that their precious son had frittered away money as though it was water running through his fingers. But how could I when, in spite of everything, I felt deeply sorry for him and for them? They had poured all their hopes into Marcus. Uncomfortable shoes I could just throw away but not my parents. They would be broken by this.

'It doesn't matter.' I inserted a pod into the coffee maker and waited while my mother gathered steam, stoked by Dad's constant encouragement in the background.

'A young man his age should be able to achieve his ambition.'

'Mum, can I point out that I'm four years older than Marcus and still renting a small flat I can barely afford?' I stifled the urge to add, 'But then I don't matter. In your eyes, I've never mattered as much as him.' What good would it do to scratch away the scab and open up the wound?

'Amy, you are the glue holding this family together,' Granny Lewis once told me. Maybe, but it was hard work being an adhesive.

So I held my peace, watched the black liquid drip into the white cup and breathed in the intense aroma, totally unprepared for what came next.

My mother was not giving up. 'You're being so selfish, dear. Can't you see that? You're denying your own brother a future. Really, how can you live with yourself when you have all that money sitting in the bank doing nothing?'

I took a sip of espresso, recoiling when it burnt my tongue. Enough lies, no more pretence. *My* life, *my* ambition was important too.

'It's not sitting there doing nothing, Mum. I've invested it.'

'What are you talking about?'

'I've bought a business.'

Business sounded better than shop, somehow. Then I remembered that my parents had visited Earth Song and, for a moment, I imagined their horror when they discovered that I wasn't just helping out that Saturday.

'What kind of business?' Mum demanded before passing on the information to Dad who growled something back. 'Your dad wants to know how much of that money you've invested.'

Batting away the question would be the easy way out but I needed time to think.

'Did you hear me? How much money has gone?' Mum was asking, her voice rising to an uncomfortably sharp pitch in my ear.

Oh, what the hell. Somewhere in London, a terrified boy had run away from a man who wanted to kill him, a boy that I was so close to helping and nearly lost because of my stupid mistake. Ok, he'd been rescued by the police but how did a child his age end up in such a state? What did anything matter after that?

'Amy, tell me the truth. How much of your grandmother's money have you spent on this so-called business?'

'Nearly all of it,' I said.

I waited for the fallout. I didn't have to wait long.

Their incredulity rushed down the phone in a breathless flood of questions and accusations. It was like being attacked by a swarm of furious bees stinging any patch of bare skin they could find. I actually flinched.

It was on the tip of my tongue to defend myself, to tell them that Marcus was up to his eyes in gambling debts but I just couldn't. Somehow, it was easier to listen to their ranting about my stupidity than to enlighten them about his. Maybe I'd just got used to taking the flak for Marcus. Battle-hardened, I suppose.

By the time I put the phone down, I was shaking – not with fear but with shock that my decisions could be so trashed by the people I loved. The one person who would have vehemently defended me was gone.

*

In the weeks before Christmas, business at Earth Song really took off. Some customers told us it was because there was so much discussion in the media about the damage we were doing to the planet – buying ethically sourced Christmas presents made them feel less guilty. We were glad to oblige, even if we suspected that some were merely virtue signalling.

Roz was noticeably light-hearted that week and had taken to singing to herself as she tidied the shelves at the end of the day. I wish I could say that my spirits matched hers but my conscience was digging at me with an enormous spade thoughtfully provided by my parents.

Ben had been on my mind as well. I knew he was safe because DI Morris had rung me to let me know they'd found him but I couldn't help wondering what would happen to him next.

Roz and I had staggered lunch hours so on the Thursday of that week, when it was my break, I headed to the coffee shop for a latte and the largest Danish pastry they could provide in the confident hope that a heavy dose of fat and sugar would cheer me up.

I'd just paid and was waiting for my coffee when a vaguely familiar voice behind me said, 'Hello there. We meet again.' I turned to see who it was and was pleasantly surprised to see Tom Brennan, the man whose Christmas chalet Ben and I had invaded. Just that morning I'd found his business card in my purse.

'It's nice to see you. And standing up this time,' Tom said, looking serious but with an unmistakably mischievous glint in his eyes.

The barista's face was a picture as she passed me my coffee.

I felt my cheeks redden. Since that Sunday, I'd had plenty of time to feel like an idiot for my behaviour although, in my defence, when you're acting on impulse you don't have time to weigh up the image you're presenting. All I hoped was that this man would overlook it and let me retire with whatever dignity I had left.

So it was a surprise when he asked if I'd like to have my coffee with him down by the river. I told him I didn't have long as we were busy in the shop so as soon as he got his order, we made our way through the marketplace and down the flight of steps that led to the riverside, finding a rare empty bench.

The river was more than usually busy that day with passing boats and flotillas of graceful swans riding the swell in neat corps de ballet formation along the bank, craning their slender necks expectantly to see if we had any food.

We chatted for a few minutes about the general topics that people who don't know each other talk about like how cold the weather was getting, how long we'd both lived in Kingston, how busy the town was at the moment, vaguely dancing around each other. Tom went on to inform me that he taught three days a week in a local high school and spent the other two days in his studio at home making ceramics to sell online and in local outlets. I said how much I'd admired the ones on display in the gallery then, when he asked me about my line of work, explained that I'd given up teaching to invest in Earth Song and how touch and go it had been financially. He seemed genuinely interested but also surprisingly impressed.

'It was a brave decision to make in the middle of a post-pandemic recession. You jumped into the deep end without a lifebelt there.'

'Some people would say it was stupid beyond belief.' These were my parents' exact words when I had finally admitted where the money had gone.

Tom frowned. 'Not stupid, no. It takes courage to follow your ambition but then you strike me as having a lot of courage, Amy. What you did to help that boy was extremely brave when you could have put yourself in danger.'

'Well, when someone's in trouble, you can't just walk by.'

I felt a sudden jolt of guilt at the fact that I'd just done exactly that to Marcus. How hypocritical of me to say that when I was about to abandon my own brother to his debtors. That wasn't the action of someone who stops to help. My mother's declaration that I wouldn't be welcome to visit them over Christmas was still stinging. Let's just say that, for me, this wasn't the jolly festive season we were promoting in the shop.

Our attention was suddenly diverted as a man leaning on the railings tossed the remains of his sandwich into the river, sending the birds into a frenzy. Ducks paddled frantically out of the way as the swans thrashed against each other, churning up the water as they fought over the sodden lumps of bread and floating shreds of lettuce.

'Just look at those eejits acting the maggot,' Tom remarked. Then, seeing my expression, he added, 'What's so funny?'

'You have a lovely accent,' I said. 'It's very musical, very easy on the ear.'

That lilt in his voice reminded me of Beth's dad who came to England as a young man but left his heart 'beyond' as he always put it. I'd always envied Beth for having such a kind, loving father which was why, as a teenager, I probably spent more time at her house than my own.

'And here's me thinking you're the one with the accent, Miss Lewis,' Tom said, with that mischievous smile that lit up his eyes. Now that I really looked at them, they were such a deep blue, like a Mediterranean sky.

'Touché,' I laughed, already feeling more cheerful and without even taking a bite out of the pastry. 'Swans are so classy but now I'll always think of them as eejits.'

Tom was looking at something out on the river. 'Talking of classy, that is one beautiful boat!'

The watery fight had died down and the swans were regaining

their composure, reforming into a dignified line as if nothing had happened, when suddenly, they found themselves rising and falling, riding the swell of water churned up by a white cabin cruiser with a long, pointed prow and darkened windows. It had emerged from under the bridge and was gliding upriver. I recognised it instantly. That racy sweep of black around the middle was so distinctive.

I got to my feet, reached for my phone and was just in time to get a photo, forwarding it straightaway to DC Clinton's number. It was only after I put the phone away that I wondered whether the driver of that boat had seen what I was doing. The image of the stocky man with the gold watch still haunted me.

'If you had a boat like that, you could be king of the river, going whenever the fancy took you, away from all the noise and crowds towards the fresh air and the green open spaces where your mind could be at peace,' Tom said, with a wistful expression on his face.

I sat down beside him again. 'That was a long sentence, Mr Brennan.'

'I know. I suffer from verbal diarrhoea – comes of being Irish, I suppose.'

Language seemed to flow out of him so easily. How different from my father. Words ricocheted out of his mouth like machine gun fire. Or Richard, the most eloquent man I knew until it became clear that what was oozing from his lips was merely a meaningless syrup of platitudes. Oh yes, he said it beautifully but it meant nothing in the end.

Strange, but I was beginning to feel completely at ease with this man. How can I explain it? The chemistry seemed right.

He sighed. 'But it's just a dream, Amy.' For a moment, he looked sad which made me wonder what was going on in his life. Abruptly, he jumped to his feet, breaking the spell.

'Well, it's been delightful seeing you again but I better go because I have work to do this afternoon before picking up Orla from school. Maybe we'll bump into each other again some time.'

'I'd like that,' I said, maybe a bit too quickly but I was already feeling worried that it might not happen. *Pull it together with a bit of dignity, Amy.* 'It's just a thought, but would you be interested in selling some of your ceramics in my shop?' Yes, that sounded quite business-like.

Tom's eyes lit up. 'Great! Yes, I'd like that. Give me a buzz then maybe you can come to my workshop to choose some pieces. Come soon.'

We shook hands and I watched him go back up the steps. At the top, he turned and waved before disappearing into the shadow of the passageway. Now it was my turn to feel sad. What a pity, I thought, that such a lovely man is married but then all the best ones are. His wife is a lucky woman.

It was late-night opening in Kingston that evening and most of the shops in the centre, us included, stayed open till ten. I sent Roz home to her family around eight and managed to cope with the welcome rush of customers by myself. I walked home on a high, proud of our success, hardly noticing that the temperature had dropped even further, chilling the air and dusting the pavement with patches of frost. Wherever Granny Lewis was now, I knew she'd be proud of me. It's mad but as I crossed the bridge, pausing to glance at the lights of the boats shimmering in the black river, her voice seemed to whisper in my ear. *You did it, Amy. The gamble paid off.*

And then, just as I was going to bed, exhausted but happy, the phone rang.

Sometimes, when you're riding high, someone will come along who knocks you over so hard that you wonder if you'll ever get up again.

20. TOM

I was having a nightmare. Orla and I were astronauts floating outside the international space station above the vast blue curve of the Earth, attached to each other by a long silver cord. I was busy painting the outside of the craft a vivid red for some reason, while she watched intently from about two metres away. Suddenly, there was a jolt and the cord broke, sending my child drifting slowly away from me towards the endless blackness of space, her arms and legs moving in slow motion as if she were treading water. Through the darkened visor of her helmet I could see her wide, terrified eyes as she screamed silently for help.

My fingers fumbled with the cord tethering me to the space station but it wouldn't unhook and every time I looked back, Orla was further and further away until she was just a tiny white speck the size of one of the distant stars. Within seconds, she was invisible among their dots of light.

I woke, wet through with sweat, my heart racing, then sat up and swung my shaking legs over the side of the bed. It was crazy, I know, but I had to go and peer round Orla's bedroom door to check she was there. Which she was of course, safely tucked up beneath her Star Wars quilt, one arm flung over Luke Skywalker's face. I nearly melted with relief.

The following morning over breakfast, she suddenly put down her spoon and made a solemn announcement.

'I don't want to be an astronaut anymore. I want to be an artist like Jack.'

'Ok,' I said, keeping my voice level. 'But you do realise that your father is a bit of an artist himself? In fact, I was an artist before Jack Morris could even hold a pencil.'

Not quite true but after such a restless night, I was worn as thin as a fag paper, as my dad likes to say.

'And before you start,' I continued, 'my name is not Michelangelo so I am not about to repaint your bedroom ceiling.'

Orla stared at me for a moment, her bows knitted together. 'I'd like some sunflowers, please, Daddy.'

I cleared my throat which gave me thinking time. 'Don't you think that since you're very nearly seven, you should be going for something a bit more sophisticated? If you really want to get rid of the planets, it's a coat of white emulsion for you, my girl.'

'Jack would know how to do it. Jack says that art is about creating visual impact.' Which is hard to say when you're six and three-quarters and you've lost a couple of teeth. I wondered if she even understood it or had Jack explained it for her? All power to his elbow if he had.

I whacked the top of my boiled egg which crackled and fractured. 'And who do you think taught him that, Orla?'

She was silent for a moment, sucking up the gloopy remains of her saturated cocoa pops and that gave me just enough time to feel thoroughly ashamed. How could I be jealous of a fifteen-year-old boy – and Jack Morris, especially? If Anna had been there, she'd have taken the wind out of my overblown sails with that way she had of making you laugh at yourself.

Orla scraped the bowl with a sound that set my teeth on edge then let the spoon clatter against the side. Her mouth was set in a firm line which meant trouble.

'Don't want white. I want flowers and trees.'

I dug the teaspoon into the egg and watched the sunflower yellow yolk ooze over the side and drip onto the plate. 'Go and brush your teeth, please,' I said firmly. 'We'll talk about this at the weekend.'

'Will you ask Jack?' she said, pausing at the kitchen door. 'Will you ask him to come and paint my ceiling?'

That did it. 'Hurry up, Orla, or we'll both be late. Subject closed; Mission Control over and out.'

It was a teaching day for me so Orla had to be dropped off at her friend Katie's house by seven forty-five. I heard her stamp up the stairs and slam the bathroom door. God help me when that girl hit fifteen. She'd probably drift away from me then to a place I couldn't reach, leaving me helplessly floundering.

You're having a sense of humour failure, my love, I heard Anna say in that warm, soft voice of hers. 'I know,' I murmured. 'But everything's harder without you, Anna.'

Fifteen minutes later, as we were about to go out the front door, Orla slipped her small hand into mine. 'I'm sorry,' she murmured, her voice husky. 'I'm sorry I upset you, Dad.'

I knelt down, put my arms around her and held her tightly. 'You didn't, sweetheart. Dad had a weird dream last night and it's made me tired today that's all.'

She lifted her head off my shoulder and pulled back to look into my face.

'What was it about?'

'Oh nothing. You know how silly dreams can be.'

'Next time you have a bad dream, come and tell me,' she said, solemnly. 'I'll make you feel better.' They were exactly the words her mother had used to comfort her.

I kissed her forehead, suddenly overwhelmed. 'Thanks, love. I'll remember that.'

*

That afternoon, Jack Morris volunteered to stay behind after pottery club to help me clear up the art room. Once I'd got over the shock, I asked him if his mother would mind him being late.

He shrugged. 'I'll be home long before her so she won't even notice.'

'She has a demanding job, Jack. It's not her fault,' I said gently, though I couldn't help feeling sorry for the lad.

'When my dad lived with us, he was always there cos he's a writer and he did all his writing in the spare room,' he said. It was the longest sentence I'd ever heard him utter.

Since the exhibition, I was full of curiosity about the conversation he'd had with Orla. Seeing them chatting away together so easily had obviously surprised his mother too. My guess was that communication was minimal in that household – not that I blamed her. It must have been tricky juggling her job and Jack without any help and without a male role model around. It was probably just as tricky as raising a daughter without her mother.

'Do you miss your dad, Jack?'

'Yeah.' He looked around for a job to do, obviously uncomfortable with my probing, so I decided to change tack.

'My daughter told me this morning that she wants to be an artist like you,' I said, as he began to scrape and stack the wooden pottery boards.

He looked up. 'Really? I mean, that's you isn't it, sir? You're the artist.'

'Apparently, Jack, it's all about youth and you score there, laddo.'

He grinned. 'Must be annoying for you, sir.'

'Very,' I said with mock indignation.

We were both quiet for a few moments while we got on with the tidying. I put the newly made pots on the drying shelf while Jack continued to scrape the scraps of discarded clay into the bin. When I turned to see how he was getting on, he was staring down at the last board on the bench, the one with the crack in it where the wood had fractured.

'Maybe we should throw that one away,' I suggested.

He was motionless, staring down at the board, and I could tell he was re-living that afternoon when he'd used it as a weapon against James Gresham. We never got to the bottom of why he'd done it so it was still a mystery. There must have been severe provocation for a normally placid student to suddenly lose all control and lash out like that. I knew James was no angel; I usually kept a tight rein on him in my classes but that day, it only took a few minutes' distraction for things to kick off.

Jack looked up at me. 'He asked for it, sir.'

'Do you want to tell me why?'

He reddened. He was curling back into his shell again, avoiding my gaze, looking shifty as only a fifteen-year-old boy can. 'The other kids know why. Didn't they tell you?' he mumbled.

No, they hadn't. The whole group had clammed up in response to my questions. Strange I know, but I got the feeling they daren't tell me what was going on, that they were afraid of someone.

'If I tell you, sir, will you keep it to yourself?' he asked.

'Of course – if that's what you want.'

He glanced around the room then went and closed the door.

'No bugs here, Jack,' I smiled. 'Do you want to check the cupboard in case there's a spy lurking among the shelves?'

Some things you wish you hadn't said. I was about to apologise but he'd already begun to talk, spilling out what happened that day in a tumble of words. Afterwards, he looked exhausted as if his secret had weighed heavily and, in spite of revealing it to me, still did. No wonder. Talk about humiliation.

'Does your mother know what happened?' I asked.

Jack looked horrified. 'No! I couldn't tell her, sir!'

'But I think you need to, Jack; it's the only way you can move on. Believe me, in her job she's had to deal with far worse. Talk to her; let her help you.'

'Ok, I will,' he mumbled, but I could tell it was more to get me off his case than a real intention.

'We've all done stupid things in our lives because we're only human beings. If I had to tell you about my moments of stupidity, we'd be here till midnight.'

'Thanks.' He went back to the bench and picked up the last clay board.

'Bin that,' I said, firmly.

21. AMY

'Sell it! Sell your stupid shop and give me the money!'

'And do what, Marcus? Starve?'

'Don't be such a fucking drama queen. Sell it, give me the money I need and go back to teaching.'

I told him there was no way retail businesses were selling at that time of year and it could be weeks before I got an offer but he kept insisting that once these people knew the money would be on its way, they wouldn't touch him. Nice of them. By nature, I'm a pacifist but right then, if I'd had a machine gun I'd have gone over there and mown them all down to save my brother.

Then, he started to beg, his voice rising and falling in waves of panic. It was a sound I'd never forget. It was the sound that broke me.

By the time Marcus put the phone down, I felt as if every bit of strength had been wrung out of me. Worst of all, I'd agreed to sell up to raise the money he so desperately needed to save him from whatever those thugs had in mind.

After a sleepless night, I trudged to work the next morning, feeling the weight of his stupidity on my shoulders. Pausing on the bridge to lean against the cold stone, I gazed down at a line of swans gliding downriver. How I envied them their smug serenity.

'Don't do it, sweetheart.' An elderly man was standing beside me. 'There are people you can talk to. You're not alone.'

'Oh, I wasn't going to... You thought I was about to...'

It should have been funny but the man was looking at me with such concern, it brought me up short.

'I'm really fine but thank you for…'

'*Thanks for, like, worrying about me,*' Ben's voice said, somewhere in the back of my head.

The man smiled. 'Oh I'm glad. You'll think I'm daft, only you did look upset, as if you were about to climb up there.'

'You're very kind, but don't worry. I'm not that athletic.'

'Just as well. Sorry if I disturbed you, love.'

I watched him walk away stiffly as if one hip wasn't working too well until, reaching the bus stop, he turned and gave a little wave as a bus slid up beside him. I was disappointed to see him go. For a moment, he'd wrapped me in his warmth and, now he'd gone, the world felt colder.

Roz had beaten me to the shop and was just unlocking the door. 'Coffee, number one priority,' she announced, bustling straight into the kitchen. 'Want one?'

'Make it strong, Roz.'

Unable to face the conversation we were about to have, I stood in the doorway for a few moments watching the marketplace come to life. Across the square, along the row of shops, security shutters were clattering up revealing windows glowing in the morning sun. Stall holders were busy setting up and a smell of frying bacon filled the air as breakfast was cooked at the take-away food hut. Ray, whose family had owned the greengrocery stall for generations, was unloading boxes of fruit and veg from his transit. He balanced two of the boxes on his shoulders and began whistling tunelessly until he noticed me standing in the doorway of Earth Song. He put the boxes down, wiped his forehead and winked.

'Morning, love. Would you like a kilo of eco carrots grown in the good old singing earth?'

Normally, I enjoyed the banter and the gentle teasing about my shop's unusual name but this morning it was all too cheerful so I just grinned, waved and stepped back inside, closing the door.

'Here, I've made it extra strong,' said Roz from behind me. She handed over a mug of coffee. 'I'm a bit stressed this morning.'

'Join the club.'

'Yes but you're so lucky you don't have kids. At seven o'clock this morning, Alex announced that he needed a shepherd's costume for the Year 2 nativity play and he needed it today for the dress rehearsal so I'm like, why the hell didn't you tell me this before?'

'Didn't you get a letter about costumes?'

'Oh sure, screwed up at the bottom of his book bag. He'd just remembered it was there.'

I realised I was missing Christmas at school when, in spite of all the tantrums, wobbles, arguments and misbehaving shepherds, the end result was always moving and, sometimes, unintentionally amusing.

No need to miss it anymore. Next Christmas it would be me pinning wings onto the backs of fidgety angels.

I wondered what part Orla Brennan would be playing at her school, imagining that serious little face beneath a blue veil or sporting a tinsel halo or proclaiming her words solemnly with that cute accent of hers with its hint of Ireland occasionally bobbing up among the London. Her father's influence, I supposed, though perhaps her mother was Irish too.

'Brown tights, black top and a tea towel for a headdress, Roz,' I suggested.

Roz raised her eyes. 'He's wearing jeans, a tee-shirt and a souvenir tea towel from Brighton and that will have to do. So what's your excuse?'

'For what?'

'For being stressed out this morning and don't pretend you aren't. I can see it in your eyes, Missus.'

'Oh, let's just say I'd give anything to swap problems with you, Roz.' I took a sip of the bitter black coffee and swallowed a need to cry.

'Come on,' she said. 'Cough up. What is it?'

When I'd explained it all, there was nothing to do except stand there and take the disappointment, bitterness and shock coming my way.

'Are you completely mad? How could you even think of selling up? This place means so much to you – and to me, as it happens. You know how much work I've put into it, how much I believe in it, Amy. You must be crazy to think of throwing it all away. And what do you expect me to do now? You can't just walk into another job these days.'

'I know, I know.' How pathetic but what else could I say?

'But that's not the point. The point is you're entitled to have a business and to run your life the way you want and just because your feckless brother – and I'm sorry but that's what he is – just because he's messed up and is in the shit, that doesn't mean he has to pull you down with him.'

Coffee splashed against the sides of Roz's mug as she gesticulated.

'I don't know what else to do,' I said, miserably. 'If I don't pay off his debts, they'll hurt him or worse.'

'Yeah, and he won't be so stupid next time. If the tables were turned, would Marcus be rescuing you? I don't think so.'

Roz punctuated the thought with a jut of the chin and, when there was no answer, added, 'And how do you know he's telling the truth, eh?'

That shocked me. She wouldn't have said it if she'd heard the heart-rending noises Marcus was making. Why is it always worse when a man cries?

'He was panic stricken, Roz. I know he's not lying. If you could have heard him, you'd understand. You know how confident Marcus is normally.'

Roz had only met Marcus once at a New Year's Eve party in my flat but had given me the impression that once was enough. That evening, he was determined to be the centre of attention and achieved it by being loud and obnoxious before drunkenly passing out on the sofa much to everyone's relief.

She put her hands on my shoulders and forced me to look her in the eye.

'Amy, please don't do this. Don't throw away your business.'

'We need to open up. It's coming up to nine o'clock.'

'Ok but we need to talk about this later.' She turned away, tutting with disgust.

I desperately needed to get out of there for a while if only to escape from the recrimination hanging in the air. Around mid-morning, I brought up the subject of Tom Brennan's ceramics. This might be a good time to have a look at his work to see if it would be a suitable addition to our stock, I told her. Her response was predictably scornful.

'Don't know why you're bothering when we're closing soon.'

It was a relief when Tom answered his mobile and said he was at home that day so I'd be welcome to visit.

Roz rummaged in her bag for her car keys. 'Take my car. It's parked in the usual place.'

'I'll be as quick as I can,' I promised.

Twenty minutes later, I reached a semi-detached Victorian cottage in a quiet back street on the edge of town. Tom opened the door wearing a splattered leather apron over faded blue jeans and a red and blue check shirt with sleeves rolled up to the elbows. I followed him as he led the way down a narrow hallway to a small kitchen which seemed to welcome me like an old friend.

His was a real kitchen, homely and far removed from those modern shiny showpieces you see in magazines, rooms that look as if no human being ever stepped foot in them let alone cooked a meal. The walls, unlike my custard fest, were a subtle shade of pale lemon fitted with wooden cupboards painted moss green. Lining the worktop was an assortment of storage jars, a large kettle and a rack of mismatching mugs. It was a room you could relax and make a mess in, just big enough to include a small table and four chairs against the end wall. The table was covered with a navy-blue oilskin cloth and in the centre was a white china bowl containing a potted poinsettia whose scarlet petals sang against the dark blue of the cloth.

Through the glass of the back door I could see a small garden. Most of it was taken up by a tired-looking lawn dissected by a paved path. At the back of this was a wide concrete shed reaching from fence to fence, with one window running along its length reflecting the house.

'That's my workshop,' Tom explained. 'It's where I spend most of my day hunched over a bench so it's grand to have company for a change.'

He ran his fingers through the thick mop of hair to push it back from his face and a couple of small wood shavings fluttered onto his shoulders. He grinned, ruefully, and brushed them off with fingers coated in dried clay.

'My work's gone to my head. I alternate between throwing pots and carving wood so it's a mad life, Miss Lewis, and never a clean one. But then if I'd wanted to be a suit and tie sort of a fella, I would have been a chartered accountant.'

I couldn't help smiling at his honesty. How different he was from Richard, a man so manically obsessed with his appearance that after he'd left, it took me ages to work out what was wrong with the bathroom until I realised that the nostril-tingling smell had gone. The glass shelf above the sink looked naked without his grooming sprays, aftershave, moisturiser pots, musky deodorants and hair gels. None of it was for my benefit as it turned out. His parting shot in the doorway had been: 'You're just one small fish in a vast, inviting sea, sweetheart.'

'Pity you're stuck in the swamp then, sweetheart,' was my retort before slamming the front door. Didn't stop me bursting into tears, though.

A chipped blue enamel pot was bubbling away to itself on Tom's stove, filling the room with the strong aroma of brewing coffee. 'Can I tempt you?' he asked. 'Or are you in a hurry? I don't have one of those fancy machines but this old thing works very well. If it's good enough for Inspector Montalbano, it's good enough for me.'

He chuckled, before explaining that Montalbano was the creation of a Sicilian author he admired, Andrea Camilleri. Nothing would have pleased me more than to sit in that kitchen drinking strong coffee like the Italians but time wasn't on my side. I reluctantly refused his offer explaining that Roz wouldn't appreciate me being away too long. One lecture a day was enough.

'Right,' Tom said, turning off the gas. 'So, would you like to see some of my work?'

'Please.' I followed him down the garden and into the workshop.

As soon as we stepped inside, I could sense the importance of this place in Tom's life. Two long fluorescent tubes on either side of the ceiling shone down onto sturdy wooden work benches. He explained that the clay bowls and jugs lined up on shelves above the bench on the left-hand side were freshly made and just drying before they went into the bulky kiln which was squatting beside a stack of white buckets. On the bench he had placed some finished bowls that had been glazed in glowing colours. An electric potter's wheel stood in the opposite corner, its legs as spattered as Tom's apron, and on the opposite side of the room, another work bench running along the length of the window was laid out with a set of woodworking tools with well-worn handles.

'Those tools belonged to my grandfather,' Tom explained, seeing my interest. 'When I hold them, I feel as if he's guiding my hand. Does that sound crazy?'

'Not at all,' I said. 'I have a fountain pen of my granny's. It's old-fashioned to write with ink now but I love the way it flows so smoothly across the page and the way it seems to connect me to her.'

He smiled. 'You were obviously close then.'

I found myself telling him how much of an inspiration Granny Lewis had been and how it was her money that had enabled me to set up Earth Song. He listened, nodding every now and then and looking into my eyes intently as if sizing me up. It was strange but talking to Tom was so easy as if we'd known each other for years. Call it trust but my confidences felt safe with him.

'I get that,' he said, when I'd finished. 'Sometimes, I can hear Grandad say, "Steady now with that chisel! You're shaping the wood not digging feckin potatoes." It's as if he's standing right behind me watching every move. Does your granny ever talk to you or am I the only mad person around here?'

'She never judged me,' I said, surprised to feel sadness welling up. 'She was the only person in my family who didn't.'

I blushed and swallowed. Why the hell was I telling a complete stranger about something so personal? But the truth was Tom didn't feel like a stranger. He felt safe and comfortable and easy and I could have stayed all day in that workshop with him, breathing in the earthy smells of freshly shaved wood and wet clay.

He smiled that slow, gentle smile. 'Your granny sounds like a real gem. We all need a visionary in our lives, someone who can see our potential when others can't.'

'So did you always want to be a potter?' I asked.

'I always wanted to work with my hands. It was a dream from boyhood.'

I told him how I'd always wanted to have my own business but my parents believed that I hadn't the brains for it.

He looked shocked. 'Really?'

'Yes, well, they invested all their hopes in my brother.'

'I'm sorry, although it's probably driven you on all the more,' Tom said, frowning.

'Even when I became a teacher it didn't impress them as much as him going into banking.'

'So you were a teacher? I bet that took some pluck, changing careers like that.'

Usually, when you don't know someone that well, you paddle about in the shallows for a while but we seemed to be treading water in the deep end of conversation. Looking into his face now, there was that sadness in those kind eyes that I'd noticed that morning by the river. It was surprising considering how readily he smiled. What was going on behind that easy-going Irish charm of his?

'It did take guts I suppose,' I said. 'Some people would say it was mad but I believe you have to take risks in life if you want to achieve your goals.'

Tom was still studying me. 'And look at you now with your own shop. I hope my daughter has your courage when she's ready to make her way in the world.'

I was forgetting the whole purpose of my visit; it wouldn't do.

'So do you have anything suitable for Earth Song?' I asked, anxious to appear business-like.

The atmosphere had changed, cooled, and it was my fault. He seemed taken aback at my sudden change of tone and subject so I pleaded lack of time and Roz coping in the shop alone. Still, it felt rude when he'd been so welcoming and I tried to make up for it by enthusiastically praising the coloured fruit bowls and ordering five of them before we shook hands on a sale or return deal. Tom promised to deliver the bowls the following day, along with some from the kiln as soon as they were finished.

'If these sell, perhaps we could make this a longer-term agreement, Amy.'

'Well...' Suddenly, I was tongue tied and nervous.

'Problem?' he asked. 'Everything's ok, I hope?'

How could it be when overnight the earth had shifted on its axis?

He was looking puzzled and I trusted him so I spilled out what was happening with Marcus. When I'd finished, he said, with surprising anger in his voice, 'So you're going to sacrifice Earth Song because your brother's been an eejit?'

'That's what Roz said but what else can I do?'

'If I were him, I wouldn't be expecting my sister to ruin her life to get me out of a hole I've dug for myself.'

He was right, of course, but to agree felt like treachery.

'You don't know the whole story,' I said, coolly.

'I can sense that you don't want to do this, Amy.' He was holding me in an intense stare.

'You're right, I don't want to sell up but he needs me so what else can I do?'

'Look, it's none of my business but I hope you're going to think it through carefully.'

I'd tried so hard that morning to carry on with dignity but now I could feel myself beginning to crumble.

'I must get back to the shop before the rush begins,' I said, turning towards the door. As I did so, something caught my eye. Lying beside the tools on the bench was a child's painting in a simple wooden frame made of plywood. 'Orla's?' I asked. 'It's very... bold.'

'Van Gogh has an awful lot to answer for. I promised her I'd frame it weeks ago but I've been too busy.'

'You could do with employing someone to help out, an apprentice, maybe.'

He sighed. 'The truth is I may have to take on more teaching. It's only the odd online customer and the likes of yourself who are interested in buying my ceramics and that won't last much longer if your brother has his way.'

Now I was fighting back tears, swallowing hard. 'I'm so sorry. I wish this wasn't happening.'

Tom moved closer. 'So do I. You could have done so well with that place.'

I nodded, too miserable to speak and wishing he would put his arms around me. I so needed a hug at that moment even from a married man with a wife and daughter. Especially from him. Unwanted tears were streaming down my face and the next thing I knew, he was turning me gently towards him, putting his arms round me, and my wet cheek was nuzzling against his warm neck.

'Sorry, I shouldn't have said that. It's me that's the eejit,' he said.

I pulled away sharply, mortified with embarrassment, and apologised.

'Don't,' he protested. 'No need.'

'I don't know why I did that. What was I thinking?'

'You're stressed, Amy. It's ok.'

He led the way out through the warm kitchen and stood at his front door watching as I unlocked Roz's car, studiously avoiding his gaze.

'So we're agreed on sale or return?' he called.

I nodded. 'Yes, and thank you, Tom.'

'You're very welcome, Amy.'

Just before I got into the car, I heard him say, 'Listen, call me if you need to talk.'

'Ok, thanks.' I'd embarrassed myself enough. Time to leave with some dignity.

Driving off, I could see him in the rear-view mirror standing by his gate. He was still there a few seconds later as I stopped to let a car out of a side road.

22. LYNN

Kids who get involved in drug selling are expendable, a conveyor belt workforce; if the bosses lose one kid, they just find another. If he'd been caught, Ben would have been eliminated because he knew too much. His battered body would have been thrown on some rubbish dump or made to disappear completely as if he'd never existed.

He got lucky. I hoped he realised how much he owed the young woman who had taken an interest in him.

Two weeks to go before Christmas. You could sense the anticipation among some of the younger members of our team and the increasingly fraught expressions of the older ones. The women with families were obviously juggling the demands of the job with the demands to get Christmas organised at home. For me, it was Jack who was constantly on my mind. He was still quiet and moody as if only half of him was ever present in the room.

At Monday morning's briefing, I reported to the team on the interview with Ben. The doctor who examined him reported finding scars on the boy's arms which could only have been caused by cigarette burns, proving that his life on the boat had been far from luxurious. Any attempt to opt out or escape was instantly punished. He and Chris lived with the threat of what the boss ironically called 'being baptised' – namely, being thrown into the river once it was dark. Even if they were strong swimmers, the boys would have found it hard to survive in the cold, dark and deep waters further upstream. What worried me now was whether Chris had been punished in Ben's place.

All in all, the prospect of them being prosecuted was rapidly diminishing. They were so obviously victims in this case.

'If James Gresham hadn't died, we might never have known this was happening right on our doorstep,' I said. 'But now that we do, our priority is to rescue the other boy and trace the people running this business before other kids get dragged under.'

DCI Kenbury pointed out the advantage of having one of their young dealers in protective custody in a safe house. 'They're probably still looking for him. They don't know we've got a witness either.'

'Who is that exactly?' someone asked.

'A Miss Amy Lewis who became concerned about the boy after meeting him a few times on the riverbank,' I explained. 'She's been extremely useful. Without her, we would never have gone after Ben.'

If I'd walked past the charity shop just a few minutes later, this case would be nowhere. Maybe we'd still be bringing in Guy Swinford for questioning, hoping that he'd give us a name before letting him go again. My gut feeling told me that he was small fry, a loner hoping to make it big. What we needed to do was find the person capable of running a business that spread its tentacles along the Thames-side towns. We needed to trace Dillon, the bloke who had picked up Ben, and we needed to trace his boss.

'Will we need some protection for this Miss Lewis?' someone else asked. I recognised one of our newly qualified DCs, a young man fresh out of Hendon who was as keen as a greyhound in the traps for its first race.

'Not so far,' I told him. 'If they knew about her and where she lived then perhaps we'd keep an eye out. At the moment, they're blissfully ignorant of this investigation.'

'So what's the plan?' The DC's pen was poised over his brand-new notebook. He was raring to go but I could see the cynicism on the faces of the more experienced people around him. These investigations take huge amounts of time and money. Anyone hoping for instant results would be sorely disappointed.

DCI Kenbury, however, seemed just as determined as the rookie to steer the team towards action.

'We do need to act as quickly as possible. There are county lines spreading out all over this country and if this is another one, we must stamp it out.'

He punctuated the last two words by slamming his fist into the palm of his left-hand causing eyebrows to raise all around the rapidly warming room. The heating in the station was always set too high, in my opinion, and what with the steamed-up windows and the steam coming off the DCI, I was beginning to feel the need for some cool oxygen.

I nodded to DC Clinton who was sitting at the laptop on the desk, and a page from Google Maps appeared on the screen at the front of the room.

'The base of the operation seems to be somewhere in this area.' I drew an imaginary circle with my finger around the place on the map that Ben had indicated. Although he'd been locked in the cabin whenever the boss took the boat downriver, the view through the porthole had given him some idea of the direction and distance they'd travelled. We'd worked out that once the boat reached Teddington lock, an hour's travelling on a falling tide and at the regulation speed limit of eight knots would bring them to somewhere near Brentford. Ben had been adamant that they'd turned into some kind of inlet near some boat yards.

The DCI looked less than impressed. 'Vague won't do, Lynn. If we carry out a raid on the wrong people, it'll be a spectacular and costly embarrassment for the Met. Plus, it will alert the right people that we're on to them. It's the equivalent of taking a swing at the ball and finding the bloody thing is still on the tee.'

Rumour had it that Bob Kenbury was a keen golfer and occasionally played a round with Greg Gresham at one of those snobby golf clubs that demands a single-figure handicap and a five-figure annual subscription.

'Ok, at present we don't know exactly where these people are,' I said with a calmness I didn't feel. 'Meanwhile, I'm going to see Ben Webster this morning to see if there's anything more he can tell us. Ideally, we'd take him downriver by boat but that's out of the question, of course.'

Even with police protection and with the boy out of sight down below, it was against normal procedure. We'd be putting a juvenile in danger which would prejudice our case in court. We had to do this by the book if we wanted these people put away.

'As I said, from what the boy's told us about the journey downriver, we've worked out that the area he described is probably somewhere near Brentford,' I continued. 'If they left at high water and passed through two locks, that brings them to about here.' I pointed to a place on the map where an inlet of the river meandered inwards for a short distance. 'Somewhere here is the yard where the boys were kept for a while and where they witnessed the arrival of other lads in a van.'

Sam and Kai planned to explore the area that morning by car and on foot to see if they could locate the yard. I could tell they were anxious to get going. We all enjoyed getting out of the incident room for a bit of investigation, me included. For one thing, it was cooler out there.

As the team left the room, I knew exactly what they were all feeling. There's a buzz of excitement when you're getting close and a raid has to be planned, arrests made.

DCI Kenbury waited until the room had emptied before delivering a warning.

'We can't afford to mess this one up, Lynn. Don't act until you're one hundred per cent sure where and what this place is.'

I looked at the craggy, contour-lined face and into his eyes which were the colour of steel. 'I've got this, sir.'

But I was not at all sure that was true.

Half an hour later, I arrived at the safe house and was shown in by the plain clothes officer who'd just come on the day shift.

'The lad's a typical teenager, Ma'am. He's not been up long so he's just eating his breakfast,' he said, leading the way into a large kitchen at the back of the house where Ben was tucking into bacon sandwiches while his foster carer sat beside him with a mug of coffee. Over the years, Yvonne Kelly had taken in several fledglings that had fallen out of the nest, teenagers being her speciality.

Seeing me come into the room, the boy froze with the sandwich halfway to his open mouth. The smudge of tomato ketchup on his top lip was a clue that this was a second helping. Just like Jack, I thought; just an ordinary kid who wolfs his food. He looked clean and tidy and his pale, pinched face seemed to have more colour this morning but then I figured that being looked after and feeling safe for once was bound to do him some good.

'Don't mind me, just carry on with your breakfast,' I said, sitting opposite him. 'I just wanted to see how you are and to give you some news.'

He resumed eating enthusiastically as if someone had just invented food and he was trying it out for them.

'That's his second bacon sandwich,' Yvonne said. 'He's a bottomless pit, this lad.'

I accepted a mug of coffee and waited patiently while Ben finished his breakfast, using the time to study him closely. Anyone would find it hard to believe that this shiny-haired lad with the extraordinary pale eyes was the same bedraggled urchin we'd brought in for questioning two days ago. Mind you, they'd also find it hard to believe that he'd been out on the streets for several weeks dealing drugs and had inadvertently caused the death of a fifteen-year-old boy.

He looked up at me, unaware that the red smudge was still there in the corner of his mouth.

'I'm in trouble aren't I?'

Yvonne shot me an anxious glance.

'That depends,' I said, 'on whether you've told us the truth and it can be proved that you're a victim of this man you told us about. If so, the courts would probably hold the view that a child who'd been physically threatened and forced into selling drugs isn't a criminal.'

He stared at me, relief bringing tears to his eyes.

'I didn't want to do it, Miss. I knew it was wrong.'

'Did the boss pay you? The people running these drug lines usually pay pretty well.'

'At first, we did get paid, and sometimes he'd buy us clothes but after about a month he said we'd have to wait for our money but not to worry because he'd sort it. Chris and I got angry about that but then he said if we got difficult there were people who would sort us out, like really dangerous people with knives and that.'

'Did anyone ever get hurt?'

'Yeah. That guy I told you about, the one we saw when we were in the shed. He tried to climb up and over the gate and they grabbed hold of him and got him on the ground...' He faltered and swallowed.

'Take your time,' I said, wondering how a fourteen-year-old child processes such violence and comes out sane afterwards. 'If it's too much, we can leave it for another time.'

'No, I want to tell you, Miss. The guy was on the ground and they were all round him, kicking and punching and all the time he was screaming and begging them to stop but they didn't, they didn't.'

'You're doing very well, Ben. What happened to this man?'

'They dragged him away and we never saw him again after that.'

Yvonne Kelly drew in her breath sharply as if she'd been stung. 'God help the poor man,' she muttered, crossing herself.

'Believe me,' I said, firmly, 'we're going to track these thugs down and put them away, Ben.'

'But what about the others?'

'The others?'

'Chris and the other dealers.'

'So it wasn't just you and Chris?' I might have known there would be a whole string of kids involved.

'We didn't know all of them but there were a couple of girls who lived in a children's home. I heard the boss call them slags because he said they were running wild.'

I opened my notebook. 'Names?'

'Dunno. We didn't have anything to do with them. We just heard the boss saying they were out of control and needed slapping down.'

'What about the men you saw? You said one of them got beaten up. What was their job?'

'They were the ones who came in the Transit van one night. They were black guys. I don't know what they were there for.'

'And do you think they were locked up too?'

'Don't know where. None of us could leave. Me and Chris, we talked about how we could escape but we didn't dare until…' He faltered. 'Please, can you help Chris? He'll be on the boat by himself now and I don't know what the boss will do to him.'

'When we find *Sea Swift*, we'll get him out of there, don't worry.'

Easier said than done but I wasn't about to tell him that.

'Is there anything else you remember about the first place you were held, the one upriver?'

'What kind of thing?'

'Anything you saw or heard or even smelled, for instance?'

Any detail however small would help us identify the location. He stared at me for a moment and was about to shake his head when his eyes widened.

'The smell! There was a smell of chocolate in the air like someone was making it nearby. It used to drive us mad when we were hungry, Chris and me. We used to dream about Snickers bars and KitKats and stuff so when we went to live on the boat, we begged the boss to let us have some and then one day, he came in and threw all these chocolate bars on the table and it was like… Christmas.'

'That is so useful. Thank you, Ben,' I said, making a note.

'What will happen to me now?' he asked, glancing at Mrs Kelly. 'Please don't send me back.'

'Back where, love?' she asked.

'I can't go back to Karl. He blames me for my mum dying. He says I made her ill.'

To me, it sounded as if all his mother's troubles began and ended with this Karl.

'You must have other relatives, though,' I said. 'Grandparents, for instance?'

He was quiet. Whatever reason he had for not telling us about his family, he was keeping it to himself. This wouldn't be an easy one for social services to solve. Then I had an idea.

'This friend of your mum's you were trying to get to, the one who lives in Finsbury Park – you said you had her address.'

The key to this boy's full identity could lie with this friend. I made a mental note to contact her when I got back, taking the limp piece of paper he produced from his pocket and putting it in my own.

'By the way,' I continued, 'I have a message for you from Amy Lewis, the lady with the dog who you met on the riverbank.'

Ben looked anxious. 'Oh. What did she say?'

'She says she's glad you like the scarf she gave you. It was kind of her to give you such an expensive present.'

I can read people pretty well and I'm almost sure Miss Lewis was covering for the boy. She had her reasons, I suppose.

Ben suddenly seemed fascinated by the pattern on his plate. With his forefinger, he rubbed at the chain of white daisies running around the edge.

'He stole it, though.'

'Who did?'

'That boy who died. He beat me up one day in the park and took it off me.'

So that explained the presence of the red scarf in the shop doorway. I remembered the CCTV images of James on Halloween night with the scarf hanging round his neck.

'I found it again, though. It's mine, really.' Ben was looking defiant.

Now I carefully steered the conversation back to the information I needed.

'You said there was a gate that one of the men tried to climb over. What does this gate look like?'

'It's dark green and really tall, like twice as tall as DC Clinton.'

I thought of Sam at six-foot-six, towering over the rest of us like a basketball player on a field of midgets.

'He says he grew that tall because his mother forced him to eat. Any more bacon sandwiches and you could end up just as tall, young man.'

A twitch of a smile then the boy's face grew serious. 'Miss, I'm really worried about Chris. What will happen to him?'

'I don't know, Ben, but tell me what Chris looks like, what clothes he might be wearing and anything you can think of that might be useful. To be frank, from what you've said about this boss of yours, he could be in danger.'

'Because of me, you mean?'

I paused before replying. Maybe this kid was carrying enough guilt.

'Because your boss doesn't exactly sound like childminder of the year.'

'Oh.' He seemed satisfied with that reason. 'Ok, Chris is Asian and really skinny with floppy black hair and he has a scar over his left eyebrow from when he was about nine and fell off his bike. He's shorter than me, like up to my shoulder cos he's only twelve.'

'What was he wearing when you saw him last?'

'A blue and white Chelsea sweatshirt, black jeans and black and white trainers. The shirt was a bit manky because he wore it all the time, even when Chelsea lost. They're crap sometimes, not like United.'

I looked up from my notes. 'Did he ever talk about his family?'

'Yeah, all the time, especially at night when we were left alone in our cabin. He told me he'd got into trouble with some local bad boys and his mum and dad were threatening to send him to some aunt in India to sort him out. They were strict, his mum and dad, but Chris was a bit crazy, Miss. Like, sometimes he'd kick off and I'd have to calm him down.'

'That must have been worrying for you when the boss was around.'

He nodded. 'Yeah, that's why I'm thinking something bad will happen to Chris without me there. I shouldn't have left him. If anything happens it'll be my fault.'

He was getting upset so I tried to reassure him. 'Look, if you'd stayed, you'd be dead by now. You had to get away, Ben, so don't go blaming yourself.'

I left him to finish his breakfast while Yvonne walked me to the front door.

With luck, someday soon I'd find myself on the other side of the interview desk facing the man responsible for the evil business that killed James Gresham and virtually enslaved these vulnerable kids. But we had so little to go on even with the photo of the boat that Amy Lewis had sent to Sam. *Sea Swift* was like a ghost that had vanished from sight since the day she spotted it in Kingston.

Yvonne gestured over her shoulder towards the kitchen and lowered her voice. 'He's not a bad boy, Inspector Morris. When you get to know him, he's a sweetheart really. If he had somebody who cared about him, it would be a very different story.'

'Well, he got lucky, Yvonne,' I said. 'He's here because someone *did* care about him.'

*

Back in the incident room, I opened up the crumpled piece of paper Ben had given me. In an untidy, obviously hastily written script, he'd written a name, Cheryl, an address in Finsbury Park and a long number which was obviously Cheryl's mobile.

The phone was answered by a woman with a strong Mancunian accent. When I explained why I was calling, she sounded sceptical.

'I don't know a boy of that name.'

She was obviously thinking this was a scam call so I quickly expanded before she had a chance to hang up.

Her tone of voice changed instantly. 'Oh of course, Julie's boy, I thought he was living with his stepdad in Fallowfield?'

'And the stepdad's name?' I asked.

'Karl Grant. He must be going out of his mind if the lad's run away. I'm surprised he hasn't rung me, knowing what good friends me and Julie were.'

'Can you tell me anything about this Karl Grant?'

'Not much apart from the fact I didn't like the way he spoke to Julie sometimes. I don't know how he was with Ben but at least the lad had a roof over his head and another adult in the house when his mam died. I'd moved down here shortly before it happened so I haven't seen him for ages. He must be about fourteen now I suppose. Yes, because he was nearly thirteen when Julie died.'

'What can you tell me about Ben? Anything would be useful.'

There was a pause on the other end of the line then the unmistakeable sound of smoke being exhaled.

'Sorry, I needed a ciggie,' she said. 'Ben? He's an average kid, likes football, lively, bit of a cheeky little git sometimes, pushes boundaries but nothing really bad. I lost touch with him and Karl after the funeral but he must have found me in his mum's address book. I don't know why he was coming down my way because I've got enough on my plate with three kids of my own so I couldn't cope with another.'

When I questioned her further about Karl Grant, she admitted that she'd had concerns about him being what she called 'a bit of rough'.

'I told Julie to watch him because he was a bit handy with his fists on a Saturday night after the pub.'

Now we're getting to it, I thought.

'I'd seen him take on men bigger than him for no reason other than they looked at him the wrong way.'

'But what about Julie?' I asked. 'Do you think he ever hit her?'

There was a pause while she took another draw on the cigarette. I could imagine her weighing up the wisdom of revealing too much to a police officer who might judge her for not acting to help her friend. Too right. But I put on my calm, neutral voice and told her that social services would need to know before they sent Ben back home.

'Well, I will tell you this,' she conceded. 'Julie sometimes had bruises on her arms and once she had quite a nasty one under her eye but she always had an excuse. "I'm so clumsy," she'd say. "I knocked into the door" or fell on the stairs or bumped into something. You name it, she'd done it.'

'And you believed her?'

'I didn't not believe her. Put it that way.'

I swallowed my incredulity. How many sodding bruises would it have taken for her to become suspicious? At least now it was becoming obvious why Ben had run away. Pity he'd just exchanged one violent experience for another.

'One more thing: does Ben have any relatives in Manchester?' I got ready to jot down names and addresses – well, we live in hope.

'There's an aunt, his mum's sister, but she and her husband went to New Zealand. She may be back by now because I think it was a work contract for a year. She was on a teacher exchange programme. Give me a second and her name will come to me.'

I wrote it down; no phone number but it was something to pass on to social services.

In the end, I thanked Cheryl and asked her to get in touch if there was anything else she thought of. I wouldn't be holding my breath, though.

When I got back to the incident room, there was no sign of Kai or Sam. They'd headed out after the morning briefing in an unmarked car to do some reconnaissance around the area the boy had indicated but should have been back by now. Both officers were in plain clothes, jeans and leather jackets, but had taken their warrant cards and radios with them. From what Ben had told us, the people involved with the yard were pretty ruthless so Sam and Kai were under strict instructions not to take any risks.

By five o'clock, still with no word from either of the DCs, I was becoming seriously worried.

23. LYNN

Sam was sounding breathless and uncharacteristically shaky. He was in the casualty department of the West Middlesex hospital.

'What the hell are you doing there?' I asked. 'And who was driving?'

Sam was a steady, careful driver. Some of his colleagues teased him about driving like an elderly man doped with Horlicks. Kai, on the other hand, was nicknamed Lewis Hamilton because of a tendency to regard every outing in a police car as a blue light run even if he was only off to interview a witness.

'I was driving,' Sam said, 'but this happened when we were on foot. Kai's broken his leg. I'm just waiting for him to be discharged then we'll come straight back. I can't talk now but I think we've found the yard.'

An hour later, they arrived back at the station. Kai hobbled into the office on crutches with his leg in plaster up to the thigh. DCI Kenbury and I took them both into a quiet room where they could have coffees and a bite to eat. Half the trauma for these two bottomless pits was that they'd both missed lunch. Since Kai was looking exhausted, we arranged a lift home for him while Sam stayed to give us brief feedback on what had happened.

The DCI closed the door to give us privacy. The damn heating and the lingering smell of canteen shepherd's pie made the room stuffy. 'I hope that your actions haven't jeopardised our plans for a raid, Sam,' he said, taking his seat.

My worry exactly. I had a sinking feeling that things might have gone badly wrong with the surveillance, and the decision to let the two DCs go had been mine.

I could tell that Sam was thinking through what he was going to say, trying to sequence the afternoon's events logically for us when his mind was probably begging for rest. My instinct as a human being was to send him home but we needed to know what had happened.

'So you followed the route we identified on Google Maps?' I asked.

He nodded, wearily. 'And our guess was right. We ended up in Brentford and discovered a side road leading into an industrial park near the river. You know the kind of place: mainly small factories, workshops, building trade outlets, that sort of thing. I drove slowly round but it was like a maze and no sign of any gates like the boy described.'

'So, a dead end in more ways than one,' DCI Kenbury observed.

Sam looked across at me. 'Yes, we thought so until DC Chauhan reminded me of something the boy told you, Ma'am. He said, "We can't see it, Sam, but can we smell it?" and that's when I remembered that in the place where he and Chris were initially held, there was a smell of chocolate in the air.'

'That's right. Well done, Kai. He's on the ball, that lad.'

Sam grinned. 'A regular Einstein. So we decided to switch to exploring the area separately on foot. If anyone asked, we were builders looking for a company I completely made up: Vertical Solutions.'

'A daft name but go on.'

He went on to say that after parking up, they went off in different directions to see if they could locate a possible match for the scrapyard from Ben's description. There were a couple of places like that on the site but both had barred metal security gates, the type with vicious points at the top to deter climbing. Nowhere could they see a tall green wooden gate.

They were both on the alert for the smell of chocolate in the air but it was Kai who first noticed it. He stopped on a corner to phone

Sam who made his way over to join him. They were on a road that was lined with bland, square, brick buildings with entry phones by each door but nothing resembling a food factory.

'So, no joy with that?' I asked.

'We wandered round for a bit then ended up in a road called Commerce Way,' Sam said. 'The smell was much stronger there and that was when we spotted the chocolate factory.'

'Not Mr Wonka's was it?' Bob Kenbury asked with an unusual attempt at humour.

Sam totally ignored it, probably out of sheer exhaustion. 'No, Sir. Commerce Way finished in a dead end but straddled across the bottom of the road, behind fancy black iron gates, was Cavendish Confectioners, a long grey stone building with several rows of windows.'

The name sounded familiar but I couldn't work out why until I remembered that DC Chauhan was fond of tucking into a packet of their chocolate-covered peanuts that he kept in his desk drawer. They were a well-known local confectionary company.

'And?' I sensed that his answer would be interesting and wasn't disappointed.

'Between the last building in Commerce Way and the chain fence that bordered the Cavendish factory was a rough path about four metres wide, bordered by a tatty wooden fence on either side,' he said. 'The path was wide enough for a Transit van to pass along. When we went over to get a closer look, we could see the path stretching some way down until it came to an abrupt end by a wall covered in ivy. Kai volunteered to go down and take a look and a few minutes later he rang me to say that the path didn't end at the wall but turned a corner and ran on for almost the same length again alongside what looked like a metal recycling yard on one side and a chain fence and allotments on the other. I was worried about him going so far down on his own and was just thinking about joining him when he told me he could see some large wooden gates – gates that meant business, as he put it.'

'What colour were these gates?' I asked.

'The colour of your Toyota, Lynn,' Sam said. 'Dark green.'

I felt a jolt of excitement. 'Did Kai take any photos?'

'Yes, some of the path and the gates before he got interrupted.'

Bob Kenbury leaned forward. 'Interrupted?'

'I was just telling him to come back when a tall, well-built guy in a baseball cap, grey painting overalls and steel-capped boots approached me from the road. He was a bit shorter than my height but built like a tank, and was carrying a serious bit of kit: a large metal box, the kind that holds heavy duty tools that most of us couldn't even lift. I didn't like the look of him so I avoided eye contact and turned away, lowering my voice to warn Kai to get out of there. Next thing I knew, the guy was standing right in front of me, looking like he owned the street.'

I heard Bob Kenbury draw in his breath and hoped that Sam had left his ID in the car as I'd told him. 'So what did you do?'

'Ok, so I trotted out my story about being a builder on the hunt for a place called Vertical Solutions when all of a sudden it occurs to me that I'm wearing an expensive leather jacket, newly pressed jeans and brand-new Timberland boots so I don't exactly look like your average builder.'

'Apart from the fact that Vertical Solutions is a ludicrous name for a building company, Sam,' I said. Mind you, I doubt I could have come up with anything better.

'So then this guy bombarded me with loads of questions about where I was working and so on and in the end, I'd had enough. I just wanted Kai to appear so we could get out of there and back to the BMW and the warmth of the station, job done. That's when I heard Kai asking me who I was talking to so I just said, "Don't get me wrong, mate, it's not that I don't like talking to strangers but I really am in a hurry. I need to find this Vertical Solutions before closing time today and I've got my mate on the other end of this phone coming to pick me up in a mo."'

'Impressive,' I said. 'You may not have looked the part but you sound quite authentic. You should have been an actor, Sam.'

He gave me a weary grin. 'Thanks. So then I said to Kai, "Where the hell are you, Des? I've been waiting here like a prat for twenty minutes now. Have you found it?" Kai said he understood and was on his way back up the path. I put my mobile in my pocket and told the big guy that my mate was in the wrong place and I had to go and find him. Then he lit a cigarette and walked away and I walked back along the road, trying to look casual. I'd expected him to walk through the gates of the Cavendish factory but he didn't. When I looked back, he was turning onto the path leading to the green gates.'

'Oh shit!' I breathed.

Sam reached for the rapidly cooling coffee on the table beside him. 'Too right, Ma'am. That's what Kai said when I warned him the guy was coming, only there was an extra expletive I don't want to repeat.'

'You're not going to tell me the two of them met each other on that sodding path, are you?'

Apparently, Kai had attempted to climb the wire fence bordering the allotments, tripped over the top of it and fallen about seven feet, landing awkwardly on a heap of concrete paving stones which was when he fractured his fibula.

Bob Kenbury and I exchanged glances, our imaginations working overtime until Sam assured us that Kai had managed to crawl behind someone's hut just in time before he was spotted. Peering out, he saw a man pause by the gates then enter a code on a keypad attached to the wall beside them. When the gates swung open, he could clearly see a large yard full of scrap metal, two concrete sheds with corrugated roofs and what looked like a couple of rusty shipping containers against the back wall. Parked up beside one of the sheds was a dark blue Transit van.

Ben had told me that a dark blue van had brought workers into the yard one night. 'Did Kai get the registration number by any chance?' I asked.

'He managed to get a photo just before the gates swung back which they did almost immediately. Whoever is in there is keen to guard their privacy, that's for sure. Kai just managed to tell me where he was before he passed out with the pain. There was an exit to a road on the other side of the allotments so I ran and got the car and was able to drag him out of there.'

'So you weren't seen?' Bob Kenbury asked.

'No, Sir.'

Sam leaned back in his chair. He looked all in. He was still fairly young and fit but I reckoned the tension of worrying about his younger colleague must have frayed his nerves.

'Good. Well done, DC Clinton. Briefing at 0700 hours tomorrow morning.'

When the DCI had left the room, a broad grin slowly spread over Sam's face. 'I didn't think we had a hope of finding that place.'

The smile faded rapidly with my reply to that.

'You two are wasted in the police force. Did you think you were in an episode of sodding *Line of Duty* or something?'

'No, Ma'am,' he said, quietly. 'We were just doing our job.'

I admired that about DC Clinton, always ready to stand up for himself and his colleagues and quite right too. I was actually proud of them both and told him so.

'Go home and get some rest,' I said. 'But before you do, will you ring Kai and get him to send the photos. We'll need them tomorrow morning for the briefing and I'd like to show them to Ben to see if he recognises the place. If he does, we're home and dry.'

We were so close now but experience had taught me not to bank on this case being wrapped up too soon. This stage of an investigation always made me apprehensive as if we were all walking a very narrow tightrope and one slip would mean failure.

When I got home that evening, a heavy smell of cooked cheese and pepperoni hung in the air, leading me to an empty pizza box on the kitchen table. Jack was up in his room doing his homework so I popped my head round his door to apologise for being so late.

He gave me the briefest of glances. 'S'ok. I'm used to it, aren't I?'

Thanks, I thought. *Just call me mother of the year.*

The photos came through from Kai a few minutes later so I rang Yvonne Kelly, told Jack I'd only be an hour, didn't wait for his reaction and, in spite of being exhausted, drove straight round to show them to Ben. Whether it was Yvonne's cooking or just the relief at being safe, the lad was beginning to fill out like a faint picture that gradually comes into sharper focus and takes on its natural colours.

He studied the photos for a few minutes then asked, 'How did you get these?' He seemed genuinely shocked.

'Foot-slogging detective work,' I said. 'Do you recognise anything?'

'Yeah,' he said, 'that's the yard. See that shed there?' He pointed to one of the grey buildings visible through the open gates. 'That's the one where they put Chris and me. And that...' He pointed to the blue Transit. 'That's the van that brought the men one night.'

'And those rusty boxes are actually shipping containers, Ben.'

'Yeah, that's them.'

'So you're one hundred per cent sure that this is the right place?' We couldn't afford to make any mistakes.

He looked up at me, surprise lighting up his pale blue eyes. 'Definitely. Does this mean you can find Chris?'

'We'll certainly try,' I said, trying to sound reassuring even though I had a nagging feeling that if these people were as ruthless as we suspected, anything could have happened to the younger boy.

On the way home, I rang Kai's mobile.

'DC Chauhan, don't ever take risks like that again,' I said, sternly.

He sounded deflated. 'I've got six weeks in plaster to think about it, Ma'am.'

'Good. Apart from that, well done, Kai. Because of you, we've positively identified the yard.' I told him the news.

'Shit! Really?'

'But no more action hero stuff or you won't have a leg to stand on.'

He laughed. 'Yeah, I'll be out on a limb.'

My elation shrivelled as soon as I set foot through the front door. Jack was in the hallway zipping up his jacket. At his feet was the large rucksack he usually took on school trips.

'What's happening? Where are you off to?' I asked.

He scowled. 'I'm going to my dad's.'

'What?'

'And you can't stop me.'

'But why, love?'

'Because you're never here and I want to live with someone who knows I exist.'

I felt the sting of his words penetrate deep into my skin. 'That's unfair, Jack.'

'It's true, Mum, and you know it,' he said, picking up the bulky rucksack and hefting it over his shoulder. I could imagine the look on Graham's face as he opened the door to find his teenage son about to invade his little love nest with Monique.

'Your dad is too busy to look after you, Jack,' I pleaded. 'He won't be pleased if you just turn up. And there's Monique to consider. It's her house after all.'

'I've already called him. He said to come on over.'

When I'd got over the surprise of that statement, panic began to rise.

'Don't go, love. After tomorrow, things will be better, I promise. We're so close to finishing this investigation and I'm owed some leave in the New Year. We could go on holiday somewhere, anywhere you like, abroad maybe.'

'I'll call you,' Jack grunted, pushing past me. The front door slammed, leaving a heavy silence.

24 AMY

Someone had made an offer on the shop. It was a positively insulting amount but as the agent enthusiastically informed me, retail businesses were incredibly hard to sell coming up to Christmas so it was nothing short of a miracle. Funny, it didn't seem like a miracle, especially when I discovered that the potential buyer intended to remodel Earth Song as yet another coffee shop.

Roz, meanwhile, had been scouting for jobs without much luck but had finally been invited to an interview for the post of manager in a small gift shop in Richmond, the kind that is so posh there are no prices in the window. She had no enthusiasm for the place. I could sense that she still harboured a faint hope that Earth Song and the job she loved could be saved so telling her about the offer was the worst thing I'd ever had to do.

'Oh,' was all she said. Then, grudgingly: 'Congratulations, Amy.'

'I haven't accepted it yet. It isn't nearly enough, Roz.' Enough to keep those criminals off Marcus's back, though.

The rest of the day was spent in an uncomfortable silence that was only broken by the arrival of Tom Brennan with the last of the bowls we'd ordered. When I told him the news, he looked surprisingly shocked.

'Your brother will be pleased if you accept it, I suppose.' His tone of voice barely disguised his disgust.

I didn't tell him that the previous evening, I'd spoken to Marcus to update him so that at least he could let the relevant people know he was about to pay his debts.

'How long before you get the money?' he'd demanded. Not a

word about how sorry he was that my business would be lost, that I'd have to look for another job, maybe go back to teaching which wasn't a disaster but not what I wanted for my life anymore.

'I haven't actually accepted the offer yet.'

'Well, get on with it!'

Something inside me snapped. 'What would you do without your big sister to bail you out? Yet again?'

He laughed, he actually laughed, then looked serious as if remembering his life was on the line.

'Let me know as soon as the money's on its way. They won't wait much longer; they're getting nasty.'

He'd clicked 'leave' before I could respond. Nice one.

Tom had brought a selection of bowls glazed in swirls of red, gold, purple and vibrant greens. I'd cleared some space in the window and watched as he carefully arranged them, draping a bunch of purple ceramic grapes inside a sunset-orange bowl in the centre of the display. The result was so stunning that, for a moment, I forgot that this might be the last of the orders we would receive from him.

Since he refused my offer of coffee, I threw my coat over my shoulders and followed him out to the back yard where he'd parked his car. The day was so cold that a thin layer of ice had covered the windscreen, and as I thanked him for trusting us with his work, the words puffed out of me in breathy clouds.

He started to scrape the ice but glanced across at me. 'I should be thanking you. It's been a great way to get my work out there.'

'I'm just so sorry that we can't continue with our arrangement.'

I sounded like some buttoned-up businesswoman trying to be formal. It wasn't what I really wanted to say at all. I wanted to say that I'd miss him popping into the shop, miss his enthusiasm for what we were trying to do, miss... him.

'It's been great working with you, Tom.'

'And you. It was a lucky day for me when you fell into that chalet. Mind you, when I saw you lying on the floor there was a moment when I thought you might have escaped from a secure unit somewhere.'

'Oh, charming. You weren't far wrong as it turned out.'

'Sure, it was a lucky day for that young lad as well,' Tom said, resuming his scraping.

For days now I'd been so preoccupied with my problems that Ben had slipped my mind. I had no idea how he was getting on, only that he was safe. Hopefully, he still had the red cashmere scarf. Knowing what he'd been through, I wanted him to have a bit of warmth.

When the screen was clear, Tom came over and held out his hand.

'Well, nice doing business with you, Amy Lewis.'

'You too, Tom.'

We shook hands like two business partners closing a deal. He walked round to the other side of the car, stopped, then came back as if he'd forgotten something.

'Excuse me for saying this but I hope you're not making a big mistake here. Not many sisters would sacrifice the business they love for a brother like yours.' The unspoken word 'feckless' hung in the air.

He obviously meant well but things were stressful enough without having my nose rubbed in the dirt like a puppy that's made a mess on the carpet so I briskly told him we'd be in touch when the bowls had been sold and wished him luck. There was an angry expression on his face when I'd finished.

'You deserve better, Amy. You deserve to make a success of this place and nobody should stop you.'

'Yes, well I don't have a choice,' I snapped. 'And I wish people would let me get on with it.'

He stared at me for a moment then turned on his heel, got into the car and drove off without another word.

I stood there in the cold feeling ashamed for being so abrupt with such a kind man, and wondering how I was going to cope with all the changes to come. It was bad enough that my landlord was expecting my flat to be magnolia by December 31st. When the sale of Earth Song went through, my whole life would turn magnolia.

Tom was right. Earth Song was my creation. I'd invested so much to make it work and letting it go was tearing me apart. By the time I got home that evening I'd made up my mind that it would only be sold to someone who gave me its correct value even if that meant waiting for the right buyer. I texted Marcus, unable to face him, and got a curt reply: 'Time is running out.'

From then on, there was no time to think as Roz and I wholeheartedly embraced our last Christmas in the shop, greeting every customer as if they were a long-lost friend. At last we'd been able to take on a temporary assistant, Clare Morris, a student home from university for the holidays. We knew from Clare's wide-eyed reaction as she walked into the shop that she would love it as much as we did and, sure enough, she proved a great asset with her bubbling, youthful enthusiasm. Best of all, she recommended us to all her friends.

In only a few months, Earth Song's past as a dreary drapery store seemed to have faded from the town's collective memory. The exception was an elderly lady who walked in one day and announced, 'Goodness! This is where I used to buy my brassieres!'

Soon, the worry that haunted me was almost forgotten.

On my next day off, I wandered into town to do some Christmas shopping in an effort to escape the tins of paint in the hallway nagging me to open them and get on with it. Time was running out but my tendency to procrastinate certainly wasn't.

Along the pedestrian precinct, crowds of shoppers drifted beneath the town's Christmas lights – rows of dangling silver stars receding into the distance. A small Salvation Army band had gathered by the entrance of the parish church and were playing carols on shiny brass instruments that reflected the glossy blue, red and green baubles hanging on the illuminated Christmas tree beside them. My heart lifted and I thought of Ben and how much I'd like to see him to wish him well for his future. Perhaps a call to DC Clinton might fix it. As the trumpets played their slow version of 'Silent Night', a feeling of sadness for this lad pushed aside the exhilaration of the last few days. What kind of Christmas was he going to have?

That thought was growing and swelling with the music when suddenly, I became aware that a small child was frozen to the spot a few yards away, dwarfed by the constantly moving stream of people around her. Shock and fear were written on her face as she frantically turned her head this way and that, obviously searching for someone. It was Orla Brennan.

Quickly, I weaved my way over, took her hand, gently drew her over to the safety of the church wall then knelt down to look into the wide, frightened eyes.

'Orla, do you remember me? I came to your stall up in London. My name's Amy.'

She nodded before saying in a small, shuddering voice, 'You're that funny lady with the dog and a boy.'

That made me smile. 'That's me. Who are you with, Orla?'

She made a face that threatened a bout of crying. 'I've lost Daddy.'

They'd been in the Bentalls Centre but had got separated on the way out by a rush of people coming in from the street. It wasn't hard to imagine the poor child's terror on looking around for Tom and finding herself alone.

'You're safe now,' I told her. 'We'll find him together.'

The band had paused between carols and their conductor was at the microphone thanking everyone who'd donated to their homeless appeal by dropping money into a basket held by the beaming, bonneted lady beside him. Before they could carry on playing, I asked him to put out an appeal for Tom Brennan to come and collect his daughter.

Minutes later, we heard a cry of 'Orla! Oh my God, Orla!' as Tom came rushing through the crowd and fell on his knees, flinging his arms around her. Orla burst into frantic sobs as he held her close. I wanted to put my arms around them both because they looked so vulnerable all of a sudden, like an island of sadness among the indifferent crowd.

He looked up at me. 'I thought...'

He was unable to finish but it was easy to imagine the awful thoughts that must go through a parent's head when their child disappears in a crowded place. I guessed that his heart would be pounding. Since Orla was still clinging on to him, her face hidden in his neck, he stood up with great difficulty.

'Thank you, Amy, thank you so much.' His voice had steadied as if he had found himself again as well as his child.

Setting Orla down on the ground, he took her hand firmly in his before looking back at me. 'Amy, are you... I mean, have you time for a coffee somewhere, in one of those places by the river maybe, out of the cold, just for a few minutes?'

We made our way to the riverside, dodging the odd cyclist and a couple of serious joggers who seemed to be in a world of their own as they pounded along leaving little puffs of breath in the still, cold air. Across the river, beneath the bare trees, one solitary narrowboat remained at its berth, smoke curling up from its black chimney. Where *Serenity* had once moored and welcomed me into its comforting warmth, there was a space to remind me that not a single word had come from Kyle and Jan since they left.

'Orla wanted to buy a present for her teacher,' Tom explained, as we headed towards a small café tucked away in a corner near the arch of the bridge. 'They break up next week. But she wanted something special, didn't you, sweetheart? Hence the trip to Bentalls.'

Orla nodded solemnly, memories of her terror just beginning to fade from her dark eyes.

'Not the usual bath oil and soap then?' I said. 'When I gave up teaching, I was so excited at the thought of having to buy my own soap. Mad, isn't it?'

'What was your favourite present?' Orla asked.

I told her about the handmade card that my most difficult pupil had proudly given me, a boy euphemistically labelled 'behaviourally challenged'. He'd smothered it in so much glitter that half of it fell out, sprinkling the carpet with clinging, metallic fragments that threatened to be a permanent fixture until my class discovered the thrill of catching the bits on pieces of sticky tape. That card meant more to me than all the other presents I got that year except for the bottles of wine from parents who recognised the slightly fraught look that teachers get at Christmas. My kitchen cupboard had about three 'World's Best Teacher' mugs in it but the wine never made it beyond the first week of the holiday.

'So, did you find anything?' I asked.

Orla shook her head.

'Dad took you to the wrong shop then. I know a place where you'll find a great present.'

A look of realisation crossed Tom's face. 'Oh, of course.' But still he didn't smile.

Orla moved closer and slipped her small hand in mine with that easy familiarity that some children have. 'I wish you were my teacher. I'd paint you a picture.'

I was expecting the usual girly obsession with rainbows, unicorns or fairies when I asked her what she'd paint.

'Van Gogh with his ear cut off,' she said, with a glance up at her father.

As we strolled along, it occurred to me that Tom hadn't heard my news about the shop so I told him about refusing the offer and waiting until a more appropriate one came along even if it meant putting Marcus on hold.

'You're right to do that,' he said. 'Don't sell that place too cheaply.'

There was genuine warmth in his voice but still that serious look on his face.

'Do you mind me asking – is something wrong? Are you ok?' I ventured.

He looked off into the distance. 'It's just Christmas. I'll be fine when it's over.'

As we went into the cafe, Orla let go of my hand and made a beeline for the only free table, plonking herself down on a chair with a look of triumph. We decided on coffees, mince pies and a strawberry milkshake.

'My treat,' Tom insisted, 'as a thanks for rescuing my daughter.'

'I'm nearly seven,' Orla said, scornfully. 'I can rescue myself.'

Tom and I exchanged glances. 'Someone's obviously recovered,' he muttered, getting up to order at the counter while Orla and I sat there in the cheerful warmth listening to the hum of chatter from other tables and the mushy Christmas music playing on repeat in the background. One of those sickly-sweet Disney choirs was schmoozing through 'Santa Claus is coming to town'.

'Amy, will you help me find a present for Miss Thomas?' asked Orla, suddenly.

'Of course,' I said. 'I'm an experienced gift shopper. Have you got presents for Mummy and Daddy yet?'

She began to sing along with the tape in her pure, childish treble. 'You better watch out, you better not cry, you better not pout I'm telling you why...'

'Beautiful singing,' I smiled.

'Mummy died.' That matter-of-fact tone again.

'Pardon?' Perhaps I hadn't heard her properly.

'She died. She lives in Heaven now.' She carried on singing. 'Santa Claus is coming to town.'

I looked from the child to her father who was now coming over with a tray. The background sounds seemed to fade as Tom put the tray down and set out the drinks and a plate of warm mince pies, each one dusted with icing sugar and trimmed with a small piece of green marzipan holly. Their spicy smell would normally have made me hungry but I'd lost my appetite. Orla immediately grasped her milkshake and bent over the straw, fiercely sucking up the lurid pink liquid in the tall glass as though nothing had happened and nothing dreadful had been said.

My face must have registered my shock. 'Are you ok?' Tom asked, passing me my coffee. 'Would you prefer something else instead of the mince pies?'

Before answering, I glanced at Orla who was still sucking away at the milkshake with intense concentration and ignoring both of us.

'No, they're fine. It's just that…'

All of a sudden, I'd become tongue-tied. In the background, the music jangled on relentlessly but now it seemed to belong to another planet, a place where everyone was in a happy holiday mood and nobody was bereaved.

Tom swallowed some coffee, looked back at the counter then at me, raising his eyes. 'Don't you hate this rubbish they're playing? Although, *you* like it, don't you, Miss Brennan?' He brushed the hair back out of Orla's eyes. 'Your fringe needs a trim before himself comes down our chimney, that's for sure. You'll frighten the life out of the poor old fella.'

She stopped drinking and stared up at him. A ring of pink froth framed her mouth. 'Mummy died, didn't she, Dad?'

Tom and I both froze, then he simply said, 'Yes, she did, sweetheart.'

I found my voice. 'I'm so sorry.' That old cliché. But it was all I could think of to say at that moment.

He thanked me with the Pavlovian response we all have to expressions of sympathy, leaving an awkward silence that I filled with my curiosity.

'What happened? Do you want to talk about it? I mean, don't if it's too painful because it's none of my business.' Oh heck, this was difficult.

But when he spoke, it was as if he'd been looking for a gate to open or for someone to give him permission to talk about a taboo subject.

'It was just before Christmas two years ago. Anna was cycling to work in Richmond. She was a designer in a highly creative company that specialises in unusual gifts. She was only five minutes away from there when she was killed by a hit and run driver.'

'A hit and run?' I repeated, numbly.

He gave me a warning look before turning to Orla. 'Would you ever go over to the counter and get us some more napkins?'

When she'd gone, he lowered his voice. 'Anna didn't stand a chance. The bastard was speeding on the main road into the town and swerved to undertake a lorry. As he did that, he veered into the inside lane, knocking her off the bike and straight under the wheels of the lorry. She died in hospital hours later. Friends wanted to place a white bicycle by the railings where it happened but I said no.'

Not far from where I lived, someone had chained a white bike with a buckled back wheel to a lamp post. It was easy to see why Tom had refused to do the same.

'Do you mind me asking how old Anna was when this happened?' I asked.

'Twenty-nine. She'd have been thirty at the end of that month and…' He faltered and I reached for his hand, swallowing back my own tears.

'Don't, Tom, if it's too hard for you to talk about.'

'She was three months pregnant. She'd told me the night before.'

Unable to speak, I gripped his hand a little tighter. I knew then that I'd always be there for him in whatever way I could.

Orla was back with the napkins and resumed sucking up what was left of the milkshake, obviously enjoying the rattling noise it was making now she'd reached the bottom.

'That's enough, now,' Tom said, letting go of my hand and pulling her glass away. 'You've had your money's worth, sweetheart.'

We finished our coffees in silence while the mince pies sulked on their plate. I volunteered to take them to Roz and Clare in the shop to have during their break and the ever-resourceful Orla solemnly wrapped them up in the surplus napkins, deftly slipping the decorative pieces of marzipan holly into her mouth with a sly glance to see if I'd noticed.

'Here,' her father said, passing her a tissue. 'You've got pink all around your mouth, you mucky little devil. Don't you know that astronauts have to eat and drink tidily?'

'Why?'

'Because it all floats away, of course, when there's no gravity. Really, Orla, you'll have to get it right before they let you go on a mission.' He winked at me.

'Doesn't matter, Dad, cos I'm going to be an artist like Jack,' Orla said, firmly.

'Oh yes, I forgot the fifteen-year-old genius of St Saviour's High.' Tom looked at me, raising his eyes. 'I have a student called Jack Morris who's become Orla's influencer, as they say. His mother is a detective in the local police force so we'll have to watch ourselves, won't we, Orla?'

That name certainly rang bells with me. 'Not DI Lynn Morris?'

He looked surprised so I briefly explained how I knew the detective. 'Small world,' he said.

Once outside, he patted my arm. 'I mustn't put a damper on *your* Christmas,' he said. 'You've had an offer on the shop at least, and I'll be fine once January comes when we can just get on and look to the future.'

My voice sounded strange as if it didn't belong to me. 'You're a lovely, talented man who's obviously been through hell and you deserve better.'

Where did that come from? As Marcus was always saying, 'You're an expert at embarrassing yourself, sis.'

'Thank you,' he said, with a sad smile. 'And you're a life saver, Amy Lewis.'

His words took me by surprise. What did he mean exactly? How had I saved his life?

'Just wait there a minute.' He darted back inside, leaving me trapped in the steady, unflinching gaze of his little girl.

'Daddy likes you,' she said, as if she was interviewing me for a job and was still assessing my suitability.

'Oh. Well, I like him too. And I like you very much, Orla,' I added, not just to placate her but because it was true. Beneath that bold, outward display of confidence there lurked a vulnerability that was all too visible when she and her father had been separated. The armour she'd built around herself crumbled.

'Good,' she said, granting me a smile. 'Are we friends, Amy?'

'Yes, of course, Orla.'

Formalities over, she held out her hand and gave mine an exaggerated shake – which was when I noticed the ragged holes in the fingers of her gloves, revealing glimpses of skin.

Tom reappeared, tucking a wallet into the inside pocket of his coat. 'Thanks for that,' he said. 'I left this on the table. So what are your plans for the holiday? Are you here or going away somewhere?'

Since I was persona non grata with my parents, a weekend in Devon was out that year so it was shaping up to be me and Max sharing a turkey crown in my newly magnolia'd kitchen. I gave a non-committal answer about probably spending the day with my closest friends, Beth and Paulo. They hadn't actually invited me yet but the part about them being my closest friends was at least true, even if I'd become a minor bit player in their busy lives.

'What about you and Orla?' I asked.

'Oh, you know, we might just pop over to Ireland to visit my parents for a few days. They'd love to see us, or there's a friend here who's asked us for Christmas dinner but I haven't decided yet.'

You too, I thought. What was it about Christmas that forced this awful pressure on single people to find someone to share it with and made you feel such a failure if you couldn't? In Tom's case, Anna's absence probably made it a time to survive rather than enjoy. My heart ached for him and for that child of his, that obviously anxious little girl who seemed so sure of herself on the outside. We're all actors in a way, hiding our innermost thoughts and worries under a coat of confidence but a six-year-old should never have to learn that skill.

We went our separate ways after that. I walked towards the steps leading to the marketplace while Tom and Orla headed for the craziness of the precinct. At the top of the steps, I turned to see that they'd stopped and were watching me. I waved and they waved back before continuing on their way, Orla's hand firmly grasped in Tom's. Already I missed them.

25. LYNN

Why on earth had this happened? More to the point, what had I done to make Jack so angry that he felt compelled to walk out?

It was the following evening while I was heating up the stiffened remains of the previous night's lasagne that the answer hit me so hard it hurt. Over breakfast, Jack had mentioned that there was something urgent he needed to talk to me about and what time would I be home? I'd promised to get back earlier than usual to make dinner at six so we could sit down together and discuss whatever was bothering him. It was important, he'd said, so important that he needed my full attention. With everything that had happened at work that day, it had completely slipped my mind.

I switched off the oven, grabbed my coat and drove over to Monique's house. Fifteen minutes later, she answered the door and raised one perfectly shaped eyebrow at seeing me. 'Your son is here,' she said, in a cut-glass accent that denied she'd ever been born French.

She was looking chic as usual in a cashmere dress that flowed easily over her slim figure and reached down to her calves. The surprise was that her outfit was matched not with a pair of beautiful shoes but what looked like the kind of towelling slip-ons they give you at health spas.

'Thank you. That's why I've come,' I said. 'I need to talk to him.'

My hair hadn't been brushed all day and my skin was probably grey with tiredness and over exposure to the office central heating which would explain why Monique was looking at me as if reluctant to let such a shabby specimen of womanhood across the threshold of her immaculate home.

Graham and Jack were in the gleaming white kitchen, facing each other over a refectory table that would comfortably seat twelve. Graham's fingers were curled around the stem of a wine glass while Jack was staring down at a mug of what smelled like hot chocolate. Graham looked up at me with that 'what have you done now?' expression that he does so well. His son, on the other hand, kept his eyes fixed on the drink in front of him. Monique joined us and took her place beside Graham without inviting me to sit.

'Jack,' I began, 'I'm so sorry I forgot about getting home early yesterday. It had been a hell of a day at work.'

'It always was, wasn't it, Lynn?' Graham sneered. 'Nothing's changed I see.'

I wanted to kill him but instead said, icily, 'Is there somewhere Jack and I can talk privately?'

Monique laid her slender hand on Graham's as if to restrain him from answering. 'The sitting room,' she said. 'But please be careful; I have just had the carpet shampooed.'

'*Oh, don't worry,*' I wanted to say. '*We'll just climb up the sodding walls, shall we?*' That's when I realised that both Graham and Jack were sitting there in their socks.

Jack got up and padded after me, closing the sitting room door behind us.

'Where are your shoes?' I hissed. 'Has she confiscated them or something?'

He looked embarrassed. 'You're not allowed to wear them in the house in case they damage the floors.'

'For crying out loud!' I looked down at my navy court shoes almost sinking into the thick pile of the carpet.

'Mum,' Jack said, 'I can't stand it here; she's driving me mental.'

'Already? You've only been here a day and a bit.'

He shrugged. 'I know but it's like I can't breathe or something. It's like there isn't any air in this house. Can I come home?'

Relief flooded through me. 'Oh, please do, Jack. You don't belong here.'

'No,' he said. 'Neither does Dad.'

When I broke the news, Monique failed to disguise her delight at losing the cuckoo in her love nest while Graham just mumbled something about it being fine by him. The perverse thought crossed my mind that it was a shame the smooth surface of their lives wouldn't be ruffled by Jack's moody presence.

Once in the car, Jack lapsed into silence until we were halfway home when he suddenly asked me to stop. I pulled into the side of the road and then, afraid he was about to take off, asked, 'Is something wrong? Have you changed your mind about coming home? Are the floors not posh enough for you?'

He grinned then looked serious. 'It's just easier if we talk like this.'

I switched the engine off then swivelled round to face him. 'Ok, fire away, love.'

'Mum, I need you not to look at me,' he said.

'Oh, ok.' I turned my attention to the windscreen as a spattering of sleet hit the glass, blurring the multi-coloured Christmas lights on a nearby house. A large illuminated Santa Claus, perched on a ladder leading to a top window, became a scarlet smudge.

'Do you think Monique would have one of those on her front wall?' I said, hoping to lighten the atmosphere.

Jack made a face. 'No. It's gross.' Then he was quiet again, fiddling with the zip on his jacket while his right leg jigged up and down. 'Dad doesn't care about me anymore, does he?'

'Hey, that's not true,' I protested. 'It's me he stopped loving, not you.'

How could I tell him the truth as I saw it? Graham had shrugged off parenthood as if it was a heavy coat whose weight he couldn't tolerate. Monique was now the centre of his self-obsessed little universe but he'd never know how much he'd sacrificed for her.

'Is that what was worrying you, Jack?' I asked. 'I mean, about Dad?'

He shook his head. 'No, it wasn't that. Remember I told you that James Gresham had been bullying me and some other kids?'

I nodded but didn't speak, sensing that this was costing him enormous effort.

'Well, it got worse, Mum, much worse.'

In my anxiety, I turned to look at him, forgetting.

'Please don't,' he said. 'I can't say it if you look at me.'

We sat there quietly listening to the rain beating against the windscreen until he was ready to talk. After several minutes, and just when it seemed that he'd changed his mind, I heard him take a breath then begin.

He told me that not long after he'd stood up to James, he received messages from a girl calling herself 'Lovesick Babe'. It began innocently enough with her saying how much she liked him. Then, one evening, things took a different turn when she asked him to send her a nude selfie on Snapchat with the promise to return the favour if he did.

'Stupid, stupid idiot! Why would a girl want someone like me?' he moaned, beating his fist against his head.

I reached over and grabbed his hand. 'Don't you dare run yourself down, Jack Morris. One day, girls will be falling over themselves to be with you because, luckily, you've got your father's looks and my brains and not the other way round.'

I tried to smile but inside I was dreading what might come next.

'If I had any brains, I would have known something was wrong,' Jack moaned.

Some questions you just don't want to ask. 'So, did you send it?'

'What?'

'Did you send the selfie?'

He stared out at the dark street beyond the wet windscreen and nodded.

'But it was really James. He saved it then sent it to everyone in our class. I only found out about it that Monday in the art lesson. People had been nudging each other and sniggering behind my back all morning and then when the teacher wasn't looking, a friend showed me the photo on his phone. I hated James then, Mum. I hated him so much I wanted to kill him so I picked up one of the wooden boards we use in pottery and hit him hard. Not hard enough though, was it? Didn't even break his nose.'

The implication of what he'd just said brought him up short. 'I didn't mean… I wouldn't really want him to…'

He lapsed into stunned silence as if he'd only just remembered that James was dead.

'It's ok,' I said. 'I know you didn't mean it like that.'

'I wish I hadn't done it. I wish I'd just ignored the message.'

'So do I, Jack. Do you realise it's an offence to send pictures like that across the internet?'

'What?' I could hear the panic in his voice.

'Sharing underage nude photos is a crime. You're a minor but you're still held responsible, although many would say you're the victim and James is… was… more culpable.'

'You mean I could be arrested?' His eyes were wide.

'No, but let's hope the photo isn't still on James's phone and his parents don't find it. You're sure he saved it? I mean, on Snapchat they usually disappear after a while, don't they?'

'Yeah, he saved it and everyone in my year group saw it and all the people he sent it to – the whole world knows how stupid I am!'

He began to sob; it was a horrible, heart-wrenching sound.

I put my arm around him, closed my eyes and breathed in the coal tar smell of medicated shampoo on his soft hair. Thank God Monique had allowed him into one of her pristine showers.

'It'll be alright. Somehow, I'll make it right.'

But he wasn't seven years old anymore and this wasn't a scraped knee or a dead hamster. This would take some managing. Even though they covered internet safety at school, kids were still thoughtlessly compromising themselves. He was the last child I thought it would happen to but maybe every parent thinks that.

'So did you tell any of the teachers about this?' I asked.

'Only Mr Brennan after Art Club. He knew something was wrong and, well, he's easy to talk to and I just got the feeling that he wouldn't think I'm stupid or anything. He said you should know about it. He said it would help.'

The man struck me as being a decent human being. If Jack had to tell anyone before me, I'm glad it was him.

But now I had to deal with my own feelings towards James Gresham. Had his parents known what he was getting up to or did they truly believe he was the innocent described in the eulogy at his funeral, the 'fine young man' his father spoke of?

A feeling of exhaustion came over me as the worries that Jack had just transferred onto my shoulders settled and began to weigh me down.

Jack wiped his nose with the back of his jacket sleeve as if he was five years old again. 'Shall we go home now?'

I switched on the engine. The wipers swept across the windscreen bringing the garish Christmas lights back into focus. A slight breeze was rocking the inflatable Santa Claus on his ladder. With any luck the stupid sod would fall off.

'What would you like for Christmas, Jack?' I asked, in a desperate attempt to restore some normality – more for my benefit than his if I'm honest.

For a moment I thought he hadn't heard my question but then he said, quietly, almost to himself, 'I'd like for this never to have happened.'

26. LYNN

Since Jack's confession, the atmosphere in the house had changed, lightened, as if someone had opened all the doors and windows and let in some fresh air. A cynic might say it was the lavender and geranium calming spray that Clare had brought home from her holiday job but whatever it was, I managed to capture the attention of both of them over dinner one night so I could explain what to expect from me in the next two weeks. 'Not much' was a summary of the situation.

I began by telling them that we were close to making arrests in an important case and so things were going to get tricky at work.

'Is it dangerous?' Jack asked, a fork full of chips halfway to his mouth.

'Not really. But the point is, I'll be busy for a while until it's all sorted.'

'Oh yeah? I thought you said…' He shrugged. 'Doesn't matter.'

'Yes, it does,' I insisted. 'I'm telling you the facts so you know what to expect, so you know that if I'm a bit stressed or a bit late home it's not my fault. And as soon as this case is closed, I'll be taking some time off.'

He frowned. 'Not much we can do in winter. I'll be back at school in two weeks, anyway.'

'Ok, how about if I organise my leave for the Easter holidays? We could take off somewhere warm if you can bear to go away with your boring old mum at your sophisticated age.'

A twitch of a reluctant smile crinkled the corner of his mouth. 'Yeah, suppose I could force myself to put up with it.'

'Big of you.'

'But next year, I want to go away with my mates, ok? No sixteen-year-old goes on holiday with their mum.'

'Of course. Listen, you could always go and stay with Dad and Monique over Christmas if you want to escape from Clare and me.'

'Not funny, Mum,' he growled. 'That Monique's a maniac. Don't know why he went off with her when he had you.'

I couldn't speak for a moment but when I finally managed it, my voice sounded hoarse. 'Neither do I. Thanks, Jack.'

Clare grinned at me from across the table. 'Suck it up, Mum. That's the best you're ever going to get.'

*

Gradually, we were compiling the evidence we needed to justify a raid on the yard. Number plate recognition on the dark blue Transit in Kai's photo provided us with a familiar name: Guy Swinford, the small-time drug dealer we'd questioned in September. We'd presumed he was insignificant but how wrong could we be? The man was obviously due an Oscar for his performance.

CCTV footage at the front entrance of the industrial estate clearly showed the blue Transit coming and going at frequent intervals. Zooming in, I recognised Swinford as the driver.

Sam drew his breath in sharply. 'That bastard sat in that interview room flatly denying everything. What I wouldn't give to have another crack at him.'

Then, an officer who'd been on surveillance pointed to a figure dressed in paint-stained overalls approaching the path. 'See this guy? He arrived about midday on Tuesday carrying a large toolbox.'

'Just freeze it there a minute,' said Sam, leaning in closer to the screen. 'Yep, it's him all right. He's the arrogant bastard who stopped me in the street.'

When we forwarded an image of the suspect to Kai, his reaction was even stronger.

'He's the reason I'm stuck here in plaster. I'd like to see him on the wrong side of a cell door.'

I couldn't resist pulling his good leg. 'What about the miscreant who put up the wire fence? Shall we bring him in too? Oh sod it, let's bring them all in while we're at it, including whoever put the allotments there and that pile of broken concrete you landed on.'

There was a pause followed by what sounded like a deep sigh.

'I miss your humour, Ma'am. I'm spending my day talking to the walls and watching Netflix. There's no edge to it.'

Later, when I showed Ben the photo, his face turned ashen. 'That's him! That's our boss.' Even a still image of the man seemed to hold power over him.

'And do you recognise anything in this one?' I asked, showing him another photo, the one that Amy Lewis had forwarded a few weeks before.

'That's his boat. That's *Sea Swift*. How did you get this?'

I told him that Amy had just happened to catch sight of it near Kingston Bridge. At the mention of her name he brightened. 'Is she ok?'

'Fine. She asks about you every time we're in touch.'

He almost smiled then collected himself as if he'd been about to do something massively uncool before asking, 'Have you found Chris yet?'

His face fell when I told him we were still looking. He knew as well as I did that every day we failed to find that boat reduced the chances of finding Chris alive.

When I got back to the station, Sam looked up from his computer.

'Ma'am, I can't stop wondering why use a boat when drug dealers normally travel by car or use public transport?'

'Maybe they thought it would be less obvious,' I said. 'After all, you expect river boats to be about pleasure and no one would associate a luxury cabin cruiser with drug dealing.'

There were murmurs of agreement. Ok, someone was thinking outside the proverbial box when they planned this operation but what a risk to run considering that *Sea Swift* was such a luxurious craft and therefore highly visible.

'Whoever it is has balls, that's for sure,' Sam muttered.

'Or not,' added Stephanie, leaving her desk to join us. 'I've been thinking about that. Either they weren't as bright as they thought or they were so arrogant, so sure of never being identified, that it never occurred to them that they were running a risk.'

Sam frowned. 'There's only one problem. Using a boat restricts you to places that aren't too far from each other. It takes too long to travel up and downriver, especially when there are locks to negotiate and a strict speed limit.'

'Yes, but they probably use other transport as well,' Stephanie said. 'After all, they had other dealers apart from the two lads. Didn't Ben mention some girls from the children's home? And there could be more kids out there for all we know.'

'A line of kids stretching from central London to the county towns perhaps.' I hoped I was wrong.

While Sam searched online for the boat's registration record in the hope of discovering the boss's name, I tried to piece together what we knew so far about the yard. Ben had told us that the place was full of scrap metal. He'd described seeing piles of rusty scaffolding, reels of cable, traffic signs and even old telephone boxes stacked around the walls. And then, of course, there were the rusty shipping containers. What were they used for? I homed into the yard on Google Earth and found shapes that seemed to confirm the boy's story. The recycling business was obviously a cover up. There was also the question of what Ben had witnessed one night. His description of the way the men in the Transit van had been treated worried me considerably.

As I panned out to the surrounding area, I noticed the narrow inlet from the Thames that connected to the end of the Grand Union Canal, close to what appeared to be a small marina. It would certainly make a convenient place to moor the boat when the boss made a visit to the yard. From there to Commerce Way at the end of the industrial estate was a short walk along the road by the allotments.

Now we needed to get in there and find out what was going on.

A couple of hours later, Sam appeared at my desk with a large coffee in one hand and his notebook in the other. He pulled up a chair and sat opposite me.

'What's new?' I asked. My head ached from peering at the screen. My eye test was well overdue but there just hadn't been time to get to the opticians. Either my arms were too short or I needed glasses.

Sam opened his notebook. 'Are you interested in boats, Lynn?'

'I know nothing about boats,' I said, rubbing my eyes. 'Never had to buy one, funnily enough.'

'So I checked the registration records and you'll be pleased to hear that *Sea Swift* is registered to one Frankie Collins. He's been the official owner for about a year.'

'Have we any info on this Collins?'

Sam checked his notes. 'Frankie Collins, aged forty-five, criminal record for GBH and robbery with violence both of which he's done time for. I recognised him straightaway as the guy I met in Commerce Way.' He handed over a photo from the file.

I found myself looking into the small, dark, resentful eyes of a stocky, middle-aged man with hardly any neck and broad, muscular shoulders. Just visible above the collar of his shirt on one side was a tattoo in the shape of a dagger. The thought of such a dangerous bastard being in control of two vulnerable adolescent boys made me shudder.

'This is the man Ben identified as the Boss. So we've now got two definite links between Collins and the boat. Do we know where he lives?'

Sam passed me another piece of paper. 'Last known address is this one in Molesey.'

'Ok, Sam, we need to check he's still there. What about Guy Swinford? Where does he live?'

'No known address. Last time we picked him up from the street. He's a bit of a vagrant. Most probably, he's sofa surfing somewhere.'

'Right, we need a warrant to arrest Frankie Collins at his home on the morning we raid the yard so there's no opportunity for him to raise the alarm.'

'What about this Dillon guy?' Sam asked. 'The one who's picking up kids like Ben for the county line?'

Now my head was throbbing. 'He's a person of interest that's for sure but for now, let's focus on the two villains on our doorstep.'

The next step was to plan two simultaneous dawn raids, one on Collins at his home address and another on the yard. Anyone found on the premises would need to be detained while we carried out a thorough search. Hopefully, there would be plenty of evidence from both the Collins house and the yard, including computers, personal phones and paperwork.

'We can discuss the logistics with DCI Kenbury,' I said, reaching for a packet of aspirin in my bag. 'We'll need some support and maybe a sniffer dog in case there are drugs hidden away somewhere.'

Sam replaced the documents in the thick file. 'Collins might well have some firearms at his house. Apparently, he was in possession of a sawn-off shotgun last time he was arrested.'

I swallowed the tablets with some coffee and made a face. 'Nice. I'll mention that to the DCI. It'll make his Christmas.'

At five that afternoon, I left the station to keep an appointment with Mr McDonald at St Saviour's High. After what Jack had told me, the school needed to know why he'd reacted so violently. More importantly, they needed to crack down to make sure nothing like that happened again.

Give him his due, he was predictably shocked by what James Gresham had done to my son and full of apologies. 'I'll have a word with Jack tomorrow morning, Mrs Morris. Why on earth James Gresham needed to behave like that, I don't know.'

'Yes, it's a shame he's not here to explain,' I said, and then, because that sounded mercenary and I certainly didn't mean it that way, added, 'I'm sure you would have found ways to help him change his behaviour.'

He nodded. 'Let me assure you that we will clamp down hard on any student who thinks sexting is a good idea.'

The word sounded so strange in his upper-crust mouth. Without meaning to, his accent gave it a sensuousness it didn't deserve. We shook hands and I thanked him, genuinely touched by his shock and sympathy for my son.

In the corridor, I literally bumped into Mr Brennan as he came round a corner carrying a large black portfolio. Seeing me, he stopped short.

'Mrs Morris! Is everything alright with Jack?'

'Thanks to you, yes. I'm glad you told him to speak to me.'

The penny obviously dropped. 'Ah, of course. It shouldn't have happened. Poor Jack.'

It was the first time I'd had the opportunity to study the man and it dawned on me that he was actually quite handsome in a sort of romantic, Victorian poet kind of way. He was the epitome of an artistic type with that wavy, almost black hair touching his collar, dark blue, soulful eyes under straight, dark brows, high cheek bones, a straight nose and a strong, well-shaped mouth. If I'd been a few years younger, I would have developed a keen interest in art, turned up for every parents' evening religiously and made appointments to see him on the pretext of worrying about Jack's drawing skills.

I must have been staring at the poor man because he suddenly looked embarrassed.

'Anyway, Jack seems to be back on an even keel now, Mrs Morris, but I'll keep an eye on him so don't worry,' he said, opening the entrance door for me.

A weight had been lifted off my shoulders.

On the way home, I stopped off at Kai's flat with a bag of shopping. I figured the lad might be starving to death so had raided

Iceland for a selection of ready meals that he could easily microwave plus a couple of packs of beer in case he needed cheering up.

It took a while for him to reach the front door and his face when he saw me was a picture of disbelief.

'So, are you going to let me in or do I have to freeze to death out here?' I held up two bulging plastic shopping bags. 'Supplies to keep you going until you can get back to the station and the delights of the canteen.'

Kai grinned, opening the door wider. 'Thanks, Ma'am. Come in.'

He led the way into a small, immaculate kitchen and I placed the shopping bags on the black granite worktop. I noted that he had one of those fancy taps that boils the water or sends it out ice cold. This lad was into gadgets in a big way.

'So how are you doing?' I asked.

Kai was rummaging through the bags, taking out some of the frozen meals and examining them as if they were pieces of evidence.

'Fine, thanks. Plaster's coming off in three weeks' time. That's very kind bringing this shopping but actually, I'm ok.'

When he opened the tall stainless-steel fridge, I almost gasped. Every shelf contained rows of white Tupperware boxes each one labelled with the date their contents had been made and when it was to be eaten by.

'My mum,' he said, sheepishly. 'She brings a week's supply of freshly cooked meals every Sunday. I've told her not to bother because she spends all day Saturday preparing them but it's like telling her not to breathe or something.'

'It's what mothers do,' I said. *The really good ones, that is.*

He nodded. 'She can't help herself.'

With the fridge door open, the kitchen was filling with the spicy aroma of curry, making me even hungrier than I was already.

'She must be a great cook. They smell delicious.'

'Cup of tea or coffee?' he asked, reaching for a stainless-steel kettle, the kind that looks as if it was designed by an aerospace engineer.

There wasn't much time but Jack was at football practice that evening so I stayed for a cup of tea and filled Kai in on what was happening with the investigation. He brightened as we talked as if hearing about work was the medicine he needed.

'So when is the raid planned for?' he asked, leaning forward. 'I really want to be there, Ma'am. I want to see that Collins guy put away.'

'Depends what the medics say, Kai. Will you be up to it?'

He looked down at the plastered leg. 'If I can get my muscles back in shape and they give me the all clear, I should be fit again soon.'

He didn't sound convinced and neither was I.

'You'll be really useful doing some research in the meantime,' I assured him. 'I'll get Sam to bring some files over. See what you can dig up about Frankie Stevens.'

'Thanks,' he said. 'I was afraid my brain was shrinking.'

'And well done. But please don't ever put yourself in that position again. If that guy with the toolbox had seen you, you could have ended up on the wrong end of a Stanley knife.'

'Point taken,' he grinned. 'Excuse the pun.'

I left him the beer but took the bags of food home with me, unable to compete with Mrs Chauhan's cuisine. Although I got the distinct impression that her son was yearning for a bit of variety in his diet. His eyes had lit up when he'd seen the microwavable toad-in-the-hole with onion gravy.

27. AMY

Unlike most of the other residents of Kingston upon Thames, who were probably doing joyous things like roasting chestnuts round an open fire, the run up to my Christmas Day was spent painting the walls of my flat every evening after work. My landlord had texted me a reminder the week before because a) he knew about my talent for procrastination and b) he's not a very nice person.

I finally laid down my brush on Christmas Eve then spent ages wiping all the magnolia splashes off the carpet, floorboards, my hands and Max's fur. To be honest, the resulting bland expanse reflected my mood perfectly.

The day before, I'd driven round to Tom Brennan's house with a gift parcel. Unfortunately, he was out, so I'd left it behind a plant pot by the front door with an intense feeling of disappointment at not seeing him. Since the day that he and Orla got separated, every moment by the river and in the cafe was playing in my head like a movie whose stand-out scenes you rewind and watch over and over again.

The parcel contained a small bottle of Irish whiskey which I thought Tom would enjoy now he'd broken up from school and a pair of hand-knitted mittens for Orla in a beautiful Scandinavian pattern of reds and greens. Seeing the ragged holes in her old ones had torn at my heart. When it started snowing, it would make me happy to think of her enjoying the feel of the thick, warm wool.

But Tom hadn't rung or texted since I left the parcel which made me feel uneasy. Perhaps he was embarrassed that I'd noticed the state of his daughter's gloves or maybe getting him a present was inappropriate when he was obviously grieving for his wife. Christmas is the worst time for people who've lost loved ones they say. Whatever it was, somehow, I'd overstepped the mark.

There was something else hanging heavily on my mind too. It felt so sad not to be in touch with my family when, through my sitting room window, I could see people crunching along the snow-covered pavements carrying bags of presents. So, on the afternoon of Christmas day, I took a deep breath and phoned my parents. Someone had to make an effort to rebuild communication and it might as well be me.

When my mother answered there were voices in the background. The neighbours had come in for a drink and were obviously being entertained by my dad because I could hear his gruff voice followed by peals of laughter. When on earth had he ever been funny? My mother was cool and distant, like someone politely talking to a stranger. It was hard to bear so in the end I decided, Christmas or not, it was time to stand up for myself.

'We're doing so well in the shop. It's become a landmark in the town.'

'Really?' she said, icily. 'Then what a shame it has to be sold. I hope you're not having second thoughts.'

That was too much. 'Do you even care how much of a sacrifice this is for me, Mum?'

There was a silence that indicated that she was taking this in, broken only when she said, coolly, 'Of course, Amy, but you owe it to your brother to help him.'

'Oh? How do you make that out?'

'He's your flesh and blood. And he didn't deserve to be so cruelly overlooked by your grandmother. That was a disgrace, leaving everything to you and nothing to Marcus.'

'Perhaps she knew which one of us would invest it wisely,' I snapped. This wasn't going the way I'd hoped.

My mother gave me one of her martyr's sighs. 'Let's not argue,

Amy. It's Christmas. There are things I could say that would only make you bite my head off and this isn't the right time so let's leave it, dear.'

In the background, my dad was calling her, saying something about getting the mince pies out for the visitors.

'Coming!' she called, brightly. 'I have to go, Amy; we've got people in.'

There was a click as she put the phone down. I could imagine her scurrying off to the kitchen then bustling into the sitting room with a bright smile to greet the neighbours and laugh dutifully at my father's jokes. It made me long to get in the car, drive to Devon and rescue her from this half-life she was living under my dad's shadow. Then I would drag her into town to see my beautiful shop again and force her to understand what she was expecting of me to give up for my feckless, lying brother.

On Boxing Day morning I was just contemplating spending the whole day in my dressing gown when the flat's entry buzzer sounded. I stood behind the door, opened it a crack then flung it wide open at seeing Beth and Paulo grinning back at me.

'Mamma mia!' Paolo exclaimed, looking me up and down. 'Have we interrupted a romantic moment?'

Beth grinned at me. 'Want us to go away again?'

'No! Don't you dare!'

I ushered them inside, making way for Luca's pushchair and manhandling the ecstatic dog back into the kitchen where he howled his outrage at being shut away from the visitors.

Beth was eyeing the walls of the sitting room. 'It's looking different in here. It's very…'

'Magnolia,' I said. 'Landlord's orders.'

Paolo grinned. 'Did he say you had to paint your hair as well? You have some magnolia highlights on the top of your head, darling.'

In spite of living in London for fourteen years, his Italian accent was still strong. The words bubbled along like a fast-flowing stream.

Of all the people I needed right then, it was these two. For weeks, there had been a wide hole in my heart that only they could fill.

'We thought you might have opened Earth Song today for the sales. We wanted to surprise you so we went there first but it's lucky we found you at home,' Beth said, lifting Luca from his pushchair and settling him on her knee. In spite of my smile, he scowled at me and blew an enormous bubble of spittle.

I explained that Roz and Clare were both tied up with their families and I certainly couldn't cope with a rush on my own. Plus, the painting was such hard work, I had no energy left. The plan had been to lie on the sofa all day watching slushy films on TV including *The Sound of Music* which always made me sob into my mulled wine. I'm an emotional wreck from the moment in the opening sequence when Julie Andrews spins round on that mountain top as the camera swoops over her and the music swells into the sky, right through to the arrival of the Nazis. It's my seasonal treat. Not cool for someone my age, I know.

Over coffee and Christmas cake (a gift from a regular customer), we settled down to some small talk until Beth announced she had some news. Paolo gave her a smile that weakened my knees never mind hers.

So soon? I thought. *Luca's barely on solids.*

Beth was always expert at reading my mind. 'It's not what you're thinking, Ames! One baby in that flat is enough for the time being. No, we've taken a big decision and decided to get out of London.'

'Oh.'

My spirits plunged again. They were about to tell me they were leaving the country to go to Italy. Paolo probably had a yearning to return to Tuscany – yes, that was definitely it. Mentally, I was working out how often I could realistically get out there to see them when Beth explained further.

'We're tired of living in a built-up area, even an upmarket one like Mayfair. We both have a yearning now for cleaner air, nature and space. It's what we want for Luca as well, somewhere a bit quieter where he can grow up away from too many traffic fumes.'

At the sound of his name, the baby looked up at his mother with that wide-eyed, slightly puzzled look that babies his age often have. It's the same expression you see on the faces of drunks when they fall out of the pub door and hit the fresh air. It's as if they no longer understand how the world works.

I waited for the bad news, determined to be brave and glad for this little family I cared so much about but dreading the thought of having them ripped out of my life.

Beth glanced at Paolo who was watching me intently with those beautiful dark eyes, as if he could read my thoughts.

'So, Amy, this is a big change for us,' he said, with a half-smile. 'At the end of January, we will have a new job managing a large hotel by the river in…'

Oh, come on, I thought. *Just get it over with.* Mentally, I skipped back to my GCSE geography searching for rivers in Italy but the only ones I could remember were the Po and the Tiber. Oh, so that was it. They were relocating to Rome. But was the air really cleaner in Rome?

'Shepperton,' Paolo said. The way he pronounced the word made it sound as if it was the most beautiful, most exotic place on earth.

'Shepperton?' I repeated, numbly, mimicking his accent unconsciously before correcting myself. 'Shepperton in Surrey?'

Beth nodded, enthusiastically. 'The hotel is a stunning Georgian country house in its own grounds by the river and it comes with accommodation for the manager and family, a converted stable block made into a cottage.'

'But, Beth, you didn't mention any of this when we met,' I protested.

'We'd only just applied and you know how these things go. It seems like bad luck to pin your hopes on getting the job before the interview. It's promotion for me because I'll be the assistant manager to his lordship here.'

His lordship winked at her. 'You must come and see it, Amy,' he said. 'It's not so far from here, just up the river. Buy a boat or swim but come and see us.'

Surely, I thought, cute as Shepperton was, a hotel in Mayfair must have a lot more kudos career-wise.

Beth, as usual, pre-empted me. 'Amy, you inspired us, actually. You of all people know what it's like to give up the safe option and plunge into a new adventure.'

I didn't tell her that my adventure might end very soon.

Christmas was turning out to be a rollercoaster of emotions. It was hard to believe that soon, I'd be seeing much more of the people I was closest to, that I'd maybe even be around when Luca turned thirteen and started mumbling incoherently.

After I'd made more coffee and let Max come in and introduce himself politely, Beth said, 'Your turn for news. Tell us the latest. What happened to that boy we saw on the south bank, the one you were so keen to catch up with?'

I gave her the news about Ben who, I'm ashamed to say, had slipped out of my thoughts in the rush up to Christmas until DC Clinton had rung me. He obviously couldn't go into detail but said they were close to making some arrests because of the information Ben had provided. He thanked me again for my part in their investigation which, apparently, had sparked off a whole new line of enquiry. Before he finished the call, there was a message he wanted to pass on to me.

'Oh, and Miss Lewis, Detective Inspector Morris would like to thank you for employing her daughter Clare over Christmas.'

'So did you know it was her daughter?' Beth asked.

'Call me thick,' I said, 'but the name didn't ring any bells. Besides, DI Morris doesn't look the motherly type so it never occurred to me that she'd have children, let alone anyone as lovely as Clare. That girl's a real asset to the shop. It's a pity she's back at uni in another two weeks.'

Beth smiled. 'You know, my dad always says that some people are like freshly baked bread: crusty on the outside but warm and soft on the inside. Maybe that description fits DI Morris.'

'Sure,' I said. 'Dream on, Beth.'

All too soon, they had to get back to the Royal Mayfair Hotel, leaving me standing in my magnolia hallway pondering how strange life can be.

I didn't know it then but it was about to get even stranger.

28. TOM

It wasn't the news anybody wants to hear let alone two days before Christmas. Dad had collapsed while they were shopping in town and had been taken to the local hospital. It was a coronary, my mother told me. They were doing their best to pull him through but it might be an idea to get to Sligo if I could.

I booked to fly out on Christmas Eve but at about ten o'clock the night before, I experienced a sudden cold feeling and knew he had gone. So the phone call minutes later wasn't a surprise just a reaffirmation that now there would never be a chance to tell him all the things I should have said, the things men never find easy to tell each other, like how much I loved him and how bad I felt for taking him for granted.

We flew into Knock airport the next morning, Orla buzzing with excitement at what she saw as an adventure, me with a heavy feeling of anticipation that deepened when we got out of the taxi at the house and a shrunken version of my mother appeared in the doorway.

In the west of Ireland, everything happens very quickly after a death. Usually, the deceased is buried within three days but in this case, because of Christmas, the funeral was postponed until the day after Boxing Day or St Stephen's Day as we know it. My mother informed me through her sobs that Dad had been brought home and that neighbours and friends had come to the house to pay their respects.

I knelt down and looked into Orla's now serious little face, gently removing one mittened hand from her mouth.

'Sorry,' she said in a small voice, all excitement dampened now we were here and she'd seen her grandmother cry.

'It's Amy you'll need to say sorry to if you ruin them,' I assured her. 'Now, listen, Orla. When we go inside, Grandad will be in his coffin. Would you like to say goodbye to him? If you'd rather not see him, that's fine.'

She nodded solemnly so I took her hand and followed my mother inside. We hung up our coats on the pegs in the hallway beside my father's dark grey overcoat and his favourite tweed cap, the one he wore for the pub. The curtains in the sitting room had been drawn, casting the usually cheerful, cosy room in cool gloom. Neighbours were sitting by the walls on a variety of chairs talking in hushed voices, the ladies with cups of tea, the men with glasses of whiskey. As we entered, everyone looked up and immediately fell silent. My mother had given them the best china teacups and the Waterford crystal that she usually kept on display in the glass-fronted cabinet. 'Too good to use,' she always said.

At the end of the room was the coffin which had been placed on two trestles. Even though you know someone's dead, it's still a shock to see the body. I stood looking down at it, trying to be the brave man of the house, conscious that all eyes were looking my way. A deep voice behind me and a hand on my shoulder made me turn to see my father's closest pal, Michael Flynn.

'I'm sorry for your troubles, Tom. This man was the best that ever lived.'

'Ah, he was that for sure,' I heard someone say from the wall. 'He was indeed,' echoed softly around the room then one sole voice like a dying whisper: 'Ah, he was, he was.'

How strange that when a person dies, they're immediately canonised in everyone's mind. No hard work is needed just the requirement to be dead. My dad was an ordinary man but he'd have been pleased with his advancement to sainthood and glad to take his place among all the other locals that death had promoted.

'And this young lady will surely miss him too,' said Michael, looking down at Orla who was still wearing the green and red mittens. Since we'd unwrapped Amy's parcel, she'd refused to take them off except at bath time, a situation I hadn't had time to resolve.

'Come and say goodbye now,' I said gently, lifting her up a little so she could see over the edge of the coffin and look into the waxen face of the man who'd once carried her on his shoulder and called her his little English lady. She seemed fascinated by Grandad lying so still in his best Sunday Mass suit clutching his wooden rosary beads between yellow, calloused fingers.

'It doesn't look like him,' she whispered.

'Well, perhaps that's because the part that made him Grandad has gone,' I said.

'Is he in Heaven now? Like Mummy?'

That was a tricky one for a part-time atheist to answer. Hopefully, the God I tried to believe in wouldn't be too fussy about Dad's swearing or his weekly bet on the horses or the time he got very drunk at my cousin's wedding and insulted the bride's mother. Maybe, He knew that, for most of his life, Eamon Brennan had been a mild-mannered, hard-working man whose footsteps made hardly an imprint on the earth beneath him.

'Oh, yes, he's in Heaven now and probably asking for a set of woodworking tools because you know how Grandad likes to keep busy,' I said, putting Orla down. She was getting heavier. 'If you took those mittens off, sweetheart, I wouldn't have such trouble lifting you. They weigh a ton.' I could tell she didn't get the joke.

There hadn't been time to thank Amy for such a thoughtful present or indeed to return the favour. Often now, she filled my thoughts. I could still picture her waving to us from the top of the steps by the riverside, sitting opposite me at the café table or lying flat on the hard floor in the chalet, one arm around the huddled boy beside her.

The door opened and my mother bustled in with a tray of fresh teas and a plate of home-made scones which she proceeded to offer along the line of mourners who took them eagerly. I understood her need to be occupied. Fussing over the visitors prevented her from thinking. I remembered doing the same after Anna died, carrying on with my work as if nothing had happened and ignoring friends' advice to take time off.

Mam looked across at me standing awkwardly by the coffin with Orla who, suddenly shy in front of all these strangers, was clinging to my side like a limpet to a rock.

'Tom, you must both be tired after your journey. Go out now and get some tea. There's a fresh pot on the stove and I'm sure this little girl would like something to eat.'

Gratefully, I ushered Orla out of that dark, sombre room and into the kitchen, glad of the sudden warmth and light.

When everyone had gone, the house became eerily quiet. My father had been, truth to tell, fond of his own voice and easy with his opinions on everything from the state of the Irish government to the price of potatoes in the local Spa. It was odd seeing his empty chair by the range and knowing that he was lying in the candlelit darkness next door.

My mother, being exhausted, retired early that evening and after Orla had gone to bed, I sat in the kitchen waiting for a small group of family friends who'd promised to come and sit with my dad, the tradition being to keep the body company during the night. In the morning, the undertaker would come and take him to the chapel of rest until the funeral the day after.

Waiting in the silence for the tap on the back door, I took out my mobile and texted Amy. She must have wondered why we hadn't thanked her for the presents so I explained what had happened and told her that the wonderful mittens had to be prised off Orla's hands at bed and bath time. My chronic embarrassment about the state of her old gloves was incidental now. How to sign off? 'Love, Tom' seemed too familiar so in the end I wrote 'All the best, Tom'.

It was totally unexpected when she rang me a few minutes later, her voice charged with concern and sympathy. For a few seconds I couldn't speak. When you're sad, a warm, sympathetic voice is enough to break you.

'Tom, are you ok?' she asked.

With anybody else I would have put on a brave face but I felt comfortable being honest with Amy. 'Not really but thanks for asking,' I said.

'How long will you be there?'

I told her we'd be staying the week just so I could make sure that my mother was ok but since Orla was back at school the following Tuesday, we'd be flying to Gatwick on the Saturday. I'd booked the midday flight from Knock.

'I'll be thinking of you both,' she said. 'Take care of yourself, Tom.'

'You too Amy, and thanks for calling. It's good to hear your voice.'

'And I wish you were here, Amy Lewis,' I said to myself when she'd gone.

*

Funerals are strange, stressful occasions. You're seated in the front pew of the church in full view of everybody, sensing waves of sympathy soaking into your back while you desperately try to hold it together. It's worse for men, really. We're expected to be strong and upright. With my mother looking grey-faced but dignified on one side of me, and Orla, wide-eyed with fascination on the other, it was my role to be the solid pillar in the middle.

During the all-too-familiar service, my mother held up well, her mouth set in a firm, determined line until the final commendation when the coffin was blessed and Dad presented to Paradise. The beautiful words broke through her defences. I gave her my hand and felt her fingers curl gratefully around mine as six of the strongest cousins and neighbours hefted the coffin onto their shoulders. We followed Dad out to the waiting hearse with a heavy sense of finality. Nothing separates more than a grave.

But then came the wake. We'd booked a cooked meal in

Sheridan's Bar and Grill for the frozen mourners who, after some warming spirits, gratefully sat down for their hot soup, roast beef and Mrs Sheridan's home-made apple pie, all of which brought the blood back to our extremities. The stories about Dad flew from table to table filling the place with gales of laughter, reminding Mam and me that he'd had another life outside of our house and another persona for his friends and colleagues.

Through it all, Orla watched and listened with uncharacteristic stillness while quietly sipping a fizzy drink pretending to be cider. The cousins on our table were clucking over her with admiration.

'That little girl is an angel.'

'Not many children would be this well behaved in company.'

'She's the spitting image of her father.'

I wanted to tell them that when I looked into Orla's dark eyes, it was her mother I saw but instead, I just assured them that, just like her grandfather, the girl had her moments. The mock cider would be rationed. Too much sugar and the 'little angel' would have to be scraped off the ceiling.

That night I lay awake for hours reliving the day and wondering what it would have been like if I'd stayed in this small, homely village like my dad who'd never set foot in another country. 'County Sligo is enough for me,' he always said. 'You have to go a long way to see mountains, lakes and fields like these.'

'But London is such a vibrant city,' I'd insisted. 'You don't know what you're missing, Dad. Or you could take Mam on a cruise to see the Mediterranean coast. You'd love that, eh, Mam?'

She'd looked up from her knitting with a hopeful smile. 'I would that.'

But he'd shrugged off my comments. 'That's as may be but I'm a country man and I'll live and die among these green fields.'

Well, at least he got his wish.

The day before we left, I managed to persuade Orla to go shopping with her grandma while I headed off to Enniscrone, a small, windswept seaside town on the Atlantic coast. My dad often used to drive us there on Sunday afternoons whenever, as he said to my mother, 'The little lad needs to run his energy off.' I had plenty of that. Somehow, try as they might to exhaust me, there was always a reserve of high spirits in my tank.

But now I needed some time to myself and that was the perfect place, open to the sky and sea, a place to clear the mind.

I parked the car and trudged along the narrow path through the high sand dunes, emerging to a sight that still took my breath away even though I knew it so well: the long, bright expanse of sand stretching in either direction with the gleaming sea beyond. As it was winter, the beach was deserted so the wild Atlantic wind had only me to buffer against as I made my way down to where the sand became soft and shiny with the licking of the wavelets.

For a while I just stood there, shielding my eyes against the brightness. Then, perhaps it was the emptiness or just the sheer beauty of the place, but my vision was blurring, merging sea and sky in a welling up of tears. I found myself crying quietly for my dad until, unexpectedly, like a piece of music changing to a minor key, a pain that had been hidden deep down erupted. I was choking on Anna's name and falling to my knees on the cold sand. Thank God nobody saw.

When it was over, I got up, took off my shoes and socks and paddled into the sea, gasping as the freezing water ran over my feet and the waves spit in my face. That's when it hit me that I was worn out by my efforts to be strong. And achingly tired of being alone.

That evening, when Orla was asleep, my mother and I sat in the kitchen drinking hot whiskies by the warmth of the range. I could sense her dread at being left by herself with that dad-shaped space in the house; the little changes would take some getting used to. Unlike me, she was new to all this.

She tried to smile. 'So what'll you do now, love?'

'What do you mean, Mam? The same as I always do.'

'No, that's not what I meant at all. You're still young, Thomas.'

Maybe I knew where this was going.

'You might meet someone else. Anna wouldn't want you to spend the rest of your life alone.'

'Women aren't exactly queueing up to marry a man with a child, Mam.'

'She wouldn't want you to suffer, is all I'm saying. You were so good to her.'

Was I? Was I good enough as a husband? Did I ever take her for granted? Was she happy being with me? These thoughts often tormented me these days.

'Maybe I'm better off as I am,' I said. 'Orla and I can manage.'

But I knew that was no longer true.

My mother took a sip of tea. 'Well, I'm going to pray about it.'

She would too. She'd be on her knees every night plaguing God and all the saints to sort me out.

Perhaps her prayers would help make me feel less of a traitor. How and when it had happened I don't know but hearing Amy's voice when she had called a few nights before, I knew now that I was falling in love again.

29. AMY

Three envelopes were lying on the hall floor when I got home from work. A couple of them were late Christmas cards from people I'd crossed off my list because I hadn't heard from them for at least three years. Making a mental note to uncross them for next Christmas, I opened the third. It was a beautifully hand-painted card depicting snow-covered fields dotted with sheep with smoke curling up from a farmhouse chimney in the distance. The glowering winter sky had been painted in shades of silver and subtle tinges of purple. The poor old sheep were in for some rough weather.

I read the greeting on the card twice before believing the evidence of my eyes – it really was from my artist friends. Folded up inside was a handwritten note from Jan. I made a coffee, shoved Max off the sofa and settled down to read it in comfort, hoping for some explanation at last for their sudden departure.

Dear Amy,

Hopefully, all is well with you and the shop is thriving. How are the ellipses coming on? We think of you often and fondly. You brightened up our Wednesday evenings with your cheerful, positive personality and you can't imagine how much we needed that sometimes.

I'm so sorry we left without telling you but something unpleasant happened. You remember the painting of the Thames that Kyle did? Well, we came home from a restaurant one night to find that 'Serenity' had been broken into and the painting stolen. Nothing else was missing but our things had been thrown around all over the place. We told the police but they didn't hold out much hope of finding who had done it or of Kyle getting his work back. There were no fingerprints and nobody in the other boats had heard or seen anything.

All we can think is that someone saw Kyle working on the painting outside on the riverbank and liked it enough to come back and take it. Charming.

Anyway, as you can imagine, neither of us felt like staying after that so we packed up the next day and left, taking 'Serenity' back to the boatyard where we'd hired her.

So we got back home a bit earlier than we planned. Come and see us any time, Amy. Bring your sketch pad and that mad animal of yours.

Lots of love.

Jan xx

I read the note a few times, hardly believing that some low-life thought it was ok to wreck their boat and steal Kyle's painting. It was worth reporting again so I texted DC Clinton to let him know what had happened. He texted me back later that evening to say he'd look into the record of the theft.

A few days later, the January sales were in full swing in Kingston town centre and we were working flat out. Clare Morris had left us with the promise to return in the Easter holidays if we needed her and I'd put on a brave face and assured her that if we were still there then yes, we'd love to have her back. We were already feeling her absence since she'd been a bubble of youthful positivity that carried us through the Christmas rush. I'd only met her mother once but you wouldn't think they shared the same genes. Maybe her job had pummelled the joy out of her.

Around four o'clock on the first Saturday in January, Roz and I were just contemplating risking a cup of tea when the door opened and Tom Brennan and Orla walked in or rather, Tom did the walking while Orla burst in, her face one big grin of excitement when she saw me. Before I knew what had happened, she had come round the counter and was clinging onto me. Tom was watching us with an expression that was hard to read. He looked tired but then, he'd had a tough time lately.

'Good to see you back,' I said.

Very gently, I prised Orla away on the pretext of wanting to see how the mittens fitted.

'Someone wanted to say thank you,' her father said. 'Since writing a letter seems to be an awful chore for some reason, it had to be in person.' He moved closer, as if gathering courage. 'How have you been, Amy?'

'Me? Ok but what about you? I mean, how did it go?'

Stupid question. How does any funeral go? It's not like a play when the scenery might collapse or someone might forget their lines.

He shrugged. 'These things go and so it went.'

I reached out and touched his arm. 'I'm so sorry.'

He smiled but his eyes were sad which made me want to hug him. Maybe I would have done if Roz hadn't been watching us from behind the counter.

'Anyway, the whiskey has come in very handy so thank you from me too,' Tom said. 'In return, madam here and I would like to invite you to dinner on an evening of your choosing.' He smiled. 'Don't I sound grand all of a sudden?'

I laughed and the atmosphere lightened immediately. 'I'd be delighted to attend your soiree, sir.' Heck, I'd turned into Elizabeth Bennett all of a sudden.

'You would?' His eyes widened and something of the old spark lit them up. 'Well, that's... I mean, wow, that's... great! Orla, did you hear that? We'll have to get the hoover out.'

Her reply was to bounce on the spot, a typical over-the-top response from a child her age but I loved her for it.

'No tidying,' I said, firmly, 'because I won't feel at home if you do.'

As far as I could remember from my first visit to Tom's house, it had a lived-in atmosphere, comfortably normal and so unlike the empty, austere places you see on property websites or TV makeover programmes. I doubted he'd have two layers of cushions on his bed either, though why that image popped into my head I had no idea.

We finally decided that dinner would be the following Saturday at seven and they left the way they came in with Orla skipping ahead of her father who turned as he closed the shop door to smile at Roz and me. 'It's good to be back, ladies.'

When he'd gone, Roz turned to me with a knowing smile. 'Happy New Year, Amy. Let's hope his cooking is as good as his pottery.' She nudged me. 'And everything else as well.'

*

By six thirty on Saturday night, I had changed my outfit three times and was still standing by my wardrobe in bra and pants wondering what to wear to a dinner with Tom Brennan and his daughter.

On the bed lay a tartan skirt (too short – more tart than tartan), a pair of black trousers and a white short-sleeved jumper (too boring) and a red silk blouse, another impulse buy meant to cheer me up after Richard left but never worn because it reminded me of him. Good riddance to bad actors. In any case, the blouse was way too sexy for this occasion so in the end, I put everything back in the wardrobe and took out my old friend – a long-sleeved, midi-length midnight-blue dress. *Oh no, not again*, it sighed. *You're wearing me out.* I teamed it with a pair of black knee-high boots and my favourite pale-blue cardigan. It was a blue fest but a safe choice for a cosy domestic setting.

Max had been watching me with that sad expression dogs have when they think they're about to be abandoned so I tucked an old sweater into his basket, gave him one of those cowhide bones that are supposed to last for hours and left the house feeling strangely excited.

It was Orla who opened their front door when I arrived. Solemnly and without speaking, she took my hand and drew me down the hallway into the cosy warmth of the kitchen where Tom, in a blue and white striped butcher's apron, was busy straining a pan of steaming potatoes into a colander. He set the pan down on the draining board, wiped his hands on the apron then came over and surprised me by grasping my shoulders and kissing my cheek.

'You came,' he said. 'I was afraid you might be scared off at the thought of my cooking.'

'Nearly,' I laughed. 'But I thought I'd give you a chance.' Actually, something smelled delicious, something meaty and salty.

Orla indicated the kitchen table, now covered with a green linen cloth. In the middle sat the small poinsettia but this time in a decidedly chunky orange pot decorated with splodges of yellow which were probably meant to be flowers.

'I made that at art club,' she announced. 'You can sit down if you like.' She pulled out one of the chairs and I obediently sat, still wearing my coat. Tom raised his eyes and sent her upstairs to wash her hands. When she'd gone, he gave me one of his wide smiles, the kind that lit up his eyes and made my heart lurch.

'Sorry, Amy, but Madam is a bit overexcited. She's been looking forward to this all week. As have I.' He took my coat and went into the hallway to hang it up.

'Now,' he said, coming back and taking the bottle of wine I'd brought. 'Thanks for this. Good choice.'

'Is it? I chose it because the label looked artistic but to be honest, I haven't a clue what the wine is like.'

'That's what I like about you, Amy. You're so refreshingly honest.' He placed it in the fridge to cool then took out a bottle of Prosecco. 'Do you fancy a glass of this stuff? I call it the poor man's champagne.' He handed me the glass. 'Now, I thought you'd be sick of turkey and rich food so it's a very basic Irish menu tonight. I hope you're hungry enough for bacon and cabbage with boiled potatoes.'

'Hmmm, sounds good.'

'The potatoes are what we call laughing spuds because when you boil them, they burst out of their jackets. And I cook the cabbage in with the gammon because it soaks up all the flavours of the meat.'

I had to smile. 'You sound like a chef on one of these TV cookery programmes.'

He poured his own wine then held the glass up. 'Not that they'd ever be cooking something as basic as this. Cheers, Amy, and a happy new year.'

'You too. It's good to have you back, Tom. I was afraid you would decide to stay in Ireland.'

'Were you?' He seemed taken aback. 'My life is here; always will be, I suppose.'

'I'm glad about that,' I said. Without thinking, I reached across the table to stroke his hand, intending it to be a comforting gesture, knowing what he'd been through. So it was a surprise when he lifted my hand to his lips and kissed it softly.

'I missed you,' he said, quietly.

We looked at each other in silence for a moment, as if seeing each other for the first time, until the sound of Orla's feet clumping down the wooden stairs brought us to our senses. When she flounced in, we both sat up straight like naughty children who've been caught getting up to mischief.

'I made the dessert,' she announced, pulling open the fridge door and bringing out a glass bowl full of some concoction topped with what looked like a whole packet of hundreds and thousands which I managed to admire to her satisfaction.

'Very pretty, Orla.'

I saw Tom smile. 'I hope our visitor has a sweet tooth.' Then under his breath, he added, 'and a good dentist!'

The meal was surprisingly tasty. Tom was right: the potatoes had soaked up all the flavours of the meat and cabbage but the meat, having been cooked slowly for a couple of hours, was tender and juicy. It was impressive and he seemed genuinely delighted when I told him.

Around nine o'clock, after Orla's trifle, which I managed to finish by spreading out the thick, crunchy top layer and hiding it under the bottom layer of sponge, Tom very gently suggested that she go upstairs and get ready for bed.

'But there's no school tomorrow,' she whined.

'No, but you have a busy day, remember? It's Benjie's party and we have to go into town tomorrow morning to buy him a card and a present. So go on now, show Amy what an obedient little angel you are and don't be showing me up.'

Orla turned to me, her sour expression brightening as a new thought came. 'Do you want to see my bedroom, Amy?'

'Ah, well... that would be lovely if your dad doesn't mind and he doesn't need any help here,' I said, half reluctant to leave the table and the company of the man opposite. Tom said he'd put on the coffee and load the dishwasher so I followed Orla upstairs to her room at the back of the house, preparing myself for a sea of pink.

As she opened the door, an extraordinary sight took my voice away. The ceiling had been painted a deep, inky blue dotted with yellow and white swirls of stars in different sizes. It was both stunning and disturbing at the same time. How long would it have taken to paint something like that?

Orla had been watching for my reaction. 'I had space and planets before but then I wanted sunflowers by Van Gogh instead.'

'Sunflowers?'

'But I got starry night instead.'

'You lucky girl.'

'Van Gogh didn't do it, though. Daddy painted it for me.'

'You have a very special dad, Orla.'

'I know,' she said, as if I'd just stated the obvious. 'It took him a long time so he says next time I change my mind, he's just going to paint it white for a grown-up girl.'

I was thinking of the lost colours in my flat. Strangely, the wide expanse of hurriedly painted magnolia in the sitting room had done wonders for the sari cushions whose vibrant colours had taken centre stage along with their co-star, my new sofa throw made from hand-dyed turquoise wool.

'It helps me to sleep,' Orla said, looking up at her ceiling. 'The stars make me feel better but this is my favourite thing.' She went over to her bedside table and picked up a bowl shaped like a sunflower with buttercup yellow petals around the rim.

'That's gorgeous,' I said, genuinely impressed. 'Did your dad make that?'

'No, Jack made it. He's an artist like Van Gogh but a bit better really.'

'Wow,' I breathed. 'He must be good.'

'Oh yes,' she said, in that matter-of-fact way of hers.

Patiently, I followed her round the room as she showed me the clothes in her wardrobe, the box of toys on the floor beneath the window, the pink unicorn with purple hair hanging from her mirror and all the treasures that make a little girl's bedroom feminine and cosy. To be honest, it could have been a bit like the trifle, overly sickly and sweet, were it not for the dramatic ceiling.

'That's it,' she said at last, throwing her arms out theatrically.

'Well thank you for this tour of your bedroom, Orla. It's been most interesting. I almost feel as if I should be paying to come and see it.'

'You're welcome,' she said. 'I'm going to bed now so goodnight, Amy.'

A solemn dismissal that left no room for any further discussion.

By the time I got back downstairs again, the dishwasher was running, a smell of freshly brewed coffee was filling the kitchen and Tom was reaching up into a cupboard.

'Mugs or posh cups?'

'What if I said posh cups?'

'You'd be out of luck. I will find the matching mugs, though.' He took out two chunky earthenware mugs and poured the coffee. 'I suppose Orla gave you the tour?'

'Yes, I thought the ceiling of the Sistine chapel was stunning until I saw *your* work.'

But how could I explain the strange mixture of admiration and concern that I was feeling?

'Thanks,' he said, 'but I don't know how much longer I can do my Michelangelo act. I still have the crick in my neck.'

'So, is this Jack the boy you mentioned before? Orla said he made the bowl by her bed.'

'Yes, he's one of my students. You could have knocked me over twice when he asked me to give Orla that bowl. We'd had an exhibition of artwork at the school the evening before and she'd latched onto poor Jack as if he was the reincarnation of Vincent himself. It did his confidence the world of good.'

'It's stunning, Tom. He's very talented.'

'Ah well, he has a marvellous teacher.'

He led the way into the sitting room, placing the tray of mugs on a large coffee table that looked as if it had been carved from a single slab of oak. 'Sit there,' he said, indicating the battered green leather sofa, with the instruction to 'move that eejit' since I was about to sit on a Paddington bear in a green hat, red duffel coat and black wellies propped up against the cushions and looking worried.

'If only Ben had had a teacher like you,' I said, once Paddington and I were both settled.

Tom sat down at the other end of the sofa and passed a mug of coffee. 'Ben? Oh yes, that boy who was with you the day we met.' He grinned. 'Or should I say the day you literally *fell* into my life? Yes, he's a strange kid for sure.'

'He's like a lost child,' I said. 'I keep wondering what his life would have been like with some stability in it because then he wouldn't have run away and got into this trouble. Or is that too simplistic?'

He looked thoughtful for a moment. 'Even kids from good homes can go off the rails. Look at James Gresham, for instance: the son of wealthy parents, a father who's a successful businessman and chair of the local Rotary club, a good home, intelligent with good grades and yet he ends up dead from a drug overdose.'

My mind went back instantly to the sight of the white flowers, the burning tealight and the coiled red scarf in the shop doorway, the markers of a place where a young life drained away.

I took a sip of the rich, dark coffee and looked around the room, anxious to banish the image to the back of my mind.

'It's very calm and relaxing in here. I like the white shutters on the window.'

'Anna's idea,' Tom said. 'Less fiddly than curtains and they give you a lot of light.'

He had filled the open fireplace with sturdy, cream-coloured church candles. Above it, on the wooden mantel shelf, was a row of framed family photos including one of Orla as a baby looking chubby and bewildered in a white, crocheted bonnet, and a family photo of Tom, Orla and the most beautiful, most elegant-looking woman I'd ever seen.

'Is that Anna?' I asked. Stupid question. Who else could it be? The truth was, her name had made me expect someone who looked very English so her appearance came as a surprise.

'Yes. Her mother was from Ghana and her father was French.' It was as if he had read my thoughts.

'You can see her in Orla,' I said, thinking of the child's creamy coffee complexion and nut-brown eyes. 'So how did you two meet?'

'She was a bridesmaid at a mutual friend's wedding and from the moment she walked up the aisle making a truly disgusting peach silk dress look elegant, my knees went weak and my heart was lost and that's the truth of it. We'd only been going out for a few months before I asked her to marry me. I'd expected her to turn me down flat but for some reason she was over the moon.'

This shocked me. 'Why wouldn't she be? You're an amazing man. Anna was dead lucky to have met you.'

An unfortunate choice of words I realised, hoping it hadn't registered.

He turned to me with a serious look in his eyes. 'I've tried to keep

Anna alive for Orla because I don't ever want her to forget that she had a mother who adored her.'

What was it like for a four-year-old to come home from school one day and find her mother gone, wiped out of her life forever?

I chose my next words carefully. 'Some day, when she's older, Orla will realise how hard you've worked trying to be two parents. You're doing such a good job.'

'Thanks, Amy,' he said. 'You know, people say, "Oh, you're so good, looking after your little girl like that." Funny, isn't it? Would they still say that if I were a widow? My mother's best friend was widowed when her three children were all young and yet nobody praised her for bringing them up on her own even though it must have been a terrible struggle.'

'That doesn't minimise what you're doing, though,' I suggested.

The room became quiet but for the steady ticking of a small art deco clock beside the photo of Anna. Frozen in time and forever young within her silver frame, she smiled out at me with bright, intelligent eyes and a wide, generous, red-lipped smile revealing dazzlingly perfect white teeth. How sad that this young, vibrant woman was robbed of a life that had so much potential. Her confident gaze held me as her husband and I sat side by side drinking our coffee.

'I'm going to tell you something I haven't told anyone else,' he said, breaking the silence. 'When I was in Ireland for my dad's funeral, I went to the beach by myself one day and broke down for the first time – I mean, properly howled my eyes out. It was mad.'

'Why mad? What's mad about a normal reaction, Tom?'

He gave me a sad smile that made my heart lurch. 'You see, I've had to hold it together for Orla, to keep her world safe but it's been so... difficult. I didn't actually realise what an effort it had taken until I was alone on that beach with nothing else to think about and no distractions.'

'You should maybe talk to someone,' I said, reaching for his hand.

'A bereavement counsellor perhaps. You've been brave for so long but bottling up your feelings won't do you any good.'

His fingers curled around mine. 'I don't know why I told you that, Amy. Maybe it's because you're a lovely woman and I trust you that I'm not embarrassed.'

That shocked me. 'Why are you so embarrassed about being human? Grieving is nothing to be ashamed of – far from it. If you hadn't loved Anna, you wouldn't have cried that day and that really would have been sad.'

He turned to look at me. 'That's true, I suppose.'

'Of course, it is. The saddest funerals are where nobody cries. Beth's dad told me that when his wife died, he was glad everyone was so upset because it showed how loved she was.'

'You'd make a good bereavement counsellor yourself, Miss Lewis.'

'It's only common sense, Tom. It's nothing magical.'

'Thanks for listening,' he said, still holding my hand. 'Sorry if I made your coffee go cold and sorry for bringing a serious note into what has been a special evening for me.'

'And for me, so no need to apologise,' I insisted. 'For one thing, you've introduced me to bacon and cabbage. My life has been changed forever.'

He gave me a mock bow. 'Glad to be of service to the English. The truth is, it's one of two things I know how to cook. Anna would be shocked at the quick and easy battered rubbish Orla and I consume on a week night. How the hell did she manage to come home from work and cook decent, balanced meals?'

'So what's the other recipe you know?' I was genuinely curious.

He looked embarrassed. 'Ok, roast chicken legs. You can't really go wrong with them I find, unless you go down to the workshop to empty the kiln and forget all about them.'

I couldn't help smiling. 'I see. Not that that's happened, of course.'

'Of course but let's talk about you now. There's so much about you that I'm longing to know, Miss Amy Lewis.'

'How long have you got? If you want to hear about my life, you're going to need to book another appointment.'

A metallic chiming from the mantelpiece reminded me that it was an early start in the shop the following morning and besides, poor Max would probably have his legs crossed.

'Ah now I've frightened you off,' Tom said. 'And just when we were jumping into deep water.'

'What are friends for? And we are good friends now, aren't we?' I hoped he would agree.

'Do you know,' he said, 'that day you and Ben fell onto the floor of Ken's cabin, I looked at you and thought…'

'I know. You thought I was a mad woman who'd escaped.'

'All right, I did, but I also thought you were the most attractive woman I'd seen for a long time. I never told you that before.' He was still holding my hands, stroking my fingers.

'Oh.' It was all I could say because inside, I was dancing. Then, I managed, 'I liked the look of you as well.' Understatement of the year.

By now, we were sitting close together. What happened next was strange because for a moment we just stared at one another, wordless and hesitant as if we were being drawn together by an invisible magnet. It wasn't uncomfortable or awkward – in fact, it felt peaceful in the silence of that room with just the ticking of the clock on the mantelpiece and Anna watching us from her frame. But then, just as we drew even closer, the spell was broken as Tom glanced sideways at the photos, breaking the connection between us. All I know is I felt such deep disappointment that it actually hurt.

'I better go,' I said, wanting to escape now.

He stood up and I followed him out to the hallway, waiting while he lifted my coat off the rack and helped me on with it. When I turned round to face him, we were so close I could smell the faint suggestion of aftershave, a pleasant, soapy smell so unlike the garish 'watch out, girls' stuff that Richard always wore. Tom lifted the collar of my coat to cover my neck then left his hands on my shoulders, giving them a gentle pat. 'There, that's you now,' he said. 'It'll be cold out there.'

Another silence as we stood looking at each other. In the end, I thanked him for a lovely evening and promised to try and make something edible at my place in return.

He gave me that broad, boyish grin again. 'That sounds almost tempting. And thanks, Amy.'

'For what?'

'For being Amy Lewis, rescuer of wayward boys, lost children and lonely widowers.'

I could feel my cheeks reddening so turned away and opened the front door. Outside, a heavy frost had glazed the pavements and crusted over my car windscreen.

'Oh shit!' I moaned, rubbing at the encrusted frost with the cuff of my coat.

'Sit in,' Tom ordered, grabbing his jacket.

'Sit in what?' I asked.

'The car, you eejit. Start the engine and give me the scraper.'

Ignoring my protests, he set to and vigorously scraped the ice off the screen and all the windows until they were clear. I left the engine running, got out and went to retrieve the scraper. We faced each other in silence, caught in the beam of the headlights with our breath clouding the air and wondering what to say until I decided we could be there all night if one of us didn't make a move.

'Well, thanks again. And thanks for all the scraping. It's been a lovely evening.'

I leaned up and kissed his cheek – after all, we were good friends now. But as I pulled back, time seemed to slow down. He put his arms around me and we stood there, holding each other, ignoring the cold and ignoring the fact that my engine was still running and polluting the atmosphere with horrible gases. It definitely wasn't an eco hug, that's for sure.

Then, suddenly, it was over as a high, demanding voice penetrated the darkness.

'Daddy, can you come back inside please?'

Over Tom's shoulder, I could see the small figure of Orla standing in the doorway of the house under the strong beam of the security light. She was wearing pink pyjamas, clutching Paddington Bear to her chest and watching us intently with a distinctly puzzled expression on her face.

'Sorry,' Tom murmured, kissing my forehead. 'Goodnight, lovely Amy.'

30. TOM

The following morning I took Orla to the children's Mass at our local church. For Anna's sake I tried to keep up our attendance, knowing how much her faith had meant to her and how she'd urged me to practise as a good example to our child.

But that morning my mind was not on spiritual matters as Orla and I walked to church.

'What are you smiling at, Daddy?' Orla asked.

'Am I smiling?'

'Yes. You have a great big smile on your face like you've heard a really funny joke or something.'

I took her hand and squeezed it as we climbed the steps to the church door. 'Maybe the funny joke is me.'

Yes, sure it was. As if a woman like Amy would ever see me as more than a friend. I was damaged goods.

All was fine until a mother and toddler slipped into the pew in front of ours. The toddler had been given a packet of crisps and a toy fire engine to keep him quiet so my concentration failed pretty quickly while Ola's gaze was fixed on the child's antics as he bashed the vehicle against the seat of the pew then pressed a button on top of the fire engine's cab producing a noise I can only describe as a growl crossed with a scream. Orla had a look of shocked superiority on her face, that middle-aged disparaging look that little girls do so well, but it had absolutely no effect – in fact, it just made him worse.

Meanwhile, the patient young priest ploughed on, tolerating the crying babies and the child running up and down the central aisle much to the fond bemusement of her parents until we reached the final blessing.

Orla took my hand as we walked home. 'Why didn't that lady give him a teddy instead?'

'Good question and I don't know the answer.' Yes I did: sheer stupidity.

She went quiet for a while and when I glanced down at her, she was chewing the fingertips of one of her mittens, something she hadn't done since she'd got them. 'Don't,' I said. 'You'll ruin them.'

She looked up at me. 'Are you going to marry Amy?' The question stopped us both on the pavement.

'No, sweetheart. Are you?'

She chuckled. 'Silly. Girls don't marry girls.'

Oh great, I thought, there's another conversation waiting in the wings.

Inevitably, the subject of her birthday in February came up as we neared the bike shop so to divert her, I stupidly asked if she'd like a party.

'Who can I invite?'

I prayed the list wouldn't be too long since our house was way too small to tolerate the lively presence of several hyped-up, over-excited little people and no way could I afford any of the outside alternatives. There seemed to be a competitive element among the parents at that school to see who could provide the most exotic venue for birthday parties, the most recent example being a boy who was chauffeured round London with ten little friends in a stretch limousine. How many of the little darlings could I fit into my Peugeot?

When we got home, I sat Orla down and calmly but firmly told her that she could invite six well-behaved, easily pleased little friends over for sandwiches, cake and coke.

'What about party bags?' she asked, frowning. 'Everyone has party bags.'

'Leave it with me.' Oh hell.

After a while, she wrote down five names headed by Benjie.

'And Jack,' she said.

'Jack? Is he new to your class?'

'No, Jack the artist.'

'Sweetheart, Jack is a fifteen-year-old boy. Sure, he won't want to have tea with a bunch of six- and seven-year-olds.'

'Why not?' she demanded. 'I like Jack and he's my friend.'

For a moment I had a hilarious vision of Mrs Morris dropping her son off at our house with a warning not to eat too much cake in case he threw up.

'Orla, no way would Jack want to come to a party at his teacher's house,' I said, trying not to laugh. 'Now please choose someone more age appropriate.'

In the end, Jack was substituted by another small girl and I managed to persuade her that if I showed each child how to make a thumb pot, then fired and glazed them in colours of their choice and delivered them a week later, that would be far superior to a party bag full of sugary rubbish.

'We should invite Aunty Rita,' I suggested. 'She loves parties and she can help me run it.'

Rita was Anna's sister, a glamorous, unmarried force of nature, devoted to her modelling career and forthright in her opinions. At our wedding she'd broken with tradition and insisted on making a bridesmaid speech, finishing with: 'Look after my little sister, Tom, or I'll be coming for you.' Nervous laughter all round, led by me.

The kids would adore her. Orla loved her aunt so was more than happy with that and, thankfully, we laid the subject of the birthday to rest. Still two weeks to go. Oh no! Only two weeks to go!

'Get your sketch pad and design an invitation,' I said, 'and let Dad have a rest with the newspapers.'

But I couldn't concentrate on the news. The scene outside the house the previous night was replaying over and over in my head. If only Orla hadn't interrupted.

Then it hit me. How would Rita react if she found out that, only three years after Anna's death, I was falling in love with another woman? Was it definitely love then?

I threw the paper down on the sofa, unable to concentrate. 'Oh God, Anna,' I whispered. 'I'm so sorry.'

31. LYNN

It was one of the coldest Januarys we'd had for a while and this particular morning the temperature had dropped even further. But we were ready, everything was in place and you could sense that the adrenalin was pumping through the veins of everyone in the briefing room.

At 4.00 a.m. we assembled in the yard of the police station in freezing cold darkness under a steady fall of snow. The only members of the team who seemed raring to go were PC Bob Davison and Bouncer, his cocker spaniel sniffer dog who was whining with excitement in the back of the dog van. By contrast, the two Alsatians and their handlers looked decidedly pissed off.

One unit set off to raid Frankie Collins' place while the rest of us drove in convoy to the industrial estate near Brentford where an officer made short work of the chain on the entrance gates with a pair of bolt cutters. We drove in, parked at the bottom of Commerce Way and made a silent approach up the path to the gates where a couple of burly officers with a battering ram splintered the silence by smashing their way in. After that, there was a lot of shouting as we swarmed into the yard, announcing our presence and warning anybody there to come out and be known.

The first thing we noticed was the dark blue Transit parked up on the left-hand side of the yard. Its roof and bonnet were covered in a layer of snow that glowed eerily under a single security light mounted on the wall above it. On the opposite side were two sheds with corrugated roofs. A beige caravan with a set of metal steps beneath its door was positioned by the far wall beside two large rusty shipping containers. Everything was as Ben had described it down to the piles of metal junk stacked up on the edges of the yard and the three battered red telephone boxes, remnants of the days when you had to press button A or B, now standing to attention in a sorry line.

Three of the support team immediately headed for the caravan, shouting a warning before entering. Seconds later, a bewildered-looking figure in striped pyjamas emerged from the caravan blinking in the harsh light of our torches. I heard Sam swear to himself as we simultaneously recognised a bleary-eyed, unshaven Guy Swinford. Seeing us, he uttered an expletive I've never heard before which is quite something after twenty odd years with the force.

'Good morning, Mr Swinford,' I called. 'I must add that word to my list. It's a new one on me.'

He shouted something very unfriendly that referred not only to my physical appearance but also to what he'd like to do to me thereby earning himself an extremely rough handcuffing from the officers on either side of him.

I just gave him a sweet smile. 'Can someone find Mr Swinford's coat? We don't want him coming down with pneumonia before he has a chance to explain himself.'

He was about to come out with some other obscenity when there was a shout from Bob Davison who was standing near the larger of the two sheds shining his torch up at the roofs. 'Ma'am, you need to take a look at this.' Beside him, Bouncer was yapping hysterically, wagging his backside off.

Immediately, I could see what was bothering him. Although the two sheds were side by side, only the smaller one had a covering of snow on its roof. That of the larger shed was completely clear and dry. We looked at each other, both realising at the same time what this could mean.

'The dog's quite interested in this one, Ma'am,' Bob said. Understatement of the year since by now, the spaniel was in a frenzy and definitely living up to his name.

But the discrepancy didn't end there. The doors on the larger shed were reinforced metal as opposed to the battered wooden doors of its neighbour in which Ben and Chris had been imprisoned. We could see why Ben was able to peer through the slats to see what was going on in the yard. Some had rotted away leaving large holes.

I called the officer in charge of the support team over to take a look. 'Do you think we could get through these doors?'

'We'll give it a go,' he said cheerfully, before waving the officer with the battering ram forward.

It took a while to make any headway but eventually, his efforts provided an opening just wide enough for one person at a time to get through. Sam went first, uttering an expletive once inside the shed. No wonder.

As I followed, winter was left behind and we found ourselves in a tropical, heat-filled summer. Neat rows of dark green plants were growing under the constant sunshine of dazzlingly bright lamps. The rattle of a fan and the thick insulation on the walls and ceiling just added to the impression of a well-thought-out operation: a hydroponic cannabis factory. The plants were reaching maturity; pretty soon they'd stifle the air with that instantly recognisable stench.

Sam whistled through his teeth. 'Where the hell are they getting enough electricity for all this?'

'Possibly stealing it off some unsuspecting neighbour,' I suggested. 'Someone around here must have an enormous bill they can't explain. It's worth asking the neighbouring businesses on this estate if they've noticed anything.'

After the shed had been sealed off, we searched the smaller one. This had obviously been used for storage since it mostly contained the kind of things you'd need for packaging, including piles of hessian sacks, boxes of plastic bags and reels of heavy-duty tape. Everything would have to be photographed and taped off for forensics.

By this time, Guy Swinford had been put into a police van so I took a look inside the caravan. Apart from the toilet, it had been gutted to provide an office space with a desk, chair and computer. Under the end window was a camp bed where he'd been sleeping and a faded blue plastic chair over which he'd draped a grubby looking vest, a pair of black denim jeans and a brown woollen jumper. Cigarette stubs overflowed from an empty, tomato-stained pizza box on the floor by the bed.

I was just contemplating this depressing scenario when Sam called me over to the desk. He'd pulled out the drawer and discovered three mobile phones, an enormous set of keys and an address book. By now, the police vehicles had been brought into the yard so that everything could be bagged up and taken away.

DCI Kenbury's voice came over the radio. 'Just one man on site? Is that it?'

I told him it looked as if Guy Swinford was the only security they had at night but there must be people who worked in the cannabis factory. We'd leave some officers on surveillance ready to detain anyone who turned up later that morning.

By six forty-five, there was a thick layer of snow covering the ground. The only objects in the yard that hadn't been searched were the shipping containers hunkered against the wall like rusty hulks with their bolts pulled across. As the first container door groaned open, we all heard a distinct scuffling noise coming from deep inside.

'I bloody hate rats,' someone muttered. Me too. It had been a phobia since childhood when my dad had decided to investigate a blocked drain and had prised open the cover only to find a nest of baby rats writhing like fat worms. That's why when Jack pleaded with me to buy him a white rat with red eyes I flatly refused. If a rat moved in, I moved out. Trouble was, the expression on Jack's face had told me that he was actually contemplating the possibilities of being a motherless rat owner.

I took a step back in case the little sods decided to run for it thereby turning me into a screaming wreck – not a good look in front of my fellow officers. Except it wasn't rats. Nothing could have prepared us for what we saw as the torch beams penetrated the darkness.

I'll never forget the eerie silence that fell on that place, over all of us as we stood there in the freezing cold trying to make sense of what we were seeing. Were there really faces staring at us from the back of the shipping container?

No doubt about it. Two young boys were huddled together on a pile of old rags.

Sam Clinton was the first to find his voice. 'What the hell is going on?'

A sudden movement jolted us all to our senses. We stood back as the two boys awkwardly got to their feet and staggered towards us, shielding their eyes against the glare of the torchlight. Once outside, the older boy, who couldn't have been more than fourteen, put his arm around the younger one, a small, frail-looking lad of about ten. Judging from their resemblance, he appeared to be the little brother of his protector who was staring at us with a mixture of fear and defiance in his dark eyes.

'Do you speak English?' I asked, with that slow, careful speech we all use when dealing with foreigners.

The older boy nodded. 'A little.'

He glanced around nervously as if checking that it was safe to speak. Shit, I thought, these kids have obviously been terrorised by somebody in this yard. I'm pretty tough but right then, it was a struggle to contain my shock and fury that some bastard thought it was ok to lock two children in a rusty box. I moved a little closer, holding one hand up in what I hoped was a reassuring gesture.

'Nobody is going to hurt you. You're safe now.'

The older lad pulled his little brother behind him defensively.

The pungent odour emanating from the open container reached into my nostrils almost forcing me back but I held my ground, repulsed that these two kids had been forced to breathe in that stench.

'Where are you from?' I asked, as gently as I could.

No answer. Both boys were staring at us all as if we were devils about to attack them.

'Where. Are. You. From?' I repeated, in case he hadn't understood.

'We come Syria,' he said.

'How did they end up here?' Sam muttered.

Good question but this wasn't the right place or time when the snow was still falling heavily and both boys were visibly shivering in their thin sweatshirts and jeans. Once we'd got hold of an interpreter, we could find out what had been going on but before then, these kids needed hot food and medical attention.

It took a while to persuade them that we wanted to help but finally, as we were about to put them in the car, the older boy stopped dead and ran back to the container, beckoning to us to follow. He pointed in at the darkness.

Sam shone his torch into the back of the container and let out a shout. 'There's a young lad lying on the floor.'

He ducked down and a few seconds later emerged carrying an unconscious boy of about twelve. The boy was Asian and was wearing a dirty blue and white Chelsea shirt.

'Chris,' I breathed.

'We need an ambulance. He's in a bad way,' Sam said.

While someone called the ambulance, I took off my coat and, though shivering, wrapped it over the bundle in Sam's arms. Chris looked like a scrap of humanity, bone thin and gaunt like a holocaust survivor. 'Who would do this?' one of the PCs muttered.

We were just walking back to the vehicles when an urgent metallic knocking sound alerted us to the second shipping container. I turned back. 'You're sodding joking. Not more of them?'

As the door was wrenched open, I peered in but was forced back by an overpowering stench of sweat and urine that made me retch. There was a scuffling sound as whoever was in there got to their feet and three young men emerged, one behind the other, coughing as the cold air hit them in the face. Like the boys, they were dressed only in sweatshirts, grubby jeans and old trainers. They shuffled together in a pitiful huddle, staring at us with that dead-eyed look that people who've lost hope often have. Once they must have been healthy and vigorous but something had turned them into frail, half-starved ghosts. It was hard to believe that here on our doorstep, human beings were being treated like this.

There was another unnerving silence as we all stood in the snow trying to make sense of what had just happened. Even the most hardened, most experienced 'seen it all' types seemed stunned. Then somebody swore, the spell was broken and one of the Alsatians began to jerk at his lead, yelping with frustration that nobody was letting him have a go at these strange people. At that, the young men began to talk excitedly in a language we didn't understand and took some calming down before they felt safe enough to come with us.

The reason none of them had suffocated became apparent when an officer walked around the side of the containers and noticed several large holes punched along the top where the metal was almost rusted through. Whoever locked them in there at night meant them to survive so they could get on with their work in the morning. Nice.

As the dawn light spread across the sky, we drove back to Kingston with more questions than answers in our heads. What we'd seen was reminiscent of the way the Nazis had treated prisoners in the camps. How could this happen in our time and under our noses in a London suburb where, five minutes away, people were living ordinary lives?

I knew that there would be no holiday for me and Jack until I'd arrested the cruel bastard who was running that operation.

Sam was driving as if the ridiculous twenty mile an hour speed limit on that particular road didn't apply to him, which was unusual for a man who normally stayed exactly one mile per hour below the limit.

'I've never needed a hot, strong cup of coffee more in my life, Sam,' I said, stifling a yawn. The truth was I was still shaken by what we'd discovered in that place. You'd think I would have built up some immunity to the horrors we often had to face, the numerous ways that man could be cruel to his fellow man. Not so. I knew officers, good friends, who'd crumbled after seeing one too many.

Sam was looking thoughtful. 'Strange, isn't it?'

'What is?'

'I was thinking how weird it is that one comment from a member of the public in a charity shop doorway led to all this.'

I was about to respond when DCI Kenbury's voice came on the radio requesting an update.

'We're on our way back, Sir,' I said. 'Has Frankie Collins been detained?'

He informed me that Collins had 'thrown a massive wobbler' but was calming down in a holding cell now he knew his solicitor was on the way. It was going to be a long day. I made a mental note to call home.

Home. Those poor sods at the yard must have felt that theirs was on a faraway planet.

Once they'd been discharged by the doctors, we brought them all in for questioning. With the help of an interpreter, they told us about their hazardous journey across the channel. They'd come in a small inflatable boat, landing at night on a beach on the south coast where two men with a van were waiting for them. The people smugglers on the Calais side had assured them that the UK would provide beautiful houses to live in, money for all their needs and, eventually, well-paying jobs. 'Don't worry,' they'd insisted, 'the men who are going to meet you will arrange everything for your wonderful new life.'

'And you believed them,' I said, thinking of the money the poor guys must have handed over to the smugglers.

Their leader, Elias, was nodding vigorously. Of course, I thought. Why else would people risk their lives in a totally unsuitable boat to cross one of the most dangerous and busy stretches of water in darkness?

Naturally, the fairy story ended the moment they climbed out exhausted onto the beach and staggered up the shingle towards the torchlight of two figures waiting for them in the darkness.

Elias told us that they first suspected something was wrong when they realised that their welcoming committee had locked the back doors of the van. He'd kept his concerns to himself since he felt responsible for the two young brothers who were already traumatised by losing their entire family in a bomb strike in Aleppo. Those kids had seen things that would make most of us insane – images that must have been permanently engraved on those large, dark eyes.

What happened next was what Ben had witnessed through the door of the shed. When the van pulled into the yard and the Syrians realised they'd been tricked, one of them tried to escape and was badly beaten by the two men who'd brought them there.

'What were the jobs they promised you and what were you paid?' I asked.

When the question was translated, there was a rush of angry answers in Arabic, everyone speaking and gesticulating at once. When the men finally calmed down, the translator turned to us with the answer.

'They were promised good jobs in London but were immediately put to work in the cannabis factory. They never received any money, only food and water. Every night, they were locked in the shipping containers in case they tried to escape. They were warned that because they were illegal immigrants if they went to the police they'd be imprisoned and deported. It was safer for them in that yard.'

Looking at these young men, I could almost feel the heat of their shame at being treated like worthless commodities. It didn't seem that long ago that statues of historical figures associated with the slave trade had been vandalised or knocked off their pedestals in cities all round the country. And yet, vulnerable people were still being enslaved right under our noses.

Later that morning, we had news of Chris. The boy had been

rushed to hospital suffering from dehydration and malnourishment which led us to conclude that he'd been locked in the container without food or water as a punishment for Ben's escape. The viciousness of his treatment appalled each and every one of us that day and, frankly, none of us expected him to pull through.

DCI Kenbury called me into his office just before lunch. 'These young men are victims, Lynn. We need to find the bastard running all this.'

'My thoughts exactly, Sir.' More of the sodding obvious. 'Has Frankie Collins talked?'

'Not unless you count the constant repetition of "No comment" as talking. He smirked all the way through the interview.'

'And what about Guy Swinford?'

'Thought *you'd* like that job,' he said. 'After you've had your lunch break, you and DC Clinton interview him and see what he'll admit to.'

'Sam and Kai brought him in for questioning in September, Sir. The guy's a bit of an actor.'

'Well, I suggest you put on a good performance yourself, Lynn. Make him think Frankie Collins has confessed and dumped Swinford right in it.'

It would be my pleasure to put the wind up the two of them.

Meanwhile, the officers who'd stayed behind at the yard had arrested two more men who'd turned up for work at eight o'clock. Judging from their muscular appearance, it was they who were responsible for locking the slaves in every night rather than the weedy Swinford.

There was a knock on the door and DS Stevens came into the room.

'Sorry to disturb you, Sir, but we've been examining the burner phones found in the caravan and this name and number appears several times. The name seems to be some sort of code.' She handed a piece of paper to the DCI.

His eyes narrowed. 'Are you sure about this?'

'Yes, Sir, it appears on all three phones. The call record shows several numbers that were used once a week but this one crops up over and over again. It matches a number we found on Ben Webster's phone too.'

Kenbury looked again at the paper. 'It looks as if this could be our man.'

'The one who's running this business?' I asked. 'Could this be Dillon's number?'

'It could be a coincidence but if whoever it is appears on all the phones, he must be important.'

'But if it's a code name, how can we work out who it is?'

Surprisingly, DCI Kenbury chuckled. 'The funny thing is, I know someone with that nickname. I'd give anything to see his face if he knew some villain was using it to commit serious crime.'

He passed the piece of paper over to me to look at. Beside the number was written one word: Ace.

32. AMY

Since Saturday night, I'd been on a rollercoaster, unable to sleep properly, unable to concentrate on even the simplest of jobs, finding my mind wandering back to that moment in the street outside Tom's house. He was so different from any of the men I'd known before, such a contrast with Richard, especially. There was so much to love about him.

But something was holding me back; a warning voice whispering in my ear. *Do you really want to put yourself through all that again? He still loves his wife, you idiot. There's no room for you.*

Time to pull myself together. I'd always be Tom's friend, looking out for him and Orla, but that was it.

Decision made, I decided it was best to keep busy. While Roz positioned herself behind the counter, I went over to the shelves to tidy the stock, starting with a basket of hand-knitted mohair bobble hats then moving on to the cashmere scarves. We'd had a new batch that were selling well thanks to the cold weather. Everyone was muffled up to the nose that January since the wind that blew off the river was cutting at faces like a sharp knife. Even the gulls looked depressed, huddling on the riverbank, no games, no fun, glaring at Max with their hard little eyes as if it was all his fault.

I was just neatening up the pile when the bell above the door jingled and a blast of freezing air rushed in. 'Good morning,' said a familiar voice, crisp and clear like ice.

DI Morris's cool, appraising gaze scanned the shop then came to rest on me. 'I thought I'd just pop by to see whether my daughter Clare was telling the truth about this place.'

Roz and I exchanged startled glances. Were we under investigation? That's what it felt like as we stood there under the appraisal of Morris's cool grey eyes and firmly set mouth. The detective seemed so tightly held together but then that was her modus operandi I supposed. I worked for a headteacher very much like her once. At school, she glided about like a grim-mouthed Queen Victoria, terrifying all of us but on staff nights out with a few drinks inside her, she became loud, raucous, incredibly funny and, often, the reason we got thrown out of restaurants. Maybe DI Morris had another side to her. Although I couldn't quite picture her dancing on tables and flashing her knickers at the waiters.

Noticing the scarves, she came across to where I was standing. 'May I?' She reached for the top one and held it for a moment, examining it closely and stroking it with her thumbs.

'It's a rich shade of red, isn't it?' She folded it with neat precision before replacing it on the pile. 'I think you mentioned to my colleague DC Clinton that someone came in here a few months ago, someone who made you feel uncomfortable.'

Yes, I still remembered the way that man overfilled the space as if he was entitled to rob me of my oxygen.

'Yes, I saw him again on the South Bank when he was searching for Ben. He makes me nervous, to be honest.'

'No need to worry, Miss Lewis. He's in custody,' she said. 'Tell me, it was one of your scarves that the dead boy was wearing was it not?'

'Yes, I checked the label but the colour gave it away too. It's unique because of the dyes our supplier uses.'

'I thought so.'

I sensed that she wasn't about to divulge any more because she was back in professional mode, sealing in her thoughts and protecting them from the public. She thanked me for my help in their enquiries and for employing Clare and turned to leave; she was about to open the shop door when she suddenly turned back.

'Actually, I'll take one of those green scarves. Green is supposed to be lucky, I believe. Don't bother to wrap it because I'm going to wear it.'

She scanned her debit card then wrapped the scarf round her neck, tucking the ends in to the top of her navy-blue coat. The leaf green sang against the dark lapels, instantly lifting her appearance.

'You'll never wear anything as soft,' I assured her.

She gave me a smile that lit up her eyes. 'Thank you, Amy. You've been more helpful than you know.'

I watched her walk away across the square towards the river.

'I wasn't sure at first but she seems a nice woman,' Roz remarked.

'Yes, maybe she is.'

*

Around twelve-fifteen, just as I was finishing with a customer, the door clicked open and a blast of cold air curled itself around our feet. When I looked up, Tom Brennan was standing at the counter, clutching a large bubble-wrapped package. Why was I so surprised to see him? The man had legs after all.

'Good morning, Mr Brennan,' I said, trying to look cool and calm while ignoring the thumping of my heart against my ribs.

'Miss Lewis.' He was mocking me with his smile. 'Listen, I have to be quick because I'm on my lunch break. I have Year 9 for double art this afternoon and they're a lively bunch. I was wondering if you'd be interested in adding my rocking horse to your stock. For some reason, it didn't sell at the Christmas market.'

'What a shame,' I said. 'Everybody wants plastic rubbish these days, I suppose.'

He shrugged. 'Sure, it's going to waste just standing around in my workshop. So, is it any good to you?'

'It could be a bit too small for me.'

'Really? And here's me thinking you'd be jumping straight on.'

I'd forgotten how easy we were with each other.

He turned to Roz who was watching us intently. 'The wood is

recycled,' he explained. 'It was given me by a friend who makes beech wood furniture.'

He set the package on the counter and unwrapped it to reveal the horse standing proudly on its black rockers staring at us with large painted brown eyes rimmed with long curly black lashes that any woman would die for. To be honest, it looked like an equine drag queen.

Roz reached over and stroked its smooth back as if assessing its pedigree. I half expected her to ask how many hands high it was. 'How much do you want for it?' she asked. Practical as ever.

'You can have it, ladies,' Tom said. 'It needs a good home.' He patted the horse's head. 'So, that's great then. Better get on.'

But he didn't move; in fact, he seemed distinctly reluctant to leave in spite of his time running short. Eventually, after opening and shutting his mouth a few times, he decided to speak.

'Well, I'm glad you'd like it and keep the money whatever you get for it because, you know, with the shop being up for sale, every little helps I'm thinking.'

Of course. After the exhilaration of our Christmas and New Year sales, Roz and I had almost forgotten that any day soon, there could be a potential buyer standing where Tom was, eyeing up the place dispassionately and planning all the changes needed to turn Earth Song into…

No, I didn't want to imagine what it might be in its next reincarnation.

Roz had fallen uncharacteristically silent and had begun tidying the rolls of silk ribbon in their cardboard box, her eyes cast down.

'Well, thanks again, Tom,' I said, trying to smile.

He must have felt the change in the atmosphere because he suddenly looked awkward. 'I should get going,' he said, backing away.

'Good luck with Year 9.' It was on the tip of my tongue to ask when I'd see him again but I stopped myself.

After he'd gone, neither of us moved for several minutes as I stared out of the window and she held onto the box of ribbons. It was Roz who eventually broke the silence. 'I'd almost forgotten. Better start job hunting again,' she said, replacing the box under the counter.

I reached out and stroked her arm. 'I'm so sorry, Roz. All my life I've been playing second fiddle to my brother but he needs my help and I can't abandon him, I just can't.'

'Honey, it's ok,' she said, her large, dark eyes full of sadness. 'I'll make us some coffee – it's got cold in here.'

When she reappeared, I could tell there was something bothering her from the deepening of the crease between her brows that was threatening to become a full-blown frown. 'What is it?' I asked.

'Tell me,' she said, looking me straight in the eyes. 'When did that boy ever do anything for you?'

I took the mug of coffee but didn't answer her. What was there to say?

As if he too had been reminded of Earth Song's fragile status, the estate agent rang later that same afternoon sounding over the top in his enthusiasm. I could imagine him rubbing his hands together over what he said was a superb offer on the shop, one that I should seriously consider this time.

'I knew things would improve once Christmas was over, Miss Lewis. This guy is keen to acquire premises for a new hairdressing business. He says it's exactly what he's been looking for.'

It was cowardly of me but I couldn't bear to tell Roz so waited until she'd gone home to ring back and accept the offer. I could almost hear the agent purring. More commission about to come his way.

'Right decision, Miss Lewis. You won't regret it.'

Regret it? He'd never know how much I hated the thought of dismantling everything I'd worked so hard to create, how much I resented handing over my shop to the guy who was going to rip out the old shelves and fill the place with basins and mirrors and the smell of hairspray and colouring lotion. I'd regret it for the rest of my life.

To add insult to injury, the agent informed me that, if possible, the buyer would like to pop in the following day to do some measurements.

I locked up and walked home over the bridge, hardly able to see because icy cold flakes of sleet were blowing into my face. The world had turned grey.

33. LYNN

With Clare back at university, Jack and I settled into our usual routine of minimal, one-sided communication in a house that felt strangely bereft of life. How I managed to give birth to such an optimistic, happy girl I don't know but when she was around, both Jack and I were lifted as if she'd injected us with a large dose of her positivity.

Meanwhile, things were moving fast at work. We'd passed on our info about Dillon to the police at King's Cross and, best of all, charged Collins and Swinford with offences relating to slavery and the dealing of class A drugs. Neither of them had any hesitation in incriminating the other since they obviously hated each other's guts but it was Guy Swinford who won the 'rat on your colleague' race. When he found out we'd arrested the two heavies who'd turned up later at the yard, he was quick to put them in it too, insisting all along that he was just the security guard and knew nothing about what was going on. As if.

After one particularly difficult interview session which ended with Swinford's solicitor requesting a few moments alone with her client, Sam turned to me in the corridor.

'When you come out of that room, do you ever feel like you need a hot shower?'

I knew exactly what he meant. We were often exposed to such grubby nastiness that it felt as if it had crawled under our skin like some parasitic worm. Then we had to go home to the people we loved and try to be normal.

On the other hand, there were times when it was the best job in the world and rescuing Chris and those Syrian youngsters was one of them. With their testimony there was no chance that Collins and Swinford would just be smacked on the wrist and told to stop being naughty boys.

Sam and I paced the corridor, playing the waiting game.

'I've been thinking,' I said, ignoring the look of mock surprise on his face. 'I seriously doubt that Frankie Collins is capable of running this entire business. For one thing he's as thick as a pile of bricks.'

'You're right. Driving a boat is about his limit.'

'And, as we know, the dirty work is often left to the likes of him while the top dog counts his profits in comfortable anonymity.'

Sam slumped against the wall as if he had no strength left. 'Why won't he tell us who it is?'

'Wish I knew. Something else has occurred to me. Remember that small-time drug dealer who was murdered back in September? We brought Swinford in for questioning about that.'

'Yes, but we had to let him go. There was no proof he had anything to do with it.'

'The thing is, Sam, we didn't know then that Frankie Collins was on the scene. Maybe we should question him about that murder.'

The thought seemed to inject new life into my colleague. He stood up straight, his eyes bright again.

'You've got a point there. The guy's ruthless. If that dealer strayed onto Frankie's patch, he was asking for trouble.'

'And the weapons that were found in Frankie's house don't exactly make him look like Mother Theresa.'

Down the corridor, the door of the interview room opened and the solicitor popped her head out. 'Thank you. We're ready now.'

I turned to Sam. 'We're barking up the wrong tree here. Let's bring Frankie Collins in tomorrow and ask him about the dear departed drug dealer.'

The following day, Kai Chauhan returned, plaster off and raring to go. It was good to have him back. I'd missed that keen-eyed puppy dog enthusiasm and that urge to get stuck in, even if it had got him into trouble. Thanks to his mum providing meals on wheels, he'd put on a bit of weight. Hopefully, he wouldn't have to scale any more wire fences.

While he and Sam tried to trace the numbers on the burner phones we'd found in the office at the yard, I arranged to bring Frankie Collins back in for questioning about the murder back in September.

I'd hardly put the phone down when an unexpected break came our way via a phone call from a sharp-eyed, off-duty beat officer from Brentford. He'd been walking his dog beside the river early that morning and had happened to spot *Sea Swift* nestled between two elderly Dutch barges moored close to Kew Bridge.

Sam looked up from his computer as I passed on this information. 'Kew Bridge? That's not the best place to hide a cabin cruiser, surely?'

'Unless it's just a temporary stop on the way to somewhere further downriver,' said Kai.

My thoughts exactly. 'I think Stephanie's right about this guy's arrogance. I have a strong feeling that whoever's behind this thinks that he's — or she's — invincible. Let's take a look. I'll see if there's an available car.'

Sam picked up his sheepskin jacket. 'Want me to drive?'

'No, Sam. I need someone who can drive really fast. Kai, get your coat. Can your leg cope with the clutch?'

Kai was already on his feet. 'I'm on it, Ma'am.'

Once the three of us were in the car, Kai gave it the full works until Brentford High Street then slowed down and stopped at the beginning of the riverside gardens. From there, we had to continue on foot along a pedestrian path.

It was a bright day, chilly but covered by a clear, blue sky. We left the car, walked down into the gardens and set off towards the bridge, keeping the distant boats in our sights. The river was unusually high against its banks and running fast is if trying to escape from something upstream. Every now and then, I glanced across at the people on the opposite side, envying them as they strolled along beside the wall of Kew Gardens, a place I hadn't been to for years. When this was all over, I'd maybe spend a day there by myself just being bathed in green.

As we got nearer to the bridge, the white hull of *Sea Swift* appeared, looking sleek and incongruous between its bulky, grey neighbours. One of these had a line of washing strung across its deck making it look even more downbeat in comparison.

'What now?' Kai asked. 'Do we go on board?'

I was about to answer when the cockpit door of *Sea Swift* opened and a man emerged into the seating area.

Sometimes when you see something totally unexpected, you think you've imagined it and that when you blink it will be gone. But I did and it hadn't. He was still there.

Beside me, Sam swore under his breath. 'Shit! Is that who I think it is?'

Finding my legs, I moved closer, shielding my eyes to look up at the man I recognised all too well.

34. AMY

When I got home that evening, I couldn't even be bothered to eat. For ages all I could do was stare out of the kitchen door into the darkness wondering what I was going to do with my life now that my dream had shattered.

Then, because if I didn't do it straight away terrible things might happen to my brother, I rang Marcus. It would be seven-thirty in the morning in Melbourne – no doubt he'd be up getting ready for work. I could imagine how the relief at being saved would lift his whole day just as it had plunged mine into gloom but there was little point in sharing that with him. Marcus was at the back of the queue when empathy was dished out.

I waited for the FaceTime call to connect and was surprised to see a young woman appear on the screen looking tousled and bleary-eyed as if she'd only just woken up.

'I'm so sorry,' I said, staring into a pair of large sea-blue eyes beneath a white-blonde fringe. 'I wanted to speak to my brother Marcus.' How embarrassing to wake a complete stranger on the other side of the world and one who, by the looks of it, was sharing my brother's bed.

She yawned, revealing a row of perfect white teeth. 'He's in the shower but I'll get him to call you back when he's out. Who shall I say?'

'It's Amy, his sister.'

'Oh, hiya Amy. I'm Tanya, Marcus's fiancée.' She laughed a tinkling laugh.

'His fiancée? He never mentioned he was engaged,' I said, feeling stupid.

'Oh yes, you'll all get invites.' Tanya smiled benignly as if she was bestowing a great gift.

'Invites to what?'

'To the wedding, dear.' She sounded as if she was talking to a small, rather dim child all of a sudden. 'Though we haven't actually set a date yet.'

My jaw tightened but I forced myself to say, 'Congratulations.'

'Thank you so much, Amy,' Tanya continued. Her voice rose with excitement. 'As soon as Marky's inheritance comes through, we're getting out of this poky flat and moving into a great little house we've seen on a new development near the beach.'

The information shot across the miles like a bullet and hit me square in the chest. 'His… inheritance? What exactly has Marcus told you, Tanya?'

'Just that he's come into some money from his nutty old grandmother. His words not mine, Amy, but she does sound like she was a bit of a screwball. Still, who cares when she's left him a pile of money, right?'

I stared at her open mouthed, unable to process what I was hearing.

Tanya, however, was on a roll. 'If you can send it over as soon as possible, Amy, we're going to use some of it to put down a deposit on the house.'

'The house?' I repeated numbly.

All I could do was stare at her like an idiot. That's not what he'd told Mum and Dad – or me, for that matter. So all that melodrama about debts and people wanting to kill him… Why didn't I realise it was all too much like the plot of a bad film or a BBC drama on a Sunday night? And the crying – he must have known how effective that would be. How could he treat me like such a fool?

'Stupid, stupid!' I muttered. Shock was turning into blind rage as I thought of poor Roz being jobless, of some stranger prowling around my shop – *my* business, that I'd worked so hard to create – of a future being thrown away. My heart was pounding against my ribs. If Marcus had been standing next to me, I swear I would have hit him.

'Just let me get this straight. You and Marcus are buying a house and that's why you need my money?' I asked, ice seeping through my veins.

'*His* money, dear,' she corrected. 'And yes, it's an adorable house only five minutes' walk from the beach. You must come and visit.'

While I took in this bit of information, Tanya cocked her head on one side like a cutesy poodle. 'He'll be sorry to miss you.'

'I bet he will,' I said, between gritted teeth.

'He's told me so much about you.'

'Really? Well, he hasn't told me anything about *you*, Tanya.'

Tanya raised her eyes and tutted. 'Oh, he's such a dark horse that Marcus!'

I gave her a tight smile. 'Yes, isn't he? But that's Marcus for you.'

A ball of anger was forming in my stomach; no, not just anger but outrage, disappointment, a feeling of complete betrayal, and the whole ugly mixture was threatening to boil over until it vomited out of me. I took in some deep breaths and forced myself to stay calm even though I felt like the stupidest, most gullible idiot in the world.

'Are you ok?' Tanya asked, her blue, blue eyes widening.

I nodded. 'So, let me get this clear. You and Marcus are going to use the money to buy a house? Right?'

'Yes, that's it, dear, like I said.' Her face expressed her sympathy for poor Marcus having such a thick sister.

'Then, would you mind giving him a message from me, Tanya?' I asked, sweetly.

'I'm sure he'll call you back when he's finished his shower,' she said, using that patronising tone again and setting my teeth on edge.

'Yes but I'd really like to leave him a message,' I insisted. 'There's no need for him to call me back.' *No need ever to speak to me again, actually.*

'Ok, fire away then, dear.' She gave a little sigh as if sorry that she'd failed to make poor Amy understand.

I took a breath then spoke slowly and distinctly between gritted teeth.

'Would you mind telling him –'

'Just a minute.' She was reaching for a notepad and pen on the bedside table. 'Ok, I'm ready.'

'Would you mind telling him,' I repeated carefully, 'that he is a world class, twenty-four carat…'

'Wait a second, please.' She was obviously a slow writer. 'Yes?'

'A twenty-four carat…'

'Is that carrot as in the vegetable, dear?'

Unbelievable. I spelled it out for her. She looked out at me and smiled, pen poised expectantly. 'I see. Yes? A twenty-four carat what, Amy?'

I looked down at Max asleep on the other end of the sofa.

'Just tell him he's a pile of dog shit and I can't forgive him. Thank you, Tanya.'

No, I didn't say that. How could I? The poor girl was as much a stooge in my brother's life as the rest of us. He'd obviously lied to her about the money and now she was going to start her married life on a bed of deception. I actually felt sorry for her. So I restrained myself without losing the gist of the message.

'Just say "Goodbye and start saving." Thanks, Tanya, and good luck. You're going to need it.'

I ended the call abruptly before she could reply and that's when the anger erupted.

'The bastard! The lying bastard!' My yell woke Max and probably startled the woman in the neighbouring flat as well.

On the top shelf of one of the kitchen cupboards was my emergency alcohol supply including a bottle of single malt whiskey that Richard had left behind. I hate whiskey but right then it was the only drink that was strong enough. I poured a large glass, threw in some ice cubes, took a gulp, practically choking as the bitter liquid burned the back of my throat, then stood for a moment looking out of the kitchen door into the darkness of the garden. How had this happened? And what now?

Swallowing the whole drink in one grimace, I poured another then picked up my mobile and rang the estate agent, leaving a message. He'd be peeved but who cared? Then, after a few more swigs of whiskey (which was growing on me now) I rang Roz who burst into tears which made me cry too so we both ended up sobbing and incoherent.

Her relief brought home to me the madness of losing Earth Song. What on earth had been going on in my head those past few weeks? Although, as Roz put it, there *were* some disgustingly violent people in this world so my believing Marcus's story was only about eighty per cent insane. Needless to say, her words did nothing to reassure me.

Of course, it was only a matter of minutes before Marcus rang sounding spluttering and furious. By now, I was feeling deliriously mellow thanks to the whiskey, in a happy place and not caring a jot about the insults flying my way.

His attack was unrelenting, continuous and brutal so I waited until he seemed to have worn himself out before telling him as calmly and clearly as the whiskey would allow that I had a business to run and a life to lead so he'd have to bloody well grow up and learn to respect other people especially me.

'You're drunk!' he shouted.

'Yesh I am. What'zz your excuse?'

Before he could answer, I switched off the mobile, disconnected the landline and collapsed into a deep, sozzled sleep on the sofa, waking at six the following morning with a thundering headache.

The alcoholic euphoria had worn off. Reality hit me hard in the stomach as my head gradually cleared, the fog became more of a light mist and I remembered what had happened.

So this is the way it was going to be. I'd always hoped that in spite of his cavalier attitude, my brother loved me in his own way, just a bit. Now I knew for sure that he didn't, not at all. If I'd lost everything, Marcus wouldn't have given a toss as long as he got what he wanted, and that was so hard to accept. He made me feel as if I didn't matter.

Early as it was, I texted Beth. She was the only person who would understand how this felt. I wasn't expecting an answer knowing what busy mornings she and Paolo had so it was a surprise when she rang just as I was making some strong coffee. She sounded outraged on my behalf.

'Listen, Amy,' she said, firmly, 'don't you dare give Marcus a second thought. You're a talented, creative and clever woman but you nearly let him ruin your life.'

'Can you believe he'd do a thing like that?'

There was a pause. 'Yes, I can. You deserve better, Amy.'

'That's what Tom said.'

'Tom?'

I explained who Tom was. 'Well, he's right,' Beth said. 'He sounds ok.'

'He is. He's the exact opposite of Marcus and Richard and maybe any man I've ever known.'

I heard her sigh. 'The trouble is, you always think the best of people even when they don't deserve it. Neither Richard nor your brother deserve you. You're too good for them, Ames.' She sounded like our old headmistress who would lay down the law, leaving no room for dissention.

Already, she was making me feel better. The fight was coming back.

'And listen to this Tom guy. He sounds just what you need, Amy.'

Yes, Marcus was on his own now and I was going to make a success of my life by myself without any help from anyone.

And now, there was one person I longed to see.

*

Spirits were high in Earth Song after that. I was flooded with positivity because the shop was saved and Marcus wasn't about to be murdered by the Ozzie mafia. The sheer relief had filled my head with creative ideas for the business which I couldn't wait to start planning.

Mid-morning, a young man came in, not to buy but to ask us if we'd like to take part in a documentary his company was making for Channel 4 about the rise of independent businesses in the high street. Would we mind being interviewed by Mary Portas? Would we mind having a crew filming in and outside the shop?

Mind? I couldn't think of anything better. The publicity would be amazing. They were coming the following Monday, he said, and the programme was going out two weeks after that.

After he'd gone, Roz and I hugged each other and jumped up and down a few times like lunatics before the reality kicked in.

'Oh shoot,' she said, her eyes wide. 'I've got nothing to wear and isn't Mary really elegant?'

But that didn't bother me. I was too busy planning what to say to a famous woman who'd made her name helping high street shops to boost their sales.

35. LYNN

'Good morning, Mr Gresham,' I said, keeping my voice steady as if it was perfectly normal to find him on the boat we'd been searching for.

Greg Gresham was looking down at us with shock blanching his already pale face. 'What the hell are you doing here, Mrs Morris?'

'It's Detective Inspector Morris,' I said, coolly. 'And I could ask you the same question, sir.' He seemed to have frozen, obviously trying to work out what we were doing there. That made two of us. He was the last person I'd expected to see on that boat.

Since he hadn't answered my question, I changed tack. 'We'd be grateful if you could help us with our enquiries, Mr Gresham.'

'Don't be ridiculous. How the hell can I help?'

'You wanted to know who killed your son.'

It was a buffer to keep him calm, allay suspicion while I frantically tried to make sense of this. What was he doing on a boat belonging to Frankie Collins?

'About bloody time,' he almost shouted. 'Don't tell me that after all these weeks, you've actually got an answer?'

'These are my colleagues Detective Constables Kai Chauhan and Sam Clinton. Can we come up there?' I asked, wondering how I was going to do that in a tight skirt.

'No, no. I'll join you.' He put down the mug and the newspaper he'd been carrying, pulled up the collar of his sheepskin coat and climbed down onto the riverbank.

'So who was it? Who killed my son? Who gave him those drugs?'

Ignoring the question, I continued calmly. 'I have to tell you that this boat has been used for criminal activity so it will be impounded while we carry out a thorough search. It would be best if you accompanied us to Kingston police station to answer a few questions.'

Anger flashed in his eyes. 'Look, this is nonsense. I haven't got time for all this. I've got to take this boat back to Kingston for a friend. He's asked me to sell it on for him. Now if you don't mind, that's exactly what I was about to do.' He turned away.

My mind was racing. The man was lying. He hadn't been in a hurry to leave. He'd been about to put his feet up with a mug of coffee and the newspaper so what else was he lying about?

'What's this friend's name, sir?' Sam asked, taking out his notebook.

'What business is that of yours?'

I glanced at Kai who nodded to show he understood and took out his mobile phone.

'Look, this is all bullshit,' Gresham hissed between gritted teeth. 'I'm going to have words with your superior. I'm a personal friend of DCI Kenbury and he's going to hear about this.'

'Yes, I know,' I said, calmly. 'I believe you play golf with him but that doesn't change anything, I'm afraid. Since I'm not satisfied with your explanation as to your presence on a boat that's crucial evidence in a police enquiry, it would be in your interest to cooperate and come with us to answer some questions. Or, I can arrest you. It's your choice, Mr Gresham.'

Surprisingly, I didn't feel any triumph at exercising my authority over him. His protests just made him seem pathetic.

'Forensics are on their way,' Kai said, 'and they've notified the local police to send an officer to stay with the boat in the meantime.'

I turned to Greg Gresham. 'Let's go, sir. This won't take long.'

Outrage was giving his face an unusual flush. 'I intend to put in a formal complaint about this. It's absolutely ridiculous. You know who I am. You know my reputation in Kingston and yet you're accusing me of...'

'Of what, sir?' I asked, innocently. 'I haven't actually accused you of anything, just asked you to come and answer some questions.'

All the same, I was seriously wondering what DCI Kenbury would make of me bringing in his golf buddy for interview.

When we reached the car, Greg climbed into the back seat muttering something about needing his solicitor; I reassured him again that, at this stage, he was merely answering some questions, helping us out. However, at the back of my mind, a terrible thought was forming – if this man had anything at all to do with Frankie Collins and the yard, the answer to his question about James's death would haunt him for the rest of his life.

I texted Stephanie to say we were coming and asked her to do a check for me. Sam had already discovered who *Sea Swift* was registered to but now I wanted to know where Frankie Collins had bought it and who the previous owner was.

*

Two coffees later, Gresham was still sticking to his story that he didn't know Frankie Collins except as a client and that his instructions were to pick up the boat and take it back to his dealership to sell on. It was all perfectly feasible and no matter how I probed, the answer was always the same. We weren't getting anywhere. Greg knew it too judging from the look of triumph on his face.

Just as we were contemplating releasing him, there was a knock on the door and Kai came in.

'Forensics have sent a photo of something they found in the saloon area of the boat. It's on our records as being stolen, Ma'am.' He held out his phone for me to see.

I was looking at a painting of the River Thames near Kingston Bridge at sunset. The sky was a bit too red for my liking but that didn't bother me nearly as much as what was in the centre of the picture. *Sea Swift*, the name clearly visible on its side, was midstream heading towards the grey stone bridge with swans riding its wake.

There was no doubt in my mind that this was the painting in the photo that Amy Lewis had shown us, the one she'd reported stolen from a houseboat moored along the river. Frankly, it wasn't my cup of tea but then I haven't my son's talent or interest in art. No doubt Jack or Mr Brennan could have described its merits but try as I might, they eluded me. It was nice enough I suppose.

My eyes scanned down to the bottom right-hand corner of the painting where the letter K was painted with a flourish of black. For a second or two I was lost for words which rarely happens.

Sam leaned in to take a look. 'Beautiful! Wouldn't mind that on my wall.'

'Do you recognise this painting?' I asked, showing the photo to Greg.

His eyes flickered. 'No, why should I?'

'Perhaps you can explain why it's on *Sea Swift* when it belongs to an artist living on a houseboat near Kingston Bridge?'

'It's nothing to do with me. Ask Frankie – it's his fucking boat.' He was reaching for his jacket. 'That's enough. I'm leaving now. You've embarrassed yourself enough, Mrs Morris. You'll be sorry you ever started this charade.'

Just as he stood up, there was a tap on the door and Stephanie came in, holding a piece of paper. 'You might like to see this.'

I shared it with Sam. After we had both read the information, we looked up at the man opposite. 'Please sit down again, Mr Gresham. I'm afraid we're far from finished.'

*

It took a couple of days for us to collate the evidence from searches of the boat and the Greshams' home, along with the record that DS Stephanie Davies had found. Frankie Collins had obtained the boat at Gresham's Car and Boat Sales but even though it was registered to him, he was actually renting it from the real owner who was none other than Greg Gresham.

Faced with the findings from the searches, he was unable to

provide an explanation for the discovery that the numbers on the burner phones from the scrapyard could be traced back to mobiles found on board *Sea Swift* and in the desk in his home office at The Oaks. Beside the mantelpiece in the same room was a tall cabinet lined with trophies. Taking a closer look, officers discovered that two of them were football trophies belonging to James but the rest were golf shields won by Greg for achieving a hole in one. At the base of each shield, inscribed in capital letters, was the word ACE.

The photo of James that I'd captured on my phone at the crematorium was the final proof. I'd almost forgotten it but seeing the photo on Kai's phone reminded me. When I zoomed in on the background, I realised that what was behind James was the side of a white boat. Just visible to his right were three navy blue letters, an S, E and A, the beginning of a name: *Sea Swift*.

Nobody in my team could get their heads round the fact that a man with such a high profile in the town could be living a secret life in such a sordid business. I suppose that's what he'd been counting on. Arrogance and greed were Greg Gresham's specialities.

Faced with the evidence, he dropped the pretence and stopped asking me who had killed his son. He'd known the answer all along. Now he had to live with it.

From then on, he stuck to 'No comment' which was appropriate in the circumstances. There would be plenty of time to live with the terrible guilt and to wonder why the boy he and his wife had indulged had turned to drugs. In a way, James had been no better off than all the needy, unhappy creatures that his father and his gang had exploited.

Had his wife known what he was doing, been involved even? He insisted that she had no idea but I remembered how she had shrugged him off at the funeral. In any case, the poor woman was about to discover the unbearable truth about her son's unnecessary death.

On the day that we finally charged Greg Gresham, I drove home so exhausted that it felt like every drop of blood had been drained from my body. Stopping at the Chinese, I bought some sweet and sour chicken, unable to even contemplate cooking a meal that evening. Sleep beckoned but there was one thing I desperately needed to do first.

'Hi Mum,' Jack said. He was in the kitchen reaching up into the cupboard for the biscuits.

I dumped the Chinese takeaway on the worktop and held out my arms. 'Come here a minute.'

'What? What have I done?' A frown creased the line of pale skin above his right eyebrow.

The cloying smell of sweet and sour sauce hung in the air around us as I drew him close to me in a hug. 'I just wanted you to know that I'm so proud of you, Jack,' I said.

After a few seconds, he pulled away. 'Ok. Thanks. Um...'

Good, we were about to communicate. 'Yes? What is it?' I asked, bracing myself for a mother/son heart-to-heart.

Jack glanced over at the worktop. 'Did you get prawn crackers with that?'

36. TOM

Orla was bent over the kitchen table writing invitations, her tongue sticking out with the effort, her forehead nearly touching the paper. The way she was gripping the pencil you'd think the poor thing had plans to escape from her fingers.

'Whose is this?' I asked, peering over her shoulder. She sat up straight revealing a little drawing of a space rocket beside the words *Benjie plis cum to my party*. 'How do you spell Saturday?' she asked. There was a little crease in her forehead where she'd been concentrating. Surely, I thought, writing shouldn't come this hard to a child who'd be seven in five days' time but maybe I was too used to teenagers. Anna would have had a better idea. Anna would have helped her more. That familiar pang of guilt stabbed at my stomach.

Laid out on the table were the other five successful invitees, each one with an Orla original drawing to fit their interest and the same painstakingly handwritten words. The activity had filled in a good hour and a half of Sunday afternoon.

When she'd finished colouring Benjie's rocket, she leaned back in her chair with a long sigh like a labourer who's laid down his pick at last.

'Well done, sweetheart. They'll all be thrilled with their pictures,' I said, wondering what these children's mothers were going to make of my daughter's awkward handwriting. Ah well, it was her own and no doubt it would improve one day when she found her feet. Come to think of it, mine wasn't all that great until I hit seventeen and started exchanging love notes with a girl in my class. Hers, I remembered, replaced all the dots on the i's with heart shapes – cute.

Orla turned to me with that look in her eyes I know so well, that *'Ha, now I've got you'* expression. Oh no, not this Jack Morris obsession again. I geared myself up for an argument.

'And can I ask Amy?' she said.

My heart did a funny little skip at the sound of that name. 'Well, you could try but she's always very busy in the shop on a Saturday.'

How long would that be true? It depressed me to think that everything Amy had worked for would be lost because of that feckless, feckin brother of hers. I filled the kettle for some tea, hoping to distract myself from the fury that was rising up inside me. Being an only child, I'd had nobody to compete with growing up but the notion that Marcus and her parents just expected her to give up everything was beyond my comprehension. Why was she worth less than him? What the hell? This wasn't the eighteenth century for feck's sake.

'Are you cross with me, Dad?' Orla asked, looking up from her work.

'No, love. Why?'

'Because you banged that mug down on the worktop and it made me jump.'

'Oh, sorry, did I?'

I poured a mug of tea and stared out into the garden at the grey February sky, the sodden grass and the lumpy black earth beneath the laurel bush, thinking about that moment outside the house when Amy came to dinner. Just a few seconds more, that's all I needed and I could have told her how I felt.

Orla, meanwhile, had taken another piece of my A4 printing paper and was already drawing and colouring a picture of a blonde lady in what looked like a ball gown standing beside a small dog with its tongue hanging out. Looking over her shoulder, I was impressed at how she had captured the essence of Amy, that way she had of looking directly at you and into you with those green eyes and that smile that made you feel as if you were the only person in the room.

Max hadn't come off so well, however. He looked like an unravelled ball of wool on two sticks.

'I'll drop by the shop in my lunch hour and give it to her, shall I?'

'Thanks, Dad.' She bent over the picture and out came the tongue.

The following day, I left school at twelve and ran the mile down to the town centre, arriving in an undignified, breathless heap at the counter of Earth Song where Roz was serenely holding the place together.

'She's just gone down to the riverside to have her lunch. You might just catch her.' She gave me an enigmatic smile for some reason so I just thanked her, quickly crossed the marketplace and ran along the passageway that led to the steps down to the riverside.

And there she was, leaning on the railings staring at something out in the river, her honey-coloured hair ruffled by the strong breeze.

I stopped to catch my breath then called her name.

37. AMY

I was leaning against the railing in my usual spot by the riverside, anxiously watching what was happening out in the middle of the river. February was living up to its reputation and we'd had a lot of rain lately. Some places further out had been flooded so the tide was running high and fast carrying with it some small gulls who were being swept along sideways in the strong current. Did they need rescuing?

'Roz said you'd be here. Glad I caught you.' Tom was standing beside me at the railings sounding breathless for some reason. 'What are you looking at Amy?'

'It's those birds, Tom,' I said, pointing out the little flock of white gulls still madly careering sideways and now only a few metres from the bridge. 'Will they be ok do you think?'

The birds looked so vulnerable, held captive by the racing water.

'They've got wings, Amy. They can fly themselves out of trouble.'

'But what if it's too fast for them, if they're dragged under?' I was genuinely concerned.

'Look now,' he said, putting his hand on my shoulder.

All of a sudden, the gulls rose as one into the air, flew back upriver and landed on the brown water to glide down all over again.

'They're having the ride of their life, see?'

'Oh thank goodness. I was just wondering how we could rescue them.'

He gave me a quizzical look. 'So which one of us was going to dive in there and grab them?'

I gave him a friendly nudge. 'You, of course!'

It felt so good to be with him again, to be completely comfortable in his presence. No need to make any effort or put on any show, I could just be myself even when that meant being a complete idiot. I'd come to love this man who could make me laugh and turn the world the right side up again.

'What are we all looking at?' someone asked. We both swung round, surprised to see DI Morris standing behind us. She was dressed casually in blue jeans, white trainers, an orange puffa jacket and the green scarf wrapped snugly round her neck.

She must have read my mind. 'It's my day off, Miss Lewis. I do have them every now and then. Hello, Mr Brennan. It's obviously yours too.'

'No, I'm on my lunch break, Mrs Morris. I have to get back in a minute.'

'Is Ben still ok?'

I felt guilty asking her a work-related question on her day off but strangely, seeing the birds captured by the river's power had brought the boy to mind.

The detective looked thoughtful, as if choosing her words carefully.

'Amy, I can't say too much but what you need to understand is that Ben has seen things no teenager should have to witness. He's been made to feel totally expendable and worthless, forced into doing something he hates and threatened with violence. It's going to take time to help him feel like a normal kid again. I'm not exaggerating when I tell you that the only act of kindness that boy has experienced in the past year came from you, a complete stranger.'

Her words sank into me, leaving a deep sadness. How many other Bens were out there living the same desperate life?

She patted my arm. 'But there's always hope. Inside, there's a good lad who just needs a bit of love and stability.'

'Thanks for telling me about him,' I said. 'I'd love to know how he gets on.'

There was surprising warmth in the smile she gave me. 'I'll see what I can do. Must go now. My son's invited a girl to dinner tonight and apparently, we need better plates.'

Tom chuckled. 'Jack's suddenly become a crockery connoisseur, has he?'

DI Morris raised her eyebrows at him. 'It's all down to you, Mr Brennan. Apparently, our plates aren't aesthetically pleasing.'

'Well, I apologise, but this is nothing compared to what he'll be like when he wins the Turner Prize.'

She actually laughed. 'To be honest, I'm just relieved that there's a girl he likes and who likes him. You probably know her because she's in the same form as Jack. Katie something.'

'Ah, Katie Moran. She's a lovely girl, feet on the ground, hardworking and a very talented artist. It's a good match, Mrs Morris, worth getting new plates for.'

She nodded. 'Good to know, Mr Brennan. Well, it's nice to see you both – and together as well.' Was it my imagination or did she wink at me before walking away? Surely not.

Tom checked his watch. 'I must go too. I'd love to stay and have lunch with you, Amy, but it's a working day.' He reached into his pocket and handed me a folded piece of paper. 'Nearly forgot the reason why I had to run the marathon to find you. I told Orla you probably wouldn't be able to make it so don't feel bad.'

Then he was gone and I was staring at a rather glamorous lady in a long dress and very high heels who I think was supposed to be me judging from the scruffy little dog on the end of the lead she was holding.

As it turned out, Roz was happy to hold the fort on Saturday afternoon for a couple of hours and even offered to lend me her car. I parked at the end of Tom's street and headed for the house with the bunch of orange and purple balloons tied to its door knocker.

The first surprise was that the door was opened by an elegant, beautiful woman wearing a spotless white apron over a knee-length, tight-fitting orange dress and a pair of matching heels. She looked at me askance as if I was about to sell her something or ask her to sign up for a monthly charity donation. To reassure her that I wasn't a chugger on the hunt, I gave her my brightest smile.

'Hello. Is Tom in, please?'

The look changed to: *what is a woman like you doing at this house asking for a man like Thomas?*

Behind her, the sound of high-pitched, excitable and very young voices floated down the hallway.

The eyebrows raised. 'And you are?'

My goodness but she was some gatekeeper.

Once I'd shown her Orla's invite, she opened the door wider. 'Go through to the kitchen please.'

I obeyed and soon discovered that the kitchen was the source of all the noise. Six children were seated round the table which had been pulled out from the wall to make room for them. Orla was in the high-status position at the head, queening it over her little guests who were busy guzzling a selection of sandwiches and assorted savouries. A large birthday cake covered in white icing dotted with purple and orange stars stood in the centre of the table waiting for the moment when its pink striped candles could be lit.

Seeing me, Orla shrieked, 'Amy! It's my birthday! I'm seven!' as if I had no idea.

Standing by the sink was a small, neat woman in jeans and a pink sweatshirt who gave me a welcoming smile. 'Hi, I'm Benjie's mum.' She indicated the lone little boy at the table who was stuffing his face with cocktail sausages.

'Where's Tom?' I asked. 'Is he hiding?'

'Oh, Tom's in his workshop. They've all been making thumb pots,' she said. 'He's just tidying up, I think. God love him but it was brave doing something like that.' Her accent told me she was from Tom's part of the world.

The woman who'd opened the front door was obviously in charge because as she came into the room, Mrs Benjie meekly asked if it was time to light the birthday cake candles. Orla started bouncing on her chair. 'Oh please, Aunty Rita!'

Aunty Rita pursed her lips. 'In a minute, dear. Some people haven't finished eating their savouries yet.' She nodded towards Benjie who had just plunged a hand into a bowl of crisps and was stuffing a fistful into his already crammed mouth, leaving fine crumbs on his cheeks.

Orla seemed delighted with the giant card I gave her. 'Get Dad to bring you to the shop and you can choose something suitable for a young lady of seven,' I said, pleased to see her eyes light up at the thought. You're never too young for retail therapy and this girl was raring to go.

While Rita was refilling the glasses of coke, I turned to Benjie's mum, keeping my voice low.

'I'll be back in a minute. Just want to say hello to Tom.'

'Don't miss the cake,' she whispered, her eyes wide with surprise that I could tear myself away from the excitement.

It was so peaceful in the garden, the only sound being the mournful chirruping of a robin in the bare branches of the apple tree next door. I tapped on the workshop door before entering.

'Only me. Sorry to bother you.'

Tom seemed amazingly pleased to see me. 'Amy, you made it! I was afraid you wouldn't be able to get away from the shop.'

'I can't stay long. Roz is holding the fort,' I said. 'Orla and her friends seem to be having a great time.'

'Has anyone been sick yet?' He dusted off the stool next to his with a bit of rag and gestured to me to come and sit beside him at the work bench.

'I think Aunty Rita has it all under control.'

He grinned. 'Yep, she would.'

In front of him on the bench was a row of thumb pots, some more lopsided than others. 'Kept the little treasures quiet for all of fifteen minutes,' he said.

'Good idea. It looks as if you're trying to straighten them out.'

'Just Benjie's pot. It looks as if it's drunk ten pints with a whiskey chaser.'

Carefully, he inserted his fingers into the wobbly pot and, with his thumb on the outside, pushed gently against the walls until they stood more or less upright. 'There, it's sobered up a bit now.'

'I take it that one there is Orla's.' At the end of the row was a perfectly formed little bowl looking smug beside the more amateur efforts.

'That's actually my demo,' Tom laughed. 'So, tell me, what's new? How's the sale going?'

Of course, he didn't know. I told him what had happened with Marcus and how Earth Song had been saved. At first, he looked pleased but then he said, frowning, 'I hope you told him where to go.'

'Yes. He's on his own now and so am I. My parents are furious.'

Since our last phone call, I'd not heard anything from my mother though to be honest, I'd not called them either, unwilling to face any more recriminations and blame. Enough was enough.

'You're *not* alone Amy.' Tom put his hand on my shoulder then realised that he hadn't wiped the clay off his fingers. 'Oh, sorry.' He quickly removed it and reached for the bit of old rag to dab at the shoulder of my cardigan. What had just been a bit of dust was now getting rubbed into the wool.

'I've been meaning to thank you,' I said.

He looked surprised. 'For what? Leaving dried clay on your shoulder? That's very generous, Amy.' There was a mischievous glint in his eyes.

'No, but if you could stop rubbing it in, that would help.' I took the rag out of his hand and dropped it on the bench.

'Sorry,' he muttered. 'Is it ruined?'

'It's ok. It's washable so...'

The trouble was, now the moment had come, my courage was

fading. For days now, I'd wanted to tell him how much he meant to me but was I about to make an idiot of myself and ruin everything? What if he was embarrassed, shocked even? We were good friends so why not leave it at that?

Tom must have seen the struggle on my face because he suddenly got up and went over to the corner where a kettle was plugged in beside a couple of earthenware mugs, a clay-spattered box of tea bags and a carton of milk.

'Listen, if we're to have a serious conversation, I need a cup of tea. I haven't had anything to drink since those children arrived and I'm parched. Want one?' The kettle clicked on.

'No thanks.' This was all a mistake. It would be better to leave with some dignity before I said too much and spoilt everything. My feelings were overflowing, running fast like the river, rushing towards possible disaster and humiliation.

Tom smiled that warm smile that reached his eyes and lit a spark in them. 'Tea is what my mother always gives people in distress,' he said. 'As soon as she offers to put the kettle on, you can see the gratitude in their eyes as if the very act of boiling the water could begin to put things right. Are you sure you don't want one? You look a bit stressed.'

Too right. What else do you call it when you're in love with a man who can never love you? Yet again. You'd think I'd be used to it by now.

I got up off the stool and pushed it under the bench, telling him that I'd just pop back to the party for a few minutes, watch the candles being lit then get back to the shop to relieve Roz.

'Shit, have they got that far?' Tom said. 'I better come too.' He was wiping his hands, taking his apron off, telling me to wait for him.

By the door I remembered something else that was news.

'Oh, Mary Portas is coming to the shop next week. She's making a documentary about people who've set up independent businesses in the high street. It'll be on Channel 4.'

Tom was staring at me as if lost for words while the kettle began to boil, filling the sudden silence with its furious bubbling.

Puzzled by his reaction, I turned to go.

'No, wait,' he said. 'Say that again.'

'She's interested in people who've set up independent shops. Listen, I'll be in touch about another order of bowls but maybe not those.' I grinned, indicating the thumb pots.

As I opened the door, I could see Rita peering through the kitchen window, straining her eyes to see what was happening. *Don't worry,* I thought, *nothing going on here, nothing to see.*

'Wait,' Tom said. He'd come up behind me and had put a restraining hand on my shoulder.

I turned to look up at him, surprised by the urgency in his voice.

'Tom, I've hardly spoken to the birthday girl.'

'Right now, it's the birthday girl's father who needs you,' he said, with surprising firmness. 'So please, just give me a few more minutes.' He reached behind me and pushed the door shut. What Rita made of that I couldn't imagine.

'I'm so proud of you,' he said, taking my hands in his. 'And knowing that you're not going to lose Earth Song is the best news in ages.'

I looked up into his face, at the warmth in that smile, realising that he meant every word. My heart gave a little jolt as he moved closer.

'I knew you'd be glad for me,' I found myself saying. 'That's what I wanted to thank you for; that's why I love you, Tom.'

For what seemed an age, the two of us just stood there looking at each other while the kettle worked itself up into a froth of bubbling fury in the corner.

'I should go,' I said at last, not taking my eyes off his.

'No,' he said. 'I need you to stay. For me.'

Without thinking, I walked into his arms and we held each other close, not saying a word for several minutes. It felt so peaceful, so… right.

The kettle had now switched itself off and the room was quiet apart from a sporadic tic from one of the fluorescent tubes in the ceiling as I closed my eyes and breathed him in.

'You have the most amazing green eyes,' he said, when we eventually parted. 'They're the colour of spring grass when it's newly grown.'

Nobody had ever said anything about my eyes before. Richard had been more concerned with what was below the neck.

'That's so poetic,' I murmured.

'That green of the grass when it's newly grown and untouched because the cows haven't been let out in the field yet.'

'What?' I gave him a gentle shove.

'Sure, they'll look beautiful on the television when you're talking to herself.'

'If you want me to mention your work to Mary Portas, you'll need to be very nice to me, Mr Brennan.'

'Oh I will be,' he smiled. 'I can think of a million ways to be nice to you, Miss Lewis.' He bent his head until his lips were on mine. It was a kiss well worth waiting for.

By the time we'd finished kissing, the candles had been lit and blown out, the cake had been sliced, Benjie had thrown up over the crisps and his mother was just taking him up to the bathroom.

'Daddy, you missed the singing,' Orla said, scornfully. A ring of icing circled her mouth.

Tom stroked her hair. 'Sorry, sweetheart.' He gave me a smile that melted my heart. 'There was a bit of sorting out to do.'

***

Three weeks later I called my parents. The rift had gone on long enough and it was time to mend things.

'We saw it,' my mother began. 'We saw that documentary on Channel 4 about high street shops.'

I braced myself for a spirited defence. 'Mary Portas?' The name felt like a charm that would protect me from the coming onslaught.

'We saw your shop.'

'Did you?' I waited, dreading her next comment, no doubt laden with disappointment.

'You lied to us, Amy, that day we came in.'

'I know, Mum, but you and Dad thought I was still teaching so what could I do? What did he say when he saw the programme?'

'He's here. I'll let him tell you.'

There was a muffled sound as she covered the receiver. Never mind, I'd just put the phone down if it got too bad. I didn't need that negativity anymore.

'Amy, we saw you on television,' he said.

'I know, Dad.'

He coughed, that clearing of the throat he always did when he was nervous.

'Extraordinary.'

'Pardon?'

'What you've achieved in such a short time.'

'Really?'

'Could be a successful business if you're lucky.'

'Luck doesn't come into it, Dad. I've worked hard to build it up.'

He coughed again.

And then he said the words I'd waited so long to hear.

'Well done, Amy.'

EPILOGUE

SIX MONTHS LATER

BEN

'Are you ready, Ben?' my aunt says, and I don't know if I am so I don't answer. Everything happened so quickly after the trial. It's like I've just woken up after a dream, a weird dream, actually.

DI Morris comes into the room. 'There's someone here wants to say goodbye,' she says. Chris flies towards me, the lunatic. I stop him just in time before he can jump at me and we high five instead.

'You ok, man?' he asks.

He looks good, I mean, really good like he grew more skin and muscle.

'I'm ok, kid. And you?'

Behind him, his mum and dad are watching us, smiling like they're happy to see us back together. His mum joins her hands like she's about to pray or something. 'Thank you, Ben,' she says. 'Thank you for looking after our boy.'

But I didn't, not really. I left him alone when I should have taken him with me. What does she mean? Her words hurt.

Chris's eyes are the brown of shiny new conkers – I've never seen them so bright. 'Good luck in Scotland, man,' he says.

I wink at him. 'If I don't like it, I'll be back.' I say it so quietly only he can hear. We fist bump and then he's gone, taken away by his parents. I feel choked up, like I might cry, so I bite my lip. DI Morris puts her hand on my shoulder and it makes me think she knows what I'm feeling.

My uncle picks up my bag and we go outside. I wait on the

pavement while he loads the bag into the boot of the car. Hmmm, big car, SUV, so maybe I've landed on my feet.

I'm just about to get in when DI Morris stops me. 'Someone else wants to see you before you go.' I turn and see Amy being pulled up the pavement by that mad dog of hers.

'Just wanted to wish you good luck, Ben,' she says.

I find my voice. 'Thanks. Thanks for, like, helping me, Amy.'

I bend down and stroke Max and he lifts his head up into my hand until his cold nose is under my fingers, the nutter. He still has the red collar on and that reminds me, so I reach into my rucksack and hold out the scarf. 'Sorry,' I say, glad that Mrs Kelly washed it for me. It's soft again and smells like fresh air.

'Keep it, Ben. It's yours,' Amy says.

She shakes hands with my aunt and uncle and tells them she's pleased to meet them. 'We're Ben's back-up team,' my uncle says. Thinks he's a comedian.

That's when I notice a tall man and a little girl standing by a tree not far away watching us. Amy sees me looking and smiles. 'That's *my* back-up team.'

I'd like to hug her but instead we shake hands like she's my social worker or something except I don't think I'll ever forget Amy and that's the difference.

'Do well,' she says. Then she turns and walks away, dragging the nutter of a dog who'd like to come with me, I think. The little girl reaches for her hand and gives me a look like she's saying, 'She's mine' and the man smiles at me before they walk away.

Aunty Kath looks across at DI Morris. 'It never ceases to amaze me,' she says, 'the kindness of strangers.'

DI Morris puts her hand on my shoulder again cos I know we're both thinking the same thing, so I turn to look at her. 'Have they found Dillon yet, Miss?'

'Not yet,' she says. 'They're still looking but don't worry about that, Ben. Go and enjoy your new life.'

So he's still out there picking up kids like me, making us do bad things – him and all the other Dillons.

We get in the car and drive away from there and I know I should feel safe now, like a normal kid, but I don't, not yet.

'Do well,' Amy said.

I'll try.

ABOUT THE AUTHOR

I have always enjoyed writing stories. At a young age, I filled up piles of exercise books with implausible adventures featuring fearless schoolgirls and brave ballerinas, providing plenty of entertainment for my mocking older brothers!

As a teacher, my special interest was in children's writing while always keeping up with my own projects including sketches, duologues, plays and stories. Three of my short plays were selected for performance in local playwriting competitions and members of the drama class I attended for many years have won medals performing my scripts in drama festivals.

My interests include art, music and theatre but, in common with many people, it is nature that holds me together. During the 2020 lockdown, walks in the forest and in a nearby field that is home to skylarks were absolute godsends. As well, I love the river Thames with its wildlife and history. That is why, in this novel, the river, in all its moods, is a constant presence flowing through the lives of the main characters.

I live in West London with a very patient and supportive husband. Michael knows exactly when a cup of tea and a biscuit will aid flagging inspiration.

BY THE SAME AUTHOR ALSO AVAILABLE ON AMAZON:

THE HEALER (2018)

Printed in Great Britain
by Amazon